DISTANS

by
Derek Bull

1

DISTANT ECHOES

ISBN: 9798848172218

For my father and mother, always supportive and very much missed.

Chapter One

He woke with a snort into the misery of a slate grey morning and stared at the spread of worn leather just an inch from his cheek. Where the hell was he? Squeezing together swollen eyelids, he looked again and this time recognised the horsehair couch Roy had bought at a second hand furniture auction some months ago. The panic which had threatened to rush up inside him dissipated and with a groan, he eased himself into a sitting position.

My name is, Danny Stephens and I'm doing fine.

Only he wasn't, not really. His head felt as though a steel band was tight around it, while his insides threatened they might soon be on the outside. Last night he had been drinking at his local and the world had seemed a pleasant place. Now he knew how wrong that impression had been and he groaned once more, only quietly this time.

Migraine! Another one! Which made three in as many weeks!

He really shouldn't have drunk so much. He'd lost count somewhere along the way, something he was doing a little too often these days.

"Never again!" he croaked the age old mantra.

He should know better by now, he really should.

Light as cold and sharp as polished steel sliced mercilessly into his brain through the open slats of a Venitian blind. He'd meant to have shut the damned thing last night but had forgotten, now it mocked him with the evidence of his own negligence.

"God..."

It was a cold morning two decades from the end of the twentieth century. His century as he like to think of it and he had not been doing fine for a long while. Perched there on the edge of the couch, he knew exactly how Lazarus must have felt when Jesus raised him from the grave.

Not grateful. Not grateful at all.

Surveying the chaos of the room around him he sighed. He'd been living here for a few weeks now, a two room flat cum storage area above Roy's second hand record shop. Roy was letting him stay there rent free and Danny paid him back by helping out in the shop every now and again. Hopefully it was only a stop-gap, until he managed to talk Chrissie round the way he usually did and he could move back home again.

He rose slowly to his feet, almost fell back onto the sofa as the pain in his head swelled but managed to stay upright. He counted silently to ten, then he shuffled across to the window, where he made two attempts to grab the blind's draw string. Catching it on the third, he jerked it hard enough to plunge the room into watery false twilight.

He rested his forehead against the cool window frame. He was sure he had been dreaming, something with music and bright lights, lots of random noise and - fear.

Fear?

Through slitted eyes, he found and lifted one of the blind slats, peered cautiously out at the bleak morning. A fine dusting of snow covered the back yard and the sky was full of winter.

He let the slat fall into place and stepped away from the window. It had been cold since Christmas but it was New Year's Eve before the first snow had fallen. Juat a taster but the TV weather man was predicting more to follow.

It wasn't the first time he'd had dreams of late, which was surprising for someone who in the past, rarely dreamed at all. Each time it had been followed soon after by a ferocious headache, which also was odd because he couldn't remember the last time he'd had migraine before this current spate.

As a youngster it had been different. He'd suffered from them quite often and they had usually laid him low for a whole day. His mother had told him that they had started around the time of his eleventh birthday, following a bout of meningitis, which he'd been lucky to survive. Not that he could remember a lot from back then and nothing at all from before the illness, for the disease, having spared his life had robbed him of those early memories. By the time he'd reached his late teens though, the migraines had stopped.

So why the hell had they returned?

He had been to the doctor a couple of weeks back, who had proscribed ergotamine pills. These did the job but sometimes had the unpleasant side affect of making him vomit and all but wiping him out for the day, so he'd decided to take them only if he couldn't ride the thing through.

As for the dreams....?

Walking to the couch, he rescued his overcoat from the floor, where it had fallen from his body in the night. He had pulled it over him when the cold had briefly roused him from his stupor. It was a good job he'd left the heating on, because the flat was like a fridge and without it, he could well have been suffering from hypothermia.

Slipping the coat on, he started on the trek to the bathroom, all five meters of it, which seemed a daunting prospect with everything inch of him protesting. His eyelids felt fat and sore and his mouth tasted like a tomcat had peed in it while he'd been asleep. If he didn't get some medication inside him soon, the rest of the day would be a right-off.

Alcohol's legacy.

Which just went to prove that he could not handle drink the way he used to be able to. In his youth, he'd been at it every weekend. Even after he'd got together with Chrissie, he'd still managed a regular Saturday night with the boys, usually rounding off with a fish supper or an Indian take-away. No worries then about indigestion keeping him up all sodding night or hangovers dogging him the following day. No tormenting little voice telling him that he was getting too old to party any longer.

And him still with four years to go to forty!

Not too old at all, it just seemed that way sometimes.

He located his medication in the wall cabinet, threw an ergotamine pill onto the back on his tongue and washed it down with water straight from the tap. An hour or so he should start to feel better.

Shutting the cabinet, he looked at the putty coloured face gazing back at him from the mirrored door. Sunken eyes, underscored by heavy purple tracks above a beard, which like his hair, was more salt than pepper these days and he was sure there were more creases on show than there had been the last time he'd looked.

He grunted and turning away, reminded himself that alcohol was a migraine trigger. He had found that he could get away with the odd pint or two but the problem was, last night it had gone way past that.

Way, way past that!

His local watering hole these days was the Bargeman's Rest, a small real ale house down by the river, where on

Friday and Saturday nights, the landlord booked various old-time bands to perform the sounds that had started the Sixties swinging. He'd gone along to hear the music and have a couple of pints but things had soon got out of hand. With the music taking him back to the days when he could drink into the early hours and still manage to be ready for work the next morning, he had just kept tipping them back.

Arm in arm with Roy, he had finally emerged from the Rest at closing time into a night that felt brittle enough to crack apart at the first hint of a sharp disturbance. Both wrapped in a blanket of boozy bonhomie, thay had sung their way along the river tow path, telling each other how lucky they were to have been teenagers way back when.

Now alcohol, his fickle friend, had deserted him, leaving him with the consequences of its passing.

"Never, ever, ever again!"

In the kitchen, he spooned coffee powder into an almost clean mug, filled the kettle and was reaching across to turn on the electric when the muscles of his lower back give a sharp twinge and he straightened up carefully. The injury was the result of a road accident back in the summer, although technically it was not a road accident because it happened in a car park.

He turned on the kettle and pressing the small of his back against the edge of the worktop, waited for the pain to subside. He'd been driving for Taxi Ragg at the time, a local outfit that had been going for a while in the city. It was the only permanent job he'd been able to get since Cousins Electrics had gone to the wall.

On this particular day, he was doing the shopping run, ferrying senior citizens to and from the massive supermarket on the outskirts of the city. He had just been dropping off an old dear, when a gleaming Range Rover, driven by an even older old dear, had slammed into the back of the cab.

The five year old Vauxhall Viva, one of George Ragg's aging fleet of cars and no match for the heavier vehicle, had been shunted forward with him half out of the door, causing him to wrench his back badly.

"I missed the brake," the old girl had explained, like that excused everything.

Returning to work a few days before the doctor advised him to, he had discovered that he'd lost his job.

"It wasn't my fault, George!"

"I know but I have to keep my fleet on the road."

And that had been that. On the dole again!

Chrissie had insisted he moved out of their house a month later, after one of their regular fallings out, only this one had gone further than usual. Things had been said by both of them, sharp and hurtful things which he for one had not really meant.

All stemming from the fact that he'd said he didn't see any point going out to celebrate their twelfth wedding anniversary.

With reason after the business with the ring.

He thought that they had everything they needed right there and she had itemised, loudly, just what they did have. As far as she was concerned it was not a lot and not just in the food line. Now he was living in his friend's storage space with no idea of how, when or, if he was honest, whether they would patch things up.

The kettle started to boil. He turned it off and was pouring water into the mug when his world was ripped apart by the harsh roar of the front door bell. It reverberated around the walls of his skull like a pinball, scoring points off of every jangled nerve-ending it hit.

"Christ almighty!" he snarled as hot water splashed onto his hand. He quickly turned on the cold tap and shoved the hand into the flow. Whoever was leaning on that bell-press better have a damned good reason for doing so, otherwise he might have to kill them!

Wrapping a wet tea towel round his fist, he turned off the cold water and pulling the overcoat close around his body, went onto the landing. He managed to get down the stairs to the front passage without falling flat on his face but seeing the open letterbox, his step faltered. The pair of eyes peering through stopped him altogether.

They were Carol's eyes.

"Danny, open the door!"

What did she want at this time of day?

Carol ran a small but successful inquiry company (she did not like it being referred to as a private detective agency) and worked most Saturdays, as there were always so many jobs to deal with.

"It's cold out here!"

She could be a pain in the arse at the best of times and he was not sure that he could take much of her company right then. He briefly flirted with the idea of slipping back upstairs, pretending that he was still asleep but with her gaze locked dead upon him, he knew that this was not even close to being an option. With a heavy heart, he opened the front door.

"I've been trying to ring you!"

She swept over the threshold trailing a slipstream of Chanel No.5 that made his stomach roll dangerously.

"Is your phone out of order?"

He vaguely remember unplugging the line from the wall socket last night, although his reason for doing so eluded him. Whatever it had been, he wished that he had disabled the door bell too and his spirits, already at a low ebb, nose dived. Outside, another day was gearing up, drab and grey under a sullen sky. He gazed at it for a moment with the eyes of a condemned man, before closing the door and plodding up the stairs behind her.

"Mind what you're doing!" Carol squealed.

He had been so caught up in his own misery, the headache, the hand, what was to come, he had not realised that she had stopped in the front room doorway. His size ten foot had clumped down on her dainty size four.

"Sorry."

She wiggled the foot, then took two steps away, putting space between. "You stink!"

"Thank you."

"Come to that the whole place does."

"You don't have to stay."

"It's dark in here!" She said, stepping into the living room. "No wonder, the blind is closed!"

"I know, I closed it."

He went over and opened the slats enough to ease the gloom but not enough to hurt his head. It was a sash window so he raised the lower frame about two centimeters to get some fresh air into the room.

"How can you live in this hovel?"

He looked around the space, at box after box of unwanted vinyl. The addition of the two large suit cases containing a lot of his clothing did not help the situation.

"It's better than a bench in the park."

"It's not as if you couldn't afford somewhere." She gave him a pained look. "We have been through this already."

They had, on a number of occasions and he did not want to go through it again. She could fix him up with a nice flat in the city, if he let her pay for it, which he did not want to do. Taking on a place of his own would seem like finally giving up on his marriage and anyway, he didn't want to be in debt to her anymore then he was already. It was a fact that she could not seem to understand.

"I need to talk to you." He grunted unenthusiastically and she gave him one of her looks, the kind he was all too familiar with. "Chrissie came to see me."

"What about?"

"She wants to put the house on the market."

"It's only been a month!" he said, aggreived. "We'll patch things up eventually."

"I'm not so sure. This time, you've really done it."

His hopes of a reconciliation dipped considerably.

"She wants a new start."

The pain in his head swelled. "Can we do this another time? I don't feel good."

"You'll get no sympathy from me."

"I'm not looking for any."

Carol had a way of getting under his skin without really trying. A natural capability she had possessed since childhood and she had been working on it since.

"It's time you pulled yourself together. I know you're hurt and feeling sorry for yourself and that's fine, up to a point. But wallowing in self pity is not going to help."

"How would you know?"

"I know, believe me!"

Considering who she was married to, she probably did at that.

"Chrissie wants to move on. She feels she has wasted enough years on you already."

Wasted! She'd really said that?

He wasn't stupid! Nor was he completely insensitive. This seperation was nothing to do with him not wanting to go out for a meal on their anniversary. That was just the straw that had broken the camel's back. Things had not been as good as they should have for a while and he knew that that was mostly down to him. He just never had the energy to deal with it. Far easier to ignore things, hope that by plowing on, the situation would sort itself out.

But wasted!?

"The last thing I need is you here, telling me how my other half is feeling!"

Jesus! She was the only woman he had ever properly loved and in his mind, he hadn't given her any real reason to doubt that. At lease, no reason she knew about.

"You've been drinking, haven't you!"

"A couple last night," he lied.

"The doctor told you to avoid alcohol."

"He's my doctor, I know what he said!"

"It can have a bad reaction with the medication you're on."

She meant the pain killers for his back, which he had stopped taking days ago. He'd not wanted the damned things in the first place but had been talked into taking them. They'd had him walking around like a zombie in no time, so he'd ditched them.

"You have to get a grip, Danny. You really do."

"You're my sister, not my mother!"

"Adoptive sister," she said pointedly.

"All right, adoptive sister!"

His head was pounding and his eyes that felt like they had been sprinkled with powdered glass. He wanted her to go but short of physically throwing her out onto the pavement, which he felt too frail to try anyway, he had little option but to put up with her.

"For goodness sake!" She had spotted the unplugged telephone cable and went across to reconnect it. Danny tried to think of a good excuse to explain why he'd unplugged it in the first place.

"I won't even ask," she said, straightening up.

Thank God for small mercies.

Carol looked at him with distaste. "Go and get some clothes on. I do not intend discussing anything while you're lolling around in your underpants."

Had he felt better, he would probably have lolled to his heart's content, but fragility and bravery do not often go hand in hand. All the same, he put up a show of resistance,

"Hurry up," she said. "I'll make you some coffee."

She walked from the room, tall and slim, attractive in a tight-arse kind of way with her designer casuals and her dainty feet. Anyone seeing the two of them together, would never guess that she was three years older than him. Standing there in his overcoat, with his gut distending the elastic waistband of yesterday's boxer shorts, he felt very inferior indeed.

He shucked the coat, scooped up his shirt from the floor and managed to get it on over his head without too much trouble. His luck ran out though when battling with his faded Levis. One leg had magically turned itself inside out and he wasted precious seconds wrestling with it before finally pulling them on.

He had to admit, he owed Carol a lot. She had been there for him every time he'd needed a reliable shoulder to lean on and, to his shame, an even more reliable bank account. He had been driving cabs long enough to have paid back some of what he owed her but now he had lost that job too, who knew when she would get the rest?

"It's only instant," she said, coming into the room just as he zipped his fly.

"Instant's all I have."

He took the mug from her in the same way a drowning man might grab at a passing branch and took a drink. It was no more than a sip but he had to struggle to keep it down.

"Hangover?"

The answer to that was self-evident so he said nothing. He would let her say what she had to say but if she tried any more ambassadorial work for Chrissie, out she went.

She watched him lower himself onto the sofa. "You need to get away."

"Where do you suggest? The Canary Island perhaps, or maybe a brief sojourn in the Carribean."

He wouldn't get far on what he had in the bank after his share of the mortgage repayments. Even if he were to give in to Chrissie, call it a day, sell the house, there wouldn't be much left over after the mortgage was cleared up and his redundancy money from Cousins was already quite depleted.

"I was thinking more of a change of scene." She smiled and he braced himself. "I have a job for you."

"I've already got a job."

"Oh yes, I forgot. Part-time in your friend's second hand record shop. Your career prospects are blooming."

Sarcasm became her.

"I think you could do better, don't you?"

She was probably right but he couldn't care less what she thought right then. His head was pounding and his stomach had started to churn ominously. The idea of having to dash for the lavatory in front of her filled him with horror.

She glanced at a wristwatch, which was small, and gold and no doubt very expensive. "I have an important appointment this morning, so I'll have to be brief."

Please! He had his buttocks clenched so tightly, he was sure that they would lock that way, have him waddling around like a penguin for the rest of his days.

"You remember I mentioned Kavanagh Mansions?"

"You've been bending my ear ever since you heard about the place. I don't want to go through the whole bloody saga again!"

She glared at him. "I can't talk to you when you're like this! Come for lunch tomorrow. We have some friends coming over, a buffet affair, nothing special. Smart casual will suffice."

He would have worried about that!

"Thea leaves tomorrow afternoon. It will be nice for you to see her before she goes."

Thea, Carol's only child, was at Sussex University studying Art History. She co-rented a flat in Worthing, a place to live both in and out of term time, as she liked to keep her home visits to a minimum. He didn't blame her. The heavy taint of resentment that often hung over the Waring home was enough to darken the most optimistic spirit. Having endured yet another heart warming family Christmas, it was time for her to flee back to Sussex until duty next forced her to return to the fold.

This year's Festive debacle had been made doubly memorable for her when, having imbibed a little too much after dinner brandy, he had risen to one of Nick's all too frequent jibes. They had ended up rolling around on the living room carpet, throwing ineffectual blows at each other until Carol and Thea had eventually prised them apart. Danny couldn't see that being reminded of that was going to make the past couple of weeks seem any brighter to her.

"Oh, yes," Carol said, rising to leave. "I have surprise for you."

He grunted unenthusiastically. Carol's surprises usually had a way of biting him on the backside. At another time, when he was feeling brighter, he might just have had a stab at talking his way out of the luncheon. The way he felt though, all he could do was follow her out of the room, moving like a man twice his age.

At the bottom of the stairs, she paused on the doorstep, holding the front door open.

"Funny how life turns out," she said wistfully. "When we were younger, everything seemed so simple."

For her, it had been.

She stepped forward suddenly and kissed him smartly on the cheek, something she had not done for a long while. She eyed him with a sad intimacy, which he assumed was meant to show him that she understood exactly how things were for him and which lasted all of thirty seconds. The wistful tone vanished like it had never been.

"Sunday. Don't be late!"

Then she was gone, walking off along the road to wherever it was that she had parked her car. He watched until she was out of sight before closing the front door on the world.

Chapter Two

That afternoon, he went to see Dad. He had slept for a couple of hours and felt, if not good, certainly better than he had done earlier. The headache was all but gone, although the pain in his back hung stubbornly on. He showered, shaved and dressed in fresh clothes, then went to the kitchen to fix himself something to eat.

Sunday lunch!

Christ, how had he fallen for that one? If he could get through the afternoon without crossing swords with Nick, it would be a miracle. They did not like each other, never had, never would, so the chances of a peaceful encounter were not great.

Nibbling his way through a piece of toast, he thought about what Carol had said regarding Chrissie and felt his spirits dip once more. He shut the thought down and turned to the job Carol had in mind for him. She wanted him to do some work for her, which meant it would be something she thought he could manage without cocking it up. Something it was not worth tying up one of her regular agents on.

Some bloody delivery boy job probably.

However, she had mentioned Kavanagh Mansion, so it might mean the job involved going to London and that he found appealing. He liked London, it was where he was born and had lived for the first eleven years of his life. No matter he couldn't remember a thing about those childhood times, some whisper of the city lingered on inside him and was re-awakened every time he went down there.

With a grunt, he pulled on his overcoat and scarf, the woollen beanie that Thea had given him for Christmas and his gloves. He picked up the plastic supermarket bag, containing the Louis L'Amour westerns he had bought from Marvin's second hand book stall in the market and headed for the street.

The books were for Dad, because he liked his cowboys and Indians, although he would no doubt say that he'd already read them, as he always did, then accept them gracelessly anyway. Next time Danny took him some, they would go through the rigmarole all over again, as though for the first time.

A watery sun greeted him but any promise of warmth it held was quickly dispelled by a steady breeze from the north. He jerked up his coat collar and headed for the alley between the building he lived in and the neighbouring one. He was brooding about what lay ahead of him, in the shape of that querulous old man and sighed heavily, tried to find some blessings to count and failed miserably.

He looked at his hand, which was sore inside the glove. If it were not for his conscience, he would turn around right away and go back upstairs to the flat and to hell with the old sod for now. Instead, he turned down the covered alleyway to where his old Ford Cortina Mk II was parked in the cobbled yard behind the building. It was a sorry sight, needing a new near side wing thanks to rust and had a nasty crack in the windshield, which he would have to get fixed before the police pulled him over.

It was a 1968 model, dark green, 1600 engine and he loved driving it. The trouble was, the battery was weak and in this cold weather, he would probably spend all afternoon trying to get it started. The alternative was getting a bus, which would be full of shoppers returning home after a morning raid on the New Year sales.

He opened the driver's door, climbed behind the wheel and inserted the key in the ignition. Offering up a silent prayer to the god of internal combustion engines, he pulled the choke right out, held his breath and turned the key. To his amazement, the engine fired first time. When the tone of it changed to a steady, quieter pulse, he pushed the choke almost shut, slipped the gearstick into first and drove slowly out of the alley.

Traffic was moving freely out of the city, which was more than could be said for that coming in and he was soon clearing the outskirts. A wide spread of of washed out sky loomed before him as the road opened up and he increased his speed. Within minutes, he was heading past the road, which led to the newish estate where their house was and it crossed his mind that he could call in and see Chrissie.

"Best not to push it," he muttered, glancing at himself in the rearview mirror. If he stopped off she might get the wrong idea, think he had gone there to discuss selling the place and that would end in another row.

When the road turned into dual carriageway, he overtook a lorry and accelerated away up the central lane, turning right at the next set of lights. They had settled on the two bedroomed semi because its garden was big enough for a child to play in, but of course, there had been no children. Chrissie had always wanted one of each and he had gone along, to make her happy, although fatherhood had never been a burning ambition of his. He couldn't understand anyone wanting the responsibility of bringing new life into what he considered a world that was getting dirtier all the time.

He flipped the indicator arm up and turned left onto the council estate where Dad's block was. Following a maze of narrow, grass lined streets until a block of sheltered flats loomed up on the left. He quickly turned into the kerb, squared off in the last parking space there was and switched off the engine. Sitting there behind the wheel as the engine clonked and bonked, he grimly considered the prospect of what awaited him.

Duty was becoming an onerous task these days, as being in the Old Man's company for too long was often more than mortal patience could endure. If he wasn't moaning about his lot, then he was telling Danny all the things he had done wrong in *his* life and warning him to pull his finger out before it was too late.

Danny got out of the car clutching the bag of books, locked the door and cut across the communal lawn fronting the two storey block. As he reached the entrance, a gang of kids erupted from an alleyway to one side of the building. A moment later, the Old Man burst through the front doors onto the lawn, shouting after them in a querulous voice and shaking his fist like some demented scarecrow.

"Little bleeders!" he wheezed. "I'll have you!"

Danny groaned inwardly.

The gang, all boys around the fourteen mark, stopped on the pavement and looked back at Dad who, having run out of breath, stood panting and gesturing helplessly. Laughing, they walked indolently away, strutting their stuff in their fashionable jeans, then turning to give the Old Man the finger and the hollow fist.

Why did the silly old devil have to get involved?

There had been trouble in the area for a while, kids from the tower blocks over near the dual carriage way kicking off at night, a couple of muggings and a break-in, plenty of vandalism and grafitti. One elderly woman claimed to have suffered a minor sexual assault in the parking bay at the front of her block, although no one seemed to know exactly what form the assault had taken. Dad, all heart as usual, had said that it was probably wishful thinking on her part.

"You want your arses kicking!" Dad shouted after the retreating gang.

"What's going on?"

Dad glanced at him as he walked across to him and jerked a thumb up at the big picture window of his front room. Looking up, Danny saw two thick, slimy tears running down the glass.

"Eggs!" Dad said. "They nick 'em from that darkie's place down the road."

He meant the Asian grocer's shop in the small precinct at the edge of the estate, but no matter how many times Danny told him, he could still see nothing wrong with the casual racism his generation had grown up with. He wasn't a racist, he'd tell you, never had been, never would be. Anything he said was said with a cosy informality, almost affectionate, according to him.

"I'll give them a slap, next time," Dad said.

Danny massaged his forehead with the fingers of his right hand. "You're too old to be slapping anyone. Go inside."

"I was doing fine. I didn't need you!"

He looked like a straggly old fighting cock and in spite of everything, Danny felt a grudging respect for him, well into his seventies and just as feisty as ever.

"I know you didn't."

Danny took his arm in his free had and walked him towards the flats, noting the wasted feel of him, little more than skin and bone, no meat at all. He wondered if this was a natural sign of aging or was there maybe some more serious underlying cause?

"Did you hear the language?"

"I heard."

Dad started up the stairs, gripping the handrail as though his life depended upon it. Danny followed him up to the first floor landing and saw that the front door to the flat was on the latch. He was always telling him about closing it when he stepped out and here it was, the same situation all over again!

"They need a few strokes of the birch."

"You disapprove of corporal punishment."

"I'd make an exception for them."

Through the large landing window, Danny saw the boys had reached the end of the road and felt a stab of concern. Supposing those little yobs decided to come round late at night, maybe pitch a few rocks instead of eggs.

"You want a cup of tea?" Dad asked. "There's a pot under the cosy."

"Not for me." The thought of the stewed brew soured his mouth. "I can't stay long."

"I don't know why you bother to come at all."

I sometimes wonder myself, Danny thought, following Dad into the flat. At once he caught the familiar aroma of stale pipe smoke and over cooked cabbage that permeated the place. Closing the front door, he looked along the hall, which was a familiar and somewhat depressing sight, with its strip of threadbare carpet over cream vinyl flooring tiles.

The walls were a bland, buttermilk colour, unadorned by pictures or nick-knacks, nothing to break up the space. Carol had offered to pay for a make-over but Dad wouldn't hear of it. This was an old man's flat with just the bare necessities and he liked it that way.

Stopping in the kitchen doorway, Danny watched him pour thick, brown liquid into a large mug from the same old chipped teapot he'd been using for more than thirty years.

"If you have anymore trouble from that lot, call the police. Don't try anything silly."

"I'm old not stupid."

That wasn't how it had looked downstairs but he didn't say anything. "I only meant..."

"I know what you meant!"

Dad pushed past him, heading for the front room and he felt the usual sinking feeling that generally accompanied his visits here.

"Maybe I'll have a cup after all," he said.

"Help yourself."

He had called this man Dad for as long as he could remember. His real father's best friend, Dad had married his widowed mother and raised him as his son.

Stepping into the kitchen, he poured a stream of dark liquid into a mug and watched grouts floating around on the surface. When he added a splash of Dad's full fat milk, greasy puddles spread out, engulphing them. For a moment, he was tempted to empty the mug down the sink but if drinking it appeased the Old Man to some degree, he would give it a try. It would be worth it.

As soon as he walked into the living room his eye was drawn to the egg stains on the big middle window, which resembled two lines of drying snot. "I'll clean that before I go."

"You needn't trouble yourself."

"It's no trouble." Danny went over and looked out at the shell fragments lying on the cill.

"I'll do it myself! I'm not helpless."

He had known this man nearly all of his life, yet there were times he felt as distant from him as he would from a stranger. Danny glanced at the framed photograph of his mother, sitting on an otherwise bare shelf unit beside the TV. If he was hoping to find sympathy in her eyes, he was disappointed. They were as flat and dead as the rest of the monochrome image.

Outside the street was empty, the gang of boys had gone. He stood the mug of stewed tea on a small table, hidden from Dad's view by another armchair and took the books from the bag. "Here's the westerns I told you about on the phone."

Dad sat in the big, worn armchair he liked best, sipping his tea and frowning. Danny felt the pressure starting to build, earlier this time than it usually did. That lingering finger of headache twitched, just to let him know that it was waiting in the wings for
an encore.

"I expect I've read them," Dad said. "You always bring me ones I've read."

Danny gazed enviously at the cowboy on the front cover of the top paperback, who was riding towards some distant snow-capped mountains, free as the wind. Just for once it would be nice to come here without having to subject himself to this pressure.

"If you have, I'll change them."

He took the books over to a table close to Dad's chair.

"That old chap they mugged is still in a bad way."

There were times when Dad imagined that he had told him things he hadn't. Glancing surreptitiously at his wristwatch, Danny tried to remember whether he had heard about this particular incident or not.

"Which old chap is that?"

"Don't you listen to anything I say?"

He took a deep breath, held it for a moment. The Old Man was in a really dirty mood today.

"So, how are you?"

"Same as you'd expect."

"What's that supposed to mean?"

Ten minutes in and already his spirits had dropped into his shoes. Would it have been like this with Jack Reed, his biological father?

"I'm an old man. Old men are a mass of aches and pains."

"Is that general aches and pains or is there something specific?"

He was thinking about the feel of the wasted arm and small stirrings of alarm pricked up inside him. Dad ignored his question and gave the books an half-hearted inspection.

"What's this about you going to London?"

Danny looked at him, surprised. "You've seen Carol then?"

"A flying visit. Earlier. She's another one who's arse barely touches the chair before she has to go."

"She wants me to go to London, does she?"

Typical Carol, stopping by after her meeting, looking to get the Old Man on board. Why was he surprised? She'd be hoping he would add his tuppeny worth to the matter.

"She mentioned a job. I don't know anything about it yet. I'm going to her's for lunch tomorrow to get all the gen."

More pressure for him to do what she wanted him to do. If he showed any reluctance, she would be counting on Dad to wag his finger and lecture him on the merits of family loyalty. Always a big thing with the Old Man, which he had never tired of drumming it into them as children.

Carol had learned long ago that to get Dad batting for her team, all she had to do was charm him and the soft old devil would be eating out of her hand in minutes. He might complain incessantly about her not coming to see him as often as he would like her to but Danny was not deceived, it meant nothing. He had never known Dad to be really angry with her and when the chips were down, it was on her side of any argument that you would find him.

"She probably thinks it might help me out. I'm up for any bits and bobs until something better comes along."

"How likely is that, the way this sodding government is acting?"

"We live in hopes," he said easily. A political diatribe was something he didn't want right then.

"And they had the bloody cheek to have the campaign slogan, 'Labour Isn't Working'!"

"Well, that's politics for you."

Dad, a diehard socialist, eyed him beligerently. "Did she tell you it was London?"

"I told you, she didn't say much at all."

"Putney," Dad growled. "Of all bloody places."

Danny had been warming to the idea of a day in the capital and with the mention of Putney, that warmth turned to excitement. Putney was the area in which he had lived for those lost years of his life. He had no memory of it and had never visited it before but the idea of taking a look around the place suddenly seemed to be just the thing he needed. And who was to say, touring around there might just wake up something in his brain.

"She's worried about you," Dad said. "She's a good girl, but this time she's wrong."

Danny stared at him, "How so?"

"She just is."

Well, this was a first, Dad going against Carol in anything.

"She must have someone else who could do it. I mean, what good would you be?"

"Thanks for that."

"I mean, she could send an experienced person, someone who knows what they're doing."

"I expect it's some sort of delivery job. Probably quicker to do it by hand than through the post. What's there to know?"

"It's not for you!" Dad said sharply.

Danny stared at him. He didn't know what was going on here at all. He'd normally expect the Old Man to be singing her praises, looking out for her brother, putting into practice everything he held dear. Now, here he was, more or less telling him to refuse her.

"This might lead to a permanent position, Dad. I need a job."

"So what's new!"

Danny clenched his fists so hard, his finger nails dug deep into the palms of his hands. "Even if it is a delivery job, it might lead to something more substantial?"

"You live in dreams. You always have done. It won't lead to anything, because you're not trained in that line of work. When it's done, you'll be high and dry again."

"You never know, she might keep me on. Train me."

"And pig's might fly."

Danny had to struggle to keep the lid on his temper. He was used to Dad's verbal swipes about him not having a decent position. He'd have thought by being open to what Carol wanted might earn some credit from him.

"It's a chance," he said, lamely.

Dad ignored him, staring fixedly into whatever dark thoughts were going around inside his head. He was quiet for so long, Danny began to think that he had said all he intended to on the subject, then suddenly he looked up.

"So what will you do?"

He shrugged. "Go, I suppose."

Dad shook his head in disgust. "Sometimes I wonder about you, boy."

Sometimes, Danny wondered about himself, allowing the Old Man to talk to him the way he did. He wasn't a kid anymore, he was a grown man edging his way towards forty. The annoying
thing was, he could not help feeling like an errant child under that rheumy old gaze.

"If only you'd listened to me in the past."

Not this again! It was the same old thing, his supposed lack of direction being a direct result of his under achieving at school.

As a kid, Dad had been on at him all the time about working harder, pushing himself to go beyond the boundaries of his limited capabilities. He was already doing the best he could, only Dad either couldn't or wouldn't see that. He'd just go on and on about making the most of the opportunities that came his way. Opportunites that Dad's own generation had never had.

The weight of a thousand years bore down upon Danny, memories of cold winter nights, shut away in his bedroom, struggling with homework he did not understand. Never a natural scholar, he'd spent hours trying to equal the standard of his peers, always falling short of Dad's expectations. Finally he'd left school with two fair GCE passes, in English and History, fails in all the rest and Dad hadn't said a word. He hadn't needed to, his face had said it all for him.

"And what am I meant to do?" Dad said.

"How do you mean?"

"I promised your mother, I would never let you go back to Putney."

Danny threw a guilty look at the photograph of his mother, searching again for some sign from her but there were no such things as ghosts. "When I was a child, maybe. I'm a grown up now."

"That's debatable."

Danny went over to the window and looked out at the empty street. The flood gates were open in his mind now and a great tide of resentment came rushing out. After school, he had drifted from job to job, something you could do in those days, when there had been plenty of work around. Labouring on building sites, working as a postman, a dustman and a bus conductor in that order, all to show this old bastard that he was capable of earning a living.

By the late Sixties, he had joined Cousins, a local electronics firm, where he'd trained as a Progress Chaser. It was interesting work, calling for degrees of responsibility and initiative not asked of him before. He'd loved it. Even so, Dad had taken every opportunity to criticise him and now, all these years later he was doing the same thing.

"Your sister doesn't always know best," Dad said, sounding as though the words might choke him.

He avoided Danny's questioning gaze, shifting about in his chair, as though he had splinters in his trousers. What was all this? Was the cantankerous old fool really worried about him going to Putney? If so, why?

"Are you feeling OK?"

Danny had accepted that fact years ago that Carol was Dad's favourite, telling himself that it was only natural, her being the fruit of the Old Man's scrawny loins. It mattered little how close a friend Jack Reed had been, blood was still thicker than water.

"You shouldn't go!"

"I'll decide that when I hear what it entails." Dad had to understand that the decision would be his and his alone.

"What do you know?"

He struggled out of his chair and walked across to the big old sideboard that had been part of the family home since Danny could remember. Opening a lower drawer, he started rummaging around inside with his gnarled and horny fingers, turning over the layers of accumulated junk.

"What have you lost?"

Dad ignored him and Danny sighed inwardly. This used to be a tough little man, slow to anger but when he did get there, watch out. When had that person turned into this irascible bag of bones, who never seemed to have anything decent to say to him? The worst thing about it was, even at his age, he would stand there and take any shit the old sod threw at him. The invisible chains of childhood being strong, lessons of respect so deeply ingrained, could not be easily overridden.

The Old Man came away from the sideboard clutching an aging photograph album and Danny's heart sank. Dad thrust the album into his unwilling hands, already opened to the right page.

"You remember this?"

How could he forget? He had lost count of the times Dad had tried to use it against him when he thought he needed his conscience pricking.

"I asked some chap to take it."

"I know," Danny said wearily. "He was walking his dog."

It was the familiar black and white photograph of a wide, empty beach, the sea right the way out at low tide, taken back in 1957, a day out to mark his thirteenth birthday. Snapped on the old box Brownie Dad had used back then, it showed a lean, almost handsome man, with a cigarette tucked behind one ear and an arm around the shoulders of the pretty, dark haired woman beside him.

"Your Mum was embarrassed."

Two children; Carol, already demanding attention at the age of fifteen, wearing a tight swimsuit that highlighted her trim figure and him, still wearing his woolen trunks, impatient to get down to the sea for a swim.

"Your mother was a beautiful woman."

The photo had started to fade, the monochrome image turning milky at the edges but his mother's face was sharp enough and the picture of her matched the image he carried in his head.

"I know."

Slim and pale, with eyes that had shone whenever she had looked at her children. Loss weighed heavily in his chest and for a moment, he could almost smell the light scent of her perfume, the way it used to linger in a room for a while after she had left it. It was difficult to accept that she had died so young from cancer, just twelve short years after this photograph was taken.

"Carol doesn't understand about Putney," Dad said.

"How do you mean?"

He looked at Danny. "The badness of the place."

"Badness? What are you talking about?"

"What it did to us! To you!"

The family had moved away soon after he was clear of meningitis, heading east to settle in Norwich, where he had joined another school, started a new life.

Gazing at the familiar curve of his mother's frozen smile, Danny sought some message, as he had countless times in the past, some secret clue perhaps hidden in her dark eyes. He'd found nothing then either, yet still the impression remained that, should he look hard enough...

"You nearly died."

"It was a virus! I could have contracted it anywhere."

Dad shook his head, "Putney robbed my sister of her son, your cousin."

Yes, Danny thought, before he was born, when his aunt Alice had moved to Putney after being bombed out of her house in Tooting. Trevor, who was four, contracted the disease and died. Alice and the rest of her family had moved to Australia soon after that and contact with them was down to a Christmas card - most years. Was the Old Man suggesting that, had Alice moved somewhere other than Putney, Trevor would be alive now?

"There was a lot of meningitis about back then."

Dad's hooded eyes slipped away from him and for a moment, he felt like grabbing hold of the scrawny old carcase and shaking it until he stopped talking such rubbish.

"It robbed you of your father," Dad said quietly.

Danny stared at him.

"It was where he went into the river."

Growing up, Dad had always been ready to tell him about the past, anything that might help him put some kind of meaning to the years he'd lost. He had never told him that Jack had died in Putney and for a moment, Danny felt light headed. It had always just been, 'The River', nothing more, no specifics. He had always assumed that the exact entry point had been elsewhere down stream, not on Jack's own doorstep, so near his home, his family.

Now, after all these years...

A wave of anger surged through him. There were a thousand things to say, questions, recriminations but the words stuck in his throat. He had to get away from there, from Dad.

The album weighed heavy in his hand and he was siezed by the urge to throw it at the old bastard. Suddenly it seemed that everything bad in his life could be laid, in one way or another, at the Old Man's door. Instead, he dropped the album into the empty armchair beside him.

"You mustn't go there," Dad said. "This is important, you have to listen to me!"

"I'm not a kid anymore. I don't have to listen to you ever again. I spent my whole life doing that and where has it got me?"

Dad sat down heavily, or as heavily as a bag of skin and bones can sit down, looking hurt, a little lost. Danny could almost feel sorry for him, almost.

"You never told me before. How could you not tell me?"

The scale of the deceit rose up, a red mist before his eyes. "You were so fucking happy talking about the past, your past, tales of you and your best buddie. Adventures and scrapes, down to the smallest detail. You never thought to mention the place he died!"

"It didn't matter before."

"It mattered to me!"

"You can't go back there!" The strength of his obsession was plain to see. He really did blame Putney for the death of his old mate.

Dad took up a pipe that was black and gnarled with age, the mouthpiece almost chewed through, the bowl thick with carbon. Using a forefinger to tamp down whatever it was that he had in there, he struck a match and held the flame to the bowl, puffing until he had a good burn going.

Almost at once he broke into a bout of coughing that turned his face from pink to red to purple and Danny found himself wondering how he would feel if the old sod keeled over right there and then in front of him. He had to admit that he was not sure and the truth of this bothered him.

"If you go, you're a bigger fool than I thought!"

"I'll let you know what I decide when I do it."

The album lay open on the chair. Mum's face looked up at him with what suddenly seemed reproachful eyes and Danny turned away. What was the point of keeping such things anyway, dead moments preserved on chemically treated paper? Shades of the past, frozen in time for people to paw over as the present slipped away!

"I'll call you," he said and left.

Downstairs, emerging from the block, Danny felt a bolt of pain in his lower back. He gazed miserably at the empty street. All his life, he had been trying to please that old man and for once it would have been nice to if Dad could respect him for who he was, what he thought.

"Damn him!"

He wanted to cling on to his anger but already fingers of guilt were stretching out inside him, diluting it. Dad could be mean, self-centred, he deserved bawling out ocassionaly. Still Danny regretted having lost his temper like that. The Old Man couldn't help being what he was, anymore than Danny could help being him. All else aside, he had been looked after, fed and clothed...loved.

A few snow flakes skittered across the pavement. He thought of Dad sitting up there in his spartan flat with no company but his memories. He had grown old, nothing more, a fate everyone had to look forward to. It was just that sometimes, he could quite happily kill him and the truth of that made Danny feel even worse about himself.

Would things have been easier with his real father?

P. C. Jack Reed had drowned in a vain attempt to save a woman from the Thames, plunging into the river on a wet evening, carless of his own safety. The silly bitch had been throwing a stick into the river for her dog to retrieve and when it had got into trouble, had gone in after it.

A dirty night, fog on the water, a tug's horn maybe, sounding low and mournful away in the dark, that was how he had always imagined it. What had she been thinking of?! They had both perished, although her body was never found. According to Dad, the dog had got out by itself.

Jack Reed's remains had turned up on a muddy foreshore the following day. The river had drawn him deep into its belly, releasing him only when the last trickle of life had been sucked from him.

Danny felt weary. He needed to get going, so he hitched up the collar of his coat and walked across the grass to where he had left the Cortina. Inside the car, he sat staring head, lost in the past that Dad had painted for him.

Jack had been Dad's best friend from boyhood. Born in London, they had run the same dirty Wandsworth pavements together, skinned knuckles and knees. Leaving school at fourteen, they went to work as milk boys for George Skinner, owner of a local dairy.

Skinner, a heavy drinker, had been unrelenting in his efforts to extract every penny's worth of graft from the youths. When drink got the better of him, he often took a horsewhip to the them for some triviality, real or imagined. One day Jack had enough of this, flooring the man with a punch to the jaw and Skinner had sacked them both at the top of his voice, still lying on a carpet of straw and horse shit.

Work was hard to find and a week later, tired of walking the pavements of south London looking for a job, the two friends had taken the King's shilling, joining the Royal Artillary. Jack's idea was that they would be conscripted anyway now war had been declared. It would be better to volunteer, for that way they would at least have the choice of the outfit they served in. So they had and a year later, had sailed away on their adventure across the channel.

Some bloody adventure!

It was a shade warmer inside the car, out of the breeze but the heat he had built up coming there was fast vanishing. He slipped the key into the Cortina's ignition but didn't turn on the engine. Leaning back against the head rest, he felt the remnants of the headache lurking above his left eyebrow.

Jack, eager to take on the Nazis, outraged by cinema newsreels of Hitler's involvement in the Spanish Civil War and later, assaults on Czechoslovakia and Poland, had had his first forray against the enemy cut short. On the wide, sandy beaches of Dunkirk, he was hit in the leg by a strafing Stuka and had been speedily shipped out, leaving Dad to fight the rearguard action without him.

Had the Old Man appreciated the irony?

Danny grunted with dark humour and toyed with the idea of going back up to the flat to ask him. As a boy he had listened greedily to Dad's stories about Jack and studied the couple of dog-eared photographs Dad still possessed. He would wish with all his heart that Jack was there with him, asking himself the never to be answered question, why had he died such a foolish death, when he had been needed so much?

He started the car and sat looking over the bonnet. He really wanted to see Chrissie, let her sooth away his troubles. But she had been doing that for a long while now and he could not blame her if she was tired of it. How many of her troubles had he taken an interest in? If he went to the house now, he would be as welcome as a stale smell.

Danny put the Ford in gear and drove away.

Chapter Three

Carol's house was one of the big, expensive ones that back onto the Wensum in one of the most expensive areas of the city. A few meters along the tow path from her garden gate, a local yacht club boasted row upon row of water craft, where restored wherries and the very latest in water-sport chic, vied for space at its limited quayage.

The house consisted of twelve rooms, five on the ground floor, seven upstairs, plus a large basement cum utility room, where Nick would occasionally rattle genuine ivory snooker balls around a full sized vintage table, an expensive present to himself on the occasion of his forty-sixth birthday. Add a couple of large, luxury bathrooms and it was easy to understand how two people could live in the same house, without seeing much of each other. A swimming pool, added to the property when Thea was a child had later been enclosed, after Nick was siezed by the idea of getting himself into shape. He had soon tired of his morning constitutional and the pool was now mostly used by guests.

Between the house and the tow path was a high wall protecting a garden stocked with all manner of bushes and trees, tended by an old chap from a local village, whose wife came in three times a week to clean and cook the occasional meal. He would fork and cut and feed, and keep the lawned areas smooth and rich enough to play bowls upon, if anyone played, which they didn't.

Having managed to get the Cortina started first time for the second day running, Danny drove there, parking in the only space available on the shingled forecourt. Sitting behind the wheel, gazing at the fabric of his sister's house, the aged red brick, the period style replacement windows, the huge, studded front door, he was tempted to turn around and drive out of there as fast as he could.

He felt out of sorts, thanks to the two cans of beer he'd consumed last night in an attempt to silence his inner voices. It had livened up Friday night's skinful and he'd woken up this morning feeling like a rung out dish cloth. He belched wetly and got out of the car, the prospect of spending an afternoon in the bosom of his family not exactly filling him with joy.

Following the flagged path that led round to the back of the house, he cursed himself for not having the nouse to have phoned Carol, explained how rough he felt and that he wouldn't be coming to lunch. She would have given him grief about not seeing Thea before she left, like the girl could give a damn about that, but at least he'd have been spared what was to follow.

He paused at the corner of the pool house, preparing himself. Overhead the sky was heavy with grey clouds, hanging ominously low. He shivered, the weather man had promised fresh snow falls across the south and east before the day was out. He couldn't wait.

The pool house glass was thick with condensation but he didn't need to see inside to know exactly what awaited him. All the usual faces would be there, the hangers-on, the ones who never missed one of Carol soirees because, in spite of Nick's disgrace, he still enjoyed considerable influence in high places. The up and coming business types who had arrived in the collection of expensive metal parked out front, were anxious to keep in with him, hoping to benefit from anything he might toss their way.

He winced as a spasm of pain from his back went running down his right buttock and he moved along the back of the property, feeling like a beggar at the feast. Reaching the pool house door, he stood there doing an al fresco hokey-cokey with his right leg to ease the pain, while listening to the muffled sound of jollity from inside. Finally, with a sigh, he opened the sliding door enough to slip through, into the fug of heat and chlorine inside and stood there, getting used to the atmosphere, trying to quell the waves of discomfort in his gut.

The pool, to his right, looked blue and inviting, while to his left, another wall of glass sectioned off the top end of the structure, creating a sizeable anti-room, which Carol had decked out with cane furniture and lush, dark green plants in huge terracotta pots. All very classy, *Not very him!*

Shucking his overcoat, he walked along to the doorway with it draped over his arm and stepped through into a decent sized space, tiled in expensive Italian floor tiles which screamed Tuscan sunshine. Three long, cloth covered tables had been set at the top of the room all groaning under the weight of a buffet luncheon. Farther back, close to what used to be the outside wall of the house, another couple of tables groaned under the weight of enough booze to make any lush think he had died and gone to heaven.

"Hey! Hey! Listen!"

Nick's voice, raised above the general hubbub, was aimed at a group of grinning idiots fooling around like a bunch of teenagers on the edge of the pool. Danny watched with a weary knowingness of what was to follow.

"What do you do when a bird shits on your car?" but the group, play acting pushing each other into the water, ignored him until he raised the volume. "Do you want to hear this or not!"

His voice held the raucous edge it took on when he had been drinking and his face darkened ominously. His audience, four men and three women, all of them well into their thirties, caught the sharpness of his tone and dutifully settled down.

"What do you do if a bird shits on your car?"

He held them there, drawing it out to way past its moment and they stood grinning expectantly, as though they could not wait to hear the punch line. It was a pretty good performance, considering they must all have heard the gag a dozen times before, because it was one of his party pieces.

"You don't take her out again."

Nick threw back his head, guffawing and his admirers quickly followed suit. Appeased by their fawning, he began splashing champagne into their glasses, which were lined along the edge of the pool. Danny turned away and saw Carol bearing down on him like a barracuda.

"You're late!" she said. "And you look awful."

"I can go if you like."

She seized his arm and steered him towards a table at the far side of the anti-room, where a middle-aged woman sat, watching their approach over the rim of her wine glass.

"Where's Thea?"

"She had to catch an earlier train." Her tone said she didn't want to discuss the matter and he guessed that his niece had fled the impending luncheon as fast as she possibly could.

"This is my baby brother, Danny," Carol announced as they reached the table where the woman sat. "Danny, meet Hilary."

"Nice to meet you," he said, trying to look enthusiastic but his face felt all wrong. At least she was a fresh face, a hand he had never shaken before.

"Carol's been telling me about you," she said, reaching out languidly and wrapping long fingers around his blunt digits.

"I bet she has."

Hilary smirked. "You are her baby brother, after all."

"Adoptive baby brother," he said and noticed Carol's smile didn't get anywhere near her eyes.

Hilary, a tall and sinewy creature, gave a low chuckle. He guessed she was in her fifties and at the moment, seemed to be well oiled, judging from the near empty bottle of Pinot noir at her elbow. She was dressed in an unflattering outfit of orange and yellow, which clung to her rather bony body and must have been expensive.

Carol said, "Hilary's on a fishing trip. She will no doubt be only too glad to tell you that she writes for The _"

"Darling, you do me an injustice!" Hilary said in a voice fashioned by years of smoking. "I never talk shop on the Sabbath. Well hardly ever."

"She's like the police, never off duty."

Hilary raised her glass, looking over the top of it at Danny. "Your sister can be very –"

"I know. She's had plenty of practice."

Carol's smile waned even more. It vanished altogether when another loud burst of laughter came from the pool area. Excusing herself, she walked through to Nick's group, with Hilary's eyes on her all the way.

"I've often wondered at the attraction. He must be a good ten years older than her."

"Try twelve and you'd be closer. As for the attraction, just look around you."

Hilary, smiling thinly, said. "Carol's sending you to London?"

"That's news to me," Danny managed a smile of his own. "She said she has a job for me but as to the details..."

"I believe it's Putney. You lived there, didn't you?"

Carol must have told her, which slightly irritated him. What other nuggets of his personal business had she been discussing?

"Until I was eleven," he said.

"I believe she wants you to deliver a package to someone living there."

"You know more than I do, then."

"All a bit, unconventional don't you think? The way the job came about?"

"Like I said, I know zilch about it."

With an enigmatic smile, she moved across to the wall of glass that looked out onto the garden. Danny hesitated a moment then followed her over.

"You lost your memory, I believe?"

Carol really had really gone to town! It wasn't as though the matter was secret, it had been discussed with family and friends so often over the years, there was nothing left to say about it. But it was his business and it was up to him with whom he shared it!

"Your early years have gone completely, haven't they?"

"Anything before I was eleven," he said. "Dissociative Amnesia, they call it. I'm surprised Carol didn't say."

She eyed him speculatively, "Have you never had treatment? Is there any treatment?"

"Not really. Nothing conclusive at least. You just have to wait and hope for the best."

"You've been waiting a long time."

Danny looked out at the garden, dead now and at the heavy, grey sky full of wintery promise.

"Yes. A while."

"Must be frustrating at times."

"You get used to it. Sort of."

His anger at Carol lacked sting. He felt as though he should be outraged but talking about it with Hilary felt a kind of relief.

"There were doctors," he said. "Specialists. All said the same thing."

"Here?"

"And in Cambridge, London, I don't remember much about it, just different rooms and different studious looking men studying me, asking questions. At the end of it, the answer was always the same. Dressed up differently but the same. It will return in its own time."

"Or not?"

Before he could comment, Carol returned. He could see ice burning in her eyes. "We'll go through to the back."

"Okay."

"I'll see you later, Danny. I was enjoying our conversation," Hilary said.

"You're easily pleased." A pudgy hand slapped down on Danny's shoulder, a little harder than was necessary for a friendly greeting and Nick was standing beside him.

"Don't be naughty, darling," Hilary said.

"Anyone want a drink?" His empty glass dangled lazily between two thick fingers, his face oozing false bonhomie.

"Don't you think you've had enough?" Carol said.

"Not nearly enough, my sweet."

"If you spoil this afternoon," she said coldly, "I'll never forgive you."

He blinked, looked at her for a second, then his fat face crumpled in a huge, boozy grin. "Which implies forgiveness is an option."

"Go to hell!"

"I already did that, a long time ago."

Danny sighed, shifted impatiently and Nick's wet eyes rolled around to focus on him. "You think you'll be working for Carol, but you'll really be working for me. I pay the wages!"

Carol squeezed his arm, "Ignore him."

"I generally do," Danny said and made to walk away.

Carol stepped into the centre of the room and raised her voice to her guests. "Come on, everyone! This all has to go."

"Don't worry, old son," Nick said. "There will be enough left for you to take home a doggie bag."

He grinned nastily at Danny, obviously thinking he'd delivered a cutting, well placed jibe.

"Go back to your friends," Carol hissed, rejoining them.

Nick shoved his hands deep into his pockets, dragging the waist band of his trousers down past his navel so that his shirt was half in, half out.

"And miss quality time with my brother-in-law?"

His fat belly lolled over the top of his belt. Two top shirt buttons were open exposing a spread of hairless chest which, like his face, was the colour of dough. His eyes glinted maliciously between puffy lids as he cast a wide-armed gesture in the direction of the luncheon tables, staggering slightly in the process.

"Go on, old son, indulge yourself! You've had your hand deep in my pocket for years, so what can a few mere morsels of sustenance matter?"

Danny knew he was refering to the loan Carol had made him, which had come from her own savings. The loan had irked Nick a lot. He thought it was another example of her bailing her brother out from a bank balance she wouldn't have if it were not for him.

Heads turn towards them and a wave of anger rushed up Danny's throat. The fat bastard was asking for it and right at that moment, he was just the boy to give it to him.

"Kitchen," Carol said, quickly taking his arm again. "Now!"

"Something I said?" Nick sneered.

"Sit down, you drunken sot!" Her eyes flashed and he fell backward into a chair, as though pole-axed. She turned Danny towards the door which led through to the house, pushing him along in front of her.

"Cunt!" Nick said.

"Such eloquence," Hilary remarked, sourly.

Carol walked him through to the kitchen in silence, her face tight and pale. She feared a repeat of the Christmas set to but Danny's temper was already draining away. By the time they reached the kitchen, all he felt was washed out.

"He's drunk."

"What's his usual excuse?"

"Are you all right?"

"I've been better." The force of his rage had left him with an empty feeling inside. "I would have hit him."

"That really would have spoilt my luncheon."

He thought she was joking but she wasn't and that almost made him laugh.

"Cool down!" Carol closed the door and turned a worried face on him.

"I already have." He moved across to sit at the kitchen table, troubled by the knowledge that, had he hit Nick this time, he may well have gone on hitting him until his pent up fury had burnt itself out.

"Do you want coffee?"

He said he did and watched Carol walk across to where the percolator stood on its warming plate.

"You told Dad about the job."

She poured two mugs, put them on a tray, added the milk jug and a few Marks and Spencer biscuits on a plate, then brought it all to the table. Neither of them used sugar. Opening a drawer at the end of the table, she fished out a couple of coasters and deposited them strategically, placing one very deliberately in front of him.

"I may have mentioned it," she said, casually. With exaggerated care, she placed a mug upon each coaster, then took the empty tray back to the work-top. "Is that a problem?"

"Not for me, it isn't," Danny said.

"Meaning?"

"It seemed to be, for him."

She raised an eyebrow questioningly.

"He told me not to go to London. To Putney, to be precise."

"Really?" The tone to her voice told him Dad had said as much to her. She sat down facing him, "How odd."

Across the room was an inglenook fireplace. The previous owner had boarded it over but on Carol's insistence it had been opened up. She thought it was just crying out for an Aga stove. Well there the stove stood, its gleaming black finish as pristine as the day it was delivered. Carol rarely cooked and as far as he knew, Nick never did.

He smiled at her, "That stove really does look good, set amid all this granite and stainless steel."

"I know." She eyed him steadily, waiting.

"He was acting weird. Like he's losing his marbles."

"Can you be a little more specific?

"He seems to believe that Putney is cursed in some way. Bad news for this family and for me in particular. "

"That's ridiculous."

"You reckon?" he said pointedly.

Her eyes met his, moved away. She sipped her coffee and placed her mug firmly on its coaster, fingers toying with the handle.

"I didn't know he was the superstitious type."

"He isn't?" she said, quickly.

"Perhaps we should think about putting him in a home."

She started, jogging her mug and slopping coffee onto the table. Springing up, she hurried across the room, returning with a wad of kitchen towelling, with which she blotted up the mess.

"That's going a little far!"

"The man believes in - ," he struggled to find the right word

"What?" she demanded.

"I don't know," he saw her lips tighten. "The man seems to believe that a place has a personal vendetta against me. Like a curse or something. Perhaps he's getting senile."

They had discussed residential care many times in the past and she had always been firmly opposed to the idea. It was almost as though she was frightened to face up to the fact that Dad was growing older, frailer and that soon there would be no alternative between a home or having him to live with her.

"We might have to put him away for his own good."

"I think you're exaggerating!"

He wondered whether the Old Man had given her the full treatment, the way he had with him. Somehow, he doubted it. "You weren't there."

"He can still look after himself"

"I'd like to think so."

He thought about telling her what had happened with the gang of youngsters but decided he wouldn't. If she wanted to see things through a rosey glow of denial, that was up to her. Whatever bug had crawled up the old bugger's scrawny arse about Putney, he could deal with alone.

"What did he say to you?"

"Not a lot." She said quickly, as she took the soiled wad of towelling across to the pedal bin. "He just felt it wasn't a good idea."

Dumping the wad inside, she came back to the table and reached into the drawer from which she had taken the coasters.

"Have you thought about what I said?"

"Anything in particular?"

"Please don't be obtuse!"

"I'm not. You didn't exactly explain."

She sighed. "I need you to deliver a package to Kavanagh Mansions."

"So, Hilary was right."

She frowned, "Well, what do you think?"

"I'm not sure. Dad may have a point."

She sighed, "I don't have time for this!"

She crossed her hands on the table and stared hard at him. If there was one thing in life that he could still get some enjoyment from, it was winding Carol up. Childish, but fun, or it was when it worked. This time, she wasn't biting.

"Okay, I'll do it. I always wanted to be a private dick."

Her face wrinkled with distaste. "Please don't use such terminology, we're not talking pulp fiction novels now. This is real life."

Which meant, discrete surveillence, fraud investigations for respectable clients, serving legal papers, engaging bailiffs and occasionally gathering evidence in a divorce case. Tracing missing people was the nearest thing her operatives got to the dirty worlds of Philip Marlow and Mike Hammer.

Suitably chastened, Danny sat back, arms folded across his chest, "I was kind of hoping for something more permanent."

"This is a one off job." She looked at him for a moment, then said, "I'll see how you get on and if things work out, there could be more work later. I'm not promising anything."

"I'd need training for that," he said.

"You'd get it. But you won't need it for this job."

"So what do you want me to do?"

"I told you, deliver a package."

"What's the matter with Royal Mail?"

"Do you want the job or not?"

"Sorry."

"This is a special package. The client doesn't want to trust it to regular delivery services."

Danny looked at her. "Is it dirty?"

"Of course it isn't!"

"Only Hilary seems to think - "

"Hilary has an active imagination, much the same as you." Carol stood up and walked across the room to a cupboard in the far corner. "It's a personal item. Family heirloom or something and of great sentimental value."

"And I'm to deliver it to Kavangh Mansions."

"Precisely."

The Warning Group, Nick's family business, had acquired an old Edwardian apartment block at Putney as part of a major property deal. Real estate, being a recent addition to the company's portfolio. They already owned a number of properties in the Home Counties and around the capital and this place was to be their next venture.

Most of the flats were empty and the last few tenants were on short term leases, which were nearing their end. The intention was to renovate the place and sell the units on at a huge profit. Carol had been so excited, she had all but purred when she had told him about it.

He watched her take a rectangular package, wrapped in thick brown paper from the cupboard. He couldn't blame her being excited. With property prices set to rocket in London, eight two bedroom, luxury apartments with river views was tantamount to sitting on a goldmine.

She brought the package across to him, as though she was bearing the Holy Grail. He took it, felt it, weighed it in his hands. "There's no weight to it."

"You should be able to manage it then."

"Ha-ha," he said, pressing the edge of the package between a thumb and forefingerer. "Thin, hard object, bumps at the corners. Feels like a picture frame. What is it, eight by four in old money?"

"I haven't measured it."

He laid the package on the table. "When do you want me to go?"

She opened a drawer at the end of the table and brought out a British Rail Inter City ticket booklet, which she laid it in front of him. "Open return. First Class. The sooner you can get it done the better."

He took a biscuit, then took a couple more. They were that sort of biscuit. He pointed at the package, "There's no address on this."

"I know."

"So how -?"

"It's for the caretaker. A man named Cockle. He lives in a flat, in the basement."

"Resident caretaker? I'm impressed. There can't be many of those around these days."

"It's a temporary placement. He's there to keep an eye on the place once the tenants have gone."

He squeezed the package again. "Is there payment involved with this job?"

"Not as such. Let's say you'll be doing me a favour and to show my appreciation, I'll let you off the money you owe you."

"We'll be quits?"

"I don't know if we'll ever be that, but as far as what you owe me, you can forget about it."

"Thanks, Carol." This was a really good deal. More! It was a spectacular deal. He drew the package towards him. "Is there a pub near Kavanagh Mansions?"

She eyed him sharply.

"I'll need to get some lunch before I come home."

"Find a cafe."

"I'm sure I can behave myself."

"You're not funny, you know?"

"But I try."

"Yes, my patience."

Danny picked up the tickets. "You were so sure I'd go?"

"Of course. What else would you do?"

He was not sure he liked being thought of as so predictable. "I can't believe you asked me. I mean, with my track record."

"Even you can't go wrong with a simple delivery job."

She carried the mugs to the sink and turned on the hot tap. "This needs handling soon."

"I'll go Tuesday. I'm taking Chrissie to lunch tomorrow."

Carol turned, surprised. "She agreed to that?"

"I haven't asked her yet. I'll tell her I want to talk about selling the house."

"But you don't intend to?"

"No. That's what I'll tell her, then I'll work my charm on her."

"Should be a short lunch then."

He was quiet for a moment, thinking about the best way to approach Chrissie but every way he thought of seemed to lead to failure so he put the matter aside until later.

"What's this surprise you have for me?"

Carol dried the mugs, standing them carefully back in place on the shelf where they lived. "I hadn't forgotten."

Returning to the table, she slipped her hand into the drawer again and brought out a photograph, which she laid on the table in front of him.

"Everyone wants to show me photographs all of a sudden."

It was same type of photo Dad had in his collection, taken back in the Fifties on the same type of box Brownie camera. It showed a street scene, the fronts of terraced cottages, workman's places by the look of them, with a small group of children standing on the pavement, looking towards the camera with big smiles.

At the centre of the group was a grinning policeman in full uniform, fisted hands on his hips, helmet firmly on his head, while the children gathered round him, six in all, four boys and two girls, looking happily at the camera, at least most of them were. The two at the back must have moved just as the snap was taken and consequently, their images were blurred.

"Have you seen it before?" Carol asked.

"You know I haven't."

"That is your father, isn't it?"

Danny nodded, looking closely at the photo. It was hard to be certain at first, this man looked much older than the young soldier who had stood beside Dad in the other photos he'd seen. This man looked as though he'd experienced much more of life than anyone should have at his age.

"Where did you get it?"

"Dad let me have a box of Mum's needle work stuff for one of the women at work. Her daughter is suddenly mad on craft work."

"You mean from the cupboard?"

There were half a dozen walk-in lock-up cupboards, ground floor back of Dad's block. The Council rented them to any tenant who wanted one. Dad had all his accumulated junk in there, mostly old tat he'd picked up along the way, an old bicycle too, hidden away with just the spiders for company.

"I found that in the bottom, in an envelope."

"Hidden?"

She looked surprised. "Why on earth would it be hidden?"

Danny shrugged, not sure why he'd said it. He supposed that he'd always though it odd that Dad should have so few snaps of his best mate. The only two he knew of were the pair of them in uniform and that was it. Dad had told him that most of his momentos had been destroyed when his mother's house was bombed during the Blitz but there had always been doubt in Danny's mind.

"Funny he's never mentioned it."

"He's probably forgotten all about it?"

"You didn't tell him what it was?

"I will when I remember. I thought you might like it."

There had been times in his childhood, the section he could remember, when he had felt that things were being kept from him. He hadn't known what but the suspicion was always there. Later, no longer a child, he'd decided that his suspicions had really been more a child's wishful thinking, in the hope that something extra about his father might turn up out of the blue.

"It wasn't hidden!" She sounded like she was trying to convince herself instead of him. She had to be right though. What possible motive would Dad have for hiding it? But why hadn't he mentioned it back before he wasn't the forgetful old man he was now?

"And even if he remembered it, later. What would have been the point of telling you about it if he'd thought it lost? I mean, to tell you that it had existed but that he no longer had it. Wouldn't that have been worse?"

Dad was in the habit of writing on the back of photographs, a note of where and when it had been taken. Danny turned this one over and sure enough, there were several lines written in faded pencil.

"I suppose," he said, toying with the notion of going round to Dad's flat, of shoving the photo under his nose and demanding some answers.

Galvin Street, summer, 1955.

Jack with The Rudd Street Tykes; Joe, Raymond, Alan, Sarah, Brian and Veronica.

"Who were The Rudd Street Tykes?" Carol asked.

"You're asking me?!"

She studied the photo for a moment longer. "You're not there."

"No."

"Did you live in Galvin Street?"

"Yes. That's one thing I do know." The children surrounding the grinning policeman were all laughing, not tight, pretend laughs, genuine ones. The two at the back may well have been too. "I'll have to ask him about this."

Carol met his gaze and there were questions in her eyes as well. "Let me deal with it. It will be better if I speak to him."

He thought about it for a moment, already knowing that she was right. If he went round there, Dad might dig his heels in and there would be another row, whereas Carol would have him eating out of her hand in no time. He nodded, suddenly tired. His night's sleep had been fitful and he'd had enough. He wanted out of there, needed space in which to think.

"Are you going to eat?"

"I don't think so, do you?"

"I'm sorry about, Nick."

"You've been apologising for him since the day you met him. It hasn't changed him, so why keep wasting your breath?"

He donned his overcoat, slipping the rail ticket in the inside pocket. Then he picked up the package. "I'll go out the back way."

Following her through to a small vestibule at the rear of the kitchen, he waited while she took a chunky jumper from a hook on the back of the door and put it on.

"I'm really glad you took the job. I want to see you turn a corner, you know?"

He nodded, smiled, it was only a day trip to London, not a life changing event. They stepped outside into an almost Arctic chill. The clouds looked loaded and ominous.

"Do you think it will snow?" Carol asked, wrapping the cardigan tightly around her body.

"That's what the forecast says."

"I love snow."

"You can afford to."

She took his arm, started them along the side of the pool house. Inside, her guests were swarming like locusts around the food tables, leaving Nick sprawled in a camp chair fast asleep. His pudgy arms protruded over the fragile frame and the canvas seat bulge dangerously from the swell of his backside.

"Do you want a hand to move him?"

"Let him stay where he is." Her gaze was as icy as the afternoon air and Danny almost felt sorry for his brother-in-law. He was going to get hell when he sobered up.

A few years ago, Nick had thrown away a promising political career, thanks to his inability to keep his fly shut. Popular within his Party, it was generally accepted that it was just a matter of time before he was called upon to kiss the Prime Minister's ring. Then the story broke of the Honourable Member, sharing his honourable member with the twenty year old daughter of some minor aristocrat and the Sunday rags had had a field day.

Devouring every salacious detail over their Sunday morning Full Englishes, the great British public had been suitably outraged at the idea of a fleshy, middle-aged father, huffing and puffing on top of a girl not much older than his own daughter. The story snowballed, became a bridge too far for a Government already in trouble and Nick's fate was sealed.

Nick's father, a harsh and loveless man, had been determined that his son would follow him into the family business. Once Nick had blown apart his political career, there had been nowhere else for him to go and old Charlie

Warning had wasted no time bending his once recalcitrant son to his will.

Well, Old Charlie was dead and buried now but his daughter-in-law was twice the man he had been when it came to forcing Nick's nose back to the grindstone. It was a pity she didn't have as much control over his libido.

"I'll speak to Dad before you go."

"Look," he said, stopping at the corner of the pool house. "Any tips where to take Chrissie for lunch?"

"Where were you thinking?"

"Jack's Snacks, a really good cafe I used when I was working the cabs."

She sighed, "That's your idea of romantic, is it?"

"I wasn't thinking romance," he said but of course, he must have been.

"Well you ought to be. Surprise her. Do something different."

"Such as?"

"Take her to Julian's," she said after a moment's thought.

Danny groaned inwardly. He was never comfortable in the swanky joints she frequented. "That sounds a bit..."

"You mean, it's not a greasy spoon?" she said sourly. "It gets pretty busy at lunch time. I'll phone and provisionally book a table. They know me, so they won't mind if I have to cancel."

"Okay," he said reluctantly. "About one o'clock should do it."

She nodded and they walked round to the front of the house. Stopping beside the Cortina, she released his arm and stood in front of him, smoothing down the lapels of his overcoat.

"I'll call later about the table."

With her palms resting on his chest, she kissed him on the cheek, (twice in as many days!) then turned and walked away. Watching her go, Danny wondered how she could stand it, all those people inside, the falseness of the world in which they existed. Most of all though, he wondered again how she could stand being married to Nick. He'd been advising her to leave him for ages but she would not listen.

"I'm not taking advice on my marriage from someone who's struggling to keep his own relationship together!"

Which was a good point.

Pausing at the front door, Carol looked back. He raised a hand, smiled, saw her slip quickly inside, no doubt off to adjust her hair and make-up before re-joining her guests.

Carol's reasons for staying were right there in front of him, the house and all that went with it. She had worked hard, getting what she wanted out of life, riding her rainbow for all she was worth. There had been no long evenings swatting in a cold bedroom for her, no anxiety about what results she would get from her exams. She was blessed with the ability to soak up information like a sponge. All her life, things had fallen into place for Carol, as though her fairy godmother sat on her shoulder, casting moon dust at her feet.

Not that he begrudged her the gifts that nature had bestowed upon her. She was his sister, how could he begrudge her anything? What had always annoyed him though, was the way she had taken it all for granted, as though good fortune was her birth right. She had sailed through school into Sixth Form College without breaking sweat, emerging two years later with three GCE 'A' level passes under her belt. This had had the Old Man boasting about her abilities so much, friends and neighbours had started to avoid him. Then, she had just turned her back on academia, packing her bags to go off around Europe with some air-headed hippies, smoking pot and wearing flowers in her hair.

And the old sod had barely raised an eyebrow!

He climbed into the car and sat staring out at nothing in particular. She was right, it was none of his business how she lived her life. It was simply that, at moments like the one just now, when weariness seemed to be rolling off her in waves, he felt at his most protective towards her.

Like she needs your protection!

When he was a kid, they had not been close, her regarding herself as all but grown up with her few years over him. She did used to tell him stories at night and go with him to the park at weekends so that they could ride the swings, on the odd occasion when she stepped down from her high horse.

He smiled, remembering she had sensitive flanks and how, when he'd felt brave enough, he would tickle her until she screamed hysterically. If he were to tickle her now, he could not imagine what her reaction would be.

He started the car's engine but didn't do anything else, just sat there gazing into space. They had been growing apart for years and the chasm between them sometimes seemed so wide, it would be hard to bridge. Carol was his sister and he loved her, he was unable to like her as often as he wanted to and that made him sad.

She had returned from her wanderings after a year, in the company of a Canadian girl, whose father was something to do with the High Commission in Trafalgar Square. They had decided to go into business, with the Canadian, who was quite well off in her own right, using her money to open a shop on the King's Road in London, selling love beads and incense sticks.

Bloody cow bells!

It was there that she had met Nick, who had wandered in one day looking for what, Danny could not imagine. He had always had a big problem picturing Nick in a Kaftan and could only assume he had entered the place just to meet Carol.

In those days, Nick had been a good looking guy, more than that, a good looking guy with money, a combination Carol had been unwilling to pass up. Turning her back on love beads and exotic hookahs, she had set her mind to matrimony.

And now she has it all, he thought, well almost. There was the nice house, the thriving business, the more than healthy bank account, and enough soundly placed investments to allow her to live to a ripe old age on the interest they accumulated. She also had a husband who was a serial philanderer and a child who avoided the pair of them.

Which is still more than you have, sunshine.

A sudden gust of cold air chased dead leaves across the forecourt. He slipped the gear stick into first and was about to pull away when someone knocked on the window beside him. Looking up, he saw Hilary gazing in at him from the between the folds of a thick fur coat. She gestured for him to roll down the window and he groaned inwardly.

"Are you going?"

"Not really my scene."

"I mean to London." She eyed the package on the passenger seat beside him.

He looked at her, "What's this about?"

"Take this," Hilary said, offering him a business card. "When you get back, phone me."

"I don't understand."

"Phone me!"

She turned abruptly and walked quickly back towards the house. Looking at the card, he saw it had her name and two phone numbers on it, one private, the other business. What was that all about, he wondered as he put the Cortina into gear then, shutting the window, he released the handbrake and drove away.

Chapter Four

He drove to the city centre some time after six. He was hungry and thinking about the Indian take-away he sometimes used. He could walk it in no time, thirty minutes there and back but on this cold Sunday evening the idea of slogging through all those narrow side streets, the wind blowing at him all the way, made him use the car.

The roads were all but empty anyway and he was soon parking the Cortina in a space on the top road, above the market square. Getting out, he locked up and set off into the chill. Down through the maze of market stalls, all shut up tight and across the square, led by the stomach rumbling smell of spicy food from the Bengal Star. Already dark, the street lamps were on, their yellowish glow contributing to the need he felt for a warm meal and a cosy front room.

He ordered his food, a chicken dopiaza with Basmati rice and a side of ago saag, then sat on the bench in front of the shop window to wait for it. The air was warm and heavy, thick with the aroma of garlic and he started to feel drowsy. There was a discarded newspaper on the seat next to him so he picked it up and tried to read the front page but when his thoughts kept wandering, he gave up.

The Rudd Street Tykes.

The memory of the photo impressed itself upon him, the kids gathered around the local bobbie, who they had obviously regarded as a friend. Jack would have got to know them, like a good beat copper would do and when the photo had been taken, there was no reason why he wouldn't be in it.

And yet...

In 1955, Danny thought, he had been eleven years old, roughly the same age as the kids in the group by the look of them. Joe, Alan, Ray, Sarah, Brian and Vernoica.

Had he known them?

He tossed the newspaper aside, cursing the blankness in his head; life with no memory of then was often a drag. If Dad had shown him the photograph, he could have asked about the group, see if he was as pleased to talk about that photo as he was about the ones he *had* shown him.

Had he hidden it?

His food arrived, he paid for it and left. When he reached the deserted market square, he walked along past the closed shops, where light blazed in the windows above attractive displays for the New Year Sales, calling to no one but him. He pulled the collar of his overcoat closer around his chin as a blast of cold wind rushed at him.

The photograph troubled him slightly and not the mere fact that he had never seen it before. He could feel it nagging away inside him but couldn't put a finger on why. He didn't know the people in it, as far as he was aware, not even his own father but still he felt the pull of recognition calling him.

He stared at the empty racks of a jeweler's window display, all the valuables put away for the night. He'd been in the shop back in November, to hand over five hundred pounds he could not afford for a beautiful diamond and sapphire eternity ring for Chrissie's Christmas present.

What a bad move that had been!

She had thrown him out in September and he'd figured that the ring, wrapped nicely, opened on December 25th would not only show her what she meant to him, but might melt her resolve and she would ask him back. Instead, she'd returned the ring, wrapping paper and all and hadn't said a word. He still had the ring and still owed Carol the money he'd borrowed to buy it, or at least, he would for a few more days.

Skirting the market stalls, he climbed the stone steps to the road. At the top the huge Christmas tree standing in front of the council offices was still bedecked with coloured lights, which had not glowed since twelfth night. They made the tree look rather woebegone as it stood in the harsh up-light from the row of lamps sunken into the concrete at the foot of the building.

A couple of snow flakes, chased along by the breeze, brushed his nose as he turned towards his parked car. During Advent, carols had played across the market from banks of speakers arranged around the square and the shop windows had twinkled with fairy lights, the stores remaining open until even the most determined shoppers had finally started for home. Now those same shops were locked tight against the winter darkness, no music, no fairy lights and certainly no Santa's Grotto, just the grim reality of another New Year of strife in a world fast approaching the edge.

One distant Christmas Eve, he had walked here with his then pregnant wife, drawing in the closeness of her body, the soft pressure of her hand in his. Chrissie had been happy then, fulfilled in the knowledge that by late summer, their family would be complete, just like she had always wanted. Even he had started to come to terms with the reality of being a father. There had been no snow that evening but had they known it, a whole different kind of winter was soon to descend upon them in the shape of a miscarriage.

God bless us, every one.

He reached the car, dug into his pocket for the keys and cast a look up at the fourth floor of the Council building, where Chrissie worked. It was the Planning Department office and her desk stood at the fourth window along, from which she had often waved to him in the past when he'd spent his lunch hour in the city centre.

His eyes were watering and icy fingers caressed his neck. The windows were in darkness, like those in the rest of the building and standing there, in the after Christmas emptiness, he felt more lonely than he had for a long while. It seemed suddenly bleaker and a slight fuzziness in the head suggested the onset of another headache. He climbed into the Cortina feeling like Methusula on a bad day and shut the door.

He could do with a drink. Correction, he needed one. A couple of drinks maybe, just to drive out the coldness from his soul.

Medicinal almost.

The miscarriage had been the start of them falling apart and it was all his fault. If he'd acted differently, been more of a man, someone for her to lean on, then maybe it would have been a different story.

And Chrissie didn't know the worst of his cowardice!

He gripped the steering wheel and bowed his head. Closing his eyes, he waited for the surge of self contempt to subside. He had allowed it a peek from the cupboard he kept it locked away in and it had almost overwhelmed him. But he knew that he would have to allow it out soon, if he wanted to get her back, that was the price he must pay.

He started the engine and pointed the Cortina towards home.

Chapter Five

The phone ringing woke him up and his wrist watch told him it was eight thirty. He dragged himself out of bed, rubbing heavy eyelids, yawning and went through to answer it.

"Can you stop by the office later?" It was Carol.

"Why?"

"I'm going to see Dad at lunch time."

"Okay." He had not expected her to move so quickly. In fact, he had thought she might forget about it altogether.

"You could tell me over the phone."

"I want to tell you face to face. So you can see that I'm not hiding anything from you."

"I wouldn't think that?"

"You thought it of him."

"That's different." He did not expand on this and she didn't ask him to. "I'm phoning Chrissie about lunch later. I'll catch her at work."

"It's all booked. Julian's at one o'clock."

He thanked her and was about to hang up when she said, "Danny, don't be too disappointed if lunch doesn't go to plan. See you later."

He could always rely on her to put a dampener on things.

Or maybe she was being realistic.

He went through to the bathroom, showered, shaved, then went to the kitchen and put the kettle on to make coffee. While it was heating up, he returned to the phone. It was now quarter to ten. He held onto the receiver for a moment before finally tapping out the number of the Council offices and when the switchboard answered, he asked for Planning. A moment later the ringing was answered but a young woman.

"Can I speak to Chrissie, please?"

He told her who he was and she went away. After what seemed like an age, Chrissie came to the phone.

"Hello?" Her voice sounded wooden.

"I was wondering if you'd like to meet for lunch?"

There was long silence at the other end, then she finally said, "Do you think there is any point?"

"It's always good to talk," he said.

She sighed, asked him where and when. When he had told her, she hung up without another word.

Danny made his coffee, then toasted two slices of semi-stale bread, spreading each slice with butter and eating them at the table. He tried to figure out why he felt so down this morning. He had not gone drinking last night, he'd brought his curry home like a good boy and eaten it in front of the TV.

He thought about his call to Chrissie, telling himself he would get some dialogue going, tell her about London and the possibility of working for Carol, if everything went well.

"Like I could balls this up," he muttered.

That news should at least make her hear him out and with luck, once they'd started talking, it would go the way it always had in the past, she would come around.

How long would that last with what he had to tell her?

Last night his spirits had risen slightly. Thinking about today with a new optimism, he had treated himself to the very last nip from the half bottle of Teachers, Roy had given him for his birthday back in July and gone straight to bed. The next thing, he was dreaming of running as fast as he could along a high flat surface, arms and legs pumping, lungs burning, running for his life. When the surface suddenly ended, he could not stop and toppled into a dark void.

Falling...?

He blinked and took his dirty plate to the sink.

Julian's was in a narrow lane off the precinct, a bijou place tucked away between a shop selling wicker work and high price teddy bears, and one offering designer clothes to punters with more money than sense. The eatery was aimed at that same clientele and Danny eyed it doubtfully. Sharp, cream blinds, a crimson awning and no doubt menues in French. Typical Carol and he wished he'd ignored her, arranged to meet Chrissie at Jack's Snacks instead.

She arrived shortly after he got there, looking good in her black winter coat over dark green trousers. She'd had her hair cut very short, similar to the way she used to wear it when he'd first met her and she had kept her make-up light, green eyes highlighted, mouth clean and set in a tight line.

Danny smiled, told her she looked good and stepped forward to kiss her but she turned her head so that his lips brushed her cheek. Then she was moving towards the restaurant door.

"This is not like you," she said.

"Carol's suggestion."

"That explains it."

He remembered late and reached awkwardly round her to open the restaurant door, then followed her inside. She glanced around the place, smiled at the waitress who came towards them. Danny told the girl they had a reservation for two in his name.

"Oh, yes sir."

She led led them to a table in the window alcove, where Danny managed to get to Chrissie's chair before she did and pull it out. She eyed him strangely as she sat down and he was not sure whether she appreciated the gesture or not. As he went round to sit opposite her, the waitress conjured two menues from somewhere and handed them to Chrissie.

"Here," she said, passing one across to him.

When the waitress turned up again and asked if they wanted anything to drink, Chrissie said she'd have a tonic water, with ice and lemon, in a tall glass. Danny said he would have the same.

"You could have had a beer," she said, as the waitress moved off.

"I could have done," he said. "I'm off it at moment."

She raised an eyebrow, looking doubtful. "Since when?"

"The weekend."

She looked like she had been proven right in some way.

Danny studied the menu, which was in English and printed on thick, expensive paper, seeing dishes he'd never heard of. He glanced across at Chrissie but her eyes were firmly on her own copy. Finally he laid the menu aside and said, "I'll have a bacon roll and a mug of tea."

"This isn't a greasy spoon," she said, quietly. "They have a good choice of Club Sandwich, have one of those."

So he did, opting for one with chicken and bacon, which was pretty close to what he'd had in mind in the first place, only a damned sight more expensive. Chrissie chose an omelette with salad. The waitress popped up beside the table and Danny wondered whether she could read their minds. He gave her the order, she smiled and went.

"What?" he asked when she had gone.

"You look uncomfortable."

"Do I? Well I don't feel it."

He felt irritated. Any discomfort was down to the way she was behaving, like she doubted the wisdom of being there.

"What did you want to talk about?"

Like she didn't know!

"You want to sell the house," he said, sounding sharper then he'd meant to.

"I can't keep up the mortgage payments on my own."

"You're not on your own. My severance money covers my share."

"While it lasts."

"There's enough there for a while yet."

"What's the point? You could use it for something else if we sold up."

"I don't want to sell up!"

His voice carried, making her cheeks flush and her eyes went off on a quick tour of the room, befor settling back on him, cold as the weather outside.

"Do not make a scene."

"For Christ's sake, Chrissie!"

The drinks came. They smiled at the waitress and took their glasses, sipping at their drinks until the girl left.

"I'll leave if you start shouting."

"I won't do that." He was a lot of things, but he wasn't the type to kick off in public, she should know that by now.

Chrissie took more of her iced tonic water and watched him cautiously. He said, "I want us to try again."

"We're always trying again, it never works."

"It could this time."

He'd given their relationship a lot of thought over the last few days, not just the casual kind of thinking he'd done in the past, this time he'd really gone into it. He'd settled on the fact that their problems were mostly down to him, the way he behaved. His general attitude to life. Not that he was going to say that.

"I've got a new job."

She looked at him. "That's good news. Where?"

"With Carol."

She put her glass down and looked at him even harder, "With Carol? You!"

"Is it that hard to believe?"

"Yes, it is actually. The pair of you are always arguing and with the best will in the world, I can't see you as a private investigator."

"Why?" He felt hurt.

"You're not subtle enough. Not for her kind of agency."

He saw that she was trying to smother a grin. "I'm doing a job for her tomorrow, actually."

"What sort of job?"

He told her he was going to London. "I have to deliver a special package to an address in Putney."

"A delivery job."

"Yes," he tried to keep the positive note in his voice. "Right."

"Carol said she would think about a permanent job if this goes well."

"You're delivering a package. What could go wrong?"

The waitress arrived with their food, spent some time placing the meals before them, deftly arranging cutlery and serviettes. "Do you needed anything more?"

Danny said that they were fine and the young woman left with a chirpy, *bon apetite*. He looked across at Chrissie's omlette and fancy side salad. Saw her cut a small piece of omlette and place it delicately into her mouth.

"So, what do you think?"

"About the job? I'm glad for you, of course. But it hardly constitutes an offer of permanent employment."

"As good as. I mean, like you said, what could go wrong?"

"Let's wait and see."

"Anyway, I meant about us."

"Same reply."

"Wait? What's the point of doing that?"

She looked at him coolly. "Did you get your money back on the ring?"

He frowned, "No. I didn't try."

"I see," she said and ate some more omlette.

Danny waited for what seemed to him an age, then said, "Well?"

"Don't rush me, Danny!" Her voice was low and ominous. "I want to think about things in my own time."

"I'd have thought you'd had enough time already." He said sulkily, knowing it was the wrong track to take as soon as he'd said it.

Her mouth tightened. "Stop now!"

He opened his mouth, saw her expression and shut it again. He tried to eat his sandwich, pushing food around the plate, picking at bits of bacon and chicken, nibbling toast.

"Don't you want that?" she said after a moment.

"I'm thinking too."

"You're sulking. Can't you eat and sulk at the same time?"

A couple sitting at a table near the door glanced across. Danny glared at them and they looked away. The truth was, he had lost what appetite he'd had and eventually, he laid down his knife and fork. Chrissie's plate was almost empty, obviously she didn't feel that bad. She dabbed at her mouth with her serviette and pushed her plate away.

"Do you want coffee?"

"I'm ready to go, if you are," she said.

Danny went to the counter and asked for the bill.

"Your waitress will bring it to your table," the woman standing there said.

"I'm here now."

She looked at him, saw he meant to stay and sighed. She fed the details of their meal into her machine and gave him the ticket it rolled out. Danny paid with his debit card, dropped some change in the saucer provided for tips and followed Chrissie out to the street.

"Thank you for lunch." She stood arranging her scarf around her neck.

"You're welcome."

She turned to go but he took her elbow, stopping her.

"I'll call you when I get back."

"I'll call you when I've decided." She removed her elbow from his hand. "You're lucky I'm prepared to think about it at all."

Danny raised his hands in mock surrender. There was a new sharpness in her voice that warned him to watch his step. She turned to leave, thought of something and faced him again.

"I know what happened on the night I miscarried."

There it was, the red hot knife in his heart. It had been dancing around in his conscience since it happened and now here it was, out in the open. "You mean me not staying at the hospital?"

She continued to stare at him, from eyes now filled with tears, either from the cold or from more than that.

"I was a coward," he said. "I didn't know how to face you, what to say. I thought that by ignoring it, nothing would hurt us. It wouldn't be there anymore."

He looked away, feeling all the chewed up emotion he'd felt that night rushing in to choke him. "It was easier to run. Put as much normality between me and your grief as I could. You were looking forward so much to..."

"Pretend it hadn't happened?! "

He looked at the ground, ashamed. "I guess."

After a moment, Chrissie leaned in close and said quietly, "I know about her."

He looked up sharply, suddenly afraid. How had she found out? Who could have told her? He'd not mentioned a word to anyone, not even Carol.

"It was an accident."

"An accident?" she said in a reasonable tone. "Yes, I can see how that might be. Your clothes fell off and the next thing you knew, you were in bed with her? That sort of accident must happen all the time."

" I - How did you find out?"

"It's something a woman just knows."

He was struggling to get his head around that. She couldn't just know, surely? Someone must have seen him and told her. He saw images of the woman he had slept with in his mind's eye. Christ! he never even knew her name.

"I don't know the details and I don't want to. I simply knew you'd been with someone else.

"It was three years ago."

She said, in that same quiet voice, "I'm hardly likely to forget."

"But if you knew..."

"I thought I could live with it. You were not so - you were better then. I could still see the man that I married in you - just. But you've changed completely. It's as though you've given up. What I knew began to fester inside me."

"I can make it up to you. Now that I'm working..."

"But you're not, not really. Anyway, it's more than that. It's like you're carrying some darkness inside you that is slowly eating you."

"What do you mean, darkness?" There was a grain of truth there, undeniable no matter how much he tried to dismiss it.

He looked away, suddenly desperate, wondering what to do. Looking for something he could say to save the situation but found nothing. "I'll make a go of this job, you see."

Her face looked pinched, all sharp angles and it was not just the cold that made it that way. It had been the first and last time he had paid for sex and the thought of what he'd done shamed him. Not only for what he'd done to Chrissie but also because it was through men like him that women like the one he'd had did what they did.

"Chrissie..." he reached for her but she stepped away. When she spoke, her voice sounded flat, business like, nothing there at all.

"It's all resurfaced, the anger the resentment. I'd just lost our baby and you were... I can't hold it off anymore."

She looked at him for a moment, then she turned and walked away.

He re-ran the conversation over and over again on the walk to Carol's office and every time, what he'd done that night weighed heavier and heavier upon his conscience.

Thank God she didn't know the full story, that he'd paid for the woman's time. If the full sordid affair was known to her, he could probably give up on even the slimmest hope of saving their marriage.

Chapter Six

He walked into Carol's agency, saw her standing at a desk and made his way towards her. She looked up from the person she was talking to and beckoned him through into her private space.

"I don't have to ask how it went," she said, closing the door. "I can see that by your face."

He went to the chair she kept in front of her desk for clients and slumped down onto it.

"As bad as that?" Carol took a bottle of whisky from a bureau in the corner and offered him a drink. "You look like you need one."

He watched her bring the bottle and two glasses back to the desk. "I take it lunch wasn't a hit?"

"You could say that."

She poured a finger of whisky into each glass and handed him one. He must look bad, he decided, for her to encourage him to have a drink.

Sitting in her chair, she said, "Go on."

"I told her I wanted to try again and she said she'd think about it."

"Well, that's good isn't it? I'd say you're bloody lucky to get that much."

He drank some whisky, not a spirit he usually liked and felt it burn its way down his throat. "There's more."

"There always is with you."

So he told her everything, gazing at the floor, the walls, the ceiling as he spoke, unable to look at her. He didn't want to see what he felt reflected in her eyes.

"For God's sake, Danny!" she said when he had done. "What were you thinking of?"

"I couldn't have been thinking at all."

"You were thinking alright, only with your dick instead of your brain."

"It just happened."

He'd been running away, frightened to face her grief. In some crazy way, looking to lose himself in something else so that maybe the whole awful business would just pass him by. He'd ended up in a run down dive of a pub on the bad side of town, drinking beer like there was no tomorrow. When she had come out of the cigarette smoke, she had looked like an angel, there just for him.

"Who was she?"

"Does it matter?" He'd been seeing her in soft focus and after a couple more drinks, she had taken him back to her place. It was only when they were standing toe to toe, him already undressing beside her bed, that she has asked him for money.

"Always up front. Get it out of the way," a sexy smile.

He told Carol the rest and saw her face go through a range of emotions, none of them good. "You've done some things in your time but this is dispicable."

"You think I don't know that!" He tossed off his drink and stood up. "I'd better go, before I sully your office."

"Sit down!"

He did, suddenly feeling too weak to do anything else. "She doesn't know the details. I suppose I ought to come clean."

"Not if you think anything of her, you won't."

He looked at her, confused.

"Christ! Do I have to spell it out? How do you think she feels already? You tell her who you were with and I wouldn't give you a hope in hell of getting back with her."

"I just thought I should tell her the truth."

Feeling an idiot for not having realised, too uncomfortable to turn her down, even if he'd wanted to, he'd paid up.

"Why? To ease your conscience? Make yourself feel better? Telling her could be the rottenest thing you've done yet! You'll just have to live with it, matey!"

She was right, he knew it. It was to make himself feel better. Another selfish move. He sighed and pushed himself to his feet again. "I better go. I've things to do before tomorrow."

"Don't you want to know what Dad said?"

A that moment, it didn't seem to matter much. "Go on then."

"He was completely surprised."

"Of course he was. I thought you'd already told him about the photo."

"A photo, not what it contained. He remembers Mum showing it to him, soon after they were married but thought that she had lost it ages ago."

Did he believe it? Did he care?

"He told me to give it to you." She opened a drawer in the desk, brought out the photograph and pushed it across to him.

He glanced at it. "Hold on to it for me, until I come back from London."

"You don't seem as interested as you were."

"I am," he sighed. "At the moment though..."

Carol stood up and came around the desk. Touching his arm, she said gently, "When you get back, we'll try and figure some way for you to redeem yourself. I think Chrissie still loves you. God knows why."

He nodded, wearily and walked out into the already dying afternoon, where the street lamps were on and the dreariness of everything rushed in at him. He looked at his watch, saw it was only a few minutes after four o'clock. Where had the day gone?

Time flies when you're enjoying yourself.

He cut through the cathedral grounds and emerged into a quieter, older area of the city, lanes paved with Victorian flag stones, large aged buildings housing the offices of solicitors and chartered surveyors, accountants and insurance brokers. There was a dull ache behind his left eye but he didn't think it would amount to anything.

Why had Chrissie waited so long before bringing it up, if she'd known all this time? If it had been her who had strayed, he would have let rip the minute he'd suspected. She thought things had changed of late but was he really so different to what he had always been? Well, maybe, although the transition must have been so gradual, he hadn't noticed it was happening. There had always been a shadow hanging over him because of his forgotten past but had it grown dark enough to overpower everything he had? More likely they had both changed, had allowed themselves to grow apart.

He turned into another narrow thoroughfare, older and dimmer than the rest, where the flagstones were worn down in places by years of passing feet. There was only one street lamp here, casting its jaundiced light the length of the place. Pausing beside a small, enclosed green, he looked through the gathering gloom, past the railings to the damp, forgotten benches and scruffy, uncut grass. A neglected place, left to the ravages of time and he wondered when anyone had last visited it.

On the other side of the green there was a high brick wall, above which the steeple of an old church soared into the darkening sky and suddenly he felt more dejected than he had ever felt before. He almost reached for the packet of cigarettes he hadn't carried for years, wanting a smoke badly and it was then that the headache struck out of nowhere, gripping his skull in a vice like grip.

"Jesus!" he hissed through clenched teeth.

His legs wobbled. He tottered back from the railings until his back met the worn brick work of the nearest building and there he writhed in agony. He slapped his hands to his temples, pressing against the pain. When his knees sagged, he shoved his buttocks against the wall to save himself from sliding to the ground.

I'm going to die here!

And a child giggled out of the twilight.

The pain in his head drained away as suddenly as it had arrived and turning towards the sound, he saw a small figure walking towards him out of the street light's glow. The alley twisted and turned, out of focus, as though he was watching everything through a contorted glass.

"Who...?"

She walked smartly past him, hard heels on the flagstones, rat-a-tat-tat! Another giggle as she went and then he was alone again in a wash of coloured lights, twisting and merging into each other as they whirled by. And there was music, a tune he knew but couldn't name, something from long ago, or so it seemed to him. A tune he had often found himself whistling at moments when, engaged in some mundane task or other, his mind had selected something from its own private juke box.

Then it faded rapidly, melting away to nothing and everything was all right again. As it should be. He straightened up, looked around, emerging from some disorientating state he could not explain. He recognised the narrow alley, the tall old buildings and the forlorn open space across the way. It was all very empty still, for which he was grateful. No one had witnessed what had happened to him.

Except the girl, of course.

Except the girl!

He got himself together as best he could, which wasn't easy because he had been badly shaken. A few hundred meters from the end of the alley was Roy's shop and suddenly he was desparate to know what the tune he remembered was called and Roy was just the man to tell him.

The second he opened the shop door, Roy's head came up from what he was looking at, a glint of hope flaring in his eye. The glint immediately died when he saw who it was.

"What's happened to you?"

"Nothing," Danny said, trying his hardest to seem his usual self. But he knew he wasn't succeeding, glancing at his reflection in the window glass, seeing a pale ghost of himself. He looked away.

"What do you want?" Roy said.

"I should ask for a refund, if I was you."

"Refund?"

"From the customer care course you went on."

"Funny man."

The shop smelled even more fusty than usual. Danny saw a corner of paper had peeled away from the top of the wall near the door, exposing scabrous plaster underneath. The floor lino was cracked and the paintwork on the skirting board badly chipped.

"You can't still be suffering from the state you were in Friday night."

"You can talk!" he made himself grin. "How's business?"

Roy looked over the top of his glasses, the usual skinny dog-end stuck to his lower lip, as much a part of him as the nose on his face. "Business, what's that? I tell you, a dead horse, mate, that's all I've flogged today. I don't know why I bother."

"You've been saying that for ages."

Something moved at the edge of Danny's vision. He turned sharply but there was no one there. The shop was occupied only by shadows.

"Jumpy!"

He had known Roy since they had worked at Cousins. He'd been there a few years longer than Danny and was assistant head store keeper. They had hit it off at once and after Roy left, about a year before the company went under, they would meet up for a drink at weekends. Roy had sunk all the money he'd saved up over the years into the shop and had been moaning about the place ever since, good times or bad.

"So, to what do I owe the pleasure?"

"I need information."

"I need a big spender to walk through that door. Which of us do you reckon will be satisfied first?"

"There's a tune in my head."

"Lucky you! Music's the spice of life."

Roy glanced over his shoulder at the shelves cram-packed with music reference books, mostly record label catalogues, HMV, Parlophone, Regal Zenophone and lots more.

"What's it called."

"That's what I want you to tell me."

"You don't want much, do you?"

"I can whistle it for you."

"My day gets better and better."

Danny trotted out a few bars and looked at him hopefully.

"You can forget about, 'Opportunity Knocks'," Roy said, with a pained expression.

"So?"

"I thought it was going to be difficult. Stretch my brain."

"Forget the big build up, just tell me."

""I'll do better than that," he said and sank behind the counter.

Danny took the opportunity to have a good look round behind the racks of L.Ps, just to satisfy himself that he'd been right before, that there was no one round there. All the same, he continued to feel edgey and the image of that girl from the alley was still in his head; the way she was there and then she wasn't.

Roy emerged, clutching an album in one hand, removed the disc and placed it on the turntable of the player he had back there. He passed the L. P. sleeve to Danny.

"Side two, track four."

It was a compilation album called, "The Fabulous Fifties", with a bright front cover of pinks and golds and powder blue, a large circle of golden stars containing the beaming faces of the featured artists, Alma Cogan, Perry Como, Dean Martin and so on.

"Christmas release a few years back. Something to buy dear old Mum. Sold a whole batch when it first came out. That's the last one I have."

Danny turned the sleeve over and found the track he'd mentioned, 'Cherry Pink and Apple Blossom White' by Perez 'Prez' Prado & Orchestra. According to the footnotes, it charted in early summer of 1955 with a highest chart position of number 2, behind the cover version by Eddie Calvert.

"That's it," Danny said as a trumpet soared.

"I know that's it. Even you don't whistle that badly."

The music filled the shop and Danny found himself silently whistling along, just the way he had so many times in the past without really noticing it. Where had he picked it up in the first place? The summer of '55, when the disc had been riding high in the charts, was the summer before he became ill.

"You remember it?"

"I suppose so."

Was it possible this tune was something from beyond the mind block, an echo from his missing past? Some tune that he had been fond of?

Roy lifted the stylus, then looked at him, "Did you want to hear it all?"

"I've got my own copy," Danny said, tapping his head. "Up here. What I'd like to know is where I first heard it."

"Radio maybe?"

"Maybe," He said, doubtfully. Mum was always listening to the Light Programme at weekends when she was doing the housework, dusting or ironing the clothes she'd washed. It was probably something she had done before they had moved from London too. Had he heard it sitting doing something the kid he'd been enjoyed, or had he heard it since then? Just because the record had been released in '55, didn't mean that it had never been played again on air.

"See this." Roy had brought up an old 45 rpm single. "HMV original, lilac label, gold writing. Not worth a fortune but still not to be sniffed at."

There had been an old wind up gramophone, which Dad still had. It was stored in the shed he rented at his block of flats, the same one where Carol had found the photo. Maybe mum had owned the record and that was where he'd heard it? Maybe it was still in there with the player? He would have to check.

"Eddie Calvert got to number one with his version," Roy said.

But Danny wasn't listening, he was thinking of the flashing lights he'd seen and the blaring sound he'd heard back in the alley. The pain that had heralded the onset of both had been severe, starting quicker than any headache he'd know before and vanishing as fast. He wondered about a brain tumour and thought perhaps he should go and see his doctor?

Especially if you've started seeing phantom girls!

"I'd better get moving," he said.

"What's all this about?"

"I just wanted to know what the tune was."

"Out of the blue, just like that?" Roy shook his head. "You come in here looking like you've been through a bad bout of something and ask about an old disc. You've never shown any interest in records before."

"I just had a migraine attack," he said. "Perhaps that has left me looking a bit low."

"Migraine? Since when did you suffer from those?"

"I used to get them when I was a kid. Now it seems they've started again." He walked to the door, not wanting to go on with this conversation. "I've got an early start tomorrow."

He told Roy about going to London to deliver the package for Carol.

"Sounds good. A trip to the capital's always worth doing."

"I guess," Danny agreed, although part of him would prefer to spend the time working on Chrissie.

"I can see why you're reluctant," Roy said. "So much going on here, who would want to get away? If it weren't for having to deal with your snooty sister, I'd offer to go myself."

"Next time," Danny said but Roy had already picked up his paper and was moving the roll-up from one side of his mouth to the other.

All at once, Danny started to feel something akin to unease and he tried to dispel the memory of what had happened in the alley. The headache scared him, the thought of tumours would not go away. That might explain the sight disorientation, the music and of course, the girl. If it happened again, he decided, he would make an appointment to see the doctor.

She'd giggled!

Chapter Seven

The 9.50 Inter City train left Norwich on time and arrived at Liverpool Street Station two minutes early. Danny stepped down onto the platform clutching the package in his hand and thinking that in spite of all the jibes aimed at the long under funded British Rail, the service was pretty good. If the railways ever returned to private hands, how long would it take the great British public to realise what they had so carelessly let go?

Inside the great dark cavern of the station, the air was cold and sour. It swept up the tracks, slipping inside his trouser cuffs, between his scarf and his neck. He showed his ticket at the barrier and walked quickly across the dirty-wet concourse towards the exit.

He loved London, always had done and why not, he was a Londoner, born if not fully bred. London was rooted in him, part of his fibre and returning was like pulling on an old, familiar skin. A skin that he felt at home in, despite its blemishes.

Outside was The City. People hurried to and fro, wrapped in overcoats against a bitter wind slicing between the tall, tightly packed buildings. Two young women walked quickly by clutching Styrofoam cups, faces pinched, eyes narrowed, puffing on cigarettes as they talked at each other without breaking step.

Busy, busy!

On the kerb, he hailed a black cab, which didn't stop, then tried another one which did. On the train, he had settled on getting a taxi to complete his journey. It was a quicker, more comfortable option than the Underground, where he'd have to face two changes of train. Once he had delivered the package, he wanted time to explore the place he'd spent his first eleven years.

"Where to?" The driver, a heavy set man with a thick beard and tricksy eyes asked. Danny told him and he grumbled something about driving all the way across town.

So much for the chirpy London cabbie!

Danny got in the back and the cab shot off into the City. He watched the buildings go by, concrete and glass beside older, grander styles of architecture, streets with familiar names filled him with warm contentment. They passed the Bank, the Mansion House, everywhere commerce on the move, hustle and bustle, air heavy with traffic fumes, the smell of frying onions. It must have been the same since London first existed, different smells through the years of course, maybe still present somewhere in there, insidiously underlying the modern day aromas.

Not that he was blind to London's many faults. He knew that like any city in the world, London had its dark places and even darker people but he loved it warts and all.

And the Thames?

The only cloud on his horizon. It had killed his father and he would have to deal with it before long. In Putney, it would be very close indeed, so coming to terms with it and what it had done was vital.

In many ways, the river was London, always had been since the Romans first made camp beside it. Now, its might constrained by flood barriers, it pulsed through the heart of the capital, its pace often deceptive, its power immense. The Thames, benignly alluring to those who did not know it, rolling past the landmarks and tourist traps, its charm beguiling, hiding the monster that lurked beneath the picture postcard facade.

And then it was upon him, as the cab swept out of the City towards Blackfriars and the road opened up. It was there, keeping pace with them beyond the thick granite walls flanking its shores, darkly brooding, drawing him to it, sucking his imagination deep into the treacherous hidden turbulence of its belly. A monster that would swallow you up in a second, just as it had Jack Reed.

He sat back in a corner of the cab and thought about Chrissie. How was she today, what was she doing? She had told him that he wasn't the man she'd married and he knew deep inside that he never had been a completely formed individual. How could he be with no foundations to build upon? His whole being was erected on stories which Dad had laid down for him, so it was no wonder he had become such a disappointment to her, to himself. How could he be otherwise?

Back when they had first met, at a party in the late Sixties, they had been too young for in depth analysis. Faults and weaknesses of character were overlooked in that thrill of initial attraction. Those days were far way now and yet he could see them clearly, feel them as sharply as if they were only yesterday.

He remembered exactly what she was wearing the first time he saw her, a white mini dress with a turquoise pattern, he knew her shade of lipstick, the smell her perfume, Que Sera and he felt a deep longing in his stomach for it now.

He had gone there with some of the lads from work, after Robbo, with his uncanny gift for sniffing out a party, had taken them to one in a house on the north side of the city, because that was how it was back then. You took along a couple of Party Fours of Watney's Red Barrel, a few records maybe and you were in, no questions asked. There would be dancing, boozing and if you were lucky some food, sandwiches and sausage rolls, always a jar of pickled onions or gherkins. By the time you brought it up later, you had forgotten what you had eaten in the first place.

It was a warm, summer night and the place had been throbbing. An ad-hoc choir singing along with, 'Hey Jude', by The Beatles and all the windows thrown open to let the smells of beer, cigarette smoke and of hot young bodies, roll out over the front lawn.

"Yubba-dubba-do!" as Robbo, shouting in his best Fred Flintstone voice, plunged into the house with the rest of them following.

He closed his eyes and settled into the corner of the seat. What he wouldn't give to take one step back to that packed front hall, parents away, couples everywhere, on the stairs, in all the rooms, talking, smoking, dancing, bodies clinging to each other like there was no tomorrow.

He had seen her at once, standing awkwardly in the passage, beside the stairs, alone in the crowd. Slim, about as tall as his shoulder, pretty, not much make-up, features that could cut glass. He'd worked his way over to her, seen she was nursing a glass of what turned out to be vodka and bitter lemon in one hand, while gingerly holding a cigarette in the other.

"I'm Danny," he'd said without any trace of the awkwardness he usually felt when meeting a girl.

"Chrissie."

Green eyes holding his, smiling and something had happened to him, something he'd always scoffed at when it happened in films or novels, that unquantifiable feeling in the chest. It was a thrill that could not be denied and she had felt it too, he'd known that. They had chatted for a while out in the kitchen, words flowing so easily, they might have known each other for years. A dance, a kiss and he had walked her home, not worrying about the last bus back across the city.

He hadn't even tried his luck, that's how much he had liked her!

"You alright?"

Feeling woolly from a restless night, Danny had been dozing. Now he opened his eyes, saw the inside of the taxi, the cabbie watching him in his rear view mirror.

"Where are we."

Outside the streets looked different, residential, no longer on the main drag through London. He saw tall Victorian terraced places on either side of them, thin, leafless trees lining the pavements at regular intervals.

"Putney!" the cabbie said. "Where you asked for."

"Kavanagh Gardens?" Christ! How long had he been drifting? "I want Kavangh Mansion."

The cabbie didn't reply and after being eyed with the kind of look only a London cabbie can give you when you're starting to get on his nerves, Danny realised they had arrived.

He climbed out of the cab, "Kavanagh Mansions?"

The cabbie's eyes moved from his face to stare meaningfully at a spot over his left shoulder. Danny looked behind him, saw where the terrace on this side of the street ended in a wide break before branching off to the right. In the gap before the terrace started up again stood Kavanagh Mansions, just a few meters away from them.

"What do I owe you?"

The cabbie told him and Danny paid, adding what he thought was a decent tip. From the way the cabbie looked at it, he didn't agree and the next minute, he drove away. The cab paused briefly at the corner of the street before turning onto the main road, then it was gone. Danny stood alone in a cold breath of wind, that washed over the roof tops, carrying the smell of the river.

Up close and personal.

Tucking the package under one arm, he walked towards the entrance to the building, pausing in front of the place to look it over.

Kavanagh Mansions had seen better days. It was a broad, Edwardian structure, with the date 1904 set into the large key stone in its arched porch. It must once have been an elegant building but sadly, years of neglect had reduced it to a tired pile of red brick and grimy paintwork.

Danny followed the line of small windows running up the centre of the place, the landing windows of each floor no doubt. When he reached the top, a movement caught his eye, a face at the window, a girl watching him. He gazed at her for a while, then looked into the porch, across a wide front step, littered with dead leaves and the odd sweet wrapper. At the back of the porch, a line of half glazed doors.

Before advancing, he glanced back to that top window but the girl had already gone. He crossed the step, moved into the porch to the doors and trying one, found it held fast. There was a bank of security buzzers set in a plastic box, fitted to the wall beside the doors. The name on the bottom one said 'Caretaker', so he thumbed it. With any luck this would not take long, then he could go exploring, find Galvin Street, the house Dad had told him they used to live.

No answer.

He chose another bell press and gave it a jab. Almost at once, a buzzer sounded and the door clicked open. He turned the knob and let himself into a musty smelling foyer, with worn brown carpet, high walls of either a dirty white or faded pastel and a high ceiling, which was flaking and cobwebbed at the corners. As the door shut behind him, he found himself cloaked in silence.

It was gloomy in there. Looking around, he found a light switch on the wall, a fat, Bakelite thing with a button in the middle. He pressed the button and was rewarded with a watery glow from a spidery chandelier at the centre of the ceiling. It hung there on three short lengths of chain, with only four of its six bulbs working.

"Par for the course," he muttered but his voice sounded loud in the thick silence.

There were radiators on either side of the foyer, fat and round, old things like they'd had in his school, which skulked against the walls as though embarrassed to show themselves. An old fashioned lift shaft, metal caged, wrought iron gates, behind which an ornate car waited patiently to be of service. Beside the shaft, a staircase wound its way up to the floors above.

Danny walked over to the lift and looked inside the car at the gleaming wooden walls and the trim of polished brass. Turning back, he eyed the cherry red doors to flats 1 and 2 on either side of him and another door to his right, unnumbered and tucked away in the far corner of the foyer. Moving to it, he saw there was a nameplate screwed into the wood bearing the one word,

'CARETAKER'

At that moment he jumped violently at the sound of staccato clattering from way up the stairs, hard heels on an even harder floor and immediately he was back in that alleyway at home, the sound exactly as it had been back there. He turned sharply back to the lift cage and peered up between the car and the mesh sides, where the shaft rose through the building in a dark column. There were areas dappled with light from the landings where the shaft passed each floor but there was nothing else to see, no shadow of movement.

The kid he'd seen?

He waited for the sound to repeat itself, thinking of the child's face at the window. The dream that had disturbed his sleep last night had been about children running, playing, lots of laughter and clattering shoes. Had she scampered about up there for his benefit? Having seen him arrive, was she now playing some game with him?

All at once, he became conscious of the weight of silence bearing down upon him. The building itself seemed to be holding its breath in anticipation. He had never known such stillness and found it somewhat disconcerting.

Stepping away from the cage, he walked over to the door in the corner and was reaching to open it when there was a clunk and the lift car started up the shaft. There she was, playing more games and he smiled grimly. Let her play all she wanted, he had a job to do and then he was away, free to do what he wanted.

He grabbed the brass door knob and was opening the door when the lift car stopped ascending. The next second there was another clunk and the low whirring sound started again as the car began its way back down.

This should be interesting.

He waited, watching through the cage side as the dark counter weight slid by with a whisper, on cables darker than the shaft they ran through. The kid was coming down to see him. The thought for some reason made him uneasy. He waited anyway, hand tight around the door knob and moments later, the car slid quietly into place behind the gate.

Danny found he was holding his breath. He let it out in and watched the gate, waiting for it to open. When nothing happened, he stepped away from the door so that he could see the inside of the car. It was empty!

"Okay! Very funny," he said, loud enough for her to hear him from wherever she was up there.

The car waited silently behind the gate for someone to get in. Danny made a dismissive noise and stepping up to the door marked - CARETAKER - opened it. Inside a short flight of concrete steps ran down to an L shaped lobby. He went down and at the bottom, saw another door facing him,this one marked

'BASEMENT - NO ENTRY'

It was cool down there, the hard floor covered only by a length of thin carpet. The air smelled of concrete dust. Looking around, he saw the front door to the caretaker's flat tucked away at the other end of the lobby, under the stairs.

Out of sight, out of mind.

'Until you're needed', he thought and walked along to the door. He wanted to get this done, get away. He didn't want to linger in Kavanagh Mansion any longer than he had to.

There was a bell press, fitted to the frame beside the door, he pressed it. When no one answered, he pressed it again, only this time letting his thumb linger. He could hear the bell ringing inside.

"Come on!"

He put his face close to the frosted glass panel in the top half of the door to see if there was any sign of movement but all he saw was grey nothingness. He should have expected this, no one home.

"Great!"

He eyed the letterbox speculatively, already knowing there was no way the package would go through there. He supposed he could leave it beside the door. It would be safe enough, as no one was likely to spot it under the stairs and he really didn't want to have to call back later.

"Bloody nuisance!" he said.

Bending down to place the package beside the door frame, he gave the door an irritated jab with his fingers and to his surprise, it clicked open. He found himself peering through a wedge of space into Cockle's hall.

On the latch.

Who went out and left their front door on the latch? His silly Old Man for one. But this was the caretaker, who might be somewhere else in the block carrying out some mundane duty or other.

"Hello. Anyone home?" He pushed the door open wide and nothing happened. After a moment's hesitation, he stepped inside. "Hello?"

The place was as cold as the rest of the basement area and there was a faint, unpleasant smell in the air, fusty but tinged with something else. He wouldn't want to live here, he was sure of that. He should just leave the package where it was plainly visible, on the telephone table next to the front door maybe. Once it was delivered, it was no longer his responsibility.

So why was he walking further into the flat?

"Mr. Cockle. Are you there?"

He took another step and stopped. He had heard something. A soft, wet sound, like a drop of some liquid falling onto a hard surface.

PLOP!

It seemed to him that it had come from the room in front of him to the right, possibly the kitchen or bathroom. A tap not shut properly maybe? A worn washer? He'd leave the package in there and go.

"I've a delivery for you," he called out and walking along to the half open door, used an elbow to push it wider.

He was right, it was the kitchen, an L-shaped room with old fashioned units, a big old cooker, fridge, a new microwave oven. He eyed the chunky Butler sink and next to it, a twin-tub washing machine, its grungy outlet hose looped over the edge of the sink, like the tentacle of an emaciated octopus.

But there was no tap dripping.

PLOP!

He turned into the shorter foot of the L-shape and stopped dead.

"Jesus!"

There was a man sitting at the kitchen table, one of those 1970s formica top jobs, four chairs with yellow plastic seats, arranged around it. The man was dead. He sat slumped in the chair at the far end, the furthest from him, facing him across the length of the table. His head was thrown thrown back at an impossible angle over the rear of the chair.

"Oh God!"

Danny gagged, unable to look away from the huge, gaping wedge shaped cut in the man's throat, so deep the head was almost severed from the body. The arms of the corpse, for that is what he was now, no longer a man, hung down on either side of the chair, finger tips pointing to a wide puddle of blood. Inches from the finger tips of the right hand, lay an open cut throat razor.

PLOP!

He realised then that the sound was of the last droplets of blood falling from the savage wound into the puddle on the floor.

Released from the grip of shock, his stomach heaved. He struggled not to vomit as the smell. a kind of brackish, metally stink, flooded his nostrils, coated his tongue. Yet he could not look away from the dead man, whose corpse looked as though it had been set there, posed, as though in death, Cockle wanted Danny to feast his eyes on the horror of what he had become.

And the face, Its expression. Like he had faced the Devil himself.

Finally Danny managed to tear his gaze away from the corpse, turning his back then stumbling through to the passage. It was the first time in his life that he had seen a dead person. He'd watched his mother in hospital gradually fade away to nothing but had not seen her once she had died. That had been bad enough but this, this was on a whole different level of awful.

It must have happened quite recently, judging by the fluidity of the blood. Was it possible, had he got there sooner, he might have been able to stop him?

Danny got out of the flat as fast as he could and hurried up the steps to the foyer. He stepped through the door and paused for a moment, still clutching the package in his left hand. He looked at it. He'd forgotten all about it in his haste to get away and now realised that he should have laid it on the table in the kitchen before leaving.

And the police?

He ought to telephone them. There was a phone near Cockle's front door. Should he go back inside and call them from there? He wanted to do the right thing but wasn't sure what the right thing was. The police would want to know if he made a habit of entering other people's homes without being invited. They would find out why he was there and that in turn could lead to Carol being rebuked about her staff trespassing onto private property.

Would they really do that?!

He looked at the package again. He did not want to leave it outside Cockle's front door, but neither did he want to take it back inside the flat. He did not want to see that face again, that terrible open throat. That awful expression!

Take it home.

That was the only thing to do, not bother with the police at all. The guy down there was way past caring.

It was probably an offence not to report a violent death, even if that death was so obviously a suicide but he would explain to Carol and let her decide what to do. He could walk away from this without having to worry about any of it. He hadn't left any signs that he'd been there, he hadn't touched anything. Most importantly, he hadn't left the package behind. He was in the clear.

The foyer was as quiet as it had been earlier. He waited in the shelter of the lift cage to make sure no one was about. The last thing he needed was seen leaving. When he finally stepped away from the cage, he crossed the foyer in long and careful steps and was almost at the outer doors when a sly little giggle stopped him in his tracks. He'd completely forgotten about her!

Bloody kid! She could tell the police that he'd been there.

As though in confirmation of this, another tattoo of heels rapping the hard floor shattered the silence. The next second, the lift car jerked and started upwards, making Danny squeak in dismay. Throwing caution to the wind, he walked quickly to the doors and out of the building.

Chapter Eight

This time, his train was delayed, arriving at Norwich almost half an hour late. Danny was worried about contacting Carol before she went home and checked his watch for the umpteenth time since leaving Diss. It was getting on for five o'clock and the daylight had turned to twilight a while ago. He would phone her from the station, tell her he was on his way to the office and that she should wait until he got there. She would want to know what had happened, why he sounded the way he did but he wouldn't tell her until he could do so face to face.

Why hadn't the girl been in school?

This had been on his mind all the while from London and now it was there, right in front of him, demanding an answer. Sick maybe, but if that was the case, what was she doing playing out on a chilly staircase? Bunking off then? But why return to the very place she might easily be caught by someone who would mention it to her parents?

If the police had any doubts about Cockle's death, they might ask if anyone had seen anything suspicious that day, strangers in the block perhaps. She might tell them about a man who had arrived, gone downstairs and then left in a hurry.

But why was he worrying, it was an obvious suicide, wasn't it? And even if they did learn he'd been there, he would say that he left when he got no answer from ringing Cockle's door bell. Why should he have tried the door?

"Christ!" he breathed.

He shifted uncomfortably as the dead man's face rose up before him. He tried not to think about it, pushing the memory away. He had seen enough of the face to know that Cockle had been terrified the moment before - he did what he had done. Something had scared him, almost out of his mind. The realisation of the act he was about to commit, or something more sinister? He shook his head, clearing the picture of it from his mind.

Why hadn't the bloody kid been in school?!

When the train drifted into Norwich Station, Danny got off before it had fully stopped, hurrying down the platform and onto the concourse. The phones were near the entrance, three cubicles in a row and he entered the nearest one. He watched snow flakes drifting lazily by the open station entrance as he dialled Carol's office number. She answered on the third ring.

"I wasn't planning to leave just yet," she said. "What's happened?"

He told her he'd be there soon and hung up with her still talking.

Leaving the station, he walked across the car park into the street, then across the bridge and down onto the towpath with only the snow flakes for company. He followed the river along to where he wanted, the footpath which ran up along the side of the cathedral.

It was surprisingly quiet when he cam out onto the main road, evening hanging heavy over everything like an icy blanket. By the time he reached Carol's office, the snow had upped its game a little, falling steadily through the amber glow of the street lamps.

The office showed muted light from deep inside where Carol was working on in her office at the back. She had left the front door open and he entered the low ceilinged main office, which was still warm.

Continuing through to her inner sanctum, he found her sitting at her desk reading some document or other and she looked up when he entered.

"Alright, what went wrong?" She put what she was reading aside.

"You can take that look off your face," he said.

He moved to the desk and laid the package before her, watched her eye it briefly, then raise her eyes to look at him. Snatching off his beanie and shoving it into a pocket, Danny slipped out of his coat and sat down in the client's chair.

"Can I have a drink?"

She nodded, walked across the office to where she kept her bottle and poured whisky into each of the two tumblers, a couple of fingers this time. She brought them back to the desk and stood one down in front of him.

"Go on then."

"There's a chance I could be in trouble," he said and swallowed half the contents of his drink.

"Tell me."

So he did and watched her expression darken with every word. When he had finished, she looked at him for a long while before saying, "Only you could be so stupid."

"I was shaken, the way he was just sitting there. You didn't see him!"

"You left the scene of a violent death. The police will want to know why?"

"They won't know I went in. I didn't touch anything inside."

She was looking at him as though she could not believe her ears. "You didn't report a violent death!"

"It was suicide!" he studied his drink.

"He'd cut his throat! I'd say that was pretty violent."

"Yes, but -"

"There's no chance it was...something else?"

"I don't think so," he said, remembering the dead man's expression again.

"Christ!" She poured herself another whisky without offering him one. "I'll have to phone the local station, tell them what's happened. I'll get the blame for this, you know that?! The police can make things bloody awkward if they want to."

"What's the point? No one knows I was there and suicide isn't a crime any more."

"Who the hell are you to decided what it was? The police will have to investigate and report their findings. Only the coroner can judge whether a crime has been committed."

"They will do that whether you phone them or not."

She sat there nursing her drink, contemplating all the awful things that could happen to her business and blaming him for every one.

"Someone will find him sooner or later. I left the front door open. It stands to reason that somebody - "

"Yes, yes!"

Danny emptied his tumbler and reaching across for the bottle, poured a refill. "The look on his face. You'd think, if he'd made up his mine to do that, he would have looked more resigned..."

For a moment, he was back in the flat, blood on the floor, more dripping from the wound. Cockle should have looked resigned, shouldn't he? Not terrified. Not like he had seen something so horrible, he would rather be dead than face it.

"It was a deep cut. Almost through to the spinal cord. His head was hanging right back over the chair, like it might fall off at any minute."

Carol watched him, her face slightly paler than it had been. "I read somewhere, if a person is serious about killing themselves that way, there is usually one test cut before the real one."

"I didn't examine him!"

Carol regarded him long and hard. "*Could* someone else have done it?"

"Open the package," Danny said, not wanting to face that possibility.

She blinked, "What?"

"What's in there might tell us something."

"I don't see how."

He was remembering Hilary's words on Sunday. "The way you were hired to do this. Didn't it seem odd, a woman walking it at closing time like that?"

" It was a bit unusual, I suppose."

"Did she give you her address?"

Carol opened the top drawer of her desk and brought out one of her printed forms, pushing it over the desk for him to read.

"Granlock Farm?"

"Other side of Aylsham. On the old Cromer Road."

"You already looked it up?"

"I was curious."

"Let's go out there," he said, standing up.

"Now?"

"Why not?"

Carol looked at the drink on her desk, thought better of it and stood up. She put on her coat, fished the car keys from the drawer in front of her and led the way through to the general office.

"I don't know why I'm doing this."

He didn't comment.

When she had locked up, she turned off the main

lights, leaving just the one in the lobby where he was.

"We'll go out the back way,"

She led him along a short corridor, past the staff toilets, to the rear exit.

Outside, Danny saw that she was driving Nick's big Mercedes W123, white, expensive, large enough to take up all the space in the narrow lanes they would encounter once they had left Aylsham.

She locked the back door and walked around the front of the car, which already had a thin covering of snow on the roof and bonnet. She opened the vehicle and slid in behind the wheel. Climbing in beside her, he fitted his seat belt.

"I'm surprised he lets you drive this."

"He doesn't know I've got it."

"Wouldn't you rather go home and get your Mini?"

She just stared at him.

"I was thinking of the narrow country roads."

She drove from the car park and pointed the Merc towards the city centre, joining the lines of cars driven by people going home from work and it took a while to get out as far as the airport.

The flow eased slightly once they hit the A140 but was still heavy enough to force Carol to keep their speed to just above forty until they reached the Aylsham turn off. It started snowing heavily.

"Damn this," she said and flipped the wipers to fast.

"I thought you liked snow."

She didn't answer.

They passed through the town and were soon driving dark country lanes into the weather with only the Merc's main beams to see by. The night seemed full of driving flakes, some as big a 2p pieces, pelting straight at them.

"I can't see properly," Carol said, leaning forward to peer through the clouding windscreen.

The car hit a pot hole, pitching them violently to the left, then a moment later, hit another, pitching them to the right. Carol cut her speed to just above twenty and Danny looked at his watch. It was already well after six o'clock. The Merc was crawling along and at this rate, he thought irritably, the woman would be tucked up in bed long before they got there!

He glanced into the back seat where the package lay. He wished she had opened it as he'd suggested. He had a funny feeling about that package. He had a funny feeling about the whole affair and it was getting funnier all the time. He wanted to know what was so damned important it had to be specially delivered.

Could it have any bearing on what had happened to Cockle?

"Maybe we missed the turn off," he said.

"Just outside Aylsham, she told me."

"We seem to have been driving for ages. Maybe you went the wrong way."

"Will you shut up!"

They went on in silence. Danny watched the snow flakes rushing at them through the headlight beams and tried hard to see beyond the darkness ahead. The snow was settling and he didn't want to get stranded out there in the wilds where it might take ages to get help.

"There!" Carol said, suddenly making a sharp left turn onto a mud track, which was even narrower than the lane they had been travelling. "I can see the house."

He could too. Some way ahead, at the end of the track, a watery glow showed in the darkness. Then the Merc bucked, something hit the off side wing with a hollow thump and Carol winced. If there was a mark left on the bodywork, Nick would go ape.

"I hope that's not dented."

"That would be a shame," he said, biting back a smile.

They hit a couple of dry puddles before emerging onto a churned up forecourt, deep mud and chicken shit that was quickly freezing into ruts. There were hulking farm buildings looming darkly on either side of them and Carol drove carefully, bringing them as close to the farmhouse as she could get. When she killed the engine, they could hear the wind sighing across the surrounding fields in the new silence. It was an eerie sound, with only the clicking of the cooling engine beaking into it.

"This place seems deserted," Danny said.

"It certainly doesn't seem like a working farm. At least in any big way anymore."

They sat there a moment longer, staring into darkness.

"Let's get this done," Carol said finally, releasing her seat belt.

Danny watched her get out of the car, then reached into the back seat for the package before following her.

The muddy, rutted surface of the forecourt was gathering snow. They crunched their way across to the front door, seeing the house was in darkness apart from the light they had seen on their approach. This, a watery yellow glow through a frosted glass panel in the front door. As Carol was reaching to press the bell, Danny stopped her and pointed at the front door, which he had noticed was ajar.

"We can't just go in. I expect there'll be a dog," Carol was wary of man's best friend.

Thinking about the door to Cockle's flat, Danny said, "It was the same in London."

Carol pressed the door bell, heard it ringing along the passage and touched the front door. It opened a little and they could hear the sound of a television playing loudly, an audience laughing, clapping, then the sound of a man's voice saying words they could not distinguish. Carol thumbed the chunky bell press again.

"No barking," he said.

He looked at her, feeling a sinking feeling inside. They waited, with him moving the package from one hand to the other until Carol hissed at him to keep still.

"I'm telling you, it's like before." His voice was hushed.

"I heard you the first time."

She pressed the bell again, holding her thumb there for a couple of seconds, turning her back to the driven snow, narrowing her eyes. "Who goes out and leaves the TV on and the front door open?"

Danny didn't bother to tell her.

"Perhaps she's out here somewhere."

Danny looked back at the darkness beyond the Merc's headlights. "I doubt that very much."

Reaching around her, he pushed the door open.

"What are you doing?" Carol snapped.

"I'm not standing here all night."

He didn't relish the thought of going inside, of possibly discovering another horror show, but neither did he want to stand there freezing his balls off.

The sound of the TV, louder now, was coming from a room at the end of a short passage, the room with the light on.

"Come on," he stepped inside."

"Stop!" Carol hissed. "You can't just -"

"After the first time, it gets easier," he said.

By the time he reached the room, Carol was beside him.

"What's that smell?" she whispered.

He'd caught it as soon as he'd crossed the threshold. It was sinilar to the smell back in Cockle's kitchen, only fuller, fouler and it was getting stronger, so much so, they had to cover their mouths and noses. They exchanged glances and went into the room.

"Oh God," Carol said, grabbing his arm.

It was a parlour, obviously the main room of the house from the lived in look of the place. There was a huge old stove, fire embers dead behind a glass door, a large oak table and four chairs in the centre of the floor.

There was a big armchair over in the corner, which was where she sat. She was, or had been, a short, heavy set woman, dressed in a thick jumper and tight jeans, She was sitting with her hands in her lap, legs sightly apart and between her meaty thighs was the stock of a double barreled shotgun, which had jerked away from her following her pulling the triggers. The baarrels had fallen forward to point at the floor, inches from her feet.

What was left of her head was thrown back and her face, from chin to forehead had been splattered up the wall behind her, so all they were looking at was an oval mess of raw meat and bone and hair.

Carol said, "That smell..."

"She's been dead a while." Danny was looking at the dried blood, both on her chest and splattered on the wall behind her, a dirty, crusted mess.

"Call the police," Carol said. "There's a phone out there on the wall."

He knew she was right. It had to be different to London, but he stood there all the same. Unlike with Cockle, he found it hard to look away from the corpse.

When he didn't move, Carol went without comment, leaving him alone with the dead woman and he eventually managed to drag his eyes away. He started a quick examination of the room from where he stood, looking for something to focus on, knowing only too well that eventually his eyes would go back to her.

If it was summer, the room would almost certainly be full of flies, homing in on the banquet laid out for them and he wondered when she had shot herself. How soon after handing the package over to Carol had she done it? Could the contents of the package have something to do with her taking her life?

And Cockle? But he hadn't received the package before he did what he did.

"Christ," Danny muttered.

He eyed a framed photo standing on the mantle shelf, the only photograph anywhere in the room as far as he could see. It showed a short, thickset woman standing beside a huge horse and grinning at the camera. She was wearing what were obviously working clothes and he guessed that the woman was the same person who was sitting near him now. At least, what was left of her was.

Sure enough, he glanced across at the armchair, saw her legs and torso but managed not to go any higher. He could hear Carol talking on the phone out in the hallway. She sounded shaken. He heard her replace the receiver and a moment later, she came back looking pale and drawn. Her eyes seemed too bright.

"They're on their way?" She stole a look across the room, then turned her head quickly away. "They asked us to leave the room and not to touch anything."

But Danny had spotted a crumpled sheet of brown wrapping paper on the floor beside the table that looked familiar. He looked at the package he was holding, then back at the item on the floor. Walking over to it, he picked it up.

"Don't touch, they said!"

Holding a corner of the paper between his thumb and forefinger, he turned it round and saw the sealing wax, a cake of red broken on two edges. Written on the paper was the name, Miss S. Eadel and her address.

"What is it?"

Danny did not reply. He saw now that there was something on one of the chairs, tucked under the table, something thin and rectangular. He moved round the table, pulled the chair out and stared at the cardboard envelope lying there.

"Open this," he said over his shoulder and held out Cockle's package for her.

"I can't," she said, taking it anyway.

"Open it!"

He laid the brown paper on the table and picked up the envelope from the chair, aware of the dead woman's legs very close to him.

"The police said not to touch anything," Carol repeated.

"Is this the woman who came to see you?"

"How can I tell?"

He pointed to the photograph on the mantle shelf, "Is it?"

"No. She was tall, thin. She said her name was Sarah Eadel but this isn't her."

Danny stared at her for a moment, then he turned the wrapping paper so that she could see the address on the front. Carol looked from the address up to his face.

"That's not her, I'm positive."

"I believe you."

He lifted the cardboard envelope again and slipping two fingers under the corner of the sealed edge, prised the tongue all the way open. He had a bad feeling about what he would see inside.

"What is it?" Carol said.

He drew out a framed photograph, a copy of the one Carol had given him and stared at it. He was aware of Carol moving to stand beside him.

"How is that possible?"

He nodded to Cockle's package, which she had still not opened. "Do it."

"Danny, I..."

He held her gaze and after a moment, she broke the seal and tore the brown paper off, revealing the same type of card envelope as the one Danny held. She glanced at him then peeled back the tongue and removed the contents. It was the same.

Danny laid the photo he held on the table. "You remember any of the names written on the back of Dad's copy?"

"A couple," she said. "Joe and Veronica. Brian. Why?"

"Alan, Sarah and Ray," Danny finished for her. He nodded towards the corpse, "Her name was Sarah, Cockle's initial was A. Does that suggest anything?"

Her eyes searched his face. "Are you saying they might be the same Alan and Sarah?"

He shrugged, "Makes you wonder, doesn't it?"

"Not me is doesn't." Carol put Cockle's copy of the photo back in its envelope and crunched the paper around it as neatly as possible. "It's one heck of a jump."

"Maybe." The idea had sprung into his head and he'd spoken without thought. Now the kernel of the idea started to grow and the more he weighed it, the more it seemed to make sense.

"Let's go somewhere else to wait," Carol said. "It seems a bit disrespectful, standing here talking."

Danny followed her into the passage, shutting the door behind them. It seemed the decent thing to do. When the police got there, they would be all over the room but until then, let her have some privacy.

Carol already had the front door open and he had to admit, leaving the house, even for a short time felt good to him. Once they were seated in the car, engine on, heater running, he took Cockle's opened package from her and tossed it into the back seat.

"What I said, it's worth considering," he said. "I know it sounds fanciful on the face of it but think about it."

"If by some wild chance, you're right," Carol said, "It would be one hell of a coincidence."

"Both of them committing suicide around the same time?" They gazed at each other. "When did you find that photograph at Dad's, before or after you got the London job?"

"Before. About a week, why?"

"Well, it's a bit odd. You get the job of delivering a copy of the same photo to Kavanagh Mansions. Even more so, just after finding the original."

"And Sarah Eadel received one - whenever."

He glanced back towards the house. "The real Sarah Eadel."

Carol eyed him nervously.

"What did your client look like?"

"I told you, I couldn't see much of her," she said. "I heard the door open and came out of my office to see who it was, so late in the day. That end of the room was in near darkness, lit only by light from outside. She stayed just inside the door, so her features weren't clear. She was standing there, holding the package."

"You must have seen something of her?"

"Only glimpses of her face. She was taller than me, thin and I got the impression that she may have been ill recently."

"How so?"

"What I could see of her face seemed drawn, wasted... She told me her name and address and what she wanted. She paid cash."

Carol looked at him, waiting but he was unsure what to say.

"I told her we were very busy and short of operatives."

"You accepted the job anyway."

"I thought about you, something for you to do." She frowned, as though unsatisfied with that explanation, seeking the words to be more precise. "She made me feel..."

"Afraid?"

"Of course not!"

Danny could see from her expression that his remark had been closer to the truth than he would have thought possible.

"Compelled," she said. "I felt... She told me it was urgent and that she was unable to get to London herself due to prior committments. She told me I must know someone I could trust who could take it."

"Did you tell her about me?"

"I didn't need to."

He stared at her, surprised. "What does that mean?"

"She seemed - so sure I would find someone."

There was the sound of a car and light washed over them. A moment later, doors slammed and there was the sound of indistinct talking, as two figures emerged from the night.

"Well, they're here," Danny said.

Carol got out of the Merc and Danny heard a man's voice asking her if she was Mrs. Warning. She went and opened the front door of the house and stood aside for the policemen to enter, two uniformed officers and a CID man, who looked into the car at him before entering. With a sigh, Danny got out and followed them inside.

"Where?" said the CID officer and Carol pointed to the door in front of them. He went through followed by one of the uniformed officers, while the other stayed with Carol and Danny.

"In case we do a bunk," Danny said and smiled at the man, who ignored him.

"Not funny!" Carol hissed. She looked tense.

The CID man came back into the corridor. "You didn't touch anything?"

From the way he said it, Danny knew it was just a casual question but Carol shot him a look, as though she had every unsolved crime in the county on her conscience.

"The front door and the door to that room," Danny said. Then added, "I touched the photograph that's on the table. It was on a chair. I picked it up and put it on there, the wrapping paper too."

The policeman looked at him hard. "Why would you do that?"

"I wanted to look at it," he said.

"Why?"

Before he could reply, the man turned to the uniformed officer, "Get on the radio, let them know what's hppened."

The officer left and the CID man's eyes came back to Danny. "What about the photo?"

"I just picked it up without thinking."

"I am Detective Constable Mills," the policeman said. "I think we had better go into that room and have a chat."

He led them through to a sitting room at the front of the house and once inside, turned to face them. It was obvious from the smell of the room that it was little used.

"You'd been asked not to touch anything."

"I did it when my sister was on the phone to you lot. When she came back, she saw me holding it and gave me hell. I put it on the table."

Carol began to make excuses but the look Mills gave her stopped her mid-flow. Danny wished he possessed the same ability. Mills looked at Danny and his face grew stonier and stonier. "Don't you know it is an offence to interfere with a possible a crime scene?"

"I wasn't thinking. I -"

"I know. You just had to have a look."

"That's about it," Danny said lamely.

Mills looked at Carol. "You have been in this business long enough, Mrs. Warning. I'd have thought you would ensure that your operatives have a basic knowledge of how to act under these circumstances."

Danny said, "I am not one of her operatives, I'm her brother."

"He was doing me a favour, officer."

Mills looked at her and she quickly went on, explaining that she had been engaged to get a package delivered to London and had asked Danny to take it.

"She was up to her neck with work and short staffed," Danny said. "She couldn't spare an agent for such a little job and as I'm unemployed at the moment, I volunteered to do it for her."

"When do you intend to take it?"

"I already did, this morning."

"Conscientious then?"

"That's me," Danny replied, catching the slight sarcastic tone in the copper's voice.

"Well, in future remember what I've said."

"I hope I'll never be in a similar situation."

Mills stared at him but before he could comment, the uniformed constable returned. "I reported back. They're getting onto the lab team."

"Bring them through when they get here, will you Jack?"

Mills watched him leave, then turned to face Carol.

"Have either of you seen that photograph before?"

Carol opened her mouth but Danny jumped in quickly. "Why would we have?"

"What was it about it that made you so anxious to see it?"

Danny shrugged, "I just...You know."

Mills shook his head wearily. Obviously he wasn't satisfied but could not think of anything else to ask them.

"Very well, you can get off," he said. "But we might want to speak to you again. You'll probably be wanted at the inquest."

They left then with Mills eying them all the way out the front door. Once they were in the Mercedes, Carol turned her head sharply to look at him.

"What the hell was all that about? Don't you think we are in enough of a spot as it is!"

"The photo?"

"Yes, the photo! Why did you say you'd never seen it before?"

"What good would it have done? Anyway, I wanted time to think."

Carol started the car. "It's about time you started bloody thinking. This could all end very badly, for both of us."

And with that, she drove out of the yard and into the dark towards the lanes that would take them back to the city.

Chapter Nine

Danny arrived at Carol's house just after ten the next morning and noticed that the Mercedes, which was parked on the forecourt, had been cleaned of the muck it had picked up last night. The bump on the wing had hardly left a mark and he wondered whether Nick would notice it.

She had called him around eight o'clock last evening and suggested they go round to Dad's today to try and learn more about the photograph. Danny had been struggling with conflicting feelings about what had happened at the farm house and was glad to hear that she was suffering similarly herself.

"You think there is something to all this then?"

"I didn't say that."

"So why?"

"Because it is obvious that you do.

She had told him to be at the house by ten and had rung off. Afterwards, Danny had sat pondering for most of the evening, unable to concentrate on anything else. Finally going to bed around midnight, he'd slept fitfully, plagued by dreams and eventually had given up around five in the morning.

Thinking about it now, he remembered waking, or at least dreaming he had awakened to find a figure, tall, thin, possibly female, although its features were indefinible. A grey wraith, with arms and hands that were reaching for him and he had awakened properly with a small shout, drenched in sweat and very unsettled.

"Car's open," Carol said, emerging from the house.

"Right," he said after a moment and climbed into the passenger seat. He sat watching her locking up as he fitted his seatbelt, wondering how she had slept. She wouldn't tell him if he asked, so sat back with his mouth shut. When she climbed in beside him, she was holding the package, still wrapped.

"Here," she said, handing it to him. "He knows we're coming,"

"I bet that pleased him," Danny said.

"He said he'll make tea."

"I can't wait."

Carol managed a smile as she fitted her seatbelt. She started the car and they drove out of the forecourt, turning towards the city centre. As they passed his Cortina, parked at the kerb, she said, "Nick called, to tell me what had happened in Kavanagh Mansions."

"Was he his usual charming self? You didn't mention me?"

"What do you think? He's staying at the London flat for a few days."

"Right." Danny wondered who was there with him but decided it prudent to keep that question to himself.

She made a right onto the main road. "He was actually really helpful."

"I bet that hurt him." He must have a guilty conscience, Danny thought but kept that to himself too.

"He's going to contact, Joe Singleton of Hellman and Strapps."

"Who?"

"He's the guy from the estate agents that's handling the Mansions. The renovation contracts and the sale of the apartments afterwards. I met him once when I was having a look at the place."

"Cockle's employer?"

"Mmm." She checked her mirror then indicated left. After she had made the turn, she said, "I've asked Nick to make an appointment for us for tomorrow."

"In London?"

"No, Timbucktu." She gave him a look, "I think we need to find out a bit more about Cockle and he's the best bet we have."

"Didn't he ask why?"

"Funnily enough, no." It seemed as though this had only just occured to her.

"Just remember, there's a Joe in the photo too."

So she may not have entirely dismissed what he'd said last night, although her expression told him she wasn't that close to agreeing with him either.

"It's a common name."

"It might be good to know the surnames of those kids," Danny said after a moment. "You think Dad might know?"

"We can ask. If only to stop you going off on some wild theory."

Wild, maybe but Danny had a gut feeling that was growing stronger all the time and he knew he wasn't going to give up on it. He had learnt over the years never to ignore a feeling like that, especially one as insistant as this one. Not that he would try explaining that to Carol, he knew she would dismiss it as another of his ridiculous notions.

Traffic was light amd they made the journey to the estate in no time. Turning onto the road where Dad's block was, Carol slotted the car into a space right outside. Danny unbuckled and got out before she had turned off the engine. He was looking up at the cloudy sky when Carol joined him.

"I think that's the snow they keep talking about on the TV forecast."

As though to prove him right, an icy breath of wind blew in their faces, making them narrow their eyes. Carol shivered and started towards the entrance with Danny following behind her. Twice in one week, he thought, it had to be a record. When Dad answered their knock, he stood in the doorway staring at them, even though he had known they were coming.

"This is an event," he said. "Both of you here together."

A wave of stuffiness, thick with those same endemic smells, rolled out over them. Dad led the way up the passage to the kitchen door.

"You'll want tea?"

"Thanks," Carol said. Danny didn't answer.

They went through to the living-room. Danny, eying the lines of dried egg on the window, walked over and was looking at the shell on the outside cill when Dad arrived, carrying two mugs.

"I said I'd clean this for you."

"And I said, I can do it myself."

Danny caught Carol's eye, saw her smile sympathetically. He took the mug Dad offered him and looked at the greasy brew inside. Sitting on a hard backed chair to one side of the dinning table, he put his cup down and glanced at one of the Louis L'Amour novels he had brought sitting on Dad's side table, a bookmark several pages into it.

"So, to what do I owe this pleasure?" Dad asked, lowering himself into his armchair. "I hope you haven't come to tell me you want to put me in a home."

"Don't be silly, Dad." Carol said. "You've got years to go before you need worry about that."

"Course you have," Danny said in an unconvincing voice. "Actually, we need to speak to you about that photograph. The one Carol asked about before."

Dad reached for his pipe, began fiddling with it. "Oh yes?"

Danny took the picture from the envelope and laid it on the table. "We need to know about these children."

"What makes you think I can help?"

"You must know something about the photo," said Carol, patting one scrawny arm.

"We thought - " Danny started.

"You thought wrong," Dad said, cutting him off.

He began scraping the inside of his pipe bowl with the little pipe knife Danny had bought him years ago. When he was satisfied, he tapped a small pile of carbon into the big ashtray beside him. "It was your Mum's photo. I thought it had gone long ago."

"Why would you think that?" Danny asked.

Dad blew twice through the empty pipe, then fixed him with a hard gaze. "Your Mum had a way of getting rid of things, photos she had of Jack, others too, wedding ones. I don't know whether it hurt too much, keep seeing him or she thought I might be jealous."

"You wouldn't have been," said Carol.

"Course I wouldn't. He was my mate. I missed him, still do. I wouldn't be jealous of him."

"These kids," Danny said, pushing the photo towards him. "The Tykes. Who were they?"

"Just kids from the area. Jack was a beat copper, he knew them. They liked him." He looked at Danny, "They were just kids."

"This is taken in Galvin Street?"

Dad nodded.

"So why aren't I in the line up?"

"I don't know," he said, concentrating on his pipe. "Maybe you weren't around when it was taken."

Danny watched him filling the pipe bowl from his creased old tobacco pouch, tapping it down, sucking air through the stem to make sure it was not packed it too tightly.

"Do you know any of their names?" asked Carol, in a silky tone that made Danny sick.

"They were just kids, like I said. The local bobbies in those days were mates with the kids on their patch. It made the job easier. It was Jack's job to put himself out there, get the community on side. He was one of the family to most of the people who lived round there."

"You don't get that these days," Carol said.

"Too bloody right you don't! They're all in cars these days," Dad said. "Look at those little bleeders who slung those eggs at my windows. Still out and about round the estate, no worries over a copper pulling them up."

"Have they been back?" Danny asked.

"No."

"Remember what I said."

"You only said it two days ago. I'm hardly likely to have forgotten already. I'm not bloody senile!"

Danny sighed.

"You've written their names on the back of the photo, Dad," Carol said.

He picked it up, turned it in his hand to read the back. He said to Danny, "That's your Mum's writing."

"It looks like yours."

"Well it's not! Your mother's writing was much better than mine is."

Dad struck a match and for a while, the only sound in the room was of him puffing the pipe into life. Danny looked at Carol, making his impatience plain.

"Who took the photo, Dad?" she asked.

The Old Man said, through a cloud of smoke, "Don't know. Your mother, I expect."

"She'd have been working, wouldn't she?" Danny asked.

"She had days off, you know? Holidays - even with pay!"

Danny ignored his tone. "It says there, Rudd Street Tykes. Was Rudd Street far from Galvin Street?

"Five minutes walk or so."

"But they used to play round our street?"

"Kids wander, holidays, nothing to do. People used Galvin street to get down to the river. Perhaps they were going off down there to play."

"I must have known them."

Dad puffed his pipe. "It's possible, I suppose."

Danny stood up.

"Going already?" Dad asked.

Carol drank as much tea as she could stomach. "We have a lot to do. I'll come and see you again soon."

Rising, she held her hand out for Danny's mug, which was still full. She went off to the kitchen, leaving Danny standing in the middle of the room, watching the Old Man strike another match and resume puffing at the pipe.

"I see you're reading one of the books."

"I've read it before but I don't have any new ones. I didn't have much choice."

"I'll look for some more next time I'm in the market."

"I expect I'll have read them too. You always get me books I've already read."

Danny was at the point of telling him to go and get the bloody things himself, when Carol returned from the kitchen.

"Ready?" she asked.

"More than ready."

She walked over and kissed Dad on the cheek, then said something close to his ear and he smiled. "We can see ourselves out."

Out on the landing, Danny waited for her to close the front door.

"That was touching," he said.

"It was nothing,"

Back in the car, they were silent until they were driving towards the city. Danny could not help feeling a little jealous of that intimacy she had with the Old Man, enough for them to share a private joke that he was left out of.

"Now what?"

"London, tomorrow. We'll see what Joe Singleton can tell us." She glanced over at him, "It wouldn't hurt to call in to the local police station and make our peace with them."

"What's the point? If they want us, they'll tell us."

He got her to drop him at the traffic lights up ahead. It was not far to walk to the house and he wanted to pick up a few things while Chrissie was at work, some heavier garments, just in case his stay in London turned out to be longer than expected. He had a feeling it just might be.

"I'll see you at the station," Carol said as he climbed out. "We'll catch the nine-thirty, give us plenty of time."

He watched her drive away until the green man came up on the crossing, then he crossed over. He realised that he had left the photograph in the car and hoped Carol spotted it when she got home. He wanted that signed one to go to London with them, even though they would be taking Cockle's copy. He would ring her later to make sure she remembered it.

It started to snow as he turned into the street where the house was. Small flakes again, dancing on a steady breeze. If they got a really heavy fall, he thought, the trains would be delayed. Some may even be cut, which would make them late getting to London, reducing the amount of time they had, no matter how early they planned to leave. The possibility of staying over became even more likely. He really would like to visit Galvin Street this time.

"Hello," he said, surprised when Chrissie opened the door as he was fiddling with the key. "I'd have rung the bell had I known you were home."

"It's your house as much as mine," she said, walking ahead of him along the hall.

"Yes, but I wouldn't have just come in." He followed her. "Are you on holiday?"

"Flexi-day."

"Right."

"Can I get you anything?"

"No thanks, I won't be long. I just wanted to pick up some more clothes, underwear, a shirt or two."

"Your holdall is on the floor in the airing cupboard."

He nodded, then hurried upstairs to their bedroom. As soon as he entered, he smelt her perfume and felt a tugging sensation in his chest. Running his eyes over the clutter on her dressing table, make-up, various aerosols, the perfume bottle, he sighed at the wave of longing that engulfed him.

He busied himself sorting out what he wanted from his chest-of-drawers, three pairs of long johns, vests and from the next drawer up, his thick plaid shirt that he only brought out in winter. He laid the articles on the bed and went onto the landing, opened the airing cupboard door. The large, tan holdall that she had referred to was there and he brought it out. It was more than roomy enough for what he wanted to take with him.

With the clothing packed, he carried the holdall downstairs and found her in the lounge. She had been watching some news programme on TV and turned off the set as he entered. "Will you sit down?"

Feeling strangely awkward, he did, opening his coat but leaving it on. "I have to go to London again tomorrow."

"The same job?"

"Sort of. It's grown."

Chrissie was sitting on the sette. There was orange peel on the table beside her and the Radio Times was open on the cushion next to her.

"I thought it was just a delivery," she said.

"Long story. I'll tell you about it later."

"Okay. If that's what you want."

"Look," he said after a moment. "Will you hold off on deciding anything. I know it's your decision, how things go with us and I can't blame you if you want to call it a day. I know I haven't been worth hanging on to lately but I intend to do better. If you could wait until this business I'm involved in is settled?"

"I had a job keeping up with that."

"Sorry. I needed to get it out, in case you stopped me."

"I've already made up my mind. I'm not making any final decisions yet."

Relief swept through him. "You mean you think we might -"

"I mean I am not making any decisions yet."

"Right."

She stood up. "We have a lot to sort out."

"You mean, I do."

She didn't argue, looking at him steadily. "I still love you, Danny. I just need to be sure that we can live with each other."

"About what I -"

She turned away. "I don't want to hear about that. Not yet. Maybe never."

He nodded, "Fair enough. If you do - whenever - just let me know..."

She watched him stand, pick up the holdall. "Do you have any idea how long you'll be in London?"

"Not really." He hesitated, then stepped up to her and kissed her cheek. "I'll call you when I get back."

She saw him as far as the hall, "Take care."

He let himself out into the cold and pulled his beanie down to cover his ears. Deciding to walk home, he turned away from the direction of the main road, cutting back and forth through streets of houses much like the one he had just left. The wind drove snow at his back, so that he soon wore an icy pelt across his shoulders.

Dad had lied again, he was sure of it. The way he'd answered, ready for any question they put to him, as though he'd been rehearsing. And another thing, not a word about London.

Why?

Probably he hadn't wanted to risk further row over the matter with Carol present, in case she got drawn into it?

"Fuck him," he muttered. There was no point mentioning it to her, she would simply dismiss what he said as him being unnecessarily suspicious. Anyway, he didn't want to think about Dad anymore. Not when he could think about Chrissie.

Leaving the house just now, he'd felt conflicting emotions, joy that she'd decided to possibly give them another chance and disappointment because she hadn't asked him to stay a while. He had to play things her way though, no rushing in, trying to sweep her along in the direction he wanted her to go. She knew what happened the night she was in hospital, at least most of it and she'd held that knowledge inside her all this time, slowly poisoning her. She had a lot of forgiving to do.

So don't screw it up!

It was a good thing he had this business in London to keep him busy. He was really eager to take the matter further, pretty sure there was more to it than what had happened so far. What's more, he felt certain that whatever was behind all this would impact on him in some way. It was part of that same gut feeling he had.

Maybe tomorrow, when they saw this guy Singleton, found out if he had known Cockle before the man started working at Kavanagh Mansions, things might seem clearer. Show him the photograph, see what he had to say, how he reacted if he didn't say anything.

He reached the street he lived on and lengthened his stride. If Singleton *had* known Cockle from way back, had employed him because of that, Singleton could tell them if he was the same Alan in the photograph. If he was, then it was likely that Sarah was the same one and almost certainly, Singleton the same Joe. With two of his old friends dead, he should be only too willing to help in any way he could.

Chapter Ten

Danny worked his way back along the train carrying two styrofoam cups of coffee, fitted with plastic lids to stop spillage. Swaying with the movement of the carriage, he thought about Chrissie, how she had been watching afternoon TV, something unheard of before. Did it mean that taking a flexi-day in the middle of January presented so few options, or was it a sign of something more meaningful? Something to do with him, with them?

He turned sideways to let a woman pass then carried on through the automatic doors between carriages. Once this was over, once they were back together, he would make sure there was more to her life than some poxy afternoon game show. Spain, he thought, they had gone there for their honeymoon, thanks to the wedding gift from her parents. He was sure that would please her and he would like to go back. Majorca maybe, it was supposed to be nice there; Palma had a great cathedral.

He reached the first class carriage Chrissie had booked them into. As he stood the cup down on the table between them, he wondered when was the last time his sister had ridden second class, with the common people. Riding first class had not done a lot for her mood, which had been worsening steadily since they left Norwich.

"Here you are," he said, slipping his knees under the table and moving along to the window seat across from her. "Don't say I never get you anyhting."

"Why would I say that? Who would be interested?"

"It was a joke."

She turned her head and stared out of the window.

Danny sighed, tried his coffee, which he found was too hot to drink and clicked the lid back in place. "Go on then."

"Go on what?"

"Tell me what's crawled up your arse."

She took a quick look around, then turned back to him. "Do you have to be so coarse? We are on public transport."

"I've heard worse on trains before now. Anyway, the carriage is practically empty."

She did not reply, just went back to gazing at the passing countryside. It was a bleak sight. The snow had stopped last night, leaving a thin coating on the grass verges but little on the brown,barren fields. Skeletal trees reached their arms into a heavy, grey sky and seeing them, Danny's own spirits took a little dip.

"I had a dream last night," he said.

"Good for you."

"I've been having a lot lately."

He had, the type of thing he would normally have dismissed out of hand in the past, in the days when he rarely dreamed at all. Recently he'd had so many, it was troubling and he was starting to wonder whether, in some inexplicable way, the dreams might be linked to whatever it was he getting involved in. Last night's, with the figure reaching for him was the latest but it was another, which he'd had a earlier that he was thinking of now.

It was about the kids in the photograph, one of two or three featuring the same cast. In this one, they had been sitting around someplace, talking nonsense, messing about. One of them had sung a verse of the ABC Minor's Saturday Morning Pictures song, putting in his own words and they had all laughed. It had been so real, he might have actually been there, one of the gang. He repeated the dream to Carol who, turning from the window, gazed at him with bored eyes.

"Is there any point to this?"

"There was a girl, older than the rest of us. I think they were all a bit scared of her."

Carol sighed, "For God's sake!"

"She was humming a tune, to herself. The same tune had popped into my head a couple of days ago."

"Really?" she looked away. "This is riveting."

"I remember it. From way back."

"Way back when?"

"When *we* were kids, I think."

"Which means what exactly?"

"I don't know," he said, irritably. "I just think it's a bit odd. Don't you?"

"I'll tell you what I think is odd, you. All this weird nonsense you keep coming out with."

She turned away, dismissing him. He tried his coffee again, feeling slightly hard done by, and found it had cooled enough to sip without risking removing the skin of his palate.

He remembered the morning he'd woken up after that particular dream, with the sound of the girl's voice playing in his head, humming, 'Cherry Pink and Apple Blossom White'. He'd had the dream after the business in the alley and it had seemed important to him, although he could not understand why. Then, last night, the figure with the reaching arms, no music at all, just those grasping hands.

Carol said. "I'm starting to think this is all a waste of time. I have enough work on to keep me busy for weeks and here I am, swept along on a fool's errand by your imaginings."

"It's more than that."

"Is it? What facts do we have? Two people commit suicide within a short while of each other, miles apart. It must happen all the time."

"And if they knew each other?"

"There's nothing to suggest they ever heard of each other."

"There's the photo. Both of them getting a copy of it. How come, if the original belonged to Mum, *they* should each get a copy?"

"Yes, that is odd," she said grudginly. "It's one of the only reasons I'm here."

"And the other?"

She looked away again.

"What about the names?"

"Coincidence," she said, still gazing out the window. Two dead people share Christian names with a couple of kids in a photo taken almost thirty years ago."

"There's more to it, I can feel it."

She sat back in her seat, regarding him with a strange, searching look. "It's unusual to see you animated about anything these days. I haven't known you show this much enthusiasm for ages."

"So what are you saying? Do you want to stop what we're doing?"

"Let's just get this wild goose chase over and done with."

She turned her face back towards the window, gazing out at nothing in particular. Watching her, Danny felt more and more disgruntled. After all it was she who had got him involved with her so called, run-of-the-mill job. A simple delivery to London, a train ride, a day out and then it had all turned sour.

She was right about his reaction though, he did feel driven. It was like he had suddenly found some purpose to his life after a long, stagnant period. This was something he had to do and he would keep at it somehow, even if Carol pulled out.

"I phoned the police this morning," she said suddenly.

"Why would you do that?"

"To let DC Mills know that we were going to London."

"For Christ's sake! We're not suspects in anything."

"I don't want to antagonise him any further than we might have done already."

"Than I've done, you mean."

"Maybe, but it doesn't matter much now. The pathologist has come back with it looking like suicide. No one else involved."

"Mills is happy then," he said.

"I wouldn't say happy but he's more or less accepting it. Of course, it's up to the Coroner in the end."

She sighed to let him know just how much of a trial it was for her, then reached for her coffee. When he judged he'd let enough seconds tick by, he said.

"Doesn't it strike you as just a tiny bit peculiar that a client gives you her name and address, which turn out to be the name and address of a completely different person? Not to mention the fact that that person has recently killed herself. Then you've got the other little fact that, the intended recipient of her package also commits suicide a few days later?"

Carol shifted uncomfortably but said nothing.

"On top of all of that, they both received copies of that photograph, which has only just come to light after years hidden away."

"It wasn't hidden!"

"Whatever you want to call it."

Her face looked drawn, concerned but about what? The amount of work she had back at the office or the fact that try as she might, she could not quite managed to dismiss things as easily as she wanted to?

"You'll be saying next that she hired me just in order to get you involved."

"The thought had crossed my mind. If I was in that photo, then I would say that might well be the case."

"Well you're not. You should be glad, otherwise who knows how you'd end up if your reasoning is correct?"

The train arrived at Stowmarket and Danny watched a few passengers get off and a couple of fresh ones get on. When it was moving again, he uncapped his coffee once more and took a proper mouthful.

"Both front doors were open."

She glanced at him but said nothing.

"Almost as though they had each received a visitor. A visitor who - "

"Who did what? Made them kill themselves?"

He had already thought about that but couldn't find a convincing argument. Was it possible for a someone to scare a person into killing themselves? It sounded far fetched even to him.

And yet both doors *had* been open and both victims *had* been sent copies of the photograph.

"The more I think about this, the more I believe we're only seeing the tip of the iceberg. I can feel it, inside. I don't know how to put it any better than that."

The feeling had started soon after he'd found Cockle, and had been growing ever since. Discovering Sarah Eadel had turned that feeling into something more substantial, a sort of conviction that there was something larger in play.

"Do you think they let someone in?"

Carol glanced at him over her coffee cup, "How would I know?"

"You're the detective, I thought you might have some intuition."

"I have and it's telling me to ignore you."

Danny gave her a tired look but didn't say anything. There were all sorts of notions floating around his mind Like the shifting, restless feeling he'd had recently and how it had grown stronger over the last couple of days. Add to this the headaches returning and the dreams. Most of all though, what had happened to him in that alleyway in Norwich.

He had often felt that he half remembered things, incidents, or at least shadows of incidents which he just could not pin down.

Was it possible his memory was coming back?

The specialists he had seen as a boy had all said the same thing, that it would return at its own pace. Maybe this was it, it was starting to return. The possibilty suddenly scared him. If he was right, then what would he be faced with?

It was half past three by the time they exited the cab outside Hellman & Strapps, which was on the corner of High Street and another busy Wimbledon road. Carol paid the driver and as he drove off, Danny opened the shop door for her to enter first.

It was an office like most other offices he'd been in, same tough cord carpet, same beige decor, the same smells of coffee and paper. There were women working at two of the four desks, either side of a door that Danny assumed led to Singleton's office. One of the women asked if she could help and Carol explained who they were and why they were there.

"I'm afraid we're late. The train was delayed due to the weather."

The woman smiled and went through the door behind her. The other woman, mid thirties, attractive, looked up from her work. Danny caught her eye, smiled and she smiled back, which drew him a look from Carol. The first woman reappeared, asked them to go through and held the door open for them as they did so.

Singleton was behind a larger desk, covered with several tidy piles of paper. He stood up as they entered, coming round the desk to meet them, "Mrs. Warning."

Carol shook his outstretched hand. "This is my brother, Daniel."

"Danny," he said, surprised when Singleton held onto his hand longer than he expected, regarding him with a long, searching look before finally releasing him.

"Please sit down. Would you like coffee? Tea?"

They both said they were fine.

Singleton was a thick set man, a little shorter than Danny, with dark blond hair and bright blue eyes. Danny had seen eyes like that before but couldn't remember where. He watched the man return to his chair, then sat down next to Carol.

"I'm so sorry we're late. The trains..."

"The weather," Singleton said, with a sympathetic smile. "Well, that's British Rail for you"

Danny sighed heavily and Singleton's eyes touched him briefly before returning to Carol. He leaned casually back in his chair. "Now, I believe you wanted to talk to me about Mr. Cockle, our unfortunate caretaker at Kavanagh Mansions?"

Unfortunate was one way to describe him, Danny thought.

"We were hoping you might tell us something about him," Carol said. "You see a situation has arisen that's rather - well, puzzling."

"A situation?"

"That's what she said."

Carol glanced at Danny, then told Singleton everything, starting with being hired to deliver the package to London and through the subsequent events leading them to the discovery of Sarah Eadle's body.

"I see," Singleton studied his hands for a while. When he finally looked up, Danny was sure his face was paler than it had been and that there was something uneasy lurking in his eyes.

"That must have been awful for you, finding her that way," he said eventually. "And you say she hired you to deliver something to Cockle?"

"No. The woman who hired me was not the woman who killed herself."

Singleton stared at her. "She used the dead woman's identity?"

"Yes. So you see, I want to learn as much about Mr. Cockle as I can, in the hope of shedding some light on things."

"Well, I don't actually know much. I mean, it was a terrible business. Quite a shock for those people still living in the block and for me too, of course."

"Of course," Carol said. "As his employer, I - "

"In a roundabout way." Singleton took a pack of Benson & Hedges gold from his jacket pocket and offered them each a cigarette. When both declined, he selected one for himself and used a small chrome lighter to start it.

"I know my husband was technically the man's employer..."

"Well, actually I was," Singleton interrupted, with a tight smile.

Carol glanced at Danny with angry eyes. In a tight voice, she briefly explained what had happened with the package. "So you see, I was hoping you might know if he had any close relation to whom we might deliver it?"

"Do you have it with you?"

"We do," said Danny quickly, before Carol could answer.

The package was tucked away in his holdall but he took his own copy from the inside pocket of his shoulder bag, laying it on the desk for Singleton to look at. "The actual one is framed but otherwise identical."

"You opened it?"

"Actually, the police did," Danny lied.

"The police! In Norfolk? Why would they be interested?"

"Because another copy was delivered to Sarah Eadle before she died."

Singleton gazed at him for several seconds, trying and almost succeeding in hiding his discomfort. He looked at the photo again, for longer this time and finally pushed it away.

"Why didn't you leave it by Cockle's door?" he asked in a thick voice. "You should have left it by the door."

"It doesn't matter really. He'd never have seen it."

"How do you know that?"

Carol fidgeted beside him, obviously uncomfortable with the way things were going.

"I'd been told to deliver it," Danny continued. "Which to me meant handing it to him, not leaving it for anyone to walk off with."

Singleton tried to out stare Danny and the silence dragged on. Eventually he looked away, said to Carol, "How did you find out what had happened?"

"My husband told me," said Carol. "I believe you phoned his office?"

Singleton nodded. "The body was discovered on Tuesday afternoon. A friend called to see him, found his door open and went in..."

"Not the child then?" Danny said.

"Child?"

"The one that lives there. I heard her playing while I was there."

Singleton frowned, "There are no children living there. Most of the flats are empty"

"She was playing on the stairs."

"There are no children living in Kavanagh Mansions, I can assure you of that."

Danny stared at him. "She must have been visiting then."

Singleton tugged at the knot of his tie, where it pressed against his Adam's apple and said stiffly, "It's possible, I suppose."

Carol said, "Mr. Singleton should know."

"I saw a kid looking out of the top floor landing window. Later I heard her playing on the stairs."

"Then you're right, she must have been visiting," Singleton said. "I don't think any of the remaining tenants have family."

"You'd know, would you? Are you that friendly with them?"

"I suppose not. I see your point."

"I believe two of the remaining tenants are single women?" Carol said.

"That's right," Singleton stabbed out his half smoked cigarette in a big ashtray close to his right hand. "Miss Weller in Flat 5 is a middle aged librarian. Mrs. Kershaw, the old lady with the short term lease in Flat 2, is a widow. I do know that she doesn't have any children, she told me. So obviously no grandchildren."

"There's that Major on the first floor." Carol said.

"Now you mention it, I believe Major Clarke does have grandchildren."

"There we are then. One must have been visiting."

"I believe they are away at boarding school."

"Tell me," Danny said. "Why engage a live in caretaker? I've seen the block and it's nothing special. Once maybe but not any longer."

"We'll need one when the building is empty, more a watchman to keep thieves away. There are several original features in the building which would bring a good price on the market. It made sense to hire in now, give the man a chance to settle in, get used to the place."

"You're right," Carol said to Danny. "That sort of thing went out decades ago, except for the more prestigious properties."

"And that's what we are aiming for, I believe?" Singleton smiled wanly.

"Quite," Carol replied.

Danny didn't like the way the man had of staring at him, as though he was trying to see inside his head. "Did you know Cockle before he came to work here?"

"A little. He had filled in at other premises at short notice. When this job came up, he applied for it and I thought he was just the sort of chap I was looking for.

"He was happy to move in?" Carol asked. "I mean, didn't he have a place already?"

"He was living with his father in a council flat in Wandsworth. I believe there was some friction between them and he was anxious to get a place of his own. The flat that came with the job was just the thing he was looking for. He was happy with it."

"Not that happy," Danny said.

Carol shot him a look, then said to Singleton, "Can you give me the father's address. I'll make sure the photo gets to him."

"As far as the father goes," Singleton said. "I shouldn't think you'll get much appreciation from him."

"We'll have the address anyway," Danny said.

Singleton nodded, scribbled something on a pad beside him and tore the sheet off, passing it across the desk to Carol.

"Thank you," she folded the sheet and slipped it into her bag.

"Well, is that it?" the agent asked. "I have a viewing to get to."

Carol stood up, "Of course. It was good of you to spare us the time."

Standing up, Danny took the photograph off the desk. "And you've never seen this photo before?"

Singleton's sighed, "Should I have?"

"You'll notice the names written on the back." He turned the photo over so that Singleton could read the writing.

"Does this have some relevence...?"

"It was when I got back from London that we tried to return the package to the woman who'd hired Carol. We took it out to the address she had given but when we arrived, we found her."

"You mean the real Sarah Eadel?" Singleton asked quietly.

"The very same. That's when Carol realised she wasn't the person who had hired her."

"How had she...?"

"Shotgun," Danny said. "Under the chin."

"Oh God!" Singleton's face creased.

"You knew her?" Carol asked.

"No, of course not," he said after a moment. "It's just so..."

"Quite," Carol said quietly.

"It seems a bit of a coincidence, Don't you think," Danny said, holding Singleton's gaze. "I mean, the woman who hired Carol knowing both of them?"

"I suppose so," the man replied. "I hadn't thought of that."

"Alan and Sarah. There's an Alan and a Sarah in the photograph. The same people possibly?"

"How should I know?" Singleton looked away, a thin film of sweat on his forehead.

"There's a Joe too."

"It's a common name."

"Thank you for your time," Carol said quickly. She took Danny's arm, "We won't delay you any longer."

The next thing Danny knew, she was pushing him through the doorway, into the outer office, then outside into the street.

"What the hell was all that about?"

"Don't tell me you couldn't see that he was lying?"

"I could see that he was a little defensive. Quite naturally, I would think, with us seeming to question his competence."

"He didn't give a damn what we thought of his competence! He was scared."

"Scared?"

"He was really shaken about Sarah Eadel. And when I said about the kids in the photo... "

"As far as I could see, he was doing his best to help us."

"Doing his best! Well, I'd hate to see him doing his worst."

"Why is it, when anyone doesn't agree with what you're thinking, they're automatically telling lies?"

"Everyone?"

"Dad, for instance."

"Don't get me started on him."

A taxi dropped its fare at the kerb and Carol walked over to it. She told the driver where she wanted and climbed in, leaving Danny to scramble in behind her, just before the driver moved away.

"Anyway," he said. "I didn't like the way he kept staring at me, like I owed him something."

"What are you, ten years old?"

He sat silently as the cab drove across the traffic lights in front of them and up Wimbledon Hill. When it reached the top and started along Wimbledon Parkside, he said, "Now what?"

"Now nothing. I'm done."

"What about Cockle's father?"

It was obvious she thought that would be another wasted journey. "You can go and see him if you want to. I intend to get back home and tackle some real work."

"And you'll not be thinking about this at all?" he still believed that she was more interested than she was letting on.

"I'll be calling at the flat before I leave."

Nick's place in Fulham, to see what was keeping him so busy. Now Danny knew what had really brought her to London. Yes, she wanted to make sure he didn't make matters worse for her in any way but mostly, it was to try and catch Nick up to no good.

"Does he know you're coming?"

"I want to surprise him."

She turned away to gaze stonily from the cab window. He opened his mouth, thought better of it and looked out of his own side of the vehicle. Nick aside, she'd seen the way Singleton was acting. She must have thought he was holding stuff back, she wasn't stupid!

Outside, Wimbledon Common was passing by, patches of settled snow here and there, deserted. Thinking about it, her attitude to this whole affair was puzzling. She agreed it was odd, that there were questions that needed answering and yet..

"I want to be dropped in Fulham Palace Road," Carol said, as the cab started down Putney Hill. "What are you going to do?"

"You can let me out on the bridge. I want to have a look round the area."

Carol opened her bag and brought out a couple of twenty pound notes. "Here!"

"What's this for?"

"You'll need some money. Food, fares, whatever."

"I have some money," he said but took the notes anyway. Glancing at his watch, he saw it was twenty five minutes to four. "I'm still on the payroll then?"

"You never were. The job is finished. You did what I asked you to do, it's not your fault the way it turned out. Your debt to me is cancelled."

"That's really good of you, Carol."

She looked at him. "But?"

"There's no job for me?"

"Maybe I could use you. We'll see when you have finished with this."

"So you do think there's more to it?"

She pursed her lips, looked at her hands. "You still think there is. But even if you're right. it's not for us. Let the police deal with it - or not."

"I can't do that."

"It's done as far as I'm concerned. Call the money a bonus."

Danny's first instinct was to try to pursued her but the look of resolve on her face told him it would be a waste of time. She opened her bag again and brought out a pen and note pad. "You have your rail ticket. I'll give you the number of the flat and you can call me when you're ready to leave. We can meet up at Liverpool Street."

She wrote down what he needed and handed the sheet to him. Danny glanced at it. It was on the same sheet as Singleton had written Cockle senior's address. Danny folded it and put it in his coat pocket.

"How long will you be at the flat?"

"Long enough," she said."

The cab dropped him off and he watched it move off towards Fulham. A cold breeze off the river plucked at his collar and he turned towards Putney High Street. He couldn't really blame Carol, putting her business first, she had a reputation to protect and he'd already upset the local coppers. As she said, they could make things awkward for her if they wanted to. He didn't think they would but she was making sure not to get in too deeply. After all, this wasn't personal for her.

Is it for me?

He wasn't sure but it certainly felt that way and that feeling was getting stronger all the time.

Back when Carol had tired playing housewife to a man who was away as often as he was at home, she had put away her microwave cookery book and engaged the gardener's wife to keep house. She had started looking round for some occupation into which she could throw herself and found Rex Tanner, a shabby operator with a detective agency in the city. Tanner was just about scraping by on whatever dirty little job he could find and had about reached rock bottom, his reputation being so low, he was almost treading all over it. He was barely making ends meet.

Tanner had a couple of good people working for him, both keen to stay on when Carol had bought the whole she-bang and they had taught her all they knew, enabling her to employ a couple more agents and build the business into the respectable concern it was today.

All the same, Danny knew it wouldn't take a lot to potentially threaten her reputation and that was why, quite naturally, she was so reluctant to persue whatever was going on here.

Coming off the bridge, he turned right onto the Lower Richmond Road. Daylight was draining from the sky and soon the street lights would come on, he wouldn't have a lot of time in Galvin Street when he found it. All the same, it was worth it to him to take a look and following the page in his London A-Z, he set out with a building excitement inside him.

Chapter Eleven

Galvin Street was a narrow throughfare lined with small, terraced houses, workman's cottages, with bay windows up and down. Each property was fronted by a cheap, meter high wall of sandstone and each property had a metal five bar gate. There were no garages, so cars lined the kerbs on both sides and saplings had been planted to give the street an added air of respectability.

Danny slipped his A-Z back into his bag and walked slowly down the left pavement, the side where the odd numbers were. He had studied the relevent pages on and off during the train journey down, looking mainly for Rudd Street in the local area without locating it. It wasn't even listed in the index for SW London.

Dad had told him long ago that they had lived at number 9, so when he found that number, he stopped and reached out with all his concentration, playing a game he sometimes played, hoping that this time something unexpected came from it.

This was where Jack and his mother had lived, where they had been a happy family until Jack had done what he did on that fatal evening. This was the house and he could be forgiven for thinking there might be something left here, some shade of what had gone by that might reach out to him.

Standing there the way he was gave him a funny sensation anyway. Here on pavements he must have played on as a boy, in a place he once had known as home but didn't know now. It was the place where The Tykes had had their photo taken, after all so there had to be something, some residue left behind.

But there was nothing, nada, zilch! Only the same old blankness there always was when he tried to find those long lost memories.

The house had recently had a face lift, expensive replacement windows, chunky double sealed front door. There was nothing left to suggest that in former years it had been divided into two flats, one up, one down, no hot water, no bathrooms and a shared outside toilet in the small back yard.

According to Dad, their flat had been the upper one, comprising two rooms and a scullery, with a baggy ceiling and bulging plaster, a coal fire that had never drawn properly. Dad had talked about it so much, he felt he knew it and of course, he had done and raising his eyes to the upper window, he could almost see his mother standing there, joggling him in her arms, watching for Jack to come home.

Occasionaly it might have been Dad of course who, living with his own mother and daughter since being demobbed, had become a regular visitor to his best mate's home and later, to his best mate's widow, going on to marry her later.

"Can I help you?"

Danny came back to the present to find a small, stout man wearing a chunky cardigan over a yellow checked, 'Mr. Toad' waistcoat, glaring at him belligerently.

"You've been standing there looking at my house for several minutes," he said. "What do you want?"

The small man's balding head was as round as the rims of his spectacles, through which his wide, blue eyes seemed much larger than they could be. Under their scrutiny, Danny felt himself squirming guililtly.

The eyes moved to a point above Danny's left shoulder and looking round, he saw a neighbourhood watch sign screwed to a nearby lamp post.

"I think you had best move along."

"I used to live here, when I was a child," Danny blurted out and immediately felt ridiculous. He added quickly, "We rented the top flat."

"There are no rented properties here now!" the man said crisply, as though the suggestion of rented flats in this particular area was an insult. "No flats! We're all owner occupiers in this street!"

Pompous prick!

Danny wondered why he was standing there, explaining himself to this little arsehole. Because he felt, what, homesick? That was the closest he could get to describing what held him there.

Jesus!

Homesick for a place he couldn't even remember. How did that work? Did he want this man to know that part of him belonged here? As if by the telling, he would somehow help himself to feel less lost?

"There's nothing here for you now."

"No," Danny said after a moment. "I guess there's not."

It was just a street, thousands like it scattered across the country. People came, people went, but the buildings, the bricks and mortar, went on regardless. The ghosts that lingered there kept their own council.

Mr. Toad continued to watch him until he was well on his way. Glancing back from the corner of the street, Danny saw him hurry back into the warm and shivered slightly, the afternoon seeming suddenly colder. Well he'd been there, seen what he came to see. Now he would leave Galvin Street once and for all, the whole experience a waste of time.

He walked on. A snow flake brushed his cheek and two or three more danced across along the pavement in front of him. Remnants of the last fall or the advanced party of a new one, he wasn't sure. He had passed streets without noticing, lost in thought and now, aware of a person in front of him, looked up to see he was at the corner of Kavanagh Gardens.

"Hello!"

It was a woman standing there, smiling a little uncertainly. Short and round, bundled up in a fur coat that reached almost to her ankles, a fur hat on her head, with ear flaps that were pulled tightly down around her chubby cheeks and tied beneath her chin.

"I thought it was you. I saw you before. On the day you came to the Mansions?" She pointed down Kavanagh Gardens. "The day poor Mr. Cockle died."

A name jumped into Danny' head. Singleton had mentioned it, the woman with the ground floor flat. "Are you Mrs. Kershaw?"

"That is me," she spoke with a slight accent, European, possibly German. The gigantic coat shifted as she moved inside it. "But how did you know?"

"Mr. Singleton mentioned you. I saw him this afternoon."

Her cheeks, reddened by the cold, looked like two rosey apples. She had a small, birdlike nose and the darkest eyes Danny had ever seen.

"And he told you about Mr. Cockle?"

"The caretaker? Yes, he did," Danny said because it was easier to lie.

Her bright eyes regarded him steadily. "You went to see him that day."

"Yes."

"The day he died."

"That's right."

"I saw you at the front door and let you in. You went down to his flat."

"I was delivering a package."

"There was no answer."

"No. Well..."

"Of course there wouldn't have been..."

"No." He said, self consciously, "I understand a friend found him?"

"Yes. A terrible shock for the poor man. He came to me and I called the police." She shook her head, thinking back, reliving the moment. Then she remembered he was there. "Look at me, keeping you here in this weather. I can't imagine what Walforf is thinking."

"Waldorf?"

She made a little sideways shuffle and he saw a weary looking Dachshund, clad in a tartan coat, waiting patiently at the end of its lead. "He is old, like me, and only has little legs, so we don't go far."

Danny nodded, smiling at the dog but all he got for his trouble was a baleful glare and low grumble.

"Hark at him! He's a grumpy old man." She beamed at the dog, then looked back to Danny. "Would you like to come in for a moment, I'll make tea?"

Danny said he would and followed her to the Mansions, glancing up before stepping into the porch. There was no face at the top landing window this time.

"They took him away in a black bag," she said, leading him across the foyer to her front door. "His poor friend was devastated. I believe it was a little more then friendship that they had and who cares these days?"

Mrs. Kershaw opened the front door and stepped into the hall. She removed the huge coat and hung it on a hall stand in a corner. Dumping his holdall, he followed her along to the sitting room, Waldorf toddling along behind her.

"This weather! It makes my bones ache."

Danny made sympathetic noises as he removed his beanie and slipped his overcoat off, drapping it over one arm, as he followed her into her sitting room.

"Take a seat and I'll make the tea." She beamed, "I have pastries. The baker says they were fresh from the oven, but he's been telling me the same thing for too many years to remember."

She disappeared through to the kitchen and a moment later, he heard the rattle of cups and saucers. Danny looked around at huge items of furniture, big wooden cabinets, a sideboard to match and a giant leather three piece suite that looked like it might swallow you whole.

He shoved his beanie into a coat pocket and laid the coat over an arm of the settee as he walked across to look out the wide bay window facing over the back garden. He saw a tangled mass of snow covered growth and beyond it, a tall boundary wall.

According to the A-Z, the road beyond the wall was Embankment and of course, on the other side of it was the Thames. He imagined the line of grey water he would see beyond the wall if he were high enough, then turned away as a few snow flakes drifted by the window.

Mrs. Kershaw came in carrying a tray with cups, saucers and side plates. She nodded at a long coffee table standing in front of the settee.

"Would you mind?"

Danny went across and cleared the table, which was littered with last Sunday's news papers, magazines and supplements. He freed enough space for the tray, dumping the papers into one of the armchairs. She stood the tray down, then went around the room turning on more lamps.

"Such weather! So gloomy all of the time."

It was clear that in reality, the room was large but made to look smaller, being crammed with the massive items of furniture. Like the rest of the building, it had seen better days, however images of what it must have been like continued to shine through.

"You are from around here?" she asked, sitting on the arm of an armchair.

"Norfolk," Danny said. "I did live down the road a little until I was eleven."

"Then you know the area," Mrs. Kershaw said, smiling up at him.

"Only from the A-Z."

She was puzzled.

"I suffered an illness when I was eleven and ever since, I haven't been able to remember anything before it. We moved soon afterwards, so..." he shrugged.

"How dreadful for you."

"You learn to cope," he said, "My sister engaged me to deliver that package, that's why I was here."

"And today?"

"Something else for her," he said with a wan smile. "That's done now, so I thought I'd have a look round the area before going home."

"Your sister runs a delivery business?"

He corrected her.

"A detective agency! You are a private investigator?"

"No. She asked me to bring it down to save using one of her regular employees. They are very busy at the moment."

"Mrs. Warning?" she said thoughtfully. "Isn't she the landlord's wife?"

He smiled, wondering how Carol would like being referred to in that way. "Her husband's company own the property."

"I met her once, She paid a visit last year when her husband came to see the building with the agent, Mr. Singleton. Who would have thought she was a detective. She seemed a very nice woman."

"She has her moments."

Mrs. Kershaw chuckled, waggling her head from side to side. "Sibling rivalry! What would we do without it?"

"Indeed," Danny said noncommittedly. Whatever his relationship with Carol was, he always seemed to come off second best.

"I've lived here for over thirty years. I don't know where all that time went."

"You must have made plenty of friends."

"Not so many. People come, people go. You lose track. My best friend, Rosa used to live here, Flat 1. She moved to the house on the corner, other end of the street."

Out in the kitchen, the kettle started a tentative whistle. Mrs. Kershaw stood up with less of a struggle if she had been sitting on the sofa.

"She is off visiting her son in Israel, for her sins. Second time this year! Like he is a baby and not a fully grown man. Eighty-two years of age, you would think she'd know better!"

Danny smiled, nodded, wanting to get her back to Cockle, see whether he might learn more about the man.

"Twice a day, I check everything is well with her house. It is a great responsibility, but it gives me something to do." She started for the door, "Excuse me. Sit! Sit!"

Danny watched her hurry from the room, then settled gingerly on the front edge of an armchair, which immediately tried to engulf him.

The room was cozy for all of its clutter, with heavy flock curtains that screamed yester-year and enough assorted Kershaw detritus to fill a small skip.

He became conscious of being surrounded by scores of framed photographs, austere looking people from another time. They all seemed to be staring at him, as though knowing exactly what had happened the last time he'd been in the block.

"Family," Mrs. Kershaw said, re-entering the room holding a huge teapot. She followed his gaze, as he shifted uncomfortably under the weight of those eyes. "Mine and Maurice's. All long dead."

Some of them were fading, all were black and white or sepia, a little like those in Dad's collection but older. There were groups of people, dressed formally, posing awkwardly for the camera, sour looking men with big moustaches and even sourer looking women in stiff, black clothes, which held them rigid. They all seemed affronted to be standing there on display.

She departed again after placing the pot on the tray, hurrying through to the kitchen and returning with a large plate, which held a selection of Danish Pastries. She was shaking her head sadly, as though continuing a conversation already started.

"A shame, the way this building has been let go. I remember how it used to be; such finery!"

She put the plate on the table beside the tray and began arranging the cups and saucers, one for him, one for her, pouring milk into each.

"You like sugar?"

"No thanks."

"Please, help yourself to a pastry."

Picking up one of the side plates, Danny lifted the smallest onto it. He smiled, "Did you ever have Mr. Cockle in for tea?"

"I invited him one time but he never came."

"Did you know him well?"

"Not well, no. Enough to know he was an unhappy man."

"Really? Why he was unhappy?"

"I think he was lonely. He said he only had his father and they did not get on."

"What about his friend?"

"Not a word about him. I reminded him about coming to tea but he muttered something about being an employee and that it was not right."

She sat back down on the arm of the sofa and took a pastry for herself. Biting a large piece from it, she spilled flakes into her lap and Waldorf looked up alertly from the wicker basket he had retreated to but.

"He wasn't the sociable type, then?"

"He would stop to talk whenever I saw him. He was polite, no more. Thin, anxious, always with the cigarette in his mouth." She shook her head, "He seemed frightened of his own shadow."

"I wonder what he was frightened of?"

"Once he said that he didn't like it here. I could see that for myself. He was anxious all the time, jumpy. His eyes were never still."

"Did he give any reason for not liking the place?"

"Noises. Things bumping all the time, he said. I told him, don't worry, that it was probably the water pipes. An old building like this."

"Did he tell Singleton?"

"I think so. The last time I saw him, he said that Mr. Murkin was going to call. That's the plumber Mr. Singleton always uses."

"Murkin..." A faint echo in his mind, an unusual name.

"Whether or not he came," she shrugged her shoulders and rolled her eyes. "A strange man. A law unto himself."

Danny ate some more pastry, washing it down with a swig of tea, which was strong but palatable, not like Dad's. He wondered whether Cockle's fears had anything to do with the way he'd ended up.

"Mr. Cockle's friend was younger than him, I think. An Asian man, a very smooth looking complection and large, brown eyes. Like Bambi. You know, the cartoon fawn?"

Danny said he knew the film she meant.

"He kept saying that Mr. Cockle was just sitting there - that his face was contorted, as though he was terrified..."

Danny saw the face again, said quickly, "Better he found him than the child."

She frowned, "Child?"

He explained about seeing a girl looking out the top floor landing window when he'd arrived and then the noise of her shoes on the floor upstairs. "As I was leaving, I heard her again, scampering about up on one of the landings."

She looked thoughtful, "Possibly one of the Major's grandchildren, although they would surely be away at school? They are normally very well behaved when they visit but that is usually during the summer holidays."

"There are no children living here?"

"There have not been any children for a long while." She said and popped was left of her Danish into her mouth. "There was Mr. and Mrs. Wiloughby back in the

Sixties, they had two girls. Before that, it must have been, Mrs. Hayden. Just a moment."

She got up again and went through to the kitchen, returning moments later with two sheets of paper towelling, one of which she handed to Danny. She sat down, wiping her mouth and fingers on the other sheet.

"Now where was I? Oh yes, Mrs. Hayden. A widow I think but she never said and I never asked. She had a daughter, Veronica, thirteen, fourteen."

"Veronica," Danny repeated and thought of the names on the photograph. When he became aware she was looking at him, he managed a smile. "Sorry, I...something...sorry."

"You have heard the name, Veronica Hayden? She disappeared."

"Disappeared?"

"It was all over the news at the time. Broke her poor mother's heart."

"Was she found?"

"Not to this very day." Mrs. Kershaw shook her head, reflectively. "What a terrible thing. I do not have children, so I can only try to imagine the heartache the poor woman felt."

A distant bell ringing in his head as he remembered the children in the Tykes photograph. The pair who had turned at the moment of exposure, a boy and a girl.

"It's a long time ago now, the nineteen fifties." She sat for a moment reflecting on what she had told him.

"So there are no children you can think of who might have been here on Tuesday?"

"None."

Danny emptied his cup and stood up. "Well, thank you for the tea and Danish. They went down well."

Mrs. Kershaw lifted herself from her perch on the sofa arm. "You are off home now?"

"Soon, maybe. Now I have to go to see Mr. Cockle's father in Wandsworth."

"Oh!" she made a face. "From what Mr. Cockle intimated, I don't think the father is a very nice man. I think he drove his son out of the flat they shared."

"I heard they didn't get along," Danny said, getting into his coat. "Still, I feel I ought to tell him about the photograph."

"Photograph?"

"I'll show you."

Opening his shoulder bag, he reached inside. When Chrissie had given him the bag, he'd been reluctant to use it. Now he wouldn't be without it. He removed his copy of the photo and showed it to her.

"The one for Cockle is a duplicate of this."

"Children?"

"I think it's a photograph of Cockle as a boy, with some of his friends."

"Ah," she said, looking at it closely.

"I should ask the father the copy intended for his son. I don't think the police will want to see it."

"The police?"

He explained about Sarah Eadel and the copy he had discovered in the dead woman's room.

"Someone else died? Another of these children?" she sounded alarmed.

"It's only supposition on my part that the photo has anything to do with Cockle. But if I'm right, then yes, another of those children." He pointed to the skinny urchin on the end of the line. "I think that's Cockle, there."

"The same photo," she said, focusing on the boy. That seems - a coincidence." Her voice held doubt and Danny turned the photo over, showing her the names on the back.

"That boy was called Alan, the girl there is Sarah."

"She was the other victim?"

"I think so."

"Are you there?"

"No, I'm not there. I think I must have known them though. Of course, I can't remember anything from back then."

Mrs. Kershaw gazed at the young faces for a moment more. "Two of them in the same picture. That is a coincidence."

"If I'm right, it is. Two matching names is not a lot to go on though."

The old woman's eyes gleamed darkly, black, intelligent eyes that showed she was already thinking as he was. "More than a coincidence."

Danny nodded, "Much more. I think the boy Joe might be the man Singleton."

"And this Ray just might be Mr. Murkin."

"The plumber?"

She eyed him shrewdly. "He is a friend of Mr. Singleton. I understand they have known each other for some while."

Danny thought she could be right. Singleton had admitted having known Cockle from before and employing another friend, Murkin to deal with all the plumbing problems the block encountered would be a natural thing to do.

"I can't say much about the two that are blurred, Brian and Veronica."

"This girl is called Veronica?"

He watched her bring the photo close to her face, squinting at it. "If I could see her better, I could tell you."

"Tell me?"

She looked at him. "Veronica, the name of Mrs. Hayden's daughter?"

"Of course," he said, although he had not forgotten what she had said just moments before.

"This might be her. And this photo was taken in the summer of 1955, which would be around the time the Hayden girl went missing."

"Are you sure it was then?" he felt as though the floor shifted a little under his feet. This was something more solid. Not out and out proof that his suspicions were correct but certainly an indicator that they might be. His head began to ache slightly.

"Yes, yes. I remember because it was soon after Ruth Ellis was executed. You know Ruth Ellis?"

Danny nodded, "The last woman to hang in Britain."

"That was in the summer of 1955, July I'm sure. Veronica vanished in the August."

"Veronica must have been a common name back then," Danny said.

Any doubts he had about his theory melted away and the implications of it suddenly scared him. All his senses were screaming at him that this must be the same girl.

"Ah, now there is a face that I recognise."

He looked at her, saw she was pointing to Jack Reed.

"He was our local policeman. The, 'Bobby On the Beat', as they say. Such a nice man. He drowned, trying to save someone from the river."

"I know. He was my father."

"Your father!?" she said, regarding him closely. "That was a man to be proud of."

Proud? Was he? He supposed he was, but the feeling was tempered somewhat by the anger he felt at Jack, sacrificing himself when he'd had a wife and child who needed him.

"I don't remember him."

"That is indeed a tragedy," Mrs. Kershaw said.

Danny took the photo from her and returned it to his shoulder bag, "I'd better get off."

Waldorf barked and she beamed. "He wants his supper, so I should let you go. And I must be free when Rosa phones. If I do not answer at once, she thinks her house has burned down, with me in it!"

Danny put on his beanie and walked along the hall to the front door. Opening it, he looked back and she waved to him.

"Don't be a stranger. And keep me informed about, you know."

He said he would and left.

Chapter Twelve

Twilight was deepening when the bus driver told him they had reached his stop, the one for Gutteridge Lane. He stepped from the bus and stood for a moment at the side of the busy main road, watching a few flakes of snow drifting through the light from the nearest street lamp.

Gutteridge Lane, or the fifty meters or so that was left of it, was before him. It ran away to meet a wide grassed area which fronted an estate of 1950s built Council flats.

He walked to the corner and started up the stump of the street and guessed that it used to run into a labyrinth of similarly narrow thoroughfares, lined by row upon row of identical decrepit, bug infested slums.

They had probably been swept away after the war in the push towards better housing. Now here was grass and trees and neat little paths, one of which he followed to the front of the nearest tall block. Satisfying himself that it was Kipling House, he glanced at the sheet of paper, where the address had been written by Singleton and, stepping aside for a young, Asian man who was leaving the block, walked into the building.

He hoped Cockle senior was in, otherwise he would have had a wasted journey, also that, if he was in, he was in a good mood, going by what had been said about him. When he saw a sign on the wall which said, Flats 13 - 22, he grunted. Cockle lived at number 15, next floor up and there was no lift.

Danny climbed to the first landing, a strip of concrete with a flat at each end. Number 15 was to his right, a half glazed front door, dark blue paintwork and no door bell, just a brass letterbox/door knocker unit, which he used. When nothing happened he repeated the action, only louder and thought about standing at the younger Cockle's front door back in Kavangh Mansions.

He put the thought away as a light came on behind the frosted glass front door panel, stepping back just as the door opened.

"What do *you* want?"

Danny looked at the busted up face of Cockle senior, a big man, turning to fat, with a neck like a bullock and the bumpy, scarred features of an unsuccessful boxer.

"Mr. Cockle?"

"Who wants to know?" the man said from deep in his belly. Small dark eyes glared at Danny from between pudgy lids, giving him the look of an angry wart hog. Although there were not any tusks, the thick lips moved continuously around several yellow, broken teeth.

"My name's Danny Stephens. I work for a private detective agency and I'd like to talk to you about your son."

"He's dead," Cockle said. "What's there to talk about?"

He eyed Danny suspiciously, weighing him up.

"I know what happened and I'm sorry for your loss."

Cockle grunted. "Not much of a loss. You better come in, I don't want the neighbours earholing."

He walked off into the flat, leaving Danny to close the front door and find his own way to a shabby front room. The TV was on playing some sort of local news programme and Cockle turned the sound down. Danny noticed a crumpled copy of the Sun newspaper open on the table and a quart beer bottle next to it.

"You want some?" Cockle asked, seeing where he was looking.

"No thanks."

"Wine man, are you?" he sneered.

"Not especially. I drink most things but it's a bit early for me."

"Suit yourself."

Cockle sat down heavily behind the table and poured some beer into a pint jug, all but emptying the bottle. He drank, belched and bumped the glass down on the table. Dragging the back of a hand across his scarred lips, he glared at Danny.

"So what you got to say about my boy?"

There was something unpleasant in the way he said, *my boy*, as though questioning his son's gender.

"I want to show you a photograph. I think it's of your son and his friends when he was a child."

"No good showing me anything like that. I wasn't around much when he was a nipper. If I had've been, perhaps he would have grown up to be a real man."

Danny took the framed photo out of his holdall anyway and placed it on the table for Cockle to look at. The man stared at him for seconds, then drew it closer, glancing at it. He stabbed at the slight figure on the end of the line of children, "That's him, there. Dunno who the others are, 'specially the copper. Back then, I done what I could to avoid the police, if you know what I mean?"

"Did you ever see the photo before?"

"Should I have?"

"You lived with him."

"He lived with me. This is my flat!" Bending over in the chair, he clicked on the controls of an ancient gas fire, mounted in the hearth behind him. "I took him in when he was thrown out of his last place by his boyfriend."

"Where was that?"

"Tooting." He peered up at Danny and gave a phlegmy chuckle, "So, what's this all about? Are you another of his little mates or something?"

"I didn't know him. I had a package to deliver to him, that's all."

"What sort of package?"

"You're holding it. I took it there on the day he was found. He didn't answer the door so I left. It was only later I heard about what happened."

"You sure you ain't one of his buddy-buddies. With your handbag and all?" He was positively glowering now and Danny took a step back.

"I told you, I didn't know him."

Cockle poured himself what was left of the beer. He seemed to have lost all interest in the photo and leaning forward, Danny picked it up. He was shoving it back into the holdall when Cockle spoke again.

"He was living with a bloke, you know? Pair of Nancy boys. Made me sick. A son of mine, a bloody arse bandit!"

It was a long time since Danny had heard words like those, and dripping with so much venom. For his own son! He shifted uncomfortably.

"You know what it's like to have a son that's not a man? Everybody laughing at me behind my back."

He couldn't imagine anyone daring to laugh at the man from the front or from behind.

"I was a seaman," Cockle said. "Seen plenty like him over the years and we knew how to deal with 'em too. Then I get one for a fucking son!"

Danny watched him turn round in the chair, bend over to reach into the bottom of a sideboard he had there. He brought out another beer bottle and opened it, catching the froth that erupted from the top in his mouth. Another belch and he refilled his glass. "You got kids?"

"No."

"So how would you know?!"

Danny hadn't said a word. "I wouldn't."

"So don't come here telling me about my kid!" Cockle growled. He stood up smartly, staggered and sent his chair tumbling over. His fists were clenched and there was murder in his eyes. "Go on, fuck off!"

"If you want the photograph -"

"Why would I want the fucking thing!"

Danny backed away from the man, half expecting him to throw the table aside and come at him. He didn't and by the time he'd reached the hall, Danny was pretty sure he was safe.

The meeting with Cockle senior had been just as unpleasant as he'd been warned it would be but at least something had come out of it. He now knew for sure that it was Alan Cockle in the photograph, so it was natural to assume that Sarah Eadel was there too.

He walked out of the stump of Gutteridge Lane feeling vindicated, thinking about his talk with Mrs. Kershaw. Veronica Hayden had vanished around the time that the photo had been taken. If that Veronica was the one in the picture, it was probably the last impression of her before she disappeared. He'd still been living in Galvin Street then and it was more than likely that he'd had a passing acquaintance with the Tykes, in which case, her too.

If only he could remember!

It was snowing now at a leisurely pace, dusting the pavements and melting on the road. He spotted a telephone box away to his right and walked along to it. Inside, standing among the miscellaneous items of debris that littered the floor, he fished the number that Carol had given him from his pocket, popped a coin in into the slot and dialled it.

"Hello?" Her voice sounded thick, like she had been crying.

"It's me. Are you okay?"

"Yes." There was a sound of her blowing her nose, then she was back on the line. "I shall be staying over tonight and going home in the morning."

"I take it you managed to reach Nick?" He waited but she didn't reply. He decided to leave it. "I'm staying on for a bit. I'm just off to find a hotel. I do get expenses, don't I?"

"You can stay here," she said. "I could do with the company."

"What about - ?"

"He's staying at his club."

On the Mall, which didn't allow women, so his evening would be ruined. Had he said as much? Was that why she'd been crying? If it was, then hopefully her tears were of anger. She had been through the same thing too many times in the past for them to be anything else.

"Where are you?"

He told her.

"So stay on the bus into Fulham." She told him where to get off. "I'll keep an eye out for you."

Coming out of the phone box, he felt glad she had asked him to stay. He hadn't fancied searching round Putney for a suitable hotel.

He was about to cross over the road, when he spotted the Asian man he'd seen earlier standing in the shadow of the old viaduct that ran across the road to his left. Once eye contact was made, the man approached him.

"Excuse me! May I talk to you?"

"Something wrong?" Danny wondered, had the man been following him?

"You've just seen Mr. Cockle."

Danny just looked at him.

"I saw you go into the block," he said. "I know you went up to his floor."

"There's more than one flat there."

"My name is, Aakesh Sah. Alan Cockle was my partner."

Danny could see the man had readied himself, as though expecting a familiar reaction.

"I did see him. Why are you so interested?"

The man blinked, lowering his guard slightly. "May I ask, was it Alan you talked about?"

He was softly spoken, direct but polite and Danny found himself warming to him.

"Let me ask you something. Why did you kick Alan out?"

"I didn't. Alan left of his own accord. I was trying to get him to move back in. I loved Alan. We'd lived together for three years."

"In Tooting."

"Yes."

There was a small pub further along the road. It was a little early to start drinking but he wasn't anticipating a session. At least it would be better than drinking with Cockle senior.

Danny suggested they went there to talk. The man's partner probably knew more about Cockle than his awful father did. Maybe Cockle had told him things about when he was a boy.

It was a one bar establishment, small and cosy with a fire crackling in the grate and the smell of beer calling to him. He asked Aakesh what he wanted then pointed out a table by the window and went to the bar to order.

They were the only two in there and the heavy lidded barman dealt with the order as swiftly as the beer pump allowed. Standing the two halves of bitter before Danny on the bar, he let his gazed roll over Aakesh as he took the money.

"So," Danny said, joining the Indian at the table. "What did you want to ask me?"

Aakesh thanked him as he took a glass and sipped at the contents. "Did you know, Alan?"

"No."

"So why were you there, talking to his father?"

"I wanted to let him know I had something that belonged to his son."

"Belonged to him, how?"

Danny gave him a long, appraising look, decided to give the photo to him and got the framed copy from his holdall. "The old man doesn't want it. Maybe it would be better for you to have it anyway."

Aakesh took the frame and gazed at the photo, then looked at Danny questioningly. Danny explained about trying to deliver the package.

"The boy on the left is Alan," he said.

"His only child. You would think that he'd want it."

"I think Alan would prefer it came to you."

Aakesh looked at the photograph for a moment longer, then brought his eyes up to Danny. There were tears in them. "I found him. So much blood. His face..."

Danny, feeling guilty, said, "It must have been a shock."

"Yes. It was not just what he had done, and that was bad enough. It was the look on his face, frozen there, like a mask. I believe he was terrified just before..."

"It must be an awful thing to contemplate...."

"Then why do it?" Aakesh said loudly and the barman looked over.

Danny asked quietly, "How was he before? The last time you spoke to him."

Aakesh thought about it. "There was a phone call. That's when it all started."

"What started?"

"A month before he left. A woman. I answered and she asked for Alan Cockle."

"Who was she?"

"She didn't say. Just repeated his name.

"Didn't he explain when he'd finished?"

"Not a word. I could see that the call had shaken him badly but he wouldn't explain it. He retreated into silence. Day after day until our relationship became strained. He was edgey, short tempered, especially if I tried to bring up the phone call. Then one day, I came home from work and found that he'd gone."

"Just like that?"

"Moved out. Not a word, just a note saying he was going to stay with his father for a while." Aakesh took a drink, thinking about what had happened. "I new something was wrong then. He hated his father."

"I should think he's an easy man to hate. Did you contact him there?"

"I found the address in a book Alan left behind, his phone number too. I phoned once but Alan told me not to call again. I thought I was owed some kind of an explaination. I thought we were good, our relationship was going places. He said something had come up, something from his past and that for now, it was safer he moved out."

"Safer? Who for?"

"He said, for me. I tried to get him to tell me more but he wouldn't. I offered to meet him after work, he was a porter then at St. Georges hospital. He told me he'd already left there. That he had a new job, with accomodation included and was moving out of his father's flat."

"Kavanagh Mansions," Danny said.

"Yes."

"Did you go there?"

"He said I shouldn't. Said he would contact me when things were better, that we could continue our life together. I waited but he never contacted me, so I tried to find his phone number. I even went to see his father to ask if he had it. You can imagine the reception I received. It seems he doesn't like Asians either."

"There's a surprise."

"In the end, I went to Putney. I wasn't sure where the place was so I took a cab and let the driver find it."

"And discovered him..." Danny said quietly. He took a drink and the beer helped a little to dilute the taste of guilt.

"I was there this evening to try and speak to the man again. Maybe he would be more receptive now that Alan..."

"He wouldn't have been."

"When I saw you, I waited, heard what you said to him and then..." He gestured with his hands and shoulders, indicating that now they were here.

"It's a pity Alan didn't tell you anything about the woman who called"

"I would like to speak to her now. She may not even know...what happened."

If the woman was who he thought it was, she was well past caring, Danny thought. He was quietly trying to work out how much he should tell Aakesh and decided, not a lot.

"There was something Alan let slip after the call," the Indian said. "I could see that he'd had a shock, hearing from her out of the blue. He muttered something about Norfolk. That she should be safe living there."

Safe!

Danny reached slowly across the table and placed a finger on the photograph. "This shows Alan with some friends back in 1955."

Aakesh looked at it again. "These children?"

"I think it was taken in Putney, where they all lived. Probably friends who always went round together."

As he studied the group, the shade of a sad smile formed on the man's mouth. Danny let him have a moment, then said, "And Alan never told you anything about his past?"

"He hardly ever spoke about his life, not that far back. Only places he'd worked. people he'd know as a man. Never about his childhood. I thought perhaps it was something he wanted to forget, with a father like the one he had."

"That's a fair assumption."

There was a pause, they sipped beer, then Aakesh said, "Forgive me but I think you know more than you're saying."

"I have ideas, notions, I don't actually know much at all."

"Can you tell me?"

Danny cautioned himself not to get carried away. It was all supposition really, drawn from what might just be coincidences. Maybe Cockle had killed himself. Maybe Sarah had too. It was the most comfortable answer and he might well be better off accepting it as such.

But there was that little inner voice, screaming at him and while that continued, he had little choice but to carry on the way he was.

"You think it was someone from his past that called?"

"I don't know. It's possible, I guess."

"One of these children?"

"Honestly, I don't *know* anything. I have theories, nothing I can prove. It's best I keep them to myself at the moment."

He could see Aakesh was desperate for more and was likely to persist until Danny gave him something. He had to cut this meeting short, before that could happen.

"Let me help." Aakesh was staring at him.

"With what?"

"Whatever it is you're doing."

The last thing he wanted was someone getting in the way. What he had to do was for him alone to follow through.

"I have ideas, nothing more. It would be wrong of me to share them with you until I see if there's anything in them."

Aakesh accepted this reluctantly and dipped into a pocket of his waterproof. He brought out a small note book and scribbled something into it with a pen, then tore the sheet from the book and gave it to Danny.

"You can reach me at this number, if you find anything."

Danny pocketed the sheet and they spoke for a while longer, with Aakesh asking more questions that Danny could not answer. Eventually, when there was nothing else to say, Danny finished his drink and made a show of looking at his watch.

"I have to go," he said.

They stepped outside into the lightly falling snow. Aakesh, shivering, drew his coat closer. peering over the collar at Danny.

"I can't understand any of this. There has to be reason for what happened but nothing makes any sense."

Danny saw a bus approaching in the distance and said his goodbyes, promising to phone if he found out anything new. He left the man standing there, hurrying across the road to the bus stop. When the bus arrived, he paid the driver and went to sit half way along the vehicle. As the bus pulled away, he saw Aakesh was still there, where he had left him, a lonely figure in the snow.

Chapter Thirteen

The bus stopped at traffic lights close to Munster Road in Fulham and as the exit door folded back on itself, Danny spotted the private block of flats he was headed for on the corner. He got off the bus and walked along to the entrance and there was Carol, coming out of the front door to meet him.

"Hi," she smiled, hugged him briefly and they went inside. "I saw the bus from the window."

"How did you know I was on it?"

She smiled sheepishly and he knew that she had been coming down every time a bus arrived from soon after he'd phoned her.

There was a small lobby, with a staircase off to the left and a stainless steel lift door in front of them. Carol pressed the call button and the door slid silently open. They stepped into the small lift car, a metal box with none of the elegance of the one back at Kavanagh Mansions and she hit the up button.

"It's only the first floor but I don't feel like climbing the stairs."

He didn't either.

The car moved swiftly upwards, gliding to a stop almost immediately and they emerged onto a quiet landing.

"That way," Carol said, pointing him towards a door to his right. "You'll like it here."

Thinking of Nick he said, "I feel welcome already."

"This is my flat as well as his, remember," she said, opening the door onto carpeted lobby.

"I'll try."

"There's one bedroom," she nodded to the door on the right. "You're on the couch in the living room."

The flat was modern, comfortable and without doubt very expensive. The living room took up the whole of the front portion of the place with the galley kitchen off of it, bathroom and bedroom sharing the remainder of the layout.

Heavy, wall length curtains hid the windows and peeling one back, Danny saw a balcony, which overlooked the main road. It must have been from here that she had been watching for buses.

"Very nice," he said, removing his coat. Carol took it from him, through to the hall. Danny unlaced his Dr. Martins, took them off and stretched his feet, wiggling his toes.

"I'll see what's in the freezer, then we can eat," Carol said as she returned and disappeared into the kitchen. "Fix us a couple of drinks, will you?"

Danny parked his boots in a corner of the room and went across to a large, oak drinks cabinet. He poured them each a whisky, hers with soda from the chrome syphon and took them back with him to the couch. He sat down with a sigh and felt mild satisfaction joustling with his weariness for recognition.

Smiling to himself, he sipped from his tumbler. He was getting to like the taste of whisky, which could be worrying as well as expensive. He looked around the room. Nick may be all sorts or things but he certainly had an eye for style, expensive furniture and a carpet, which had to be Axminster.

No flat pack here.

Carol popped her head round the door and asked him if he could eat a curry.

"Are you cooking it?"

"It's in the freezer. Ready meals."

"In that case, yes please."

She made a face and disappeared back into the kitchen. He drank some more whisky, heard her messing with the oven and as the expensive single malt slipped smoothly down his throat, he leaned back and closed his eyes.

He had learned a lot this afternoon, from Mrs. Kershaw, from Aakesh. He was looking forward to relating it all to Carol.

"They will take half an hour, " she said, coming into the room. Opening his eyes, Danny watched her collect her drink, sample it and sit down in an armchair across from him.

"How long have you had this place?"

"A few years. It's a bolt hole for Nick, when he works over or...whatever."

"Was he planning 'whatever' this evening?"

"I've no idea and I'm not in the mood to speculate."

"Fair enough. Do you mind if I use the phone?"

She waved a hand, "Be my guest."

He stood up and went through to the hall, where the phone was fixed to the wall. He dialled the number of the house and waited through five rings before Chrissie answered.

"It's me."

She sighed, "Are you still in London?"

"Were you sleeping?"

"I dozed off on the couch."

He told her that he probably wouldn't be back until tomorrow evening. "There's a couple of things I want to do."

"How's it going?"

"Slowly. You know. I may be barking up the wrong tree, for all I know."

"Does it feel like that?"

"No it dosen't. If only things would start coming together."

"I'm sure they will. Stick with it."

"I intend to but there's a long way to go yet."

"Call me when you get back."

He said he would and hung up with a warm feeling inside. He liked the fact that she was glad he was sticking with it, as though she really wanted him to succeed. As though she might even be proud of him. He grinned and allowed himself a small air punch.

His eyes found his overcoat, hanging across the hall. Walking over to it, he delved in the left hand side pocket and felt his fingers meet a small square card. He took it out and read the numbers that Hilary had given him at Carol's last Sunday. It was worth a try, he thought. After all, she had approached him in the first place.

He went back to the phone and called her home number first. Half a dozen rings and he reached the answer phone. He hung up and dialled her office number, which rang and rang and he was about to give up when she answered.

"This is Danny, Carol's brother."

"Well, hello." Her voice sounded weary.

"Bad time?"

"End of a shitty day. What can I do for you?"

She sounded different to the woman he had met before, more business like. No hint of booze to her voice now.

"I was hoping you could do something for me."

"Go on."

"There was a child went missing, years ago in Putney. A girl named, Veronica Hayden. Nineteen fifty-five I think. I was hoping you could dig up something for me about the case."

She said. "Does this have to do with your trip to London?"

"It might do."

There was a long pause, he could almost hear her thinking.

"There was a body found in a Kavanagh Mansions in Putney the other day. Is that the same Kavangh Mansions as the one you were delivering to?"

"Yes, it is."

"Could this have any relevance to what you're asking me to do?"

"Yes it could." Danny wondered how much more he should tell her on the phone. "I'll fill you in when I know more."

She thought about that, finally saying, "Okay. But don't leave me hanging for too long."

"I'll call you tomorrow?"

"Do that."

They said goodbye and he returned to the lounge.

Carol wasn't there, so he went to stand in the kitchen doorway, where the aroma of their dinners cooking made his stomach rumble.

"How's Chrissie?" Carol was opening a bottle of wine and looking at him over her shoulder.

"Fine. I thought you didn't like me boozing."

"I hate drinking alone."

She nodded to two glasses on the side and took the bottle through to the lounge. Picking up the glasses, he followed her, standing the glasses on the extendable dining table, which she had already pulled out. He watched her pouring wine, a dark and hopefully very dry red. This on top of the whisky, was she trying to prove some point or other?

"I called Hilary.

"My Hilary?" She looked at him, surprised. "What on earth for?"

"She's agreed to find out what she can about a girl that disappeared from the Putney area thirty odd years ago."

"A girl?"

"A fourteen year old who went missing in the summer of 1955."

Carol stared at him.

"I'll tell you all about it later."

"And Hilary gave you her number?"

"Both, home and work. At your place, Sunday. Apparently she's writing a series of articles on cold case crimes, murders and such. I don't know the details but something you told her about being hired to deliver that package sparked her interest."

"Her antenna's never down far. What I don't understand is what you going to Kavanagh Mansions can have to do with anything."

"The girl lived there. It seems likely she knew the Rudd Street Tykes too." She gave him a long, hard look which he couldn't fathom. "You don't mind, do you?"

She shook her head. "Of course not, but she should have spoken to me."

Maybe she should, Danny thought but if Hilary found anything for him, he wasn't going to stand on principle about accepting it.

"I'll tell you about Cockle senior once we've eaten," he said.

The curry was supposed to be chicken Vindaloo but he found it was more a Madras in strength, otherwise it was fine. He was surprised at just how hungry he was. In fact, when they were done, he felt he could still eat more. He helped Carol take the dishes into the kitchen and watched her load them into the dishwasher.

"Coffee's on," she said as they returned to the lounge. She curled up in an armchair. "So, what's this about a missing girl."

"I'll come to that in a minute."

Out in the kitchen, the percolator started to bubble. He lowered himself onto the couch and took her through his meeting with Cockle senior. When he had finished, she looked underwhelmed.

"So you learned nothing."

"The man did confirm the boy in the picture was his son. Then I met Aakesh."

"Tell me."

"He was Cockle's long term partner."

He told her about their meeting and subsequent conversation in the pub. "I think the woman who phoned Cockle was Sarah."

"You think?"

"Okay, there's no actual proof but it does seen likely, don't you think. I mean, if that is Alan in the photo, then it's just as probable that the girl in it is Sarah Eadle."

"All right, it's possible. But I still think you're chasing smoke and sooner or later you'll realise it."

"The phone call from Sarah is interesting. You have to admit that."

"If it was her. As for the Indian chap and Cockle, it could well be no more than a lover's tiff."

And he's inventing the phone call?"

"No. But he might well be over emphasising it."

"Why would he do that?"

"Guilt. If they'd had a bust up and Cockle was so distraught, he killed himself, then perhaps Aakesh blames himself."

"You're wrong there. Take my word for it.

She regarded him for a moment. "You're hiding something."

"Not hiding."

"What then?"

"Waiting for the right moment."

"That kind of something, is it?"

In the kitchen, the percolator stopped bubbling. Carol unfolded herself from the chair and went through to the kitchen. Returning with two mugs of coffe, she placed one before him and sat down again.

"Do you intend contacting this young man again?"

"Maybe, maybe not."

He knew already that he probably wouldn't and felt bad about it.

"You'll have to have a lot more than you've got to convince me."

"I spoke with Mrs. Kershaw, the old woman in Flat 2. She's lived there or years."

"I know," Carol said. "She took over a ninety nine year lease with thirty left on it. She's coming to the end of it now."

"We had a long talk over Danish pastries."

"Intimate terms already?"

Danny ignored her. She wasn't taking him seriously at the moment but he was determined to change her mind.

"I showed her the photo."

"And?"

"She didn't know any of the kids but she recognised my father."

"Kavanagh Gardens was probably part of his beat."

"It was."

"There you are then."

"I'm just saying, her memory's good."

"Lucky her."

He took a sip from his mug. "I told her, I thought the boy on the left of the line was Cockle."

"She couldn't see a likeness?"

"She was non-commital. But she listened."

"I am listening, honestly."

"Two suicides, two photographs, two open bloody doors. Come on, Carol, you're supposed to be the detective, not me. You must have some feeling for the undertow here."

"I deal in the real world, everyday problems which people need sorting. It's not a pulp fiction world! No shadowy alleyways, or femme fatale babes crossing your path, just dull routine most of the time. Trying to help people whose lives have hit a bad patch."

Danny looked away. She knew her business but seemed devoid of any trace of imagination for something outside the norm.

"Mrs. Kershaw said Cockle was a frightened man. He didn't like working there, kept hearing things, noises. He couldn't rest."

"Don't start bringing in the supernatural, please!"

"I'm not!"

"Face it, Cockle was depressed, he'd broken with his lover and had been living with his father, who sounds pretty vile. Then there's this AIDS business, which seems to be spreading like wild fire. The tabloids are already referring to it as, 'The Gay Plague', building stigma against gay men. A lot of people believe the poor sods who have it have only got themselves to blame. That they have got no more than they deserve. That sort of thing would be depressing enough before the bust up with this, Aakesh."

"In which case, surely he would have confided in Aakesh, told him how he felt. They loved each other!" he took a breath. "Aakesh is convinced the phone call from the woman in Norfolk started the whole thing, opened up the past in some way."

"The past?"

"His past! He was frightened of something alright but not public opinion. I think it was of something from his childhood coming out of the woodwork, a secret, something The Tykes had seen or done, which they hushed up. The same with Sarah. They were haunted by it. The others in the photo probably are too."

"Haunted!"

"I don't mean by ghosts!"

"Well that's something."

She picked up her mug and sat back in her chair, waiting pointedly for him to produce his rabbit from the hat. Danny turned the photo on the table so that she was looking at it right way up.

"Mrs. Kershaw told me about the girl upstairs who disappeared in 1955, around the time this photo was taken. Her name was Veronica Hayden and she was fourteen years of age."

"This is the child you asked Hilary to find out about?"

"Yes." Danny placed his finger above the two blurred figures in the photograph. "Say this Veronica is the same one."

"You showed this to Mrs. Kershaw. She would know, wouldn't she?"

"Come on! Would you?" He tapped the top of his finger against the blurred face of the girl.

"Okay, fair point."

"Now imagine this. You have a bunch of kids getting up to all sorts in the school holidays. I bet they were a rough and tumble lot, playing where they shouldn't, daring this, doing that. Then say, something happened, something bad, worse than they could ever have imagined."

"To her, Veronica? Are you suggesting they may have harmed her in some way?"

"Yes. An accident, maybe in a place where they shouldn't have been. Along the river or in one of the bomb sites that were plentiful back then?"

She looked at him. "Alright, let's say you're right. Do you honestly believe five frightened kids could keep quite with the police all over the place? They'd have been questioned, separately, just a parent with them but without the gang to back them up." She stood her mug down and leaned towards him. "I'll tell you what happened. She was abducted by some twisted, dirty bastard, murdered and buried somewhere."

"That's the assumption everybody made at the time, no doubt. It's the obvious one and it's held sway ever since. But I think it's an easy option."

"No. What you mean is, it doesn't fit in with your theory, so you don't want to consider it. You honestly think those children killed her?"

"I'm not saying they murdered her! I'm just saying it's possible something happened and that they have been covering up ever since. Now, for some reason it's all coming back into focus for them. Someone is sending them copies of this photograph, say. They feel their story is about to unravel and panic is setting in."

"Then why not go to the police?"

"Would you in their shoes? I'm pretty sure I wouldn't."

"I might."

"You wouldn't."

"I would if two of my friends who were involved in this imaginary incident of yours had died. I certainly would't kill myself!"

" But you're not one of them. Anyway, maybe it wasn't suicide."

She stared at him, then sat up in the chair and stared at him even harder.

"I asked you if you thought there was any doubt."

"I'm not an expert."

She thought for a while and shook her head. "It's nonsense anyway! Something out of an Agatha Christie. The forensic people would pick up on anything out of the ordinary and it can't be that easy to make a murder seem like suicide. That's what you're suggesting, isn't it?"

"I don't know. That's what I want to find out."

In spite of her argument, he could tell he had given her something to think about.

"Alright," she said after a moment. "I'm willing to conceed there are some features that could warrent further examination. We need to be sure this is the same Veronica."

"I'll do that."

"How?"

"For Christ's sake! I don't have all the answers. That's why I need to keep digging."

"I don't know. Maybe the police...?"

"The police would laugh me out of the station, you know that."

She was looking at him as though the enormity of what he was suggesting had just dawned on her. "You really think these two could have been murdered?"

"Maybe. Those photos didn't send themselves and I just can't convince myself that seeing a copy of it would be enough to make them kill themseves." He paused, facing the same brick wall he had arrived at before. "Veronica must have had family, people who loved her.

Her mother for instance, aunts and uncles, cousins, even a father somewhere."

"Sounds like you're grasping at straws again."

"I admit it's a bit far fetched but it's possible. I think Singleton is wirried about much the same thing."

"You think he's afraid too?"

"I think he suspects something's going on. Only he would know why he feels that way."

She drank some coffee, turning it over in her mind all the time. "What do you know about the missing girl's parents?"

"Not much. According to Mrs. Kershaw, the woman was a widow."

"But?"

"But they might have been seperated. Mrs Kershaw didn't know the family that well."

"They'd be getting on now."

"Not that old, if they were in their thirties then."

Carol let out a sharp breath and said irritably, "This is all pretty flimsy."

"I know. But someone did hire you using Sarah Eadel's name. The woman took pains to keep herself hidden, arriving at the end of the working day. Almost as though she'd been watching, waiting until the staff had gone."

Carol looked away. He could see her inner conflict playing out on her face. Part of her thought he had a point but the other part, the part she wanted to be right, kept highlighting the thinness of his argument.

"I can't help thinking that there's something more here," he said.

"Such as?"

He shook his head and they relapsed into silence.

It had to do with the past, he was sure of that, the Rudd Street Tykes and with him. "Perhaps the Old Man might know something."

Dad had been a regular visitor to Galvin Street before and after Jack Reed died. He had often spoken about them. Occasionally, he had brought Carol along, mostly after his mother died and the friends across the road, who had two daughters of Carol's age, were unable to look after her.

"Are you sure you can't remember anything from when you first visited Galvin Street?"

He had asked her about those visits before, hoping she might shed some light on the years he couldn't remember. Her visits had been seldom though, she had preferred spending time with her friends to playing big sister to a kid she hardly knew.

"You know I can't. I didn't want to go in the first place, so I was hardly taking notice of anything."

"I thought you might recall seeing the Tykes. You know, just vaguely, at the periphery of your mind."

"I don't." She sounded weary. "I remember your father in his uniform, and Mum of course, because she was so nice to me. You were just an annoying kid iI did my best to ignore. I was three years older than you and a boy."

He sighed heavily. "Perhaps I am grasping at straws. I'm just so sure there's something there, if only I could see it."

"We should call it a night."

She was right. It could do no good sitting there going round and round in circles. He was continuing with this no matter what she said, so there really was no point of discussing it further.

"Have you thought that if you're right, this could be dangerous?"

He had but hearing it from her brought the truth of it home to him with deadening force. If there was someone else behind these deaths, they wouldn't take kindly to him poking his nose in. But he couldn't think about it any more now, he was so tired his mind was turning sommersaults.

"We'd better get your bed made up," Carol said, standing up.

Yawning widely, he didn't argue.

Chapter Fourteen

Carol got up the next morning and found Danny sitting in an armchair, wrapped in Nick's bathrobe. He had folded up his bed clothes, which now sat in a pile on the couch, and had the BT Phone book on his lap, leafing through it.

"Good reading?"

He smiled, "There's coffee in the kitchen."

"That bath robe suits you."

"It's roomy, I'll say that for it. You could get two of me in here."

Carol went through to the kitchen and returned with a mug of coffee. "Who are you looking for?"

He shut the book and drained his own mug. "I was looking for Ray Murkin and I've found him."

"Who?"

"Ray. The Ray in the photo."

"Maybe!" she corrected. "You can't just look for a Murkin with the initial, R and decide that he's the person you want."

"I admit I'm taking a gamble but Murkin's an unusual name. He's the only one in the book and Mrs. Kershaw said a plumber by that name has the contract for Kavanagh Mansions."

"Another link to Joe Singleton."

"Exactly! He must have engaged him. Doing a favour for an old friend?"

"So you'll knock on his door and ask him?"

"Something like that."

"How long is this going to take? I want to be gone before midday."

Danny got up and walked to the door. "You go, I'll catch a later train."

She was not happy but she accepted what he said.

"Is it okay if I take a shower?"

"You know where it is."

He stood for a long time in hot flow, feeling the knots in his body ease under the relentless pounding needles of hot water. When he had finished, he towelled himself down and went to the bedroom, where he selected a T-Shirt and underpants from Nick's chest-of-drawers. He had some of his own in his holdall but had an idea that he would be staying in London for more than one more night and wanted to save them. Not that he would say as much to Carol, not yet.

The T-Shirt was baggy and most of the under pants he tried had been stretched at the waist and were loose on him. He found an unopened pack of three from M & S and breaking the seal, took a pair out. These fitted comfortably. He put on his shirt and jeans, finishing off with a pair of expensive woollen socks from Nick's collection.

Walking through to the kitchen in search of something to eat, he found that Carol had prepared breakfast, cereal and warm milk, fresh coffee in the pot. She had been talking on the phone and now returned to the kitchen. "That was the office. The police want me to call them when I get back."

"Mills?"

"Probably."

"You expected that." But she still looked worried. "It'll be a formality, a few more points to clarify."

"That's what I'm worried about."

"You can only tell him what you know. A carefully trimmed version."

"Yes and we know who to thank for that, don't we?!"

Danny finished eating, washed their dishes, then walked through to the lounge to put on his Dr. Martins.

"What's the weather like?"

Carol opened the curtains to reveal grey light heavy with the threat of snow. "I've called a cab for ten thirty."

"I'm nearly done." He glanced at his watch, saw it was just after half past nine and put a spurt on, asking for a plastic bag to put his dirty underwear in. She took it for him and shoved it in the washing basket, which made him smile. Nick would get a surprise when he next put his smalls through the machine.

"I borrowed some undies."

"Mine or his?"

"Your's would have been a better fit."

By the time the taxi arrived, they were standing out front of the block, wrapped up in their winter coats and hats. She touched his arm and looked him straight in the eye.

"I like the enthusiasm you're showing for this business but don't get carried away. If you're right, things might turn dangerous."

"I'll be fine."

"I mean it, Danny. If it looks like it's going bad, promise me you'll walk away."

"You have my word."

With a last long look at him, she climb into the cab. He told the driver she wanted Liverpool Street Station and the cab moved off. Danny waved once, watching as it did a right at the traffic lights. When it had disappeared in the morning traffic, he crossed the road to the bus stop to wait for a bus back to Putney.

The snow had stopped and all that remained of yesterday's fall lined the gutters and edges of the street.

The road was clear and dry and the traffic was running smoothly. Staring in the direction the bus would come, he thought ahead to what he had planned.

He had matched the address in the phone book to the street location using his A-Z and would go straight there, see if the man was in. If he was, he would play it by ear, learn what he could without divulging too much himself. Not that he had much to divulge in the first place. If this Murkin was the person he was looking for, he would try to get him talking about what had happened to Cockle and Sarah. Try to provoke a reaction.

When the bus came, he got aboard, paid his fare and sat on the seat next to the exit. Looking out as the streets passed by, he replayed Carol's parting message, the way she had said it and how she had looked when saying it. He would never have admitted it to her, but there was already a sense of unease lurking inside him that he could not shake. Not so much about what had happened so far, more about what might be to come.

He no longer harboured any doubt that this whole business was somehow pre-ordained. That somehow, he was being led along a route already mapped out for him. A route laid down long ago and that he could not veer from even should he try to.

The bus dropped him on the Putney side of the bridge and he paused momentarily on the pavement to take stock. According to the A-Z, Stacy Road was two off the High Street on what would be his right. On the map, it was a long and narrow throughfare which widened half way down and changed its name to Woodside. After that it ran all the way through to Putney Common.

Turning up his collar, he walked off into the gloomy morning, passing shops already showing light in their windows, lending a late afternoon feel to the morning.

People drifted here and there like ghosts, each with their mind fixed on where they were going, scrunched down into their coats, trying to ignore the bitter cold of another winter's day.

By the time he reached the entrance to Stacy Road, tiny intermitent flecks of snow were falling, drifting on the air. They brushed his cheeks like ghost kisses and settled like dandruff on the shoulders of his coat, only to quickly melt away.

On the corner, he stopped and stared about him, feeling his mind jump ahead of him, as though knowing the street and yet not recognising it in his conscious mind. A trong sense of deja vu insisted itself upon him and he stood there looking round, for what?

Recognition seemed barely a fraction away, if only he could reach it. It was more than twenty-five years since he had lived in Putney, a quarter of a century and yet there was this undeniable feeling that everything was so familiar, while at the same time alien to him.

He stepped back into the lee of the big. granite corner building housing a bank, feeling a tightness starting up in his head. A second later, a burst of pain blossomed in his left temple, quickly settling into a throbbing ache above his left eye.

Children laughing!

He squeezed his eyes shut and when he opened them again, he saw the sky was lower, greyer and snow flakes were falling steadily. No longer the tiny drifting fleck of before but fully formed flakes, which danced this way and that on the strengthening breeze.

Flakes scampering across his shoulders, patting his face and all at once the day suddenly brightened into a wintery, Christmas card scene. He saw a parade of small, shabby shops outside of which a bunch of children played, running from pavement to road and back again in their excitement.

Leaning against the building, feeling the solid granite dig uncomfortably into his shoulder blades, he watched the children, all aged around the ten or eleven mark, as they scampered around throwing snow balls at each other, squealing delight and...

I remember this.

But did he, or was he just telling himself that he did because he believed he should?

He stared at the snow covering the street, three or four centimeters and wondered how he had missed such a heavy fall. There had been hardly any a moment ago.

But this isn't now!

No it wasn't and as the realization dawned on him, the pain drained away down the side of his face. This was a scene that had been, a picture from way back when.

A memory!?

Stepping away form the bank wall, he moved along the pavement, closer to children. There were five of them, four boys and a girl, wide eyed and ruddy cheeked, puffs of breath blossoming from their mouths as they played around a large, wooden kiosk standing on the pavement outside a junk shop across the way.

As with all the shops in the parade it had a seedy, neglected look, in need of a facelift. Brown paintwork, thick with road dust, plate glass windows thick with grimw. Fixed to the Junk shop's wooden cill was a thick metal hasp, a length of chain stretching to the kiosk and fastened to a metal eye, screwed into the back, by meaty padlock.

The kiosk itself was a solid looking affair, wooden and about the size of a telephone box. There was a glass panel halfway up the front side, beneath which was a brass slot waiting for the required coin to be dropped into it. The kiosk, front, sides and rear were painted the same dull brown as the shop and in sign written letters of chipped gold paint, above the glass panel, was the legend

JACK TAR - A PENNY WILL MAKE HIM JOLLY!

Standing across the road, Danny could see through the glass panel, a painted beach scene, brilliant blue sea, sand of an impossibly deep yellow and painted seagulls in motionless flight across a cloudless sky.

Sitting upon an upended wine barrel, was a dummy, similar to the kind used by ventriloquists. The same glowing cheeks, the same bulging eyes. Huge tombstone teeth stretching across the mouth in a wide and vaguely disturbing grin.

He had seen something similar to this, on holiday with Mum and Dad, Yarmouth possibly, or further afield, Skegness. Then it had been a laughing policeman in the box, wearing full uniform of a bygone age and not the hooped jersey and navy trousers that Jack Tar was wearing.

He vaguely remembered watching the policeman go through his routine and wondering whether Jack Reed had ever laughed so raucously when he was on duty.

Now the children, taking a break from their snowballs, had gathered in front of the kiosk and stood gazing wistfully at the frozen figure within. From the way they were reacting, it was obvious that no one had the required amount to set Jolly Jack performing.

Danny looked closer at them, familiar figures, faces almost hidden by winter hats and scarves, small oval faces peering through clouds of exhaled breath, the same faces he'd seen in the photograph, only in colour now instead of grainy black and white.

The Tykes!

In that instant, a movement to one side drew his attention to a passage between the junk shop and the next door establishment. A figure, another girl, emerging from the half light of that narrow place, a girl in a sandy coloured duffle coat, a brightly patterned bobble hat on her head, two blonde plaits hanging down either side of her pretty face.

Veronica?

She directed a sly, knowing look his way then she was running off to join the others. Meeting her eyes, be it only for a split second, had sent a frisson through him, a tiny electric shock that left his toes and fingertips tingling.

Danny started, realized he was holding his breath and let it out in a long stream. He saw her join the others, showing them what she held in one gloved hand - an old penny. She had saved the day! and they gathered around her as she she inserted the coin into the slot at the front of the kiosk.

The next moment, Jack exploded into life, rocking to and fro, sending peals of crackling laughter into the space around him. It was all waist movement, wooden legs pinned to the wooden beach, torso rocking back and forth, teeth flashing, eyes glowering at the children.

Danny knew a feeling of unease, as was wondering where she had obtained the coin when, right on cue another movement at the corner of his eye drew his gaze back to the alley.

A small, skinny, bespectacled boy emerge into daylight with tears and snot running down his face, blood from a nasty cut on his cheek. His clothes were dishevelled, his coat front yanked askew at the throat, where a hand had gathered it into a bunch.

Jack Tar sent out raucous cry of delight. Danny took an involuntary step towards the the boy, who having turned to look at the group, slunk away towards the High Street.

She did this!

Danny watched the retreating figure for a moment, then turned his attention back to the children and to one especially, the girl in the bobble hat. She stood at the back of the joyful group and to his surprise, she turned her head suddenly and for a moment, her dark, solemn eyes bored into his.

Danny shuffled backward a couple of steps, as though prompted by the intensity of her gaze. He opened his mouth but no words came out, just a puff of air, squeezed through narrowed tubes. The next thing he knew, the children were leaving, walking off in a huddle away along the road.

Danny watched them go for a moment, then turned his head to look at the kiosk where the dummy sat motionless. No more laughter, just a fixed grimace and those scary bulbous eyes, glaring directly at him.

Not such a Jolly Jack Tar after all!

And then it was over. Whatever it had been just stopped. He staggered slightly, as though released from an invisible grip and looked about him at a street almost devoid of snow. The same heavy sky that had been with him since he'd left the bus, the same chilly wind blowing scattered flakes at him.

Across the way, the shops were brightly painted and the junk shop window was now filled with carefully arranged flowers, bright in the dull light. No kiosk, no dummy and no sign of the children.

A snow flake settled on his nose and melted. He felt as though he had woken from some kind of dream, a cold empty feeling, a sense of aching loss in his chest. He needed to get moving, people were starting to eye him curiously, concern or fear? He turned away and walked off in the direction of where Murkin's home should be.

Had it been a daydream? A resurging memory perhaps?

A full blown hallucination?!

That was scary.

It took him ten minutes to find Murkin's address, at the very end of Stacy Road, just before it was dissected by another narrow thoroughfare, changing to Woodside on the other side. Another short parade of shops, like those he had left behind, half a dozen perhaps, only these, at the wrong end of the road were mostly closed and forgotten, a newsagents, a laundrette and that was that.

Murkin's place of business turned out to be at the centre of the parade, a run down, shabby looking place, with sun bleached paint work and the same dirty plate glass window as its closest neighbours.

Above the shop window it said, R. Murkin. Quality Plumber. The shop door, half glazed and slanting back from the street, shared a small tiled doorstep with another door, presumably to the living space above.

Danny stood on the pavement, gazing at the shop for a moment, still feeling a little spacey. What he'd seen back there had been so clear, so solid. He had actually been there but did that mean that the dark block in his head was really melting? Had he stood there as a boy and seen the same scenario play out?

The not so casual observer?

His mind steadied and he walked up to the front door of the shop and tried the handle but it was locked. Peering through the dirty glass upper panel, he made out a dingy interior, with a long, wooden counter behind which stood rack after rack of piping and other plumbing merchandise. The shop had obviously been closed to the public for some while.

Turning to the other door, he used a heavy door knocker to bang and heard the hollow echo of his bangs rolling along the front passage. A couple of stray snow flakes blew into the porch on a gust of wind, circling his head lazily before falling onto the step. He was lifting the knocker to bang again when the door was opened by a thin, drab looking woman, with a narrow face and large wet eyes.

"Yes?" she asked, nasally.

She wore no make up and her greying hair was yanked back from her face into a scruffy ponytail. It was hard to judge her age, but he would guess she was in her mid to late forties, maybe older.

"I'm sorry to trouble you," he said. "I'm looking for, Mr. Murkin."

"Is it work?" she asked and sniffed wetly. "He won't see you if it's work."

"It's not work." Danny told her. "It's - personal."

"Personal?" she said, as though the idea was completely alien to her. "Well, you'd better come in then."

The hallway smelt of old dinners and disinfectant. A floor of the same red and navy tiles as the porch led along a narrow passage, round beside the staircase and finished at the door of a room at the far end.

"He's upstairs," she said. Her washed out eyes regarded him without interest. "Go up, you'll find him."

She walked away along the passage to the back room where, through the open door, Danny could hear a radio playing. He watched her go into the room and close the door behind her.

Beside him the staircase went to the even darker upper floor and he moved to stand at the foot of it. He could still hear the radio but quieter now and he glanced to his right at another door, presumably leading to the shop. He shivered slightly in the cold passageway and started up the stairs.

It was a gloomy ascent. The single light bulb suspended from the upper ceiling gave out a meagre glow. A low wattage one, he guessed, 60 watt or less and most of its light was swallowed up by aging anaglypta wallpaper, painted in some inderminable colour which resembled mud.

At the top, he found himself facing a narrow landing running away to his right, past more closed doors, then a second flight of stairs going up to the attic rooms. He paused, listening and heard, just above the muted sound of the radio downstairs, a whining, clicking noise, which sounded like it was coming from the room in front of him. It had to be Murkin in there but what the hell was he doing?

Danny didn't knock, just dumped his holdall on the landing, opened the door and went in. If Murkin was surprised, he didn't show it. He was sitting in the centre of the room on a hard backed chair, wearing a woolly, marmalade coloured tank top over a grey flannel shirt. His trousers were dark, either washed out black or dirty grey, secured at the waist by a thin belt with the sort of entwined snakes buckle that had been popular back in the nineteen fifties. On his head perched what seemed to be a British Railways guard's peaked cap.

"Mr. Murkin?"

Surrounding him and seeming to take up most of the room, was a huge model railway layout, six tracks at least and about three times that many spurs, on which idle locomotives waited their turn to shine. Trains ran both ways around the tracks, through model towns and rural settings, each dotted with little plastic people.

What furniture was left in the room had been pushed back to the edges to make room for the layout, leaving little space for movement. around it.

Murkin, sitting directly beneath a naked light, was a scrawny looking character, with stringy wisps of ginger hair poking out from under the cap. He had washed out, blue eyes that bulged from their sockets and a struggling gingerish moustache decorating his narrow upper lip and a few spidery hairs of the same colour protruding from his bony chin.

"I don't want talk about pipes," he said.

The washed-out eyes followed a sleek, blue steam engine racing down a long, straight section of track with a line of carriages behind it.

"I don't blame you, seeing this lot," Danny said.

A small shiver of childish pleasure ran through him looking at the set up. He had always wanted a large train set like this when he was a boy but Dad's income would not stretch anywhere near it.

"A mate of mine had quite a set when I was a kid. Nothing like this though."

Murkin's eyes never left the engine, as it leaned into a bend, wheels clickitty-clacking over the joints between sections of track. It swept past Danny and round the next bend, then it was off on another long, straight section, heading for the only window in the room.

"Triang, I think it was." Danny said vaguely.

Murkin watched the engine and its coaches disappear into a tunnel that occupied the track on the bend in front of the window, then turned on his chair in time to see it emerge at the other end. He looked up, his pale, faraway gaze ignoring Danny's smile, as he reached out to the bank of control boxes before him.

"Triang stuff's for kids," he said in a toneless voice. "This is all Hornby 00."

Working one of the many knobs, he brought another train, a green loco pulling four coaches in maroon and cream livery, to a halt at a station. Danny watched that blue job go tearing around its circuit, half expecting Murkin to start making choo-choo noises. When he looked up, he found the man was watching him.

"This one's a local train," Murkin said. "It's the other one, that's special. D'you know the Mallard?"

"Not personally," Danny said but Murkin didn't smile. "Broke some record or other, didn't it?"

"Steam rail speed record of 125 mph, 1926," Murkin said and started the local train moving again.

A movement to Danny's right drew his attention to a stubby black engine, linked up to a dozen or so goods wagons, moving slowly on yet another line, in the opposite direction to the Mallard.

"You didn't come here to talk about trains though."

"No." Danny looked at him with new regard, waiting for him to continue but he didn't.

Murkin worked some signals to allow the goods train to pass into a marshalling yard and brought it to a stop in a glass roofed workshop. Mallard sped by on the very outside track, racing onward into its journey to wherever Murkin had in mind.

"I wanted to talk to you about a photograph I have."

Murkin looked back to his trains, saying nothing. Danny opened his bag and took the photograph out. He reached over the railway tracks and held it up for Murkin to see.

"This one. It was taken back in the fifties, in Galvin Street. The kids were known as the Rudd Street Tykes and I think you're there with the rest of the gang."

Murkin's eyes flicked sideways and up but before Danny could see what he was looking at, they were back on the trains again.

"Two of them are dead, Alan and Sarah," he said. "That leaves three, you, Joe Singleton and Brian - what's his surname?"

"Ellis," Murkin said.

"And of course, the girl on the end."

Murkin watched the green loco go past him, clickety-clack, clickety-clack.

"I believe her name was, Veronica?"

Murkin said nothing.

"Did you know they had died? Had Joe told you?"

"He phoned," Murkin said eventually.

"And why not? You were mates, all of you."

Murkin stopped the green loco at a second station, while the Mallard went tearing by on the outside circuit. He risked a glance at the photo.

"Where did you get that?"

"Have you got a copy?"

Once again Murkin's eyes went to the left and up, and this time Danny saw that he was looking at a shelf in the chimney alcove on this side of the breast. The shelf was jam packed with books of all sizes and at the end, on the left, pinned between the wall and a tall book called, 'Steam Locos', was a thin buff coloured folder.

"You see," Danny continued. "I think you three are in danger."

This time, Murkin looked directly at him and Danny saw a shadow cross his eyes. "It's not her. It can't be."

"Not who?"

But he looked back at the trains, watching the Mallard going up through the tunnel again, then out and into the long straight towards the next corner. There was a thin coating of sweat on his forehead and Danny glanced down at the ancient electric fire sitting in the hearth of the boarded up fireplace, both bars glowing orange.

"What's in the folder?" Danny nodded at the shelf.

"Stuff." It was hot in there but nowhere near as hot as it would need to be to make the man sweat like that. "About Putney."

To the left of the fire and far too close, was a small, two shelved structure holding lots of cleaning materials, oil, spirit and cloth, all flammable. "What sort of stuff?"

"Events," Murkin said, dragging a hand across his forehead. "Historical facts, about this borough."

"Like?"

"Like the fact that the Levellers used to meet in our Parish Church and that that poet, Swinburn lived in one of those posh houses on the Upper Richmond Road."

Danny said. "Can I have a look?"

"Thomas Cromwell lived in Putney. His dad was a publican. And Atlee, you know who Atlee was?"

Danny said he did but Murkin, who was starting to gabble, told him anyway. "Labour Prime Minister, 1945 to 1950. His government brought in the National Health service. This ain't just the starting place of the bleeding Boat Race, you know!"

"Okay."

"Christie, the murderer, was arrested down on the Embankment."

"So I heard." Danny watched the Mallard rattle past in front of him. "What about Veronica? Anything about her in you notes?"

Talking about his research had taken Murkin's attention away from the photo. Now Danny held it up again to remind him and saw the shadow jump across his eyes again.

"I was given the job of delivering one of these to Alan Cockle."

Murkin looked at him, pale eyes bulging.

"By the time I got to his flat, he was dead. I've spoken to the man who found him."

Murkin said, "It was that old woman found him. Her that lives there."

"No. It was Alan's ex. He saw him, saw his face. Alan was terrified when he died."

Murkin turned back to his trains, ran his tongue across his lips.

"The woman who hired my services called herself Sarah Eadel."

"She wouldn't!"

"She didn't. Someone was using her name."

Murkin flicked him a quick glance. "Who?"

"Dunno. By the time me and my boss went out to Sarah's place to talk to her, she was also dead, her face blown off with a shotgun."

"I don't wanna hear no more." Murkin said, jumping up. He sounded close to panic and was licking his lips over and over.

"Alright! Sit down and listen. I'm here to help you."

"If she's back, how can you help?"

"I think she is back," Danny said. He didn't know who Murkin was refering to but there was no need letting him know that. "I think she killed them, or made them kill themselves, if that's possible. I think she aims to kill you and Joe and Brian."

"It wasn't me. I didn't do it!"

"Okay! Okay!" he had to keep the man from freaking out altogether. He said, quietly, "It has something to do with Veronica, doesn't it?"

Murkin's eyes fixed on him. "She knows it wasn't me!"

"Who knows? Come on, Ray. I can't help you unless you talk to me."

"You can't help! No one can!" His lips twitched slightly, as though he was trying to think what to say next.

"I know where Joe is," Danny said. "I need to find Brian. He has to be warned."

"Don't know where he is. He moved away, long time ago."

When Murkin next looked at him, Danny could see that something had happened to the man and that he had lost the advantage. Murkin was suddenly, inexpicably calmer and was gaining confidence by the second.

"What happened to Veronica?"

"I don't want to talk to you anymore."

"Did one of you kill her?"

"Get out!"

Danny stared at him, at his wide eyes and his sweat coated face but more now, a determination that hadn't been there a moment ago. Where it had come from, he couldn't imagine but who could say how this man's mind worked?

"I think I'd better look at that folder," he said.

"Nothing there for you."

Danny smiled, as though recognising defeat. A train rattled past between them. Murkin followed it with his eyes and Danny made his move. Quickly as the cramped space would allow, he squeezed between the edge of the layout and a chest-of-drawers.

"Hey!" Murkin shouted.

Danny caught the track bed a hard whack with his hip, jarring the layout enough to cause the Mallard to jumps the rails. As the toy train ploughed into a picnicking family group and turned onto its side, Murkin let out a pained shout.

Fast as Danny moved, the plumber was faster. Moving with surprising alacrity, he ducked under the track bed and launched himself at Danny, who had just reached the bookshelf.

He grabbed a wrist at the same moment Danny's fingers closed around the folder and no matter how much Danny tried to dislodge him, Murkin clung on fast.

"Let go!" Murkin hissed, breathing sour breath into Danny's face.

Turning his head, Danny managed to force them away from the wall, closer to the layout and his hand gripping the folder held on, drawing it free from of the books. He felt Murkin, his grip strengthened by all that pipe work he had dealt with over the years, draw him closer. Once again. the man's sickly sweet breath filled his nostrils.

"I only want to look," he said, breathing through his mouth.

Murkin wasn't listening. He held on, their embrace looking almost intimate. At last Danny managed to pull back, retaining the folder, in a tenuous, one handed grip.

"Just stop!"

But the man wouldn't stop, so Danny used an elbow, jamming it against Murkin's jaw, as they renewed their struggle in the restricted space, feeling his fingers gradually losing their grip on the smooth surface of the folder. He brought up his other hand to shove Murkin in the chest, hard enough to send him staggering backwards until his buttocks hit the edge of the chimney breast.

"STOP!" Danny shouted but Murkin wasn't listening. He had lost interest in the folder and had started to shake violently.

"Hey!" Danny, suddenly frightened, tried to reach him.

All at once, Murkin's eyes rolled up in their sockets and he slowly descended into the narrow valley in which they stood. His head clipped the edge of the layout bed with a hard clunk and a loose foot caught the small shelf next to the fire that held his various solutions.

"Christ!"

The next moment, Murkin was just a twitching, jerking form on the floor. For one awful second, Danny thought he might have badly injured him. He bent over the moving body as it jerked about like a crazed marionette, white specks of foam speckling the lips, eyes rolling wildly.

"I'll get help," he said.

Beside him, the other passenger locomotive moved smoothly by on its inner track, past the wreck of the Mallard and the plastic people crushed beneath it.

Stepping over Murkin, he got out of the confined space and hurried from the room, clutching the folder in his hand.

"Hello?" he called, grabbing his holdall and clattering down the stairs.

Eventually the door down the end of the passage opened and Mrs. Murkin came out with a pained expression on her narrow face.

"It's Mr. Murkin," Danny said. "He's having some sort of - attack."

"Again?" She sighed as she made her way past him. "Trust him! Right in the middle of my programme."

As he watched her climbing the stairs, he heard the sound of laughter coming from the radio in the back room.

Turning away, he quickly left the building and outside, started walking towards the point where the road became Woodside. He was trembling. It was the first time for a long while that he had been involved in anything resembling a scuffle, apart from that drunken tussle with Nick at Christmas.

Suddenly he was overcome with shame at what he had done. It was obvious that Murkin had underlying problems and it seemed his actions had triggered some sort of fit. Yes, Murkin had started it but really, could the folder be that important? He glanced down at it, held against his chest.

Not stolen, borrowed.

He just wanted to look through it, then he would take it back, apologise to Murkin for what had happened.

He paused on the corner, looking across the road into Woodside. It was a much wider thoroughfare and clearly a more affluent area than that which surrounded Stacy Road. The mixture of property types, smart detached places and semis, some grand, three floored Victorian terraced houses of the type he had always fancied owning. The type of place that would always be beyond his reach, no matter how much he was earning.

It was not by chance he had turned this way. He had found the phone number and address of a small hotel near Putney Common in the same phone book in which he'd located Murkin's address. He had noted it just in case and now intended to take a room for the night, a place to study whatever was in the folder. Tomorrow, he would go and see Singleton again and this time, he wouldn't leave until the man was more forthcoming.

Chapter Fifteen

It was a cul-de-sac, with houses on one side of the road and the common on the other. Standing like a beacon of light and hope in the middle of a sea of snow touched grass, was a church.

The common away to his right was divided by two spurs of the Lower Richmond Road, forming a Y shaped island. One branch of the road, according to a large metal sign, led in the direction of Barnes and Hammersmith Bridge while the other went to Roehampton, Richmond and the A3 Guildford By Pass.

Beyond the island of grass, was a Victorian gothic styled cemetary with chapel and a surrounding wall topped by spiked raings. To the sides and rear of it the common continued to the red brick building which had once, as Danny had seen when passing it, housed Putney Hospital.

With the distinct impression that he knew this place playing in his mind, he turned away to look at the hotel behind him. The things that were happening to him were happening too fast. He needed time to process what seemed to be going on and would not allow himself to get too excited about the possibility that his memory block was clearing.

The hotel, which was called, 'The Heath Hotel'. Inaccurately because Putney Heath was at a completely different location but he supposed it did sound better than, 'The Common Hotel'.

It comprised of two large semis having been knocked into one, mock Georgian building, red brick with double glazed lattice styled windows. There was a open cemented frontage, so guests could park their cars safely, although there was ony one car there at the moment, a large, bright red Volvo. He walked past it and opened the front door, then stepped into to a wide reception area, where a desk waited across a sea of thick, highly patterned carpet extending up a flight of stairs to the upper floor.

The space was deathly quiet. He walked across to the desk, conscious of the small clicks and creaks the floorboard made beneath their colourful covering and dumped his holdall down in front of the desk. He looked at the bell fixed to the top corner of the desk but didn't ring it, lifting his eyes to the wall behind the desk, where an expanse of wall space was given over to a selection of show posters for West End theatres, nightclubs and things to see in London.

Beside these was a framed display, large enough to hold an A2 sized poster, containing several sheets taken from of old newspapers. The spread concerned the death of rock singer, Marc Bolan in a car crash on Barnes Common back in 1977. The newsprint had yellowed slightly but was easily reable, the text being fashioned around a black and white image of a smashed up Mini waiting to be towed away.

He remembered it happening. Bolan, a non driver, had been on his way home from an evening out, driven by his girlfriend, when somehow the car had ploughed into a huge tree at the side of a humpback bridge, killing the singer instantly.

"That happened just along the road from here," a woman's voice said.

He started slightly and turning, found himself facing the smiling face of an aging blonde, whose hair was a little too blonde, whose dress was a little too tight and whose smile, wide and rather startling, was a little too white. She regarded him from sharp, blue eyes and must have liked what she saw, for her smile grew even wider.

"I remember it happening," he said. "I didn't realise it happened around this area."

"Humpback bridge, very dangerous." She moved behind the desk, hips swinging more easily than they had a right to in that dress. "He stayed here a couple of times. If he'd done so that night, he'd still be with us."

"Well, the music goes on, I guess."

He put her age to be around the mid-fifty mark and quickly averted his eyes from the deep cleavage she had on display.

"We often get people coming here, looking for the site. Fans, I suppose you'd call them, although it seems a bit ghoulish to me. Mostly young girls who must have been children when he was around. They bring all sorts with them, flowers, badges, someone once brought a large white swan to pin to the tree."

"I'm more a Beatles man myself," Danny said. "I was wondering whether you might have a room vacant?"

"We do. Five of them actually. It's very quiet this time of year."

"I don't have any luggage except this," he said, glancing down at the holdall.

"That's fine," her teeth flashed. "Just pay in advance."

He booked a room with breakfast and followed her to an upstairs front double, ensuite, wardrobe and chest of drawers. Along the way, she told him that she was still an Elvis girl.

Once they reached the room, she showed him the facilities, pointed out the small, colour TV fixed to the wall and the courtesy basket containing tea bags, instant coffee tubes and individual tubs of UHT milk. "The kettle's new."

"Very nice," Danny said, although he would hace seen all this without her guidence.

"Right!" she smiled. Come down when you're ready and we'll get everything done."

He was ready then and followed her back down to reception. He used his debit card, which he knew would take his balance pretty near rock bottom and asked her where there was a decent place to eat nearby.

"Well, there's The Feathers on the corner," she said. "They do some nice pub grub, or there's the Tea Pot cafe just a short walk along the main road. They do a tasty meal, if you don't mind plastic table cloths."

"I use them all the time," he said and she smiled uncertainly.

Having parked his holdall up in his room, Danny tucked Murkin's folder under his arm and left the hotel. He took himself along to the cafe, because pub grub called for a pint to go with it and he didn't want to start drinking, not with the folder contents to go through.

The cafe proved to be a good five minutes walk from the hotel and when he reached it, he was feeling more hungry than peckish. Inside it was almost empty. A man reading a paper at a table near the counter and an old woman sipping tea at another about half way up the shop.

Shedding his coat, he hung it over the back of the chair beside him and placed the folder on the seat. He sat down and watched a few snow flakes drifting past the window and reminded himself to phone Carol later, let her know that he was staying over.

He would call Chrissie too, because he wanted to hear her voice, he thought and drank some tea, then finally allowed himself to addressed the possibility that being here in Putney was quietly having some affect on him.

He opted for liver and bacon, today's special, which came with peas and mashed potatoes, a mug of hot, strong tea and took a table by the window.

221

The familiarity he had felt outside the hotel, looking at the common, The Tykes around Jack Tar's kiosk.

Veronica, with her plaits. A pretty girl but with a hint of something darker behind her eyes.

He picked up the folder and laid it on the table. It was not that thick, in fact it was pretty slim and looking inside only confirmed the paucity of its contents. It seemed to be mostly cuttings, from newspapers and magazine, the odd page or two torn from books.

Nothing much at all, he thought , tasting the bitter tang of disappointment and then he saw the photograph. Even though he had half expected to find a copy in the folder, it still gave him a jolt. So Murkin had received one already!

His food came, steaming hot and laced with thick gravy, just the way his mother used to make it. He laid the folder aside and clicked into eating mode, tucking into the food with the vigour of a starving man. Using the mashed potato to mop up the gravy like a schoolboy and savouring every mouthful.

Finally, he popped the last piece of sausage it into his mouth and sat back with a warm tide of satisfaction creeping through him. He felt a glow of almost contentment until he turned to the folder again and took out the photograph.

Sure enough, there were the Tykes looking out at him, exactly the same as the others except that this copy had a second photo held to it with a paper clip. About to remove it, he paused, decided to wait until he was back in his room and drained his mug.

Slipping the photos back into the folder, he put on his coat and took his dirty crockery up to the counter, earning a smile from the woman at the till. He told her the food was wonderful, paid for it with the money Carol had given him and left the cafe feeling slightly sleepy until the cold woke him up.

The afternoon was still young but the glow of the street lamps and the cars passing by with their dipped lights on made long for the modest comfort of his hotel room. He set out at a brisk pace and when he reached the hotel, went straight upstairs.

In the room, he tossed the folder onto the bed, took off his coat, hat and scarf, then sat on the side of the bed to remove his boots. He realised for the first time how weary he felt and walked through to the bathroom to run a bath. He watched the water splashing into the tub for a moment, then returning to the main room, stripped down to Nick's boxer shorts and sat on the side of the bed.

Reaching for the folder, he removed the photos and using a thumb, pushed the paper clip off, seperating them. Moving aside the photo of the Tykes, he looked at the other one, another monochrome, probably taken on the same Brownie camera. It looked like it had been snapped at a fun fair, with the focus being a stall with high canvas walls on three sides and open at the front.

"Coconut shy!" he smiled.

He had always loved having a go on those stalls, having a pretty good eye, even if he said so himself.

The photo showed two boys caught in the process of throwing balls, one boy with his arm held back to make his shot, half turned to watch the throw of his mate.

"So there..."

Holding the photo closer, Danny saw it was the boy Joe from the Tykes photo.

The others were there too he saw, standing at the edge of the frame, half seen figures looking on. Murkin and

Cockle possibly, hands shoved into the pockets of their shorts. No sign of the girls.

Was the boy caught throwing his ball Brian?

His back was to the camera, arm at full thrust, blocking of any sign of his face. He must also have had a good aim to, the way the others were watching.

Suddenly remembering the bath, he jumped up and hurried through to the bathroom. The tub was well over half full already, steam rolling in lazily coils around the small room coating the window and wall mirror in a thin film of condensation.

He shut off the hot tap, ran enough cold water until it suited him. Stripping off the boxer shorts, he climbed in and lowered himself in the water, feeling the knots in his muscles begin to slaken almost immediately. Leaning his head back against the edge of the bath, he closed his eyes.

She's back!

Murkin had been scared when he'd said that. It was like he knew what was going on and that it had something to do with whatever had happened back when they were all kids the 1950s.

I didn't do it!

Danny opened his eyes and stared at the ceiling. Didn't do what? The very fact that he'd said it implied something *had* happened.

He used the small bar of soap provided to wash himself, lifting each leg in turn to get to his feet. Working a lather up beneath each armpit, he wondered whether that something might be connected to Veronica losing her life?

He would have to learn more about her, but if Hilary didn't come through, he wasn't sure how he could go about it. If Mrs. hayden was still alive, if he could find her, maybe she would be willing to talk to him.

And tell him what?

He laid the soap aside and sank down in the water, finding himself a comfortable position and closed his eyes.

If she believed the Tykes had hurt Veronica, then why no go to the police? With what? Unless she had actual proof, then there was nothing they could do. No, she would have to act herself, seek them out, confront them.

And then what?

Make each of them kill themselves? Hardly likely. So, murder then? She could still be a strong and agile woman, even in her late sixties, but strong enough to overpower someone twenty years younger?

There it was, that wall again. He had seen both of the dead people and even from an amateur's point of view they had both looked like suicides, raising that same question, how did you make someone kill themselves?

He sighed, maybe Carol was right, he should let the police handle it. he should go to them, tell the truth about the photos and take his punishment. They could conducted a more thorough examination of things than he could. And what if they failed to find anything suspicious? What did he do them with this driving in his gut that could not be denied?

He lay there until the bath water was losing its heat and his skin was close to pruning, then got out. Pulling the plug, he took a towel from a pile of three on a rack at the foot of the tub and walked through to the room. He would take the folder back tomorrow, see Murkin, apologise, try to win him round. If he could get the man talking again, maybe he would let something slip that would point some way forward.

He dried himself off and donned the white bathrobe hanging on the back of the door, courtesy of the management. Filling the kettle from the hand basin tap in the bathroom, he put it on to boil. He considered taking some paracetemol for the suggestion of a headache that had formed above his left eye but decided against it. If it developed to a full blown skull cracker, he would deal with it then.

He yawned widely, walked over to the window and looked out at the common. In the gathering twilight, the dusting of snow looked deeper, the glow from the street lights making a lie of perception.

Looking to the side, he saw the railings around the wall of the old Parish Cemetary, darkly menacing in the yellow tainted light. His eyes lingering on the triangular island between the two roads, he felt a strong sense that a fun fair used to pitch up on it every summer. He could almost hear music and smell the cooking of hot dogs and onions...candy floss.

"Christ..."

He shivered, as though someone had walked over his grave.

Closing the curtains, he returned to the almost boiling kettle and dropped a tea bag into a cup, dangling the attached string over the cup's edge. He opened one of those dainty little milk tubs and poured in the contents, then topped up with now boiling water, stirring the bag around the cup until the brew was the strength he liked it.

Dumping the spent tea bag in the waste bin, along with the empty milk tub, he carried the cup to the the bedside table and stood it next to the beside lamp. Reaching for the folder, he spread Murkin's cuttings out on the quilt, and thought about him writhing around beside the railway layout. He shouldn't have left them to it, although from the way his wife had acted, the fits were a common thing.

No no doubt the man would be fine by morning and he could make his peace with him.

There were all sorts of cuttings on the bed, various shapes and sizes, mostly from newspapers but some pieces torn from books and magazines. There was also a couple of sheets of lined A4 paper, each line crammed with Murkin's childlike hand writing, un-joined up letters marching across the page until brought to a halt by a full stop. He decided to go through the cuttings and book pages first, leaving the hand written stuff until the end.

It was slow going and with each piece read, his disappointment grew until he laid the last cutting aside. There was nothing, just accounts of events over the years, articles about famous people who'd had even the most tenuous of connections to Putney. There was no order to the stuff, sheets shoved in anyhow, but what had he expected? There was something not quite right about Murkin and seeing the pathetic collection before him, he felt his hopes falter.

He finished reading through the last half a page of newsprint, a story about an unexploded German bomb, taken from The Wandsworth Chronicle. It had been discovered one street away from Galvin Street in 1959, long after the time he was interested in and dealt with by the army.

Murkin obviously fancied himself a some kind of local historian and the man did have one or two interesting pieces in his collection. None of it had any relevance to what Danny was looking for and he shoved everything back into the folder.

Whatever it was that Murkin was frightened of, he had found nothing so far in the folder to even hint at it. There might be something in the written pages but looking at the lines of spidery writing, he didn't hold out much hope of it.

Reaching for the A4 sheets, he placed the photos on the bedside table and sank back on the bed with his pillows supporting his shoulders against the headboard. Lifting his cup, he sipped some tea and eyed the top page. There was no heading, just straight in, as though Murkin was talking to his reader face to face.

There were two cuttings clipped to the sheets, taken from a facsimilie of a local news paper from the 1940s. The first, a copy of a photograph taken even further back in time, showed a country house type building surrounded by acres of lawns and gardens, while next to it was another picture of presumeably the same building as a burnt out ruin.

The headline read - Local Club House Destroyed By Fire! A caption beneath the photos told him that the building had been, The Ranelagh sports club. He unclipped the cuttings and laid them aside, moving on to Murkin's written work.

I remember the Ranelagh cos we played there. Just the five of us until she came. Then it wasn't much fun anymore. The best days were when there was just us. It was our hideout where no one could bother us. Until she came. When I was a kid, my dad told me that before the war it was where all the rich people came to play tennis and polo and rowing on the lake and dances with bands and booze and all the fancy clothes. There was regular parties all very posh with all what they called the best people in their fine gowns and evening suits. Music playing on the summer air. No posh evenings of wine and cocktails and ballroom music for me no fear. Beer and

rock 'n' roll is what I like. No polo cos I can't ride
horses.

Anyway it was all gone when we used to play there. It
closed down when war broke out my Dad said then the
club house was burned down in the early fifties. When
we used to go there when we was kids me and Joe and
Sarah and Brian and Alan it was all overgrown and wild.
Just a shell all black and stinking and beams across
rooms with no floors where everything had fallen in. Just
a ruin all overgrown even the grotto.

Real dangerous if you played there so the coppers said
when they came to our school but we played there
anyway cos we knew what we were doing and that was
our place. We'd just sit around in the long grass and
other stuff at the grotto when it was hot and we'd catch
tiddlers and try and catch dragon flies. Sometimes we'd
play Germans and English which was my favorite but
Sarah used to moan cause she was a girl so we played
cowboys too so she could join in better.

They was good times. Until she was there. She used
to make fun of me.

I didn't like her.

He had managed to stretch it over two pages and then
clipped the newspaper cuttings to it, like he was leaving it
as a testament. In case something happened to him
perhaps?

Danny took up the photo taken at the fair. There was
just the five of them before Veronica came along and he
thought about the scene outside the junk shop, the way
she had run to join them after robbing the smaller kid in
that alley.

Had they been avoiding her? Had she enveigled herself into their company? Murkin's tone in his pages seemed to suggest the that.

Did something happen at the Ranelagh?

The whole tone of what he'd just read seemed to suggest that Veronica had become a disruptive influence within their group, possibly causing trouble for them. Remembering how she had seemed to look right at him in Stacy Road, the wildness in her eyes, he wouldn't be surprised.

Not that she had actually been looking at him of course but it had felt that way, like she had seen right inside him and and he remembered the distinct chill that the touch of her gaze had given him. It had been as though she'd known everything about him.

Had something taken place in that burnt out ruin, where it was dangerous, where it would be easy to have an accident? Had she had an accident, maybe been killed? Had they kept quiet about it afterwards?

Danny finished his tea, swung his legs over the edge of the bed and stood up. He carried the cup back to the shelf where the courtesy basket stood and checked his watch. It was getting on for half past six.

What had they done with her?

Time he made his phone calls.

The phone was on the other side of the bed. He walked round and sat on that edge of the mattress, picked up the receiver and pressed for an outside line. A few clicks and then he got the dialling tone, so he called Chrissie first and listened to the ringing at the other end. Thinking of the layout of the house and where she might be until he had left it long enough and hung up.

He stared at the phone. Had she gone out? If so, where to and more importantly, who with?

"Jesus, man!" he squashed the feeling of jealousy that had sparked inside him. She'd not looked for company with another man before, as far as he knew and he was pretty sure that she wasn't going to start now.

Are you sure of that? After what you did?

He got another line and phoned Carol. She answered on the third ring. "Where are you!?"

"I'm staying over."

"I've been waiting for you to call since I got home."

She was annoyed, almost chewing her way down the line to get at him. This of course was not a new experience.

"I've been busy, doing my job."

"There is no job! You did what I asked, now you're playing your own games." He heard her draw in a long breath. "You have to come home. Dad's in hospital."

"What's wrong with him?" he felt a spark of concern, remembering how thin the Old Man's arm had felt the day of the egg throwing incident. Had he collapsed? A heart attack perhaps? The way that pipe smoke made him cough, it wouldn't be such a surprise.

"He's been beaten up."

"What?!"

"He confronted a gang of youngsters playing around in and out of the block. They gave him quite a beating."

Danny thought of the ginger haired kid he'd seen, leading his gang away from Dad's shouted threats, the way he'd looked, dead eyed little bastard. If he had been behind this attack...

"How's he doing?"

"He's in a bad way. Last night, he was unconcious." She sounded all in. "How could they do such a thing to an old man?"

Depends on the old man, he thought and immediately felt ashamed. He told her he would be back tomorrow.

"I'll come straight to the hospital from the station."

She told him the ward Dad was in and that visiting was limited at the moment. "It's just family for now."

Danny was about to hang up, when he heard she was still talking. "What was that?"

"For some reason, Hilary is trying to get in touch with you."

"Did she say anything?" he felt excited.

"Just for you to call her."

"Okay, thanks."

"Did she give you her home number too?"

"She gave both to me. I already told you."

"Oh, yes."

"You can get any thoughts like that out of your head. Christ! She's old enough to be my mother."

"Not quite. And I wasn't thinking anything like that."

Now he felt stupid and was annoyed with himself for over reacting. "We'll talk when I get home."

"Don't make a nuisance of yourself."

"Fuck off, Carol!" he said and replaced the receiver.

He went over to his coat to get Hilary's number from the pocket, then dialled her at home. When she eventually picked up, she sounded rushed.

He told her who was calling. "Sorry to disturb you at home."

"That doesn't matter. Hold on. I was in the shower and I don't have anything on."

Danny shifted uncomfortably after what had just passed between him and Carol. He sat on the edge of the bed, trying not to think about Hilary naked.

Why didn't the Old Man listen to anyone?

Christ, those youngsters might have killed him. It made his insides churn. No one knew better than he did how bloody annoying the old sod could be, but to do that!

"Hello?" Hilary spoke in his ear.

"Carol said you were trying to reach me?"

"Yes. A couple of things. There were in fact two children went missing around the same time from that area."

"Two?!"

"Your Veronica was one, and she was never found. The other was a boy named Berat Soyadi."

Danny blinked as something resonated in his head.

"He was the son of a minor diplomat, based at the Turkish Embassy, which was still at Portland Place then."

"This was the summer of 1955?"

"That's right. The family lived in Putney and he went missing after visiting a fun fair at Putney Common. His body was discovered a few days later in the old Parish Cemetary by the guy employed to keep it tidy. The kid had been viciously attacked, mutilated."

A heavy sense of dread settled in the pit of his stomach "How?"

"His throat was slit. His sex organs had been cut off."

"Jesus! A sex crime?"

"A pretty twisted one. I don't know about an other signs of sexual assault, anal penetration, semen traces and so forth, the report dosen't go into details." She sighed, "Poor little devil was only eight."

The tightness he felt inside increased, something was telling him he should know about the boy. "Anything on Veronica's mother?"

"Not yet. I'll keep looking."

"I'm going home tomorrow so if you need me, you can reach me at my place." He gave her the number at the flat then, after a moment's consideration, the number of their house in Norwich. "If you can't reach me, leave a message with my wife."

She said she would do that and after he promised to keep her up to date with anything he discovered, they said goodbye.

He got up, went to the window, stared out at the common. So he was right, the fair did used to come there, the only place suitable for it, being clear of trees and heavy bush. He gazed out at where the triangular section between the two roads was a dark mass, woods behind it and the old cemetary on its far side.

The boy had disappeared while visiting the fair.

A blade of pain pierced his forhead above his left eye and he closed both eyes eyes tightly. At once he saw coloured shapes whirring, heard music getting louder and louder, filling the night. The impression of horses, fair ground ones, galloping up and down in a fixed circuit, whirring round a centre island.

His legs sagged and he staggered back, sitting heavily on the foot of the bed inside a cacophony of fairground noise, laughter, screams of joy, the rattle and crash from a host of rides and side shows.

His headache picked up a notch.

It was like the scene in the alley back home, when he'd heard the music and seen the girl go by, heels rat-tat-a-tatting off the flagstones.

It was true that since finding Cockle's body, he'd had a sense of things closing in on him, the impression sometimes threatening to overpower him. That impression had been growing stronger ever since and he was convinced that what was unfolding around him in drips and drabs were snatches of memory. They didn't make any sense at the moment but would eventually lead to a whole.

Then what?

He opened his eyes, half expecting to find the fair in full motion right in front of him but all that met his gaze was the dark night through a rectangle of double glazed window.

"Old Parish Cemetery."

The boy had gone to the fair, had walked among the lights and smells, the excitement of people enjoying themselves. Kids on roundabouts, kids fishing for yellow plastic ducks with bamboo canes and the horses, painted in gold and red and green, nostrils flaring as they went up and down, round and round.

And there he was, riding an outside horse, laughing as the fair span by, everything beyond the ride a meaningless cyclorama of faces, waving, watching. There, right before his eyes, on tan coloured mount, a small, olive skinned boy with black hair and a twisted spine, turning to grin at him with large square teeth and dark, gleaming eyes.

"Berat!"

Danny groaned, turning away from the window with the image of the boy in his mind. It was Berat who'd had the train layout he'd remembered before, in the basement room of the family home.

How nice that house had smelled, spices and incense, even the paraffin heater down in there with the trains. A homely smell, lovely parents, even a lovely sister who had loved for her deformed brother so much.

Had they been at the same primary school? The small boy was younger but still they might have been friends.

"Christ..."

His head ached badly.

And then another onslaught of flashing pictures flooding his mind. He saw a small boy clearly now, deformed by the hump on his back, with over-long arms and legs, skinny. Other kids calling him spider but he'd just laugh at them with those big teeth and those dark, shining eyes.

Danny squirmed on the bed, crawling up until his head reached the pillow and he managed to find the bedside lamp, warm light filling the room. He was cold and worked his legs under the quilt, pulling it up to his chin, closing his eyes, waiting for the pain to subside.

He thought for a moment that he might pass out but then the fair was behind him and the pain was melting away. He could hear Bill Haley singing, 'Rock Around The Clock', as he went walking through a copse at the rear of the fair site, a secluded area.

The fair noise went on in the background, muted along with the shouts and bangs, screams and laughter, but there was someone closer, singing softly, eight, nine. ten - eleven too and there she was, gazing at him with such hungry eyes.

"My Mum hates this song. I like it though. I'm going to see The Blackboard Jungle when it come to the pictures."

An X certificate film but she could pass for sixteen, if she made the effort, no doubt about that.

"I bet it's good?"

He didn't care, he was just talking for the sake of it, to try to hide the fear in his gut, the fear he always felt when in her company. Fear of what she might do, but with a little shiver of expectation too at the thought of what she had shown him before.

She shook her head slowly, like she could read his mind. "Oh, no. It's your turn this time."

She smiled at him, like she wanted to eat him. Older by almost three years, the signs of the emerging woman clear on her girl's body, small breasts pushing out her blouse and a womanly roundness to her hips. She had shown him the light scrub of dark hair between her legs a week ago, which had released a storm of conflicting emotions within him. A rush of alien excitement, which had turned his insides to water but mostly fear, because he knew that she shouldn't be showing him and he shouldn't be looking.

"Daniel," she said, laughing at him with her eyes. "You owe me something."

"I dunno..." he didn't want to.

"I think you know what you must do." Suddenly she grinned, "Daniel in the lion's den."

She was the only one that called him Daniel. Even at school, no one called him that.

He stared at her, her face still the face of a child and so very pretty. But her eyes weren't pretty, not if you really looked into them. They were older, much older than they had a right to be. She moved towards him, driving him deeper into the trees and that smile on her mouth, which had turned from mocking to hungry, more than hungry, ravenous.

He looked around, moving backwards, not wanting to turn his back to her and all the time, desperately searching for a way out, a way that would take him back towards people and light, not deeper into the common.

"It's your turn, Daniel. I showed you mine, now you must show me yours. That's only fair. Otherwise, I might get very angry."

As she spoke, he was moving them gradually to his left, bringing the fair closer with every step and when she finished speaking, he knew he had a chance. He made a feint toward undoing his belt, fiddling with the buckle, a pair of entwined snakes that clipped together. He let his hands actually touch the metal, fingertips tracing the snakes, drawing her gaze.

Perez 'Prez' Prado's trumpet was blasting out now, 'Cherry Pink and Apple Blossom White' had replaced Bill Haley. She muttered something about her mother liking the tune but her eyes never left his belt buckle and he knew it was his chance.

He launched himself away from her, turning and running for all he was worth, legs driving, arms pumping, hot breath burning his throat. Breaking from the copse into the world of light and sound from the fair, he never faltered, just kept driving himself forward until he reached the side of the dodgem tent.

Now he stopped, looked back, expecting to see her angrily staring after him. What he saw though was her moving through the trees, glimpses of her pale blouse through the branches, gliding like a wraith towards the road.

The road that went past the Parish Cemetary!

And there was movement in her wake, following behind her, caught up in her spell, a small, ungainly figure.

"Berat..."

Ice entered his heart.

Chapter Sixteen

It had started to snow by the time Danny entered the dirty-wet concourse of Liverpool Street Station, medium sized flakes that blew around in the breeze and followed him through the central arch into the station.

After learning about Dad it was obvious that he had to return home as soon as he could, one because it was expected and of course, he cared about the old an. But he was also thinking, after what he'd been through the night before, that it would be the perfect time to hit him with some questions, questions that he would answer truthfully for once.

There was an Inter-City train that had been due to leave from Platform 9 ten minutes ago but was still sitting there. He walked through the ticket barrier and up alongside it with a few fellow travellers, not many at this time on a sullen, Saturday afternoon.

The train waited in brooding silence, its livery barely visible beneath a thick coating of grime. When the cleaners had finished their whistle stop tour through the coaches, the passengers were allowed to get on and the fat woman standing next to him, pushed her way into carriage H before anyone else could move.

Danny followed her, turning the opposite way, wandering through the train looking for First Class. When he got there, he found the carriage empty and settled in an aisle seat at the far end, facing back along the train. It was chilly in there but would no doubt warm up once they got moving, so for now he sat with his coat on, his beanie pulled down to the tips of his ears and his scarf touching his chin. Leaning his head back against the headrest, he closed his eyes and sighed.

The day had started badly with him waking early, feeling heavy headed, the thought of what he'd seen the evening before haunting him. It had given him a restless night and had brought him awake in the early hours, cold and stiff and miserable. He had crawled deeper under the duvet and dozed off again but had been unable lose the memory of the fair ground.

Had Veronica killed Berat? It was difficult to believe a young girl, attractive and with her whole life in front of her would commit such a terrible act. Then he thought of the look in her eyes, the way she had regarded him in that copse and thought perhaps she might.

He was certain now that it had not been so much a dream as a returning memory. Which meant that he had stood there and watched Berat following after her like a pet dof and done nothing about it. But what could he have done at his age? After all, he hadn't known what she'd had in mind.

"Fuck!" he muttered, trying to turn away from his thoughts.

It didn't matter what he had or hadn't known, he must have been aware of her nature to a degree and therefore, should have got after them, pulled the trusting younger boy away from her.

Danny opened his eyes and looked around the carriage. No one else had entered it and he was glad, he felt like being alone. There were still doors slamming further down the platform but they should be off soon, so with any luck he'd have the carriage to himself, at least until Colchester, the first stop.

How well *had* he known her?

Considering what had gone on between them, quite well. His thoughts turned to what she had shown him and the knowledge that there had been a warm stirring deep inside him. The knowledge made him uncomfortable now. It was one thing knowing it as a child of eleven, quite another through the memory of a grown man and he recoiled, deeply uncomfortable.

He ran through what else had returned to him, searching for the edge of the memory in the hope he might snag it, reveal more but his mind was blank. Beyond a certain place, there was only that familiar darkness. If things were coming back to him, clearly they would do so at their own pace and not when he wanted them to.

The key had to be, 'The Rudd Street Tykes'. Even if he hadn't been one of them, then he must have known them, been on the periphery of their activities now and then.

The train's diesel engine started humming as it warmed up. Moments later, a whistle sounded and with couple of jolts, the train began moving slowly along the platform. Daylight fell upon him through the carriage window as the train cleared the station roof, grey daylight, the sky heavy with cloud lay leaden upon the land.

He snuggled deeper into his coat with a little shiver and watched snow passing across the window. Part of him found the idea of his memory returning somewhat unsettling. There were obviously things hidden in his mind about himself that he would rather not know, such as the memory that had returned to him last night for instance. Too many memories like that could easily challenge the way he thought of himself, his whole manner of being. The person he believed himself to be might well be based upon a bedrock of lies.

He massaged his eyelids with a thumb and forefinger. Shadows of doubt had haunted him for as long as he could remember, becoming stronger by the time ha had reached his teens, causing him to start doubting the things Dad had told him. There had always been an underlying suspicion of information be left out and it had gradually become more diffcult to suppress his doubts.

Outside the carriage window the gloomy jungle of East London houses slipped by beyond a screen of steadily falling snow. It was beginning to settle on the dull roof tops and in small back gardens. The folder was on the seat beside him, calling to him, reminding him of the detour he had taken on his way to Putney Bridge Underground station in order to stop by Murkin's home.

"Jesus," he breathed, glancing at the folder.

The street was closed, a fire engine parked at the kerb outside the shop. A few people gathered round the building, gazing at the scene before them and whispering to each other, their faces grim. Fremen were moved about, packing up equipment, sweeping debris off the pavment into the gutter.

Danny had gone over to stand close to the on lookers, close enough to smell the stink of the burned wood coming down from the empty, blackened windows on the first floor. The people gathered there, neighbours mostly, wearing their indoor clothes, top coats drapped over shoulders, standing silently.

One of two women closest to him moved closer still, an old woman, stooped and frail inside her nightgown, draped with a heavy overcoat. She had looked at him from watery eyes.

"Could have spread, that could. With us next door and my husband partially disabled."

He had asked when it happened and sucking her lower lip in over her naked gums, eyes moving to the broken windows, she said. "Stink's filled our place. Gets in your clothes and hair it do. I can taste it all the time."

"During the night?" he'd asked, wrestling with a thick finger of horror that threatened to choke him

"Early hours. Woke us all up, every house along here. Fire engines, police, ambulance, hell of a racket. Still, shouldn't say too much, not with them two..."

"Dead?" something had jumped inside him.

"Took 'em both out on stretchers." The woman, leaning in closer still, had said quietly, "She had a breathing mask on but he was all covered up."

Too late! He'd been too bloody late and now another of the Tykes was dead!

At the site they had been talking accident but he knew differently, it had been more than that. He couldn't stop thinking about the old two bar fire in Murkin's room, the stand with flammable liquids next to it, which Murkin had kicked as he'd fallen. Had something spilt and eventually started a blaze?

Not accident, design!

Surely whatever it was that had spilled would have evaporated by the time the fire started? Perhaps that old fire had been given a helping hand to finally give up the ghost, bars glowing orange, full power on it's worn filiments and its ancient, cotton covered flex? Maybe it had simply burst into flames.

Murkin had had a copy of the photograph, just like Cockle and Sarah Eadel. He may well have had it all along but Danny would bet anything on it having arrived it in the post just days earlier. Whenever it had turned up, it had had him well and truely frightened, no doubt about that.

"She's back!'

But would he have let her inside so easily?

His friends had.

And who precisely had he meant by *she*?

Veronica? But Veronica was dead, wasn't she?

Murkin wouldn't have let anyone in so easily but his wife might. She had let him in after all, without question.

"Just go on up."

Signal trouble at Shenfield meant that by the time the train reached Ipswich, the second scheduled stop, it was running even later than before. Danny stared out the window at snow dusted streets and the snow still falling. If it went on like this, he would be delayed getting back to London tomorrow. It didn't take much to throw the rail network into chaos.

And then the lights went out.

Danny looked at the ceiling and they came on again, flickered and a moment later and stabalized. The train slid into the station, stopped and he watched the passengers who had alighted trudging down the platform towards the exit, through the ever darkening afternoon.

A handful of new passengers boarded the train, doors slamming spasmodically along the platform but none joined him in his carriage. Moments later the train jolted, then began moving and the lights went through their routine again.

The natural light in there was practically non-existent, so it became very dingy when the carriage lights were off. He shivered. Not only were the lights in the carriage on the blink, the heating had faded away too and he was glad he had kept his coat on. It was perishing.

Another half hour or so and they would arrive at Norwich and he would have to drag himself out into the wintery afternoon but at least he'd be moving, not just sitting here waiting.

The lights went out again.

"For God's sake!"

Out of nowhere, the face of Alan Cockle swam up before him. The expression frozen on it had been something no one should have to see because some sights could never be un-seen. Then others materialised, Sarah Eadel, no expression there with the face gone and Ray Murkin, whose face had probably been to charred to recognise but Danny could make a pretty good guess as what his expressions the moment he'd known what was happening.

The automatic door at the far end of the carriage slid open. Danny waited for it to close again and when it didn't, he leant over the arm of his seat and gazed along the aisle. There was no one there. The door had stuck, allowing a strong blast of even colder air to rush through the carriage and over him.

"Bloody hell!"

Grumbling to himself, he got up and was half way along the aisle, intending to see to the door when it shut by itself. He gave it a long, hard look, turned around and started back to his seat, trying to ignore the snow falling almost horizontally past the carriage windows. It was going to be a long walk home once they arrived at Norwich.

He reached his seat and had just sat down when the lights went out again. This time, they stayed out and the carriage interior took on a grainy, false twilight appearance. The temperature, already cold, seemed to rapidly plummet and he snuggled deeper into his coat, his teeth chattering spasmodically.

Christ, it was dark in there, especially it seemed at the far end of the aisle, where an extra heavy slab of shadow looked to have gathered over the seats just inside the door. He found that for some reason gazing at that blackness made him uneasy and he looked away.

Outside the countryside was zipping by, fields of settling snow, black solitary trees and wondered whether Hilary had made any headway, trying to find what had happened to Veronica's mother. He'd like to know what had piqued her curiosity about Carol's mystery client in the first place. She must have developed a nose for possible stories, situations that didn't quite add up and the way Carol had been approached had started bells ringing.

He glanced along the aisle and saw that the shadow over the far end seats seemed to have grown. No, not grown, coalesced into something more solid and now all but covered them. It could almost be mistaken for someone, a rather large someone, sitting there. The form looked as though it was occupying mostly the outside seat but seriously overlapping the adjoing one.

he shifted uncomfortably. It was facing him along the aisle as though watching him but there couldn't be anyone there. The seats had been empty a moment before when he'd gone to shut the door and no one had entered the carriage since.

But the door had opened!

The shape seemed to change slightly as he watched and worse, a split had appeared in it, a small vertical slit through which a snatch of grey-white showed clearly. It wasn't! Could that be...?

An eye!

He gasped. There *was* someone sitting there!

A cold finger shot up his spine. He tore his eys away from it, looking back to the whitening fields, the skeletal trees at their far edges, reaching into the sombre sky with naked, elongated arms.

A trick of refracted light might look like a face...an eye... That's what it was, nothing more than that. It couldn't be anymore than that!

He looked again along the aisle to the far end of the carriage and found that the slit had widened, revealing a bony sharp plain of cheek beneath the glistening eye. The eye itself deep sunken in its socket - obsidian black.

She's back!

Panic welled up inside him, filling his chest, tightening it so that it was difficult to draw breath. His heart was pounding, his mouth was desert dry. She, whatever she was, must have picked him up back in Putney and dogged his heels all the way here. It would have been easy to fasten onto him, heading for Putney Bridge Station with a mind full of turmoil, so that he was more or less oblivious to what was around him.

Veronica's mother?

But he already knew that it wasn't, even as a voice inside insisted that it must be, telling him to go down there, challenge her. She had to be well over sixty and from what he could make out, shrunken by illness. Certainly nothing for him to worry about.

Then why was he worried? More than worried, scared! Was it even human?

Of course it was human! What else could it be?

He forced himself to stand up, leaden body on shaky legs. With a huge effort, he slid one foot out into the aisle, then the other, keeping his eyes on that shape at the end of the carriage all the time.

Flapping a hand behind him, searching for the door handle, he remembered it was an automatic door just as the damned thing opened on its own.

A deep, primal dread held him fast, because there was something about that figure that was more than...more than...

But he couldn't move.

His legs refused to work.

He realised the train was slowing and risking a glance outside, saw city suburbs sliding by, countryside giving way to roads, to houses. Down the aisle, the shadow spread too, melting into a shapeless dark mass.

Was this what Cockle had seen before...?

Danny didn't need to see anymore, he should get out, now, while he still could. But he was terrified to move in case his doing propelled what was down there into sudden action.

He saw Norwich City football stadium passing by, then they were slipping under the station roof. On his left, the platform sprang up and the train slowed even more as it neared the buffers at the end of the line.

Home!

When he looked back to the end of the carriage, he found the end seats were empty. The door down there was shut so whoever it was, whatever it was must have slipped out while he was looking away and he had only turned away for a second.

The train stopped and instantly doors were thrown open, passengers began alighting, jumping down to the platform, hurrying for the barrier. Danny stood there watching, searching for a figure in black, an all enveloping coat, maybe?

"Where...?"

But the flow dwindled until there no more people passing by the window.

He reached into his seat, retrieved the folder and moved into the small lobby between carriages. Climbing down onto the platform, he followed the last of the passengers to the ticket barrier, handing in his ticket and passing quickly through to the concourse.

No trace of any dark figure anywhere. He scanned the area again, then set of at a swift pace through the arched station entrance and out into the carpark at the front of the building, where evening had already begun closing in.

Beyond the car park, pedestrians wrapped up against the cold moved quickly about their business. Standing in the covered entrance, Danny took the time for a good look round before starting for the street.

There was still no sign of anyone resembling the figure, which didn't mean he wasn't being watched for some shelter or other. He considered taking the short cut along the river bank and through the cathedral grounds, it was certainly the shortest route but it was also secluded and dark, very dark.

She's an old woman, for pity's sake!

He decided to go the long way, where there would be more people around and even the light from the street lamps was better than no light at all.

The snow had all but stopped, which was good, as he would be walking into the wind and the last thing he needed was it driving into his face all the way up the road. Carol's office was closer but he would see her later. He wanted to see Dad alone if he could. There were things he needed to ask him and he didn't want Carol stepping in as a sheild should he need to get a little rough. With Dad in his weakened state, he may be able to get to the truth for once.

One way or another.

Chapter Seventeen

The shop was closed but there was a light on in the flat. Danny could see it through the frosted glass panels in the front door. He dug out his keys and let himself inside, then climbed the stairs to the landing as quietly as he could, moving along to stand in the doorway of the front room.

Roy was inside, bent over one of the tea chests. There were several record albums on the floor and he was moving others about inside. no doubt looking for those he wanted to move take to the shop. Danny felt relief wash through him.

Roy obviously hadn't heard him arrive.

"Lost something?" Danny said.

Roy jumped violently and turned. "You bloody idiot! You almost gave me a heart attack."

Danny entered the room and went straight to the window, looking down at the street below, one way and then the other. There was no dark follower out there and in some ways, he was disappointed. At least if there had been, he would know that what he'd seen in the train carriage had been mortal.

What else, for Christ'e sake!

Stepping away from the window, he drew the curtains shut and turned to look at Roy, who was speaking.

"You look like a refugee from some Siberian gulag."

"You wouldn't believe me if I told you."

"Try me." He stood up and settled one buttock on the edge of a tea chest.

"Later. I have to go see my dad. He's in hospital."

"You know then?" Roy took out his old tobacco tin. He selected a roll up and fitted it into the corner of his mouth, then fired it up with his lighter. Blowing a stream of smoke at the ceiling, he continued, "Carol told me yesterday."

Danny stared at him, "Carol actually phoned you!?"

"It wasn't a social call. She wanted to know if I'd heard from you."

"I spoke to her." Danny rubbed his face hard, suddenly feeling drained. "She reckons they did quite a job on him."

"Bastards!" Roy said, getting to his feet. "What sort of scum does that to an old man?"

Danny didn't tell him that there had been times when he had felt like doing something similar himself. "I have to get out there."

"They have visiting hours."

"To hell with that!"

"Alright." Roy noisily cleared his throat, "I'll take you. That bloody heap of yours won't raise a spark in this weather."

He lived a couple of streets away, where he kept his newish Datsun in an off road parking space. It would take him only a few minutes to go and get it.

"You want one of these?" Roy offered his tin of roll-ups.

"You know I gave up."

"The way you look, you may need to start again." He moved towards the door, paused and glanced back. "What was London like?"

"Big and noisy."

"Yeah, funny." He made a sour face and left.

Danny lifted the curtain away from the window. He heard the front door close and saw Roy walk off to the left. There were no other sudden movements that caught his eye but the street lights kicked up long shadows in every nook and cranny, so there was no certainty that there was no one out there.

He let the curtain fall into place, realising how tired he was and drifted across the room to the couch, sitting on an upholstered arm. If he sat down properly there was a good chance he would fall asleep and he couldn't risk having a fuzzy mind when he confronted Dad.

Dad!

Somehow he had to convince the Old Man that he needed to hear the truth. The little pockets of the past that had been popping up all over the place didn't make any sense on there own. He needed to see the whole picture in order to link them together, to give him a least a half grasp on what had happened back then.

Roy arrived and drove them quickly across the city. The roads were wet, the gutters slushy and the pavements were speckled with patches of settled snow. The hospital, located on the very edge of the city centre, was a sprawling mishmash of buildings grown up around the original central one, as needs required. There had been talk of building a new one for years but talk was all there was to it so far.

Roy drove behind an ambulance up the gritted road to the entrance, swung left into the seriously inadequate car park and was lucky enough to find a space in the front row. Danny offered to sort out the parking ticket but Roy told him he'd do it, to get on inside and see his dad.

"You going to wait here?"

The car park had not been gritted for some mysterious reason, so they picked their way across a hazard of half frozen slush to safer ground in front of the big glass entrance doors.

"No point me going in," Roy said, his face pinched by the cold. "Anyway, I hate hospitals."

Danny nodded and watched him walk off towards the ticket machines. "Just get half an hour," he called after him and saw Roy raise an arm in acknowledgement.

He went into the front lobby then walked through to the large general reception area, which was busy with people coming and going. He looked round, getting his bearings, down past the indoor plants, wild looking things in huge pots, dotted around in no particular order, to brighten the four ranks of cheap looking plastic chairs either side of the walkway. A wide flight of concrete stairs led to upper levels and in the shadow of the stairwell, two lifts offered their services.

The hospital was as busy as he had expected. The hub-bub of dozens of conversations competed with the constant flow of muzak coming through speakers, dotted around the walls and painted to blend in with the wall colour. A group of people waited for one of the lift cars to arrive, so Danny took the stairs up to the first floor, where Geriatrics was located.

By the time he reached the floor his back was aching, so he paused, leaning against the balcony rail, looking across a line of faux leather covered sofas down the long corridor in front of him. Hanging signs pointed the way to Obstetrics and Radiology, to Neurology, wall signs indicated the lifts, the toilets and the cafeteria but he couldn't see any sign to tell him how to find the department he was looking for.

He walked along the corridor until he found a nurse's station and explained why he was there.

"Geriatrics," she said. "That's where you want."

"I know," he said. "I can't find it."

She showed him a corridor along on the left, with pale blue walls and beige linoleum flooring. Thanking her, he followed the flow of too warm air, heavy with the smell of dinner and antiseptic until he found the ward halfway down.   Entering, he saw two nurses at another station, one working on some charts, the other standing at her shoulder, talking to her.

"I'm looking for my father." He told them Dad's name.

"We have him in a side room." The standing nurse came around the station and took him along to a door on the right of the ward.

"How is he?"

"Better than he was. He's responding well to treatment."

"But?"

"He's had a bad shock. He's still weak, so not too long, okay?"

He watched her walk away for a moment, then let himself into Dad's room, a south facing one, which on fine day would be filled with sunshine and very bright thanks to its neutral walls and skimpy yellow and white curtains. As it was, the space was full of grey-blue half light. He spotted a chair near the window and brought it close to the bed.

"Hello Dad."

The bag of bones in the bed had a puce coloured face, with yellow-purple shading around the cut beneath his right eye. Both eyes looked to have sunken into their sockets and the closed eyelids had a blueish tint to them. The slight mound of body beneath the covers looked pathetic and for a few seconds, Danny forgot how angry he was.

"Dad?"

After a moment, the lids fluttered back and a pair of vacant eyes stared at the ceiling before sliding sideways to look at him. They seemed empty of recognition but all the same, Danny had the feeling that the Old Man knew he was there.

"You want me to put the light on?"

Dad groaned softly, moved his head on the pillow.

"Okay, we'll leave it off."

The lids trembled, the eyeballs rolled, the lids fluttered. "Is that you, son?"

"Yes, it's me. I'm just back from London." He looked at Dad hoping for some kind of reaction but there was nothing. "I've been having a high old time of it in Putney."

The eyelids closed again and Dad said softly, "Told you not to go."

"Yes, you did. But you didn't say why."

"It's a bad place..."

"It can be." Danny leaned closer, "And I don't think I've seen the worst yet."

"I told her not to send you." The same whispery voice, the same waft of sour breath.

Danny sat back. "But you learn things there, Dad. Guess what I learned."

Dad's eyes opened slowly and fixed on him.

"I'll give you a clue. It concerns Jack Reed and those kids he was with in the photo you'd forgotten about."

"Jack was a good man..."

"The Rudd Street Tykes, you must remember them?"

Again something moved behind Dad's eyes, a shadow, then the eyes slid away.

"No bells tinkling? How can you have forgotten them? You remember everything else from back then."

"A brave man..."

"Some might say a stupid man, a thoughtless man. But it's not him I want to talk about."

Dad's eyelids shut. "He died a hero..."

"So you said, but I want to talk about the Tykes. About the girl that went missing. Veronica, her name was."

Dad lay unmoving, asleep or dead maybe to a casual observer. But Danny was used to the Old Man's deceit by now and frustration got the better of him. He reached out and grabbed a bony shoulder, started to shake the bag of bones.

"Look past all that bollocks! You've been filling me with shit all these years, now I want the truth!"

Dad opened his eyes. "I don't know..."

"Don't know what?"

Danny's grip transfered to a handful of gown and he slightly lifted the skinny torso from the bed. The tube in Dad's wrist became taut and the IV stand connected to it trembled dangerously.

"Don't know what I'm talking about? You must have taken a bashing."

"Let me sleep."

"In a minute. Tell me what I want to know and you can sleep as much as you like."

Dad's eyes rolled, showing thick and yellowing whites. He began to mewl, sticky throat noises.

"Was I friends with them...with her?" His mind's eye threw him a picture of that figure in the train and he lifted Dad higher. "Tell me!"

"Danny!" Her voice cut through the room like a whip lash and he looked over his shoulder. "What the hell are you doing?"

It was Chrissie. The nurse who had shown him to the room stood at her shoulder, staring at him with outraged eyes. She hurried forward, pushing him aside.

"I...was just trying..."

The nurse shot a black look his way, as she set about checking the old man over. The next moment, Chrissie was by his side, taking his arm, leading him from the room, out of the ward and along the corridor to the landing.

"What the hell was that about?"

"I needed him to talk -"

You might have hurt him!"

"I'll hurt him, the old sod!"

"What's got into you?"

He tried but failed to meet her gaze. "I need him to tell me the truth."

"Don't even think of going back in there."

The fight drained out of him. He sighed heavily and walked away from her, down to the main corridor and along to the stairs, where he sat down on one of the couches.

He had come there feeling, if not confident then optimistic about getting something from Dad. He'd thought the beating he had taken might have loosened him up a bit, made him more inclined to tell the truth. Now everything was ruined.

Chrissie approached, staring at him. "What happened to you in London?"

"Nothing. Everything. " He shrugged, "Christ knows, and Dad but neither are talking."

"I've never seen you like this before."

"For a moment..." He shuddered, back on the train for a moment. "I never felt like throttling him before."

"Danny!?"

He looked up at her with a weary smile. "I do need to talk to him."

"Then you'll have to wait until he's stronger."

It was no good arguing, he could see that. Anyhow, the way Dad was, he didn't think he'd get far, even if he were to get back in there. Chrissie sat down close, looking at him. He met her eyes, her lovely eyes and smiled again. Reaching out, he brushed her cheek with the back of his fingers.

"You win."

"Good," she said. "I was just daring to feel hopeful."

"And now?"

She smiled, "Still hopeful. Just about."

"I thought I may have ruined our chances."

"I know you wouldn't normally behave like that... Something bad happened in London, didn't it?"

"Bad..." He looked away, across the building to the wall of windows on the far side and made a small noise as the enormity of the task he faced suddenly hit him. Chrissie moved closer.

"Tell me."

"Something. I don't know. Maybe I'm wrong, reading too much into it."

Possibly Carol was right and he was chasing shadows, shadows of his own creating that would lead him on and on into ever increasing confusion. There was no end because he hadn't created one. He would love to forget all about Putney and the Rudd Street Tykes, all about Veronica and what might have become of her.

And the train?

"What are you going to do?"

He stood up and moved to the safety rail. He felt trembly inside. That figure on the train had been real enough, hadn't it? No figment of his imagination? He looked at her, gave her a tired smile.

"Roy's waiting outside for me. I'm going to get him to take me to Dad's."

"Why?"

He shrugged. "Why not? I need to look for something."

"Something important?"

"I won't know that until I find it."

"Why don't you come home afterwards?" she said quietly. "I'll cook something, we can talk."

"Home?" He felt warm inside, hearing the word. He lifted her hand to his mouth and kissed it. "I'll see you later then."

"Danny." She stood up, "I don't know what you're involved in. You can tell me or not, that's up to you. It's good to see you interested in something again but don't let it take you over."

Interested! If only she knew. Maybe he would tell her this evening. He would be glad to lay it all out in front of someone else, someone other than Carol. Get her opinion. At least Chrissie would listen to him seriously.

"I love you, you know?"

She looked away, "I'd better get back to Dad."

She had always got on well with the old sod, almost as though she was his daughter by birth and not by marriage. Maybe Dad felt sorry for her, being lumbered with him. Danny waited for her to say something more but she didn't.

"I'd best get going too," he said.

"How is Roy?"

"Same as usual."

She nodded, smiled and walked away. He watched her go for a moment, then went to the stairs and started down. Shoving a hand into his hip pocket, he felt his fingers come into contact with his door keys and he smiled grimly, Dad's keys were on the same ring. He'd take his time looking around, the outside cupboard to start with, then in the one place he might find something, the Old Man's case of secrets.

Chapter Eighteen

Roy was waiting in the Datsun, engine ticking over. The moment he saw Danny coming, he sat up and was reaching for his seat belt as Danny climbed in beside him.

"How was it?"

"Same as you'd expect."

"Is he any better?"

"Hard to say, really. He never was very demonstrative."

"Right," Roy said, as though he understood, which he obviously didn't.

"I have to get some stuff from his flat," Danny said. "Can you take me out there? No need to wait, I can find my own way back."

"Your wish is my command." Roy gunned the engine and turned the car towards the car park exit.

Driving through the city, Roy tried to make conversation but Danny's one word answers soon made him understand that talking wasn't on the agenda at that moment. When they got there, Roy let him off at the kerb outside Dad's block. "I don't mind waiting."

"No thanks, mate. I don't know how long I'll be."

They said goodbye and Roy drove away on a near empty road. It was cold and bleak, barely anyone about. There was icy patches on the pavement and snow lying on the grass verges all the way up to the entrance to the block.

Danny walked carefully, digging the door keys from his pocket. All the way out there, he had been contemplating what he may find in that old case, Dad's treasure box, as they had called it as kids. They used to joke about him sitting alone by the light of a solitary lamp, trawling through the stuff he had collected over the years, like some latter day Fagin pawing his secret stash of goodies. He almost smiled as he entered the block.

Taking the stairs two at a time, ignoring the protests from his back, he reached the landing and walked on, past the flat, right to the end of the balcony, to where three tall cupboards nestled in an alcove at the end. Dad's was the middle one and the door opened easily when Danny tried the key. There was a light inside, 100 watt bulb behind a metal grill in the ceiling. He flicked the wall switch to the on position and saw in the glow that filled the space that the cupboard was much as he remembered it, full of -

"Junk!"

Two old bicycles, Dad's large black one with round handle bars and a cracked leather seat and leaning against it, a smaller pink one, straight handle bars, which Carol used to hurtle about the streets on as a young teenager. Neither had been ridden for years and Danny couldn't understand why Dad kept them.

There was a wicker washing basket, painted gold and the monster mangle that used to decorate the kitchen before they'd had a twin tub.

"For god's sake!" he said, struggling to move a couple of suitcases, big ancient things that were filled with old bedding.

A couple of sturdy cardboard boxes behind them held ornaments from the house they had lived in before Dad moved here. There were several framed pictures; cheap prints of famous artworks, and stubby pieces of black painted wood, decorated with nails, golden string looped from one to the other, fashioned into crude depiction of sailing ships.

He paused to look into another large cardboard box, shoved into a corner and found it held a lot of his old toy soldiers, cowboys mainly and Herald American Civial War figures. He couldn't remember playing with them, certainly hadn't done so much after their move to Norwich but Dad insisted they would be valuable someday. The same with two Dinky WWII trucks in their familar blue and white striped boxes.

No sign of his train set.

Finally he saw it, pushed right to the back of the space, an HMV model radio/gramaphone in a dark wood housing, record deck in one compartment with the radio beside it in another. A piece of furniture really, with a speaker at each end and a special space at the side for storing records.

He moved closer, managed to lift the lide enough to see the velvet covered turntable beneath, the pickup secured in the way he remembered, by a retaining clip that fitted over it to hold it to its rest.

Reaching over to the door to the record space was awkward thanks to two tall, heavy boxes stored in front of the unit but he finally managed to get the door three quarters open and saw the handful of old 78 rpm discs that he remembered, bittle shellac things in paper sleeves.

Squatting down in the cramped space, he was able to flip through the discs, all by artists of the 1950s, Anne Shelton, Dickie Valentine; 'Oh My Papa' by Eddie Fisher, which drew a grunt from him. There was, 'The Man From Laramie' by Jimmy Young and 'Mack The Knife' from The Threepenny Opera by Louis Armstrong, which the BBC had banned for some reason known only to themselves.

No copy of, 'Cherry Pink and Apple Blossom White', either by 'Prez' Prado or Eddie Calvert.

Stepping back, his leg brushed the wicker basket holding all mum's sewing stuff, the same stuff Carol had been going when she'd found the envelope containing the photo of the Tykes. He grunted, stepped out of the cupboard and closed the door on the rubbish in there. It must have been a hundred to one shot that the photo would be found by Carol and it crossed his mind for one fleeting moment that maybe she was meant to find it. Fate, or something more.

But he didn't believe in fate, did he?

He didn't believe in a lot of thing but feared that his certainty in matters he judged to be impossible might be challenged in a big way the longer this business went on.

Walking along to the flat, he let himself in and a wall of heat engulfed him, making him gasp after the chill outside. He went straight along to the front room, switched on the light and saw Dad's chair, empty and forlorn and next to it, on the side table, the large glass ashtray in which his pipe rested.

Dad had lived there a while now and the walls seemed to ooze his presence. Danny wondered how long that would last once the old boy had moved on and the flat was re-let.

Going through to the bedroom. he pushed the door as wide as it would go and turned on the light. There it was, sitting on top of the wardrobe, the same old brown, cardboard suitcase that hadn't seen a holiday since God knew when, peeping over the architrave at the top of the unit, like it had been expecting him sooner or later.

Dad's treasure trove! he grinned. It had fascinated them as kids, sitting up in bed playing make believe, fantasizing about what riches were to be found inside. The treasure now would be papers, photographs he had never seen; all the Old Man's secrets, which right then were more valuable to him than any amount of the gold doubloons in Captain Flint's treasure.

Shucking his coat, he laid it on the bed, then dropped his beanie and scarf on top of it. Bringing a hard back chair from beside the dressing table, he stood it in front of the wardrobe door. Space was at a premium and it was a tight fit, less than a smidgin on either side. Steadying himself on the chair back, he climbed up onto the seat with a child like excitement growing inside him and standing there, gazed at the case.

This moment had been a long time coming, he thought, touching the surface of the case. It was smaller than a regular suitcase which was odd, as he remembered it as being larger. It had cheap extendable hinges and clasps, the chrome of which was tarnished with age and it looked anything but special now, although that same nervous thrill played on inside him.

He reckoned he could lift it clear of the wardrobe and drop it onto the bed using its brown plastic handle and a hand underneath to take the weight. He would have to be careful turning in that narrow space, just in case his back gave out but he thought he could manage and reaching over, grabbed the handle. He lifted the front of the case, which was surprisingly heavy, slipping his left hand beneath it, then he hefted it up and around in one smooth movement, so that it balanced momentarily on the top of the architrave.

Manoeuving in mincing little steps, he got himself into the correct position, where he could support the weight and bracing himself, he completed the turn and let the case fall to the bed in, where it bounced heavily.

What the hell did he have in there?

Stepping down, he looked at the case for a moment before pulling it towards him and thumbing the latches sideways, so that the locks popped open. Taking hold of the lid he threw it back and stared at a large sheet of brown paper, level with the brim, placed there as a protective cover for what was inside. Tearing away the paper, he looked down at a top layer of old newspapers and magazines.

"Treasure indeed," he muttered,

He lifted out the top bundle of magazine, which proved to be programmes for the yearly El Alemien Reunion evening. He recognised the blue and yellow banner above the black and white photograph of a soldier leaning from the turret of an armoured car, looking pretty pleased with himself. And why shouldn't he? He'd just been part of Britain's first WWII success, the defeat of Rommel's Afrika Corps. After Dunkirk, it must have been a sweet victory. Now recognised as a turning point for the Allies.

The programmes, he remembered had disappointed him as a kid, as after that cover picture, most of the rest of the thing had been writing, punctuated by the odd advert.

The Reunion itself used to take place at the Royal Festival Hall, right up until the death of Field Marshal Montgomery, who had been overall comander of the campaign. Dad had gone to almost every one, leaving his children with his mother, while she was alive and later, with a trusted neighbour that Danny and Carol had learned to call Auntie Maud, or so Dad said.

Danny smiled, laying the programmes aside and turned to the next bundle, newspapers, mostly copies of the Daily Mirror, as far as he could see. These were whole editions not just cuttings, as with Murkin's collection and each bundle tied with string. The top edition was from 1945 proclaiming The Labour Party's landslide election victory, Churchill amazingly rejected by a populace demanding change.

Finding some nail scissors on the dressing table, he used them to open the bundle and lifted the editions clear one by one, the 1952 one announcing the death of King George VI, for which the paper's usual red banner had been changed to black, Princess Elizabeth returning from a trip to Africa with her husband, now the new Queen.

Then there was a Coronation issue, June 1953 headed, 'Happy and Glorious', with a picture of a smiling young Queen waving royaly to the crowds. Inside pictures of wet streets and cloudy skies.

There followed editions covering the Suez debacle of '56, the assassination of President Kennedy in '63, and the Apollo Moon landing in the summer of '69, one small step etcetera, etcetera. The last edition was of a Sundy Mirror for 31st July 1966, England's World Cup win over Germany, 4-2.

They thinks it's all over...

He smiled at the memory. On the front cover the triumphant team were pictured waving to the happy fans gathered outside the hotel from the roof of its entrance. He couldn't afford to let himself be drawn into reading any of them though, no time for nostalgia here and he quickly re-tied the bundle.

Placing it aside, he lifted out the next one, which was thinner, a few editions of the Wandsworth Chronicle, a weekly broad sheet publication. The front page of the top one, dated April 2nd 1953 told of the arrest of John Reginald Christie, the Rillington Place murderer, arrested near Putney Pier, just as Murkin had said.

The papers left faint ink marks on his fingers, even after so long and dust up his nose. He ran through the following editions, looking for some reason why Dad had chosen to keep them but found nothing worth noting. For all of his being so anti-Putney, he was interested enough to have kept these local rags for no obvious reason.

Nothing about missing local children.

He dumped the papers on the bed, then several editions of the National Geographic magazine, Picture Post, Photoplay and to his amazement, twenty or so issues of a motor bike monthly! For a man who never even owned a car! He vaguely remembered that Dad once said how he used to go to speedway meetings before the war, so perhaps that was why he kept them. It was the only connection he could think of.

He tossed the bundle on top of the others and it fell to the floor, where he left it. At the bottom of the case were several smaller bundles, brown paper bags, creased, slack with age, old letters, documents of all shapes and sizes. These seemed to offer more promise and he took one up, opening it eagerly.

Inside he found Dad's army pay book, his medical card, a dried out packet of V For Victory army issue cigarettes, ten brittle sticks encased in a protective packet. Dad's regimental tie, red lightening stripes on a navy blue background, rolled into a neat ball and a greasy, cardboard box, not much bigger than the cigarette packet, but sturdier.

The outside of the box bore an address in fading ink and a used postage stamp stuck on the top right corner of the box, George VI's head on it. A black franking mark across the King's cheek and temple had cancelled it. The address was for the house Dad had lived in before moving to Galvin Road and Danny knew that inside were his campaign medals, as he'd seen this item before.

He opened the box and slipped out the medals, spreading them across the eiderdown, the way Dad had allowed him to so many years ago. They still looked new because Dad never wore them; gleaming metal shapes, the Africa Star, the Italian Star, the more recently issued, Dunkirk Medal, brightly coloured ribbons, as clean today as when they had been sent. Dad had always said that he knew where he'd been, what he had done and that he didn't need medals to remind him.

Where had Jack's medals gone?

There were birthday cards in a grey shoebox, for Carol, signed Mum, Dad, brother Danny and his own cards from eleven to fourteen, nothing from the years that were lost to him.

next came a bundle of long, official envelopes, one of which held Dad and Mum's marriage certificate, birth certificates for both of them and for Carol, Mum's death certificate. No birth certificate for him and no certificate for Mum's marriage to Jack either.

The last envelope and contained school reports for Carol, along with her examination certificates and then finally, something else concerning him, his final school report, the only one of his the Old Man had seen fit to keep. He didn't need to read the comments of his teachers, he remembered them even now.

Could do better!

Daniel needs to apply himself more!

"Fuck you!" he muttered and tossed the envelope aside.

The rest of the stuff in there seemed mostly more old photos, ones Dad had prefered to keep in his case rather than put into his assorted albums. All taken since they had moved east.

Danny tipped the case upside down so that it emptied onto the bed, then selected a stiff backed envelope, larger than the others. It contained a black and white photo of a grey haired, elderly woman, Dad's mother, his own step-grandmother, who had died when he was thirteen and who had apparently been extremely fond of him.

There was something else inside the envelope, a letter written on one of those thin sheets of writing paper that used to be available from stationary shops, the sort that folded up to form an envelope when you had finished writing. They were used for airmail post, being very light in weight in order to keep the postage costs down. This was a very old one of the type issued to servicemen, for them to use to write home to their loved ones.

It was addressed to Dad's mother at the house she had lived in from after the Blitz, right up to the day she died. At the top left corner was the censor's official stamp and top right was a printed on postage stamp, cancelled by a Field Post Office franker. It was in fragile condition and handling it carefully, he spread it out on the bed.

It had been sent from Sicily in the summer of 1943, a few months into the Italian Campaign. The writing, in Dad's large, curly hand, blue ink, faded over time, was addressed, *'Dearest Mother'* and attempted to tell her how things were for him and the rest of the boys without contravening censorship restrictions. Needless to say, it hardly gave any indication as to what was going on, *'Am as well as can be expected'* and *'Am awaiting the move to wherever we are going next'*, next being mainland Italy and later, Monte Cassino.

Towards the end of the letter, he wrote of his concerns for Jack, who had been sent to the far east to fight the Japanese. In her previous letter, Grandma had apparently told him that Jack had been taken prisoner and sent to one of their infamous POW camps in Burma. Dad wanted to know if she'd heard anything further, writing that those Japs were *'wicked buggers'* and that he *'feared for Jack's wellbeing'*.

Danny stared at the words for a long while. Dad had never said that Jack had been a prisoner of the Japanese, nor what treatment he had received at their hands. He could not imagine anyone going through that, witnessing cruelty every day, experiencing it, could remain unaffected. The horrors those poor devils had gone through, the beatings, the disease, the starvation, the survivors finally emerging like walking skeletons.

He folded the letter carefully and laid it aside. His focus on Jack's war had always been on the time leading up to Dunkirk, where he was wounded, because that was all Dad would ever talked about. Even when he'd asked questions, Dad had just siad they had lost contact after Dunkirk. Danny had assumed that, after recovering, he had rejoined his old unit in the European struggle against the Germans. Now he knew better and the knowledge made him wonder how the experience might have worked on Jack.

How would it work on any man?

He looked at his watch. He had to get going soon. He wanted to spend as much time as he could with Chrissie before going back to London. They had to talk, talking was important, especially the sort of talking they had to do.

But there were still items from the case to check and he quickly began sorting through the stuff he had emptied onto the bed. Ten minutes before he decided that there was nothing there that was likely to be of interest and he dragged the case round to face him ready to start putting the stuff back into it.

He reached out and gathered up a handful of items and noticed a loose sheet of newspaper, yellowing and brittle, hiding beneath some old, empty envelopes. It must have escaped from one of the envelopes when he'd upended the case. Picking it up, he saw it had been torn from a copy of the Chronical, folded neatly across its middle and opening it, he saw a photograph of Jack in full police uniform, standing outside the local police station and beneath the photo, the headline

TRAGIC DEATH OF LOCAL POLICEMAN

The story told how P. C. Jack Reed had dived into the Thames in an attempt to rescue a drowning child, only to be washed away to his own death.

Danny sat on the edge of the bed, staring at the words before him, running through them again and still not finding any sense in them.

A drowning child!

No woman!

No dog!

"A child!"

The story had always been about the woman who had got into trouble trying to save her dog. Throwing sticks for it on a wet and chilly night and he'd accepted it. Now it was only too clear what a ridiculous story it was and the truth slammed into his brain like a power hammer.

The report went on to say that P. C. Reed, off duty at the time and returning from a trip to the local cinema with his wife and child, had acted immediately upon hearing a child's cry for help. Rushing across the main road and down to the river's edge, he had ripped off his coat and shoes and without hesitation, had plunged into the river to save the girl.

Wife and child.

He had been there!

Danny laid the sheet of paper aside and stood up. A peculiar sensation ran through him, a picture struggled to form in his mind. He moved to the bedroom window and looked out at the dark, cold night and was in another place. He could could smell the evening chill, dank and fetid - the river!

"I saw it happen."

His was a child, walking between his parents, talking about something, the film they had just seen. There had been a light mist, no dense fog or damp winter's night, no tug's horn sounding from out across the Thames...

Just...

Then it was gone, vanished in an instant, replaced by the scene of the street outside Dad's bedroom window, the lone street lamp glowing valiantly in the brittle air.

Danny moved back to the side of the bed. The sheet of newspaper had slipped from his fingers and was now lying on the counterpaine. He picked it up again, folded it and slipped it into the inside pocket of his overcoat.

A corner of the original suitcase liner had peeled away from the base of the case to form a flap. He gazed at it stupidly for a moment before reaching out and turning it back. He ran his palm over it the surface of the paper liner, pressing it flat and feeling the outline of something beneath, another envelope or perhaps a photo that had managed to work itself under the there.

Tearing the flap, lengthening the original damage enough to reveal that it was indeed a photograph, black and white of course, with the usual thick white border. This one showed a small gathering standing outside the main entrance to Waterloo Station, the steps up to the entrance guarded by the stone lion which had once reclined there.

Danny pulled the photograph free. It looked to have been taken sometime during the war because it showed two servicemen in uniform and two women, one in slacks with a jacket over and the other in a two piece suit with a little hat perched on her head. All were laughing, no one less than the woman closest to the camera, with her mouth and eyes wide. She stood between the soldiers, arm through that of the man on her left, while the other two looked on. She was the only one he recognised.

It was his mother, younger and happier than he remembered. She looked like a girl, eighteen maybe, with her other arm raised towards her partner, aiming a playful swipe at the man's field cap. He was a lean, handsome sergeant with dark, wavey hair and very white teeth.

Just another uniform, nothing unusual there. British battledress by the look of it, and yet somehow different, worn with a leather jerkin. A bit of fun in wartime, it must have been happening all over the country but this was different. This involved his mother.

He needed to get away. He left the case where it was and got into his things, shoving the photo into the same coat pocket as the page of newsprint. Turning off the light, he left the room and was halfway up the hall, when the front door opened.

"What are you doing here?" Carol said.

He stared at her. "I could ask you the same thing."

She pushed her way inside and walked down to the bedroom door. "When did you get back?"

Danny closed the front door, "This afternoon. I went straight to the hospital."

"You saw him? How is he?"

"Not very receptive."

"He's still in shock," she said.

"I thought it might be that."

She gave him a hard look then with a small dismissive noise, entered the bedoom. Switching on the light, she pulled up sharply, seeing the state of the room. She stared at the suitcase sitting on the bed, then turned and looked at him questioningly.

"Are you going to explain?"

"The hospital said he needed pyjamas."

"And you thought you would find them in there?" She moved to the side of the bed, staring from the mess lying on the quilt to the opened suitcase. "To think, we used to picture all sorts of treasure being in this."

"And all there was, was junk."

For a moment or two longer, she stood thinking about the past, then her face lost its wistful look. "Is this why you came here, to open it?"

"Kind of. I needed to see what he had in there."

"Pyjamas, you said."

"I lied."

"I know. Pajamas is why I'm here." She began returning the contents to the case.

"I opened the magic box and guess what? no magic, just a load of old crap."

"What did you expect, Aladdin's cave?"

"Like you said, we used to -"

"We were children then. At least you were, I was just humouring you."

He sighed. The heat was starting to make him feel stifled. "I didn't expect much."

"You weren't disappointed, then." She put the letters and stuff back, then fitted the magazines in and started on the newspapers. "So now tell me what this is really about."

"It's like an oven in here!" Danny said. Dad's old furniture stood like tombstones in the overhead light, wallowing in the heat. How the hell does he manage to sleep with the air as thick as this?

"Don't prevaricate."

Danny pulled the photograph from his pocket and handed it to her. "What do you make of that?"

She glance at it, then looked closer, recognising their mother. "I wonder who the soldier was?"

"Search me. It's not my father and it certainly isn't Dad."

"Was it in the case?"

He nodded, "Under the bottom lining."

"Hidden?" she asked sarcastically.

"Who knows?" but he didn't believe it had been and thinking about it, he no longer thought Dad had hidden the Tykes photo either. But it had been hidden, not just left there forgotten. Which meant that his mother had hidden it. For him to find perhaps?

She looked hard at him then, holding on to the photograph, walked past him into the hall. "Come through to the living-room, the light's better in there."

Danny followed her through, saw her stop under the ceiling light and give the photo a long, searching look.

"Does this have anything to do with you going to Putney?"

"The photo?"

"You going through the case."

"Yes. There's a lot you don't know."

"So tell me."

Danny gazed at her. Something had just popped into his mind, a small thing at first but it had grown rapidly and now he thought it all made sense.

"What did Dad say, when you let him know about the photo you found."

"I already told you."

"You wouldn't have been satisfied with that."

"I wouldn't?"

"I know you, Carol. You'd have wheedled the truth out of him." He stepped close and grabbed her wrist. "No more lies."

"You're hurting me!" She pulled away, rubbing at the red marks on her skin. "What the hell is the matter with you!?"

"I'm sick of people stringing me along, like I'm some sort of idiot. I want to know everything that old bastard said!"

"This is ridiculous!" She turned away, "I'll not stay here and be interrogated by my own brother."

"Adoptive-brother," he growled.

"If you touch me again, I shall call the police."

Their gazes locked. She meant what she said, but she could see that he did too. For a moment the air between them all but sizzled, then, as suddenly as it had grown, the tension melted away.

"When Jack Reed jumped into the river, I was there, wasn't I?"

She sighed, sat slowly down on the nearest chair. "Dad begged me not to tell you."

To hear her say it somehow made it clearer than ever. All he had been told over the years, all the stories about the past, the years he could not remember. What was truth and what wasn't?

"The meningitis?"

"Yes," she said quietly. "You contracted it soon afterwards, apparently. Dad thinks the shock brought it on."

"Can it do that?" Danny sat down heavily. "It's a virus, isn't it?"

"I'm not sure. I expect your system was down after - after the shock of what you saw and..."

He felt as though he had been kicked in the stomach. "How could he keep a thing like that from me?"

"I wasn't sure how you'd react if I told you, so I agreed to keep quiet."

Danny walked over to the window again and stared out at the street. It was snowing once more but only in a half-hearted manner. Eyeing her reflection in the glass, sitting there, watching him, he said, "I've started remembering things."

"What sort of things?"

"Scenes, like cuts from different films, thrown at me. They're all mixed up but they are hinting at some overall pattern. I just don't know what that pattern is."

"Could you be imagining them? Making them up subconsciously - to suit what you want to believe?"

"Believe?"

"That you're remembering your past."

"No." He turned to face her, "Being in Putney does seem to have started something happening in my head. Trouble is, what's coming back, instead of making everything clearer it's just making it worse. I keep trying to see the whole picture but whenever I reach for a clue, I just find darkness.

"As I said -"

"I'm not making the fucking stuff up! The things I've seen are too real." He took the photo from her and laid it on the table in front of him. "I'm sure now, it has something to do with my past."

"The Rudd Street Tykes?"

"I don't think I was one of them but I knew them, met up with them from time to time."

She gave him a long, thoughtful look.

"It's here, in my gut. I can feel it."

"All right, I have a certain respect for gut feelings. I'll go along with you for now."

"Thanks."

"Does this photo fit in?"

He looked at it again and shook his head. "I don't know. If we knew who this bloke was, that would help. He might be just some casual date. It was war time after all."

"Maybe he was a friend of your father. Someone he met in the army."

"No," Danny said.

Something had been nagging at him about the soldiers in the photo. He had spotted something and now he realised what it was. The act of turning had brought the shoulder of the guy with mumder round towards the camera, so that the letters on the epaulet of his battledress were clear.

"You remember, as a kid I used to be interested in anything to do with the war?"

"Only too well." She had been forever complaining about the space his books took up on the living-room table when she was in a mad rush to complete the homework she had left to the last minute. He'd had a small library on all matters WWII, weapons, aircraft, ships and uniforms. Danny held the photograph out to her and she took it.

"I don't know what I'm looking for."

"Jack Reed was in the Royal Artillery."

"Okay." She looked at him blankly.

"Look at the epaulet on that man's uniform. He was a Canadian soldier."

Carol looked at the photo and a small smile grew on her mouth. She handed the photo back to him.

"Canadian or not, she was having a good war."

Danny didn't smile, he felt uneasy. The idea of their mother out on the town did not bother him and if that was all the photo showed him, then that would be okay. But there was more, only he couldn't put his finger on it. Something didn't sit right with him, he was sure of that.

All at once he felt tired and wondered where the hell all this was going to end. Once again, part of him wanted to give it up, get on with the uncluttered life he'd been living before. No cares, no responsibilities, that was for him, wasn't it?

And Chrissie might not have you back!

He sighed. He knew that the old him would have to go if he wanted any chance of them trying again. Already he was different, he could feel it. He knew, deep inside that no matter what happened, no matter how down he felt, he could not let this go. It had hold of him now and he would let it play out to its conclusion.

"My brain feels like mush," he said. "There are so many things vying to be recognised, I can't think straight."

She kept watching him, silent, waiting, letting him get it off his chest.

"I think someone's after me."

"Who?" Carol asked sharply.

"The same person who - killed the others - maybe." He half expected her to dismiss this as she had other suspicions he'd voiced but she didn't. "There was - someone on the train earlier. Watching me."

"Watching you? You should have challenged them."

"I know but I couldn't move. I was too frightened." He gave her a wan smile, "I'm not proud of it. I wanted to run away."

"What happened?" she asked quietly.

"I turned away, just for a moment and when I looked back, there was no one there."

They gazed at each other and time span out between them as both sought an explanation and failed to find any.

"And after, on the platform, the concourse?"

"Nothing. No sign anywhere."

"You've no idea who it might be?"

"All I know is, whoever it was could move bloody fast."

"I told you this could be dangerous! Poking around in things you know nothing about."

"It has something to do with my relationship with the Tykes.."

"You said you weren't part of the gang."

"I'm pretty sure of that." He hesitated, then said, "There's something else."

He told her about Berat. "Hilary found out about it." He took her through the scene in the copse, seeing the boy following Veronica.

"What -." She turned away, frustrated. Moving to the window, she stood gazing out.

"I believe what I saw was a memory."

"Whatever it was, you think the girl did that to him?" Turning, she looked at him angrily, "She was a child herself, for God's sake!"

"Not such a child," he said, telling her what she had wanted him to do. "I think my relationship with the Tykes was a casual one. It might have been different with her."

Carol stared at him for a long while and he could only imagine what she was thinking. At length, she said, "I don't know what to say. This all sounds so..."

"I think Veronica murdered the boy," he said. "But don't tell me to go to the police!"

"And tell them what? That you think a fourteen year old girl who went missing thirty ago, murdered a boy shortly before she vanished? Christ!"

"At least you're not telling me it's all in my imagination."

"Is it? I mean, what makes you so sure these - memories you're retrieving are not just things you're dreaming up?"

"They're not," he said quietly. "I know."

She held his gaze for a moment, eyes searching, pleading almost, then she looked away and shook her head. "Let me get the few things I came for and we'll go. I'll run you home."

"I'm going to the house."

She looked at him, sighed.

"It's okay. I've been invited."

He followed her back to the bedroom and watched her through Dad's chest of drawers, pulling out several drawers until she found what she wanted. She removed a pair of flowery pajamas and stepped away, moving unsurely, her mind not fully on what she was doing. She closed the drawer and over-folded the pajamas.

"What do you think?" he asked softly.

Another sigh, she looked at him with tired eyes. "I don't know, Danny. I really don't."

Outside in the bitter night, it was still trying to snow. Carol started for the road, where Nick's car was parked with its two nearside wheels up on the pavement.

"They should make that sort of thing a parking an offence," he said.

"If they do, you'll be forever paying fines."

Banter but their hearts were not in it.

"I'm going back to London tomorrow."

They walked across to the car and she busied herself for a moment, opening it. This done, she turned to face him. "You're still working for me by the way."

He nodded, tried a smile. "Does that mean an expense account?"

"Okay. But don't take liberties."

"As if."

They got into the car and fitted their belts. Carol started the engine. "We should hear something about the inquest soon."

"Okay."

That night at Sarah Eadel's farm, with her dead body waiting for inspection, seemed an age ago but in reality, it wasn't even a week. So much had happened in the intervening days and much more was still to happen, he was sure of that. He wondered briefly whether he would managed to survive until it was all done.

He hoped that, if the girl's mother was still alive, they could find her, talk to her. It was possible she might be able to tell them something that would give them something to work on. He really hoped they might find some smallk thing, some clue that put them on the right track. In fact he was clinging to this hope because there were other ideas trying to form in his brain, wild, alien ideas that he did not want to entertain.

Carol drove speedily along the dual carriageway, turning right at the lights and then making a sharp left onto the road where the house was. Stopping outside, she pulled on the handbrake and looked at him.

"Are you coming in?"

"You two need to be alone."

He nodded, released his seat belt. "The inquest. You think they'll want both of us there?"

"Probably." She watched him open the door and get out. "Danny!"

He looked back inside, "Yes?"

"Be careful."

He nodded, shut the door and watched Carol drive away. Standing on the pavement, looking into the empty street, he suddenly felt more alone and exposed than he could ever remember feeling before. When the feeling became too much, he turned up the front path to the house. Chrissie had the front door open before he got to it and stood back to allow him to enter.

"You look so...lost," she said gently, turning from closing the door.

It was warm in the hall and he caught the smell of something good cooking. He should feel happy just standing there but the cold inside him was not as easily removed as that beyond the front door.

Chrissie said, "Shepherd's Pie."

"Especially for me?" he said, making an effort.

"Don't kid yourself."

He shed his coat, hanging it on the wall mounted hanger, beanie, gloves and scarf shoved in the pockets. He went through to the kitchen, which was large, fitted out three years ago with modern units by a local firm that had been recommended to him. They had built an island in the middle of the floor. Somewhere to sit and have breakfast, or lunch, or if you didn't want to go to the trouble of eating in the dining room, dinner.

Chrissie poured two glasses of red wine and picking her glass up, looked at him over the rim. "Hilary phoned."

"Okay." He felt uncomfortable, even though there was absolutely no reason for him to do so. "It's work. She's a journalist friend of Carol's. She finding out a few things for me."

"To do with what you're up to in London?"

"I gave her this number, just in case."

"In case of what?"

"I just thought she could leave a message with you. In case she couldn't reach me at the flat."

"You should see your face," Chrissie said. She handed him the other glass of wine, gave him a sly smile, "I know Hilary. We met at Carol's a year or so back."

"What did she want?" Now he felt a little stupid.

"You to call, as soon as."

He cautioned himself not to expect too much and jabbed a thumb over his shoulder at the telephone, "May I...?"

Chrissie cradled her glass in one hand, "You don't have to ask."

Danny went out, pulling the door to behind him. Gulity conscience had pricked him in there, shadows of past involvements. He had kept them to himself but they sat in the corner when he was with Crissie, like a white elephant.

There hadn't been many but after what Chrissie had said outside the restaurant the other day, about the things a woman can pick up on, he wondered if she already had an inkling about them. The possibility of that was something he would have to come to terms with if he ever moved back in.

He found Hilary's card in his coat pocket and went to the phone. Lifting the receiver, he dialled her home number and she picked up on the third ring.

"It's me. Chrissie said you called."

"I've found Veronica's mother."

"What! Where?"

"Bournemouth. She lives there with her step-daughter."

He heard her swallow and knew she had a drink in her hand. He didn't blame her, he wished he'd brought his glass of wine with him, he could do with it right then.

"I called, just to make sure. I told the daughter we're journalists looking into police cold cases. She seemed happy for us to visit. Apparently Ellen Hayden is practically blind and not too clever on her feet but otherwise fine."

He felt as though someone had thrown cold water in his face and realised that he'd been hoping the old woman was involved in some way. If she was in such a state though, she couldn't be, at least no first hand.

"Are you there?"

"Sorry, I was thinking. I'm coming back tomorrow. Is there any chance we could go down and see her in the next couple of days?"

"I don't see why not."

He told her where he would be staying, the same hotel in Putney and she said she would call him there. "I can pick you up in the car."

When she had gone, Danny stood in the hall with the receiver in his hand, weighing up what she had told him. He hadn't been sure the woman would be found and now... How had Hilary found her so fast?

Chrissie came out from the kitchen, looking for him, saw him standing there. "Danny?"

He blinked, came back to the present and hung up the phone. He could see the concern on her face and without thinking, moved to hold her, but she stiffened slightly and he let his arms drop.

"I've just had a bit of a surprise," he said.

"Right." She reached out, touching his cheek with her fingers. "Good or bad?"

"Good, I hope."

"Then you had better come through and tell me about it."

Chapter Nineteen

Her smile was broader, her eyes brighter.

'What big teeth you have,' Danny thought as he walked into reception. He could see why she was so glad to see him, all the keys were hanging on the board, the hotel was empty of guests.

"It's always slow at this time of year, but this weather has killed off what trade there might have been."

"And now I'm here."

"As you say," she beamed. "You are here."

"I said I would probably be back."

"People say all sorts of things." She opened the register and wrote down his name, next to the same room number as he'd had before. She took up the room key. "For longer this time?"

"That's right," he said and took the key. "I remember the way."

Her smile tightened a little, "Of course do."

He started upstairs feeling her eyes on his back until he passed out of sight. Once inside the room, he set to unpacking his things, underwear, a couple of shirts and a decent pair of trousers to wear to Bournemouth. When he had done, he phoned Hilary, who told him everything had been arranged.

"I'll pick you up in the morning around nine."

When she had gone, he looked at his watch, saw it was almost midday and decided to walk round to The Feathers for some lunch. He arrived at the door to the saloon bar just as the pub opened, ordered a pint of bitter and an individual lasagna, then took his beer to a table near the fire to wait for his food.

The bar would soon start filling up, he thought, watching a steady file of customers arriving. A couple of drinks, a read of the Sunday paper and then home for lunch. One or two nodded as they passed him by, walking into the back of the large room with their usual tipples. All regulars, he guessed, no passing trade with the weather this bad. A bus driver and conductor came in for a quick half each and then his food arrived.

When he'd first heard that Hilary had located Veronica's mother, he'd been excitemed at the possibility of finding things out. Now that elation had melted away, he felt low and somewhat irritable. He could not loose the feeling he'd had since that incident in the train, the sense of something ominous hanging over him.

"Damn!" he muttered.

There were thoughts, ideas so wild, trying to form in his mind, thoughts he had to struggle to hold at bay because, should he once acknowledge them, might shatter his hold on his sanity.

He ate his food with little appetite, although it was perfectly edible. Finally he pushed the plate away half eaten and drank some beer. When the bar door opened, he started slightly, then saw another customer, who stood on the threshold, tapping slush from his shoes before entering.

Drinking his beer, Danny went over what Chrissie had said to him last night, when he'd told her he believed his memory was returning, that memories couldn't hurt you - physically at least.

"I hope you're right," he'd told her.

He had gone on to slowly lay it out for her, explaining the things she couldn't quite grasp, what he thought was going on and why. She had listened tight faced and when he'd finished, had turned away from him for a while.

When she had finally turned back, she had gazed into his eyes. "You're holding something back."

"No," he'd said, surprised that she could see through him so easily. Of course he was holding something back, from her but, more significantly, from himself too.

"Is it dangerous? You might get hurt, is that why you're not telling me?"

"No. I just don't know."

He'd told her he thought any danger was focused on Singleton and Brian, trying to quieten the little voice inside him.

"You said twp people had died already."

"Three, Ray Murkin too."

She gave alittle gasp. "Another suicide?"

"Accident. House fire."

"But you don't believe it was an accident, do you?"

"No. That is why I must make Joe Singleton understand and there's still Brian. I don't know where he is yet."

"He could be anywhere. He might not even live in this country."

That possibility had already occured to him, which was why he had to get Singleton to talk, although it was possible he didn't know either. Just because they had been friends as kids, didn't mean the friendship had lasted, as it seemed to have done with the others.

"I've been thinking," Chrissie had said during doing the washing up. "That woman, the one who engaged Carol. It's almost as though she wanted you involved in this."

"Carol would tell you you're being fanciful," he'd replied, managing a smile that didn't feel too strained.

She had sighed. "Maybe she'd be right."

Sitting at the breakfast bar, he'd watched her put the kettle on for tea.

"Can't you speak to that old woman again, the one who lives in Kavanagh Mansions? She knew the family, it's possible she may remember someone else who was close to them?"

He'd been glad she was taking an interest but there wasn't anything she could suggest that hadn't already crossed his mind. He doubted Mrs. Kershaw would be able to help him anymore than she had already.

"I suppose it wouldn't hurt to ask."

"What about the girl's father?"

It was a thought, he had supposed. Was Mrs. Hayden really a widow or had they separated and she didn't like people knowing? Mrs. Kershaw had hinted at something there. If the man was still alive, still active, then he might want to avenge his daughter, if he thought the Tykes were resonsible for whatever had happened to her.

He thought now that this did sound far stretched but he was glad for any straw to grab at. They had talked on long into the night and when he'd said he had better get going, she had told him to stay.

"You mean it?"

"I wouldn't have said it if I didn't."

He smiled ruefully now, remembering how his hopes had soared, only to be dashed the next moment when she told him he was sleeping in the spare room. When he'd kissed her goodnight, she had let him kiss her properly, rather than just a peck on the cheek but her resolve had held and there had been a look in her eye that told him not to push it.

He sighed, stood up and left the pub. His journey down had been long and thankfully uneventful, although he had been on edge all the time his carriage had remained empty of other passengers. Now he needed to walk, as he did some of his best thinking when aimlessly strolling.

He turned his feet away from the common in the direction of Putney Bridge. A watery sun, which had been struggling to break through the cloud cover since he had left the pub finally gave up the fight and the sky returned to it's usual spread of unbroken grey.

Kavanagh Gardens was up ahead, his intention being to call at the Mansions and talk to Mrs. Kershaw. He would ask her to think back again to those long past years, but he really didn't think she would remember much more than she had told him already.

When he came to the next side road however, he stopped. The name plate on the wall told him this was Rothermire Road, which he remembered from his A-Z was next to Galvin Street. Galvin Street ran into Benmare Road, which tailed round at the bottom to intersect Rothermire, which carried on straight down to the river.

He stood on the corner wrestling with conflicting emotions. He knew at some time, he had to come to terms with the river being so close to him in every way but could he face it up close and personal? It was a thing he'd been avoiding since arriving in Putney. Was there anything to be gained by facing it now?

Rothermire Road was almost a duplicate of Galvin Street with terraces on both sides, only the buildings in here were that bit grander, they even had small patches of garden in front of their bay windows. The newly planted saplings along the kerbs seemed more at home here.

At the bottom of its length, the road ended in a man made hump constructed to guard against flooding and indeed there was a plaque fitted to the side of the nearest building marking the high water mark when the Thames had burst its banks back in the 1953 floods, drowning several people in their own homes. Beyond the hump the river was waiting, just across the road named Embankment.

Danny could see it, smell it and he hesitated a moment before crossing over. The river did not look too pleased to see him, its waters moving sluggishly beneath the leaden sky. It seemed drained of purpose by the weather and ashamed that he should see it in such a diminished state.

He stood at the safety barrier looking down at the little wavelets kissing the concrete banking at his feet.

I know the monster you are, the tricks you play and keep well hidden, to snare the unwary. Well you old bastard, you ain't getting me!

A lick of chill breeze coiled around his neck, then slipped inside his coat collar, just as though the river was giving him an answer. He shivered and tugged his upturned collar closer together at the throat, moving on towards the bridge. He walked slowly, hands thrust deep into his coat pockets and tried to show the Thames he was indifferent to its presence.

Putney Pier was locked up and empty. In summer, there would be pleasure boats picking up people for river trips, both upstream to Kew Gardens, Hampton Court, ices in the sunshine, and downstream, past the Palace of Westminister, the Tower, the Cutty Sark to the sea.

"Southend," never his favorite seaside resort.

Nothing now though, just the Thames, sulking in the chill air, not even close to being appealing. It had been along here that Christie had been picked up after weeks on the run. His last glimpse of freedom before the Old Bailey and a date with the hangman.

A little further along, he stopped again. Embankment turned up towards the main road. In front of him, at right angles to it, was a cobbled slipway wide enough to roll a boat down to the waters edge, when the tide was in as it was now. The stink of river water was stornger here, rolling up to meet him, welcoming him as it had his father thirty years earlier.

He moved back away from the smell, a sudden wave of panic turning his insides to water. They said that the sense of smell was the evocative, bringing back long forgotten events.

"No - I..."

He resisted but images like ghosts came rushing back to him andstruggled as he might, he could not prevent them to materialising before him.

This was the place where Jack Reed had dived in...

He gasped, hearing the pounding of running feet, shoes slapping tarmac and all at once, the day peeled open for him. Jack was there running towards him, past him, ripping off his raincoat and kicking off his shoes.

"Help!"

A voice from the river, young, terrified and he watched Jack climbing the safety railings.

No! he wanted to shout. Stop! but he was mute in the face of this playback and then his memory shut down. The day came into focus, was whole again and he gazed about him, desperately looking to catch a loose end of the past as it melted away.

But there was nothing, just the river, lapping innocently as it had done before, in one of its deceptively benign moods. He was alone.

Danny lurched away from the safety railing, walking quickly up the short incline of Embankement to the main road. There had been something he had almost grasped during that flashback, something that lingered on inside him now, eating away at him and then he had it. Jack had drowned that evening, but what had happened to the girl?

When he reached Kavanagh Mansions, Mrs. Kershaw was at her window, closing her front room curtains. She saw him at once and smiling, beckoned him to come see her and as he stepped up to the entrance, the security pad on the wall buzzed. A moment later the front door lock clicked open.

The foyer was loaded with that same deep and brooding silence, waiting for him he thought as he closed the front door with care. It was strange the way if affected him, made him feel a strong sense of reluctance to disturb it. Across the foyer, the lift waited patiently behind its closed gates.

Mrs Kershaw opened her front door. "I thought you had gone home."

"I did," Danny said, stepping into her hall. "And now I'm back again, like the proverbial bad penny."

"Business or pleasure this time?"

"Not pleasure."

She looked at him hard. "No, I see that now."

Closing the door behind him, she shooed him along in front of her and into the living-room. "You'd like some tea? No pastries, I'm afraid."

"I'm fine, thanks."

Danny dragged off his beanie and shoved it into a coat pocket then, removing the coat off, draped it over the back of one of the chairs set around the dining table. He watched Mrs. Kershaw switch on two additional lamps, then move to turn off the TV.

"This light," she said. "You would think it was early evening instead of early afternoon."

"I'm sorry to disturb you," he said, sitting carefully on the front edge of the couch.

"Disturb me, huh! I was just watching a film I have seen a dozen times before. 'Brief Encounter', with Trevor Howard and Celia Johnson."

"Carnforth Station," Danny said.

"Never was a smut in the eye so romantic." Chuckling, she settled herself into her armchair. Waldorf stepped from his bed and came over to investigate Danny's boots.

"Yes, it's me again," he said to the dog.

"Go back to bed, Mr. Nosey Parker," said Mrs. Kershaw, waving a hand at the dog. Waldorf looked up at Danny with a sad eye, then did as he had been told.

Danny managed a smile. "How are you?"

"Much as I was two days ago."

"Was it only two days?"

Light glinted in her dark, intelligent eyes, weighing him up. "So, what can I do for you?"

"Am I that obvious?"

"When I saw you, I told myself, this man has something on his mind. Is it about Mr. Cockle again?"

"Indirectly."

"How did you find his father?"

"Unpleasant."

"Ah," she nodded. "He hasn't changed then."

"Not so's you'd notice. He didn't seem to care about his son."

Mrs. Kershaw shook her head and made a tutting noise, "His own flesh and blood."

Danny paused, seconds ticked by. At last he said, "I want to ask you about the girl who disappeared and her mother."

"So ask." If she was surprised, she didn't show it.

"Was there anyone else who was especially close to them? A relative or special friend?"

"Not that I know of. The woman was a very private person. I was certainly not a confidante."

"What about the girl's father?"

"She never mentioned him, not a word, other than to say she was a widow. As for friends, I did not ask. I would say that they lived a very solitary life. I do not remember any visitors at all."

Danny sighed, it was just as he had anticipated. It seemed as though nothing was going to make this business any easier. The clock ticked away from wherever it was located.

"When I say there were no visitors," Mrs. Kershaw said. "Veronica brought a boy back once, I remember. A local friend, possibly?"

"A boy?"

"It was not a common occurrence, seeing her with anyone of her own age. Of course, she must have had friends at school but someone visiting their home? It was very unusual."

"What did he look like?"

She shrugged. "A boy. Younger than her, I would guess."

Danny swallowed dryly. Could it have been him? Was this where she had brought him to show herself to him? That would explain the vague sense of recognition he had felt when he'd first entered the block. It may also have been...

"A dark skinned boy?"

"No, not dark skinned. Why do you ask?"

He hesitated, how far should he go? She was watching him, waiting. "You remember a young boy being murdered around the time Veronica disappeared? A Turkish boy."

"Disabled," she said. "I remember. A terrible thing."

"I thought maybe..."

"That he was her visitor? No this boy was English, or at least, not dark skinned. You must remember, back then there were not many dark skinned people around here. A Turkish boy, with disabilities would stand out."

Who then? Him?

"You remember nothing more about him?"

"It's a long time ago and he was just a boy. I can tell you one thing though, he did not stay long. I saw them arrive as I was finishing polishing my letterbox. It was brass and we used to do that sort of thing then."

"Did they speak?"

"That was the odd thing. I remember it struck me at the time, he seemed reluctant to go upstairs. It was like he didn't want to be there at all. As though she had in some way made him come with her."

"There was no name mentioned?"

"None. They went up the stairs, he came down soon after."

"And you saw him leave?"

"When I had finished the letterbox, I went in and put on my coat to take my dog for a walk. Not Waldorf. Even he is not that old!"

Waldorf looked up under his brow at them as though knowing they were talking about him. Mrs. Kershaw chuckled, bent over and tickled the ear that was nearest to her.

"I was just leaving the flat, when the boy came hurrying down the stairs and out, without looking back."

She looked troubled, as though she had remembered something that bothered her.

"What?"

"It was just after he had gone. I was certain I could hear her laughing up there on that top landing."

Danny felt troubled by the story. It may have been one of the Tykes, not him at all. But even as he thought this, he knew in his heart of hearts that it had been him.

"Tell me," she said, after a moment. "Do you think that someone may have hurt Mr. Cockle?"

"It's possible," Danny said reluctantly. "Do you?"

"The thought, it crossed my mind. When I saw him. His face. Such a look on that face. As though he was frightened out of his life."

"Maybe he was just that," Danny said and immediately cursed himself. He looked away. Quietly, he said, "Other things have happened since I last saw you."

She stared at him. "More deaths?"

"Ray Murkin."

"The plumber, Mr. Murkin?"

"Yes."

"Oh, dear Lord. How?"

"A house fire. They're saying it was caused by an old electric heater."

"An accident."

"It should be in the local paper when it comes out."

"You think, something other than an accident?"

He remembered the struggle with Murkin, his foot catching the shelf of spirits as he went down. Was he wrong, had something fallen, spilt it contents near enough to the fire to ignite? Was there a chance it had not evaporated?

"I'm not sure. I can't explain it to you, you would think I was out of my mind."

She fixed him with a probing look, dark eyes gleaming. "I am very old and I have experienced a lot in my life. I do not rush to judgement over things that are - what shall we say - out of the ordinary? Might this be something along those lines?"

Out of the ordinary? Did she mean, could she mean - other worldly? Supernatural? Surely not! But why not? He had entertained the idea more than once lately but had managed to dismiss it from his mind. Now the weight of the idea bore down upon him.

"I meant that someone else might be involved. Nothing more than that."

Mrs.Kershaw stared him, seeing through his prevarication, recognising his fear. She nodded eventually, allowing him to keep keep his own counsel.

"What about the other children in the photo?"

"Joe Singleton's, all right, as far as I know. I am going to try to see him in the week. The other one, the one with Veronica at the back of the group, is Brian Ellis. So far, I don't know anything about him. I'm hoping Singleton may be able to help."

She was still looking at him in the same way, those intelligent eyes seeing right into his soul. "Maybe whatever happened to Veronica has some bearing on this situation?"

Her gaze was unrelenting and he realised how much he had underestimated her. "I think something happened to her, while she was with them. An accident. I think they were responsible and have lived with the secret for almost thirty years."

"And now, it has come back to haunt them?"

He said quickly, "Possibly someone who loved her..."

"Is making them pay?" She nodded, grimly. "I can see why you would think that and indeed it is possible."

"But?"

"But you are not convinced?"

He sighed. "I don't know. The only person I can think of would feel strongly enough to carry out such a revenge would be her mother."

"If she is alive."

"She's alive. I'm going to see her tomorrow. She's living in Bournemouth, with a step-daughter. Apparently she's a semi invalid."

"Ah!" Mrs. Kershaw nodded gently. "Well then..."

"Exactly."

Danny got up and moved across to the rear window. Looking out at the garden, he sighed his frustration. "I feel so strongly about all of this but every time I feel I'm getting closer to finding something out, I end up being further away. My sister thinks I'm deluding myself. That the deaths are just what they seem to be, suicides and an accident."

"She could be right."

He was quiet for a moment, his thoughts elsewhere. At lkenght he said, "I was down by the river just now. At a place on Embankment that I knew, I mean really knew was the spot where my father went into the water."

"You mean you felt it? A memory? "

"Things seem to be coming back. Random scenes that I can't fit together."

"After so long?"

"There's no time limit on it according to the experts."

"And because you are here, in Putney. Now it starts?

"Down there, by the river. I was seeing everything that happened and then it just stopped."

"Perhaps you should stand back. Give the thing some space."

He shook his head, "I can't do that."

"Maybe that is all you can do. You believe that in some way what is happening here has something to do with your past. Running round chasing smoke will get you no where. Maybe all you can do is keep following events and let things return of their own accord?"

She stood up with some difficulty and shuffled through to the kitchen. Danny heard water running and a few seconds later, she returned.

"I'm sorry," he said. "I must be keeping you from your meal."

"Not at all. When my Maurice was here, we always dined in the evening, once he had returned from work."

"But on Sundays?"

She showed him a little smile, "Sunday is not so special to me. We were never religious and for my Maurice and I it would have been Saturday."

"Ah. Yes."

"Sitting for long periods makes my right leg stiffen up. When you are older, you'll have these little inconveniences to contend with. I get up, I walk about, maybe I go to the kitchen for a drink of water and it eases. The water ensures that I will have to get up again in a little while, to dispose of it."

She returned to her chair, sitting with a small wince. When she was comfortable, she eyed him sternly. "I have something to tell you. It is a matter I do not like to think about but under the circumstances..."

"Please don't feel obliged to - "

"No, no! You must know that this Veronica, she was not all that she seemed."

No, she wasn't, he thought and saw Berat following her through the trees.

"Oh, she was polite, that girl. Always with the smile, the quiet good morning. Butter in the mouth of that one would not melt." She shook her head, remembering. "So smart, she was, in the white blouse, the long white socks and polished shoes. Hair always neatly plaited."

"You saw the other side of her?"

"I saw! She was the Janus, with the two faces. I saw the true face, the one which she kept hidden."

She turned towards the window, as though seeing back over the years. "All this time I have tried to keep it out of my mind but it comes back. It will never leave me."

"What did she do?"

"It was a day in the Easter holidays. A windy day, beautiful blue sky, the occasional puff of white cloud. My Maurice had died of his heart in the winter, at work."

Her gaze transfered to one of the photographs on a nearby shelf, showing a lean faced man, smiling out at whoever cared to look at the picture, while those in the photos around him seemed disapproving. Mrs. Kershaw briefly shadowed his smile with a sad one of her own.

"A master tailor with a small firm in the East End, travelling back and forth everyday on the Underground, right across London. A craftsman, he was. Such hands! The finest work you could imagine. Bespoke suits to die for."

Outside the window it had started snowing again. In spite of the heat in the room, Danny felt a chill reaching his ankles and gave a small shiver.

"What does it matter now? The thing is, he died and I was still a state of mourning, staying in the flat mostly. On this particular day, I was sitting in my bedroom looking at the garden, thinking, remembering."

She raised a hand and pointed a crooked finger towards the window. "The garden is a communal one. For the residents to use. It runs right back to the boundary wall, as you can see. Bushes and trees, a small lawned area in the middle with benches, a bird bath, feeders. All overgrown now. Such a shame. Not then though."

She sighed, seeing the garden as it had been. Danny waited a moment, then said, "Was she out there?"

Mrs. Kershaw nodded her head, "She was out there. I didn't notice her at first but then she moved and I spotted her, kneeling down in the bushes, close to the back wall. At first I was not sure it was her, but then I recognised the new blue jeans, with those rolled turnups that girls wore then, very new and not suited for kneeling in the garden."

"What was she doing?"

"I asked myself the same thing, what could she be doing? She was working on something, bent over it, arms moving all the time. I could not imagine. She was there for a while, then, just as I was thinking of going out, she finished it and got to her feet. She stood there, looking down at the place for several seconds then, quite suddenly, she turned and stared back at my window."

"She saw you?"

Mrs. Kershaw shook her head, "I didn't think so at the time. I managed to slip back behind the curtain. I waited, hardly daring to breathe, which was silly because she couldn't have heard. When I was brave enough to peep out again, she had gone and a moment later, I heard a door bang at the rear of the building. I went to my front door and heard her going upstairs, her shoes clip clop, clip clop on the steps."

Danny felt a cold finger run up his spine, remembering what he had heard the day he had taken that turn back in Norwich and later, just outside Mrs. Kershaw's front door. Heels on concrete.

Rat-a-tat-tat!.

"When I was sure she had gone, I went to the garden to see what she had been up to. Being on the ground floor, I have a door in the kitchen which lets me directly onto the lawn. Just three little steps. No need to go through to the back of the building."

She paused, her face drawn and pale, the memory returning strongly was having an affect on her. What she had seen all that time ago was still difficult for her to deal with.

"I found the place where she had been, but there was nothing there. At least, that is what I thought at first. When I looked more closely...I saw it... a dead pigeon. Somehow she had caught it and killed it. More than killed it, she had systematically taken it apart, its wings, its legs. Wrung it's neck until the head had come away in her hands..."

"Christ," Danny murmured, thinking of what had been found in the Parish cemetary.

Mrs. Kershaw was watching him with pleading eyes. "I was sickened, so much so, my head felt light. I managed to get a hold of myself and turned around to come back inside. I looked up and saw her watching me from the window of their top floor flat. She was - smiling."

A hush descended on the room after she finished speaking, almost as heavy as the one that occupied the foyer. It drew out, long and uncomfortable until Danny said, "Tell me this. Do you think she was - dangerous?"

Mrs. Kershaw eyed him bleakly. "I think she was evil!"

He stared at her. Such an old fashioned word and yet here, it seemed to fit the situation perfectly. Her heard that same clock ticking ponderously off in the flat, time slipping away. Mrs. Kershaw sat back with a heavy sigh, as though sharing what she had, had somehow taken a toll on her.

"Can I get you something?" Danny asked.

"No, thank you. I'll be alright in a moment."

He waited a moment, until she seemed more settled then asked, "Did you say anything about this?"

She shook her head. "Afterwards, I found it difficult to face her and she knew it. She would give me her bright good mornings and her mother would smile beneficently but I used to see it there, behind the girl's eyes, she was laughing at me. I think I was a little scared of her."

A ripple of fear run through him too. He was suddenly back in the copse behind the fun fair and could actually smell the onions cooking in the hot dog stand, the sickly aroma of candy floss. She was, dressed in a summer frock, her hair in plaits, hanging down her back between he shoulder blades. A pretty girl, older than him in all sorts of ways, which had made him feel uncomfortable when she had leaned into him, when she had smiled.

"Now it's your turn."

"Mr. Stephens?"

He blinked, saw Mrs Kershaw looking at him. He managed a smile, told her he was fine, although he was far from feeling it.

"When you see the mother, do not repeat what I have told you. But always remember it."

"I shall." He didn't think he could forget it if he tried.

When he left, she walked him to the front door. The afternoon had settled into its long, slow slide towards evening. She had given him something to think about and in doing so, had taken a lot out of herself and he didn't want her to stand there watching him leave. He was about to say as much to her, when she took hold of his sleeve.

"Do not have the closed mind. I am old and have seen much of life, things most sane people would not believe.

Remember your Mr. Shakespeare; *There are more things in heaven and Earth, Horatio, than are dreamt of in your philosophy.* Science does not have all the answers to things that beset us. Most but not all. Very occasionally, the rational mind can endanger the unsuspecting."

He looked into her dark, unflinching eyes and knew that she meant every word she had said. For a moment his mouth worked soudlessly and he felt as though a weight had been lifted from him. Finally he nodded and watched her slowly close her front door. Did she know more than she was willing to tell him or could she see past his defences to the thoughts he was struggling to keep at bay?

Alone in the foyer, the heavy atmosphere closed in about him and he started towards the main doors, eager to get away from it. His hand had just closed upon the door handle when he was brought up sharply by the sound of a giggle.

After what he had just been told, the sound chilled him. He was gripped by a sudden sense of dread. His mouth was dry and his skin eruoted in a cold sweat. Holding his breath, he strained to hear more but there was only that all consuming silence.

More games?

It had to be that same child up to her old tricks. Nothing more, in spite of the thoughts trying to pierce his brain. To allow them recognition was a step closer to madness.

He made himself turn and look at the stairs, at the lift waiting its silent vigil. It was the same kid up there, it had to be. He would not let fantasy get hold of him, in spite of what Mrs. Kershaw had said. This time he had to prove the girl was flesh and blood.

No more games!

He walked smartly across the foyer to the foot of the stairs and stopped. He listened again and the silence pressed back at him like a solid thing, filling his ears, his mouth with smothering pressure. Then, as though on cue, he heard, drifting down from upstairs, that same familiar tune and the hairs on the back of his neck literally bristled.

"Prez' Prado."

'Cherry Pink and Apple Blossom White.'

"My Mum likes that".

His heart felt like it might burst. Who was she? How could she know that tune, released when he himself was just a child?

He laid his cheek against the mesh of the lift cage and peered up the shaft. She was up there somewhere and it was time for him to put a stop to her games. He would catch her this time, find out who she was, what she was playing at. Take her to see whoever was responsible for her.

Who had taught her that damned tune?

He climbed two steps and stopped, fear a worm in his brain. But he had to do it, he had no choice.

Take control of the situation!

Stiffly he lifted a leg and then the other, taking the steps two at a time as his muscles resisted, hauling himself on using the bannister until he reached the top of the second flight of stairs.

The singing had stopped. He stood on the landing until he was certain it wasn't going to start again and that thick, ominous silence closed in. If he didn't move now, he might give up altogether.

She know I'm coming.

A dull clonk from down below held him fast. A moment later, the lift car slipped quietly by, gracefully ascending the shaft.

"So that's it!"

He knew her game. Wait until he was almost up to her floor, then jump into the lift and descend, leaving him stranded, able only to watch helplessly as the car dropped through the shaft with her in it.

You could always let it go.

Turn right around now and walk away from this place.

Does it really matter who she is?

That was the easy option but he couldn't take it, not if he wanted to find some kind of peace of mind.

He grabbed the brass bannister rail again, forcing his protesting body up the stairs to the next floor and as he did, the lift car slipped past him, heading for the top of the shaft, cables running, clicking rhythmically as the counter weight descended like the blade on a lazy guillotine into the pit below.

He moved past flats numbers 5 and 6, one of them where the Major lived and wondered whether the old boy had his grandchildren over again. Maybe it was time to knock on his door, ask him what the bloody hell was going on. The fact was though, Danny didn't really believe the girl had anything to do with the Major.

So who?

He didn't want to think about that. Not then, maybe not even later. Certainly not until he could think about it in a logical, level headed way, because right now there were all sorts of wild notions trying to fill his head.

He went on climbing, with just the two flights to go, managing to cover the remaining stairs to emerge onto the top landing with his throat burning and a persistent ache just above his coxis.

Bitch!

Breathing hard, he slumped against the lift cage and waited until his head stopped spinning.

What was she up to?

The lift car was there, gate open, waiting for - who? He was the only person on that landing. Somehow the girl had vanished. He glanced at the landing window, the same window she had stood looking out of on the day he had tried to deliver Cockle's package.

She had not jumped into the car after all, so where the hell was she?

She had to be somewhere.

She couldn't have just vanished.

A feeling of unease rippled inside him. He stood upright and dragged in long, steady breaths until he was able to breathe normally again. The flats on either side of him, numbers 7 and 8, were empty. Had she managed somehow to get hold of a key to one of them? Was that all part of her game, to try and spook him enough to make him run away?

Veronica had lived up here. The thought hit him out of the blue and looked from one front door to the other, wondering which flat had been hers. After a moment, he moved to the door to number 8 and trying it, found it was locked tight.

This was the flat. It was the one of the pair that looked out over the rear garden. He squatted down and peered through the letterbox at an empty hall. The odd door or two open onto it. Nothing to see but dust motes drifting through grey, winter dusk.

Straightening up, he groaned softly, stretching his back muscles against the dull pain which sat above his right buttock. If she was a grandchild of the Major, maybe had a key to his flat, she could have nipped down a floor before he got there, slipped inside and was there now, enjoying his confusion.

He reconsidered going down a floor, banging on each door and if the old boy answered, asking him whether his grandchildren were staying.

And then what?

When the man quite naturally asked him, a stranger, what business it was of his what did he say? That he had chased a girl up the stairs and she had disappeared? The man would think he had a madman at his door or worse. There was no way he could do that.

He was sweaty and tired and aching. Worse, he couldn't stop suspicions of the impossible whispering in his ear.

Fucking nonsense!

He could afford to start giving credence to ideas like that.

Keeping this in the forefront of his mind, he stepped into the lift and closed the gates. With a last look at the landing, he thumbed the button for the ground floor and the lift car started its downward journey. He whould get back to the hotel, climb into a bath and then have a nap before thinking about an evening meal.

Chapter Twenty

Heels beating again, rhythmically, as ahead of him a nurse led the way through swiftly through a maze of desolate corridors. The walls were bare and there were abandones gurneies and shards of glass cluttering the way before them but in spite of this, he knew the place.

"This is Putney Hospital"

"It was," she answered cheerily. "Soon it will be demolished."

"I had my tonsils out here."

"Yes, but that was a long time ago. You were just a child."

She giggled and he felt a fist tighten inside him. He knew that giggle and tried to see her face but she was striding out ahead of him so that he couldn't get so much as a glimpse.

They entered a room, puddles on the floor and graffiti covered walls. A metal framed bed strewn with shabby covers, staff surrounding, masks pulled up so only their eyes showed. Furtive eyes, glee filled glances, the odd stifled tittter as Chrissie, giving birth.

"Soon be here," said a doctor and they all gazed down between her legs.

"Where have you been?" Chrissie looking at him, suspicious.

"Nowhere, " he said.

"Not this time," the nurse whispered in his ear.

And then Chrissie was screaming, pushing and relaxing, then pushing again, with him clutching her hand and the staff urging her on.

"It's a big one all right!" the nurse said, leaning in even closer.

And then it emerging from her in a bath of blood and mucus, a child of huge proportions, which opened it eyes and smiled at him with the sly cunning he remembered so well.

"Now you show her yours," said the nurse and started to laugh.

Danny woke with a grunt.

"Danny!"

He stared around him. Where was he? There was sunlight on his face, warm and welcome and there was movement.

"Danny? For God's sake!"

He remembered then that he was in Hilary's car and turning his head, saw her glance across at him. She looked back at the road, as he humphed, shoved himself up in his seat until his seat-belt would let him go no further.

"I must have dropped off."

"You were dreaming. Some sort of nightmare, it sounded like."

"Sorry."

Christ, in broad daylight!

He tried a laugh which sounded hollow. "Bad night."

"It must have been."

It had been a terrible night and he'd woken early, dull and unrested. He'd listened to the hushed world beyond the hotel room window and remembered how much he hated Mondays.

"At least you weren't snoring."

He wondered whether what he had dreamed held some hidden significance, a half remembered memory perhaps, which had turned to nightmare inspired by what he was involved in.

It had occured to him that the memory of the train set he'd mentioned to Murkin must have returned to him subliminally and had been with him for some little while. Only when he started to remember Berat had he realised that it was in his house that he had seen the layout, but it must have been there for a while for him to have told Murkin about it.

It dawned on him that it was the same with soldiers in Dad's outside cupboard. Yes he remembered them being there in a box in his bedroom but not of playing with them. He'd been into other things by then, things a lad of twelve or thirteen would be into. The soldiers had come with the family from London, so any memory he had of playing with them had to date from before the meningitis too.

Yawning, he looked out the car window at the passing scenery, motorway embankment speckled with patches of frozen snow. What else was lying in his mind waiting for something to introduce it to him?

"Where are we?"

"Just past Winchester. I'm pulling in at the next service station."

Good. He wanted to call Chrissie. He looked at his watch, 10:23, they had been on the road for well over an hour. He could do with some coffee and his bladder was uncomfortably full.

"I'm busting for a pee."

Hilary glanced over at him, "Thank's for sharing that."

Danny smiled, rubbed his face, made noises as he stretched. This morning, he had dressed in clean underwear, his decent trousers and a thick jumper, then had gone down to face a breakfast he'd had no appetite for. Now, as a blue sign saying Services jumped into his eyeline he still didn't feel hungry.

Indicating, Hilary turned the car onto the access road, following it through to the car park and slipped smoothly into one of the spaces near the main building.

"Jesus!" she said as she opened the car door and felt the cold wrap around her. "This sun has no warmth in it."

She was right, it felt colder than it had for days, even with the sun shining the way it was. He released his seat belt and climbed out of the car. He waited while she locked up and, flipping up the collar of his overcoat, fell in beside her, walking towards the entrance.

"Not really the weather for a trip to the coast," Danny said.

"We're not looking for sea and sand and a Mr. Whippy."

It was good to get inside the building, where the heaters soon got to work on their chilled bodies. Pausing in the foyer to get their bearings, Danny studied the big sign fixed to the opposite wall, right above the bank of sliding doors to the restaurant. The sign told them that the male toilets were to the right, female ones and the filling station shop were to the left.

"I need the loo, as well," she said. "I'll see you in the restaurant."

Danny found his way to the Gent's, relieved himself and then went to where a couple of phone booths stood at the edge of the main foyer. Stepping into the nearest one, he searched his trouser pockets for change and lifted the receiver.

He had spoken to Chrissie just a day ago but after his experience in Kavanagh Mansions, he needed to hear her voice, especially with the ghosts from what he had just dreamed haunting his consciousness.

He phoned Carol first, checking in rather than seeking solace. He told her where he was going and she'd told him to take care.

"When do you think you'll be back?"

"Not sure. Wednesday maybe, I want to see Singleton again, if I can."

"I'll call him and sort it out."

"Don't bother. I want to catch him cold."

She was doubtful but agreed to go along with him. After a few more words of caution, she wished him luck and hung up. He knew she still had her doubts but was glad she was making the effort and keeping her views to herself.

With Chrissie it was different. He'd tried last night from the hotel but she hadn't answered. Sunday night, she should have been home and he'd decided to try later, settling on top of the duvet to watch a TV sitcom that he hadn't found funny the first time round. When he had tried again, she still wasn't in.

This time, he didn't wait long. After two rings and no answer, he dialled the Council offices and got through to Planning. He was told that Chrissie had called in sick, so he rang the home number once more and waited. He imagined the phone ringing in the hall, on and on, not being answered and began to feel alarmed. Where could she be? There was so much stuff happening at the moment, stuff that might spill over and those he loved.

"Hello?"

"Where were you?"

"In the loo, if you must know," she said.

"How are you?"

"Okay. You?"

"All the better for hearing your voice."

"Where did you dig that line up from?"

"It's true!" He paused, then said, "I understand you're sick?"

"You phoned work?" she didn't sound pleased.

"I was worried. I tried to call you last night. Twice."

There was a pause, then, "I was out to dinner with Roger."

"Roger?" His hackles prickled slightly. "Do I know him?"

"He's from work. You met him at the Christmas dance the year before last. He works in Enviroment."

There was a tone to her voice that seemed to be daring him to ask more. He checked himself and managed to say, "Did you have a nice time?"

He remembered Roger now, a great bean pole of a man, with curly fair hair and thick framed glasses. He'd noticed the way he hung on every word Chrissie had spoken, eyes through the lenses like those of a doting puppy. If that bastard ever got the chance, he would make a move on her without doubt, a hesitant fumbled one maybe but a move all the same.

"Not really," she said. "His wife is screwing him into the ground over their divorce settlement and he needed a shoulder to cry on. It was a bit heavy actually."

"I bet," he said. "It was good of you to keep him company."

"Possibly," she sounded uncertain.

Here he was, worrying his guts out and she's been out with... He let it go, heard her relax and knew he had passed some test or other. He patted himself on the back for playing it smart for a change. If he'd let his jealousy take over, he might have blown his chances. Anyway, did he really have the right to get jealous, after how he had behaved in the past?

"Did you speak to that old woman?"

"Yes."

"Anything helpful?"

He thought of Veronica torturing the bird in the garden. "This and that."

She was quiet for a moment, detecting there was more on his mind but when he didn't volunteer anything, she said, "Stay safe. Say hello to Hilary for me."

Danny replaced the receiver and walked back to the restaurant thinking of Roger and his puppy dog eyes.

317

Hilary was at a table along to his left, beside one of the large windows. As he walked up, she said, "I got you a egg and cress sandwich."

He thanked her, although his appetite had dulled even more since the call home. He sat down and watched her tucking in to the Full English breakfast she had bought herself.

"You seem to have everything on your plate."

"No black pudding," she said around a corner of well done sausage. "I love a bit of black pudding."

The idea of eating congealed blood had never appealed to him. He opened his sandwich pack and took out the first half of his egg and cress. Biting a small mouthful, he drank some of the coffee she had brought him to wash it down.

"Tell me," he said after a moment. "Why are you so interested in all this?"

"I told you, I want a story."

"And you're sure that there's one here?"

"Aren't you?" She cut into her bacon and forked some into her mouth. She wiped her lips on a paper serviette and smiled. "I've been a journalist for a long while. You get to pick up on things that sound - off. I got that itchy feeling in my gut when Carol told me about her mystery client."

"Simple as that?"

"I've learned to trust my gut over the years."

Danny nodded, "Me too."

"It's about time you told me what's going on," she said. "From your point of view."

They had made a deal and she had come across with her part of it. "Okay. But it's mostly a story of returning memories and guess work."

He took her though it from the beginning, from finding Cockle to what he had learned from Mrs. Kershaw. He told her about Murkin's death and his own growing conviction that somehow, the whole thing revolved around the disappearance of Veronica.

"You saw Cockle?"

He nodded, waited for her to comment and when she didn't, he picked up his bag and took out the photo Carol had given him. "There was a copy of this in Cockle's package."

She took it, looked at the group of children then glanced at the back. "The Rudd Street Tykes." she said. The policeman is -"

"My father," he confirmed. "Sarah Eadel had already received a copy and there was one in Murkin's folder." He leaned across and touched the photo with the tip of a finger, moving it from face to face. "Cockle, Sarah, Murkin and Joe Singleton."

She looked at him. "And these two kids with the blurred faces?"

"Brian and that's Veronica."

"Our Veronica?"

He nodded.

"And you?"

"I wasn't part of the gang. I think I knew them, mixed with them off and on." He bit off a second piece of sandwich and started chewing. The bread was a little dry but he'd had worse. "I'm beginning to remember things. Not much at the moment, just bits. I'm trying to put the memories together and not very successfully. I'm feeling my way through my own early life.."

"That must be weird?"

"Weird is one way to describe it."

"You might have been the one behind the camera."

"Who knows? It's possible, I guess."

"Do you believe Mrs. Hayden has something to do with what's going on?"

"I was toying with the idea until you told me about her health."

Hilary popped some more sausage into her mouth to keep the bacon company and cut a corner from the fried slice.

"Someone followed me home the other day, on the train. At first, I thought it could have been her."

She watched him as she ate her food. Danny looked away, finding himself back in that carriage, facing whatever was at the other end.

"So, who was it?"

"It was - ill defined," he said quietly. "The lights in the carriage went out and the daylight was fading..."

"Perhaps you ought to have gone down there."

"There was a figure, which looked a bit..." he felt a shadow fall over him and shuddered. Then he came back to the present and looked into her sharp, blue eyes. "I know I should have done."

And he knew why he hadn't done it. He'd been afraid, more than that, terrified. In that second, he had been sure he was looking at something that could not be and the fear of that had held been primeval.

"Well, it's done now," she said quietly.

"Yes."

"But someone did follow you?"

"I told you!" he snapped.

Could he have been mistaken, fooled by the poor lighting? Worse, had he imagined the whole thing? He hadn't seen anybody after he left the train. He pushed the sandwich aside and reached for his coffee.

"I called in a favour," Hilary said, dragging the last piece of hash brown through the yoke from her second egg. She popped it into her mouth and ate it. "I have a contact in the Met. I know that the police are more or less satisfied that Cockle killed himself. Okay, there's still the inquest but the coroner would be guided by what the police believe. So if you're thinking murder..."

"I'm not," he said. "At least..."

"What?"

"What would have made them kill themselves so close together and don't say coincidence."

"I don't know." She searched in her bag for her cigarettes and brought out a pack of Gauloise. "If you're right, that they had some kind of pact... I don't know."

"I can't see it myself."

"The collective guilt angle makes sense, if you're right about what happened to Veronica."

"Something really frightened Cockle just before he died. I saw his face. He was terrified. I mean really gone."

"Can you think of anything that might scare someone enough to slit their throat?"

Same question, same answer and yet...

He said he couldn't but that same idea hovered at the edges of his mind. But how could he accept? To do so would mean going against everything he was sure about in life. Death was part of life, as real as being born. When you were done, you were done and to start giving creedence to anything else would probably get him certified.

Hilary pushed her empty plate aside. She took a drink of coffee and a long drag from her cigarette.

"These are disgusting things," she said, making a face. But once you've smoked them in Paris for long enough, you can't give them up."

Danny nodded and dragged in what second hand smoke he could capture.

"Do you want one?"

"I gave up," he said. "I like a little hit from other people's now and then."

She grinned and wafted some of her smoke in his direction. The moment passed and she stopped smiling.

"Have you told me everything?"

"How do you mean?"

"You seem edgey."

He'd just found out that his wife had had a date with a man who obviously fancied her, so edgey? Of course he was fucking edgey, especially when he thought how Roger would take their seperation as a green light to make his move.

"Is it domestic?"

"I don't want to talk about it."

"Fair enough," she blew smoke at the ceiling. "I've had enough of that to last me a lifetime."

"You're married?"

"Was. Is that so unlikely?"

"No. It's none of my business anyway."

She tapped ash into the aluminium ashtray on the table. "I was married. To a fellow journalist, which was a bad idea from the start. We were always breaking up, then getting back together again. It went on for years."

"Until you'd had enough?"

"Until he died."

"Ah."

"Funny, I haven't thought about him for a long time."

"How did he..?"

"Pancreatic cancer. He was forty-two. I suppose it was on the cards for someone who propped up the bar in the, 'Cheshire Cheese' as often as he did. Still, we had our moments."

"Good," he said and meant it.

The end of her cigarette glowed as she took another deep drag from it, blowing a plume of smoke above their heads. "So is there?"

"What?"

"Stuff that you're not telling me?"

"I don't think it has anything to do with this."

"But you're not sure?"

"For years, I believed my father died trying to save a woman from the river. Now I know it was a child he went in to get."

"Which makes him even more of a hero, right?"

"Yes, of course. But why should my mum and the Old Man lie to me about it? Dad told Carol that the shock of seeing him drown brought on the meningitis, which in turn screwed my memory. I don't know if that's possible but that is what the old sod is claiming and I just have this great ball of doubt lodged in my craw."

She said quietly. "You were there?"

He nodded, "I saw it...some of it. Then the shutters came down. I have no idea whether shock can do that, make you more susceptible to catching the virus. Maybe it was just coincidence it came when it did."

"And now the memories have started to come back."

He looked at his hands, then up at her. "Trouble is, I don't know what's real and what isn't. Can I be confident the things I'm remembering are really memories and not figments of my imagination? To be honest, I don't know where the hell I am anymore."

Hilary gazed at him for a moment, drained her cup and stood up. Stabbing out her cigarette in the ashtray, she gathered her things together. "Let's move. The sooner we get there, the better."

When they were in the car, she drove over to the filling station and filled up at the nearest pump. Watching her through the wind-screen, Danny decided that perhaps he had chosen well after all. The difference between the woman he'd met at Carol's luncheon and the woman out there was tremendous. He had written her off as a boozy, cynical journalist but he now saw a smart, resourceful woman who he was sure would see things through to the end.

Hilary retuned to the car, slipping in under the wheel and fastening her seat belt.

"Can I give you anything towards the petrol?" he asked, as she started the engine.

"Expense account," she said.

"Me too," he told her and smiled grimly.

Traffic was light and she soon had them back on the motorway, heading south. For a while they drove in silence, although Danny could feel questions in the air. Finally, when they had put a few miles behind them, Hilary glanced across at him.

"What were you dreaming about earlier."

"It was just a dream." He didn't want to rake all that up again.

"You said nightmare."

"Okay, a nightmare." He sighed, "There's stuff behind it. It's a long story."

"We have nothing but time."

He turned to the window, thinking about the derelict hospital, Chrissie giving birth to a monster. He knew where that came from and wasn't going to share any of it with her. The thing she had delivered though, lying there between her thighs was - was...

It had had Veronica's eyes and Veronica's smile!

After a while, he said, "On my first day at Kavanagh Mansions, I saw a girl watching me from the top floor landing window."

"And?"

"And then she wasn't. Gone, just like that. I didn't think anything of it at first but later..."

"Is that what you dreamed about?"

"Forget the dream. This is more relevent."

He told her about leaving the building after finding Cockle, how he'd heard shoes on one of the floors above.

"And that stuck with you? How old was the girl? A child or older, a teenager?"

"I don't know. Early teens, possibly."

She looked across at him. "What are you getting at?"

"Nothing. I'd just had a shock and was pretty spooked. The expression on Cockle's face... I don't know, it all felt...wrong somehow."

"It made you feel uneasy?"

"I guess so." He shot her a glance, "You weren't there. You didn't feel. That place has this atmosphere that..."

"And you"d seen Cockle's body, his face."

"That's right."

"You went into the flat?"

"The door was open.... He was sitting there, in the kitchen." He swallowed dryly. "His head was hanging off and that expression..."

He watched a big old Volvo edging past them in the middle lane, an old man clutching the wheel, white hair, hooked nose, eyes locked on the road ahead like there was no tomorrow.

"Then you heard the girl giggle," Hilary prompted.

"It was like she knew what I'd seen."

"How could she?"

"She giggled, like she was playing some game with me, hide and seek, the sort of thing kids do sometimes."

Danny shook his head and looked out of his window at the passing countryside.

"Well?"

He'd told her about seeing Mrs. Kershaw the day before but not in detail. He sighed heavily and said, "Mrs. Kershaw, the old woman who lives in Flat 2, she told me something about Veronica, something pretty horrible."

He repeated the story.

"No angel, then."

He took a deep breath, then blurted out, "I think she killed the boy, Berat. I believe I knew him."

Hilary snapped her indicator arm down and pulled into an upcoming lay-by. When she had the brake on, she killed the engine and looked at Danny with a hard, almost angry eyes.

"I want to hear it all."

So he told her, all the 'memories' he'd had, the scene with Jolly Jack and later, at the fair, the coconut shy. The copse behind the fair.

"Your turn at what?"

He felt uncomfortable but told her anyway.

"What happened then?"

"I ran off, back to the fair and when I looked round, that's when I saw them. Berat following her through the copse."

Hilary thought for a moment, running it over in her head. Finally she spoke and her voice sounded tight. "You really think she did that to the boy?"

"I've looked into her eyes. I know it."

Hilary took her cigarettes from her bag and used a small silver lighter to start one. Opening her window, she blew a stream of smoke into the air.

"Mrs. Kershaw thinks she was evil." Danny looked out at the embankment to one side of the car. The sun was bright but all he felt was the familiar creeping chill flooding his insides.

"And you?"

He didn't comment. The thought he'd kept at bay, that wild and ridiculous notion came at him stronger than before and this time, he found he was inclined to give it some consideration.

"We had better get moving," Hilary said quietly. She took a last long drag from her cigarette, then crushed it into the already full ashtray in the dash. "I said we'd be there by early afternoon."

She had been given directions by the step-daughter. so once they reached Bournemouth, she found the house with relative ease and parked across the street. Danny took stock of the area, a quiet, affluent one on the edge of town, mostly detached houses of various styles and ages. The one they were visiting was old, possibly Georgian, surrounded by a high wall backed by a screen of old trees, many of them leafless now. A couple of evergreen firs either side of the main gate stood out like good teeth in an otherwise corrupted mouth.

Lying back at the end of a long, flagstone path, the house had that olde worlde look that you saw in those 1930s American films of British classic literature, Dickens or Austen, with a young Laurence Olivier's, Darcy paying a visit to Greer Garson's, Elisabeth Bennett.

"Ready?" Hilary said.

They got out of the car and crossed the road. He eyed the growth clinging to the front of the house. "How did you manage to find her so quickly?"

"Pure luck" She opened the gate and let him through in front of her. "A friend on the paper, our movie reviewer, a true anorak who could bore for England on the subject of British Cinema, happened to see my notes. He recognised the name, Ellen Hayden and asked if she was the same woman who had married, Dick Lewis, a veteran lighting man."

"Never heard of him."

"Don't worry about it. Other than movie buffs, I shouldn't think anybody has. Lewis is dead now but Colin, that's our reviewer, knew that his widow went to live with her step-daughter in Bournemouth."

"Easy as that?"

"Not really, there was a lot of digging to do afterwards but eventually, I found her. And I got a meal out of it." Hilary smiled, blushing slightly, "We're sort of a part time number, you know? Anyway, it was his turn to buy."

"Does he know about Veronica?"

"He remembered the woman when Lewis married her. Lewis was a widower with a daughter of his own, so Ellen inherited another daughter."

"I wonder how Veronica would have felt about that?" Danny said.

The flagged path led right up to a huge stone step at the front door, worn by the passage of many feet over the ages. The garden they passed through to reach it seemed well tended but was looking sorry for itself under its thin winter coat. Stretches of frozen snow spread across the lawn and plants that edged the path, all were shut down and limp.

The door bell, an old fashioned pull type with a metal handle on a shaft, was mounted on the wall beside the heavy front door. The shaft went through the wall to connect to a mechanism on the inside, which eventually rang the bell.

"Do you thinks that's original?" Danny asked.

Hilary grunted, pushed him aside and gave the handle two sharp tugs. They heard the ringing deep within the house and shortly afterwards, the door was opened by a tall woman in her early forties. She regarded them, smiling and said to Hilary, "I'm Paula, we spoke on the phone."

Hilary shook her hand. "This is Danny Stephens, my assistant. I told you about him."

"Hello," he said as she reached for his hand.

He felt a vague sense of recognition and spent a few seconds trying to understand why. They had never met before, yet he felt sure there was something familiar about her. If the feeling was mutual, Paula Lewis didn't let on.

"Please, come in," she stood aside, so that they could step into a high, cool hallway. "You must be in need of tea after your journey?"

She showed them into a pleasant drawing room, large, with an impressive bay window overlooking the front garden. She asked them to make themselves comfortable.

"I have just made some fresh," she said, smiling. "It won't take a moment to fetch it through."

"Is your stepmother up to seeing us?"

"She's looking forward to it," Paula said. "She enjoys talking about Veronica, even though it's still painful for her. Excuse me."

"I know her," Hilary said when they were alone. "I can't think where from."

"I felt the same. She must have one of those faces."

"She doesn't seem to feel the same way about us."

"Well look at us. Do you wonder?"

"Speak for yourself," Hilary said.

There was a fire burning in the large fireplace, to supplement the central heating. Hilary stopped in front of it, looking at three framed photographs on the mantle shelf.

"Look at this."

Danny went over to join her, saw she was looking at a head and shoulders portrait of a girl in school uniform. She girl looked nothing but the model student in her blazer and tie, with her hair brushed until in shone.

"Veronica?"

Danny nodded, a feeling unease perking up inside him.

"Pretty girl," Hilary said.

He took in the perfect smile she was offering the camera and thought about Mrs. Kershaw's comments.

"All that glisters,"

He'd seen for himself how that smile could change. Just looking into the photographed eyes deepened his unease. He moved along to look at another photograph, a smiling couple standing on Westminster Bridge, Big Ben clock tower in the background.

"Who do you think these two are?" he asked. Not that it mattered, he just wanted something other then Veronica's sweet face to think about.

"Who knows?"

The last photo was of a man in his early sixties, a face with the wrinkled, weathered look of a walnut. His eyes were smiling too but with him, all they exuded was kindness. "I guess this is the film guy, Lewis?"

Paula returned then, pushing an ornate metal tea trolley before her, bearing cups, saucers, a plate of biscuits and a large, covered teapot. She steered it into the area created by the sofa and armchairs grouped around the fire.

"Is this your dad?" Hilary asked.

Paula smiled. "That was taken on the set of a film called, 'Charley Bubbles'. Back in the sixties."

"He looks a nice man," Danny said.

"It's there, isn't it, in that face? He died coming on seven years ago. He went out with the autumn."

They sat down, watching Paula arrange the cups and saucers on a coffee table in the centre of a large, circular fire rug, close enough for them each to reach from their chairs. Hilary glanced up at the mantle shelf. "And the other photo, the one in the middle, is Veronica?"

"Yes." Paula stood upright, the smile tightening slightly on her mouth. "That's my step-sister."

Hilary caught Danny's eye, saw that he had spotted the change too. "She'd be older than you?"

"By a year or two."

"You think she's dead?" Danny said.

Paula blinked, looked at him in surprise. "Well, yes. Doesn't everyone? It seems most likely and if not, where has she been all these years?"

"What do you think happened to her?" Hilary asked

Paula finished preparing the tea things. "I don't think about it. It's too depressing to dwell on. Now, I'll go and see if Ellen is ready to join us."

"Seems a bit chilly on the subject of her step-sister," Hilary said after Paula had left.

"I know how she feels."

Hilary grinned at him, "You don't really feel like that."

"Mostly not," he conceeded. "But don't tell Carol."

She nodded towards the photograph, "Must be hard, living with a ghost."

"Ever present," Danny reflected. "I can see that."

Hilary said, "I think it's more than that though."

Danny looked at her, waiting for her to expand.

"It was more like she knows something about her, something she doesn't like."

The door opened then and Paula returned, pushing a wheelchair ahead of her. Mrs. Hayden, staring searchingly ahead of her, was already smiling in anticipation.

"Hello! Hello," she said, gazing just a little to the right of Danny's left shoulder. "How do you do? Welcome to our home."

Even sitting in the chair, Danny could see that she was a tall lady and lean to within an inch of emaciated. She sat clutching the arms of the chair with skeletal hands, fingers wrapped around the arms tipped with long, yellowing nails. Her head was thrust forward, her lean face with its chiselled features, pointing from one to the other of them, as though trying to fix their position with her clouded eyes.

"Where shall I park you, Ellen?" Paula asked.

"That end of the sofa, please my dear, close to the fire." She added in their direction. "I feel the cold so badly."

Paula manoeuvred the chair into position between the sofa and the fire place and the old woman smiled absently at the flames. "I can more or less see them but more importantly, I can feel their warmth."

Paula proceeded to pour the tea and Danny saw Hilary regarding her closely.

"Ask her," he said.

Paula looked at him, then at Hilary, who blushed slightly. Mrs. Hayden looked around, without knowing what was happening.

"It's just, I am sure I have seen you before," Hilary said.

Paula smiled, "Perhaps you have heard of my books."

"Books?"

Mrs. Hayden beamed proudly, "She is quite a famous author."

"I write children's books," Paula said, blushing herself now. "I'm not at all famous."

"Paula Heffingham!" Hilary beamed, "My niece loves your stories. I usually end up reading one to her when I visit."

"That's one mystery solved," Danny said. He had never heard of Paula Heffingham but he must have seen her photograph some place because she did look familiar.

There was a short hiatus while they drank some tea, then Mrs. Hayden said. "I understand from Paula you are interested in my daughter's disappearance?"

"Yes," Hilary said.

"Is there any special reason?" The old woman gazed directly at Hilary, "You're a journalist, I believe?"

"That's right."

Danny saw her eyes move across to him and he wondered just how blind she really was. He realised then that for some reason, he didn't like Ellen Hayden. There was something avaricious about her that made him uncomfortable. She had been watching Hilary almost ravenously.

Hilary told her the paper she worked for. "I have a regular column in the Sunday supplement."

"There are so many of those these days."

"Sorry?"

"Magazines, supplements, God knows what else. The Sunday newspapers are getting so thick with extras. Most of it doesn't get looked at." She smiled thinly in Paula's direction. "You read the paper to me every weekend, don't you dear but we never finish it. It's generally used for the fire with most of the contents unread."

"Well," Hilary said smiling, "That puts me in my place."

"I expect your pieces are popular. It's just time, you see. There's not enough of it in the day." A meaningless smile hovered on the old woman's mouth. "You write about crime, I believe?"

"Not exclusively. I usually aim for six of those cases a year," Hilary told her. "So far, I have finished two and have a third ready to go. I would like to make the fourth about Veronica and was hoping it would be with your blessing."

"I always like people asking about Veronica. It means that she is not forgotten."

"Would you like your tea, Ellen?" Paula asked, lifting the woman's cup from the tray and moving it to a small table, closer to the wheelchair. She told the old woman what she had done and pointed a finger at the cup.

"Yes, yes, my dear. I can find it." Mrs. Hayden turned her face back to Hilary. "Do you think your article might re-ignite interest in the case, or is it just for - entertainment?"

"Never that," Hilary said. "My pieces certainly aren't meant to entertain. Interest people, yes and there's always hope that reading the piece might stir someone's memory."

"After so long?" Paula asked.

"It's a long shot, I admit. But it has happened in the past, a television programme perhaps or a book. Cold cases seem to fascinate a lot of people."

"As I said," Mrs. Hayden repeated. "I am pleased to talk about my daughter. Of course, for a long while after it happened I felt differently. I didn't think I would ever get past the raw grief I felt."

"I can't even imagine what that must have been like."

The woman favoured Hilary with another vague smile. "As the years have slipped away, I find remembering her a comfort. I am still hopeful that before I die, I shall learn what happened to her."

Hilary glanced at Paula, who looked away.

"Well obviously I can't promise anything," she said. "Re-examaning things may bring something new to light."

Danny asked, "Did Veronica have many friends?"

Mrs. Hayden looked his way, as though she had forgotten he was there. "Are you a journalist too?"

"He's my researcher," Hilary said. "I rely a lot on his input."

Mrs. Hayden nodded. "Veronica wasn't a great mixer. She used to enjoy her own company. Went for long walks alone, at least as far as I know. I'm sure she would have told me if anyone went with her."

"You were close?"

"She told me everything, as a good daughter should. She used to say that I was the only friend she needed."

Danny's mouth tightened and saw Paula glance at him, Their eyes met for a second and he saw the trace of a tight smile cross her mouth. She said, "What about those photographs, Ellen?"

The old woman turned her face towards her and she didn't look pleased at all. "My daughter had several hobbies. Photography was just one of them. She liked to read and was always at the local library. And drawing. She would sit by the river for hours or in the local park with her sketch pad. She would be at it again in the evenings. Polishing up, she called it. Working on the sketches she'd done that day. I still have some of her work."

"Would you like me to fetch them?" Paula asked.

"Thank you, dear. That is if our guests are interested?"

Danny and Hilary said they would love to see them and Paula went off to find them. Before she left the room, Danny called after her. "You might fetch any photos too."

She cast a glance at Ellen Hayden but nodded ayway.

"As for children," Mrs. Hayden said, her brow creased. "I believe she met some from the other end of town from time to time. Acquaintences more than friends."

"I see," Hilary said.

"She would have avoided the more common ones, of course but I believe she sometimes played with those she believed suitable."

Danny thought of the scene behind the fair and clenched his jaw.

"She must have known her fellow classmates from school ?" said Hilary.

"She did not attend any of the local schools." The old woman had a way of staring with her cloudy eyes, that Danny found disconcerting. "Veronica was a very bright girl. She attended the Gilden School for girls in Kingston-Upon-Thames. It's a grammar school and very highly thought of. At least, it was then."

"It still is," said Hilary. "Someone on the paper has a daughter there."

"Well, there you are. I'm more than a little confident that, had she been allowed, she would have ended up at Oxford or Cambridge."

Mrs. Hayden's face creased into a self satisfied smile. Watching her, Danny wondered whether she was as delusional about the girl as she made out. Could Veronica have really pulled the wool so firmly over her eyes, that she was totally oblivious of her daughter's true nature? There was something about that tight face, with its mean, narrow features that made him think she knew much more than she was letting on about the girl.

"Can you tell us about the day it happened?" Hilary asked.

"It was during the school summer holidays in 1955. I remember it had been very hot for several days, unusually so for England. Veronica had been in her room all morning, playing records and reading, that awful Russian novel, 'Crime and Punishment."

"She enjoyed the classics?"

"She took them out from the library. Although that one was not the sort of thing I was happy with her reading. She was almost fourteen and very advanced for her years."

Mrs. Hayden reached out a hand and carefully patted the air around the table until she found her cup and saucer. Lifting them, she drank from the cup, then went through the routine once more in order to replace them on the table.

"I had kept her in at the end of June. It wasn't often I had to discipline her but this time... I had given her permission to go to the fun fair on Putney Common, as long as she was home by nine o'clock. She didn't return until much later, which was unlike her. She would not say what had delayed her and so, as a punishment, I forbade her from going out for a week, even to the library. I believe it is referred to as being grounded these days."

"Yes," Hilary said.

"The frightening thing was, a young boy, who disappeared while visiting that same fun fair, was found murdered just a day or so later. Oh, I was really afraid when I heard the news and was determined to keep my girl in for even longer."

"I read about that," Hilary said. "He was murdered rather brutally."

"I believe so."

"The killer must have been covered in blood," Danny said.

"No doubt, no doubt," the woman said coldly. Turning towards Hilary, she went on, "Of course, I was frightened to let my child out, as any decent parent would be. But you cannot keep young people shut up indefinitely, especially when the weather is as fine as it was then. Veronica became a little tired of staying in, fractious and somewhat rude, which was also unlike her."

"So you relented," Danny said.

"Indeed, I did," the old woman said thickly. "Too my everlasting regret."

"You think there may have been a connection between the boy's abduction and Veronica going missing?" Hilary asked.

"I put it to the police but they didn't seem to give it much creedence."

Perhaps they had other suspicions, Danny thought.

"You can't blame yourself," he said.

She told Hilary. "It's still the hardest fact for me to deal with. If I had insisted on her staying in, if I had not relented..."

Her words tailed off and she stared into her own well of misery until Paula returned, breaking the silence. She was carrying a few sheets of cartridge paper, four or five large, off white sheets and an old chocolate box.

"Thank you, my dear," Mrs. Hayden said, gesturing vaguely towards the sofa. "Just lay them on there. Our guests can look at them as they choose."

Danny chose to do so at once. Getting up and moving across to the sofa, he spread the sheets out. There were four in all and seeing them, he realised that Veronica had been quite a talented girl. There was a drawing of the Thames done in charcoal, obviously drawn from the Embankment at low tide, with the river at rest and a tug boat, heading towards Putney Bridge towing half a dozen wide, flat barges.

"That is very good," Hilary said, looking over Danny's shoulder.

The other three had been drawn in a park, a couple playing tennis on a hard court, a childs play area, swings, roundabout and slide. A group of children were gathered around a see-saw, a boy sitting at one end and a girl at the other, suspended in the air, while the rest of the group milled about.

The Tykes!

Danny counted the kids, three boys standing, the boy and girl sitting on the see-saw making five. Any of them might be the children in the photograph.

"Who's that?" Hilary asked.

Danny had turned to the last drawing, which was of the head and shoulders of a boy of around the ten or eleven mark. He had a head of dark hair, which hung down over his forehead and he was looking off to one side, his mouth almost smiling.

"Is there no name?" Paula asked.

There wasn't but Danny was looking at the the girl on the grounded end of the see-saw, who wore a shirt like a character from a western movie and had a cowboy hat on her head. It was Sarah, he was sure of it.

"Are you looking at the boy?" Mrs. Hayden said.

"Do you know who he was?" Paula asked.

With that same tight smile, the old woman shook her head. "I remember having a joke with Veronica over the drawing. I suggested she might have a sweetheart."

"What did she say to that?" Danny asked.

"Denied it, vehemently and went to her room."

There was a pause, silence descended on them in which Danny felt he could almost hear time slipping away. This silence was different though from the one in the foyer of Kavanagh Mansions. This one was full of human emotions, the other had been full of menace.

"Are these the photographs?" he asked, lifting the chocolate box.

"Yes," Paula said, ignoring the look her step mother gave her. She took the box from him and removed the lid, showing him a few black and white photos of the type he'd seen so many of recently.

Danny took them out and spread them next to the drawings on the sofa. His hand stalled on the last one, which was the same as the one Carol had found at Dad's, with The Tykes and jack in the street. Was this and not the other one the original?

"Are these children some of her friends?"

"Possibly?" Paula glanced at Mrs. Hayden

"Is it the one with the policeman?"

Paula nodded.

"She knew them, yes."

Danny asked, "Did she take the photograph?"

"It was her camera of course but a friend of the policeman took it, I believe." Mrs. Hayden smiled in the direction of the sofa, "That's Veronica at the end, where the figures are blurred. Apparently the boy teased her just as the shutter went."

"The boy in the drawing?" Danny asked.

"I couldn't say."

Danny looked from the photo to the drawing and back again. Was he seeing his first glimpse of Brian's face?

The other photos were nothing special, at least as far as they were concerned and Danny skipped through them until the last but one, which showed the Tykes at the fair. The gang were crowding one of the boys and all that could be seen of him was a raised arm and a hand clutching a coconut.

"They were taken that last summer," Mrs Hayden said sadly. "It was a week before the schools started back for the new term. She went out and I never saw her again."

The old woman pushed her face forward definatly and Danny saw a trace of moisture on her cheeks. When she realised he was looking at her, she wiped it away with a swipe of her hand.

"The police were around for weeks, weren't they, Ellen?" said Paula.

"Yes," her voice was suddenlky hushed, defeated and she sank down into her chair. "They questioned the local children, those in the photos but they claimed they knew nothing."

"Do you think they might have?" Danny asked.

"Who knows with children like that. It wouldn't surprise me if they knew more then they owned up to."

Hilary said, "Surely they would have done all they could to help the police?"

"You think so? Well, possibly."

The police searched everywhere," Paula said. "The commons, Putney and Wimbledon, everywhere local."

"There was a nationwide search," Ellen Hayden said, wearily. "For all the good it did."

"Police boats searched the river, from Putney down to Greenwich and beyond," Paula continued. "Weeks ran into months and they kept at it, certain they would find something that would lead to her."

"But they didn't," Mrs. Hayden said.

Paula went to her, touched her shoulder, offering comfort but the old woman shrugged her off.

"No one reported having seen anything. It was as though she had simply vanished into thin air. As the weeks past. the excitement died down, the newspapers lost interest. Eventually, the trail went cold, as much of a trail as there was. Veronica faded from the public's awareness."

The old woman was gazing into the fire now, her claw-like hands locked together in her lap. Danny glanced at Hilary, who avoided his eyes. No one wanted to acknowledge the weight of despair that had descended upon the room.

"The police eventually told me they were winding the investigation down. They couldn't keep pouring resources into something which was not yielding results."

"The case has never been have closed, though," Paula said to her.

"As if that matters!" She snapped.

Hilary said, "It is possible we might turn up something new. I admit, chances are slim but you never know."

"There are those who know and there are those who know they know." the old woman said harshly. "One day, what they know will come back to haunt them."

"How do you mean?" Danny asked.

But she sat as though she hadn't heard him, her clouded eyes fixed on the crackling flames.

"What happened to Veronica's father?" Hilary asked quiety.

Mrs. Hayden continued to stare into the fire as seconds ticked by. Hilary glanced over at Danny, wondering whether she should ask again.

"My husband disappeared in Berlin in 1946," Mrs. hayden said at last. "He had been posted there by the

War Office, part of a covert operations unit keeping tabs on the Russians."

"An agent?"

She turned her head slowly in Danny's direction, a slim, humourless smile on her mouth. "An agent. As was I. In my case, at home, mostly working in Whitehall. Of course, I'd had to undergo basic training, which was where we met, in deepest Sussex. We became friends, then lovers and eventually, with all the necessary agreements in place, we were married."

Paula reached for the old woman's cup but Mrs. Hayden waved her away, adjusted herself in her chair.

"After the war, Berlin was divided into four sectors, British, French, the Americans and the Soviets. Both the Americans and our government suspected our erstwhile allies would try to take over the whole of the city, as they had that part of Germany. Berlin was an island in a hostile sea.

"Simon, that was his name, and two other agents were sent there to mount a joint mission with the American OSS. They were to monitor things at first hand."

"OSS?" Hilary asked.

"Office of Strategic Services," Danny told her. "It later became the CIA."

"And he went missing?" Hilary asked.

"Him and the two Americans. The OSS had a contact in the Eastern sector and had put together the small group. Something went wrong, a leak of some kind and they were caught. Weeks later, the body of one of the Americans was discovered deep in the Western sector but the other one and Simon were never found."

"So Veronica didn't know her father?"

"Only as much as a five year old can know a person she had rarely seen. To this day, I don't know what happened, just that the assignment was considered vital to allied interests but was abandoned afterwards. I officially became his widow seven years later, soon after we had moved into Kavanagh Mansions."

It was quiet for a moment until Danny said, "Talking of Kavanagh Mansions, I met an old neighbour of yours recently."

Mrs. Hayden looked towards him expectantly. "I'm surprised there's anyone there who remembers us."

"Mrs Kershaw in Flat 2."

The woman's face turned stoney. "She's still there!?"

"For a while longer. She remembers you well.""

"I expect she does, the way I dealt with her." Ellen Hayden's tone was sharp enough to cut skin. "She once tried to tell me that my beautiful daughter, my loving little girl had done something abominable, in the garden." She shuddered, "As though one such as she would even contemplate committing so vile an act."

The animosity in her responce had taken him aback and he remembered Mrs. Kershaw's words of caution. He opened his mouth, saw the warning glance Hilary flashed him and closed it again. The old woman was trembling with emotion and Paula moved quickly to her side.

"All right, Ellen. I think you've had enough now. You had better go and rest.

Ellen Hayden allowed herself to be wheeled away across the room. She held her head up proudly and never so much as glanced their way. When they were alone, Hilary turned to Danny.

"That business in the garden...?"

"She believed it all right," Danny said.

Paula returned, "I'm sorry about that."

"I'm the one who should be sorry," Danny said. "I didn't realise that mentioning Mrs. Kershaw would upset her so much."

"It wasn't just that. She's not as over things as she pretends to be."

"Perhaps we shouldn't have come," Hilary said.

"She insisted. Part of her thinks there is still a chance..."

"That someone will remember something?"

"I suppose I should discourage her but I don't have the heart."

"No. Neither would I have."

They left soon after, Paula showing them out. "It's seems to have grown colder."

"More snow on the way." Hilary said, looking at the sky, which was clouding over. "It was such a lovely morning."

"I'm sorry you came all this way for so little."

Hilary shook her hand. "I wouldn't say that. We wanted to hear the story from Mrs. Hayden and we did."

They stood looking out across the garden for a moment, until a breath of cold wind plucked at their collars. Hilary turned to Paula and said carefully.

"Don't mind me saying but, Mrs. Hayden seems to be a bit..."

"Overbearing?" Paula gave a tired smile. "Mostly, she's fine. It's just at times, things get...too much for her."

Danny, thinking of Dad, said, "It can get a bit trying, all the same."

The smile slipped away and she wrapped her arms around her body against the cold. "She is getting worse, if I'm honest. I'm starting to wonder..."

"How much longer you can put up with it?" Danny smiled. "I have one much the same."

"Well.." Hilary stepped away from the front door, ready to leave but Danny hesitated.

"There's something I'd like to ask you. It may seem an odd question, but does the tune, 'Cherry Pink and Apple Blossom White', mean anything to you?"

"Yes, it does." Paula's weary smile returned. "Ellen is always playing it. 'Great Big '50s Hits', the tape is called, about forty songs from that decade. That one is her favorite. Apparently, Veronica loved it too."

"That follows, I suppose." Danny shook hands with her.

"You know," Paula said, casting a quick glance back into the house. "My father once told me something about Veronica, something that Ellen let slip. The girl kept a secret in the basement of Kavanagh Mansions - in a sweets tin. Ellen never said what it was, if she knew. Veronica would fly into a rage if she even mentioned it."

"What happened to it?" Danny felt a surge of hope in his chest.

"Still there, I think. When Ellem moved, she left an old trunk down there. The tin was inside. My father never pursued the matter but was sure there was something wrong with it. I believe that played on his mind until the day he died."

They said their goodbyes and walked across the road to the car. Once inside, Hilary asked, "What do you make of that?"

Danny shook his head. "I wonder what was in the tin."

"What's all this business with the tune?" she said, fitting her seatbelt.

"Something of nothing, I expect," Danny felt drained. "It's part of the mess inside my head."

Paula was still standing on the doorstep. Hilary gestured for her to go inside and saw disappear into the house. Danny sighed and fitted his seat belt. He was tired and cold and wanted to get going.

"As far as I can see we have three options when it comes to Veronica," Hilary said. "The generally accepted story, she was abducted by some unknown person. That you're right and something happened with the Tykes, which they have kept quiet about all these years."

"And the third?"

She gazed out the wind-screen, across the bonnet of the car. "Have you ever considered the possibility that Veronica is still alive?"

Danny stared at her in amazement.

Chapter Twenty One

He sat on the side of the bed and stared into the grey light of morning, seeping into the room through the window curtains. His watch on the bedside table showed it was close on half past seven and he had been awake since just after five.

At that hour of the morning the room had been so cold, he had been unable to sleep and fed up lying there in the darkness, watching the pictures playing inside his head, he had got up and made some tea.

He'd tried to call her last night. There was no answer.

The pictures were at their worst now, when he was away from home, away from Chrissie and lonely. Supicion sent waves of jealousy coursing through his body like moulten lava, so that he felt all burned up inside.

Hilary had dropped him outside the hotel at just after seven o'clock yesterday evening, having run ahead of the weather all the way back to London. He remembered the cold wind reaching for him as he had stooped to look back into the car.

"What will you do now?"

"Home, shower." She had smiled tiredly, "Open a bottle of wine and think over what we learned today."

"That shouldn't take long."

"We'll see. There might be more there than you think."

By then the weather was catching up with them and he was already shivering. He let her believe what she liked and saying good bye, headed for the hotel thinking himself about a hot shower.

"I'd like to come with you to see Singleton tomorrow," she called after him.

"Be my guest." He was already thinking about Chrissie.

"What time? I'll pick you up."

"Lunchtime. I have to do something first."

Pausing on the door step of the hotel, he had watched her drive off towards Putney Bridge until flakes from a new fall of snow blew at him from across the common.

In his room, he'd removed his out door gear, fighting back images of Chrissie and Roger on a date. In the bathroom, as he'd relieved himself into the toilet, he asked himself again and again, where had she been?

Stripping quickly, he stepped into the shower, upping the temperature until it bordered on uncomfortable to wash the chill from his bones. Standing there under the pounding hot needles, he forced himself to think about the job in hand.

His mind was made up. He did not believe the three Tykes had died by suicide or accident in the accepted sense. Something had coerced them into acting against their will.

But how?

A shudder ran through him. What could they have seen that was so unbearable? Did he need to ask?

When he'd finished washing, he dried himself off, dressed and made himself a cup of tea. If he called home now, he could catch Chrissie before she went to work and hearing her voice might just give him the fortitude to face up to the thoughts he was now considering.

If he called and she wasn't there, what then?

Last night, his hostess had knocked on the door to ask if he would like to share an evening meal with her and he had accepted. In the warmth of her kitchen, a large space with a table big enough to seat half a dozen, the pair of them had shared a tasty spag-boll and a bottle of extra dry red wine. He had listened to her tell him about her husband, from whom she was separated and their daughter, who was coming to visit some time in the week.

"You'll probably meet her, if you are still here."

"I'll be here," he'd told her and had gone on to answer questions about his day in Bournemouth, visiting an invalid relative, all the time struggling to keep his eye lids from drooping.

Eventually the warm food and the wine had worked on him so much, he'd excused himself and returned to this room. Thinking back now, the woman had obviously intended the evening to go in a different direction, the way she'd been dressed, casual, open neck, lots of breast on show.

"Jesus!"

Another time, he might have taken up the offer.

He turned on the TV, early morning chat, the state of the Underground, delays on this road and that, an accident on Western Avenue. Then the news, Reagan and Thatcher love-in, Brezhnev defending once again the USSR's invasion of Afghanistan. He listened for a while and when he'd had enough of world problems, he turned it off.

The heating came on, Going to the window, he opened the curtain wide and saw that the common wore a new white coat, still not thick, grass tufts poking through the snow. Should he try Chrissie again?

The telephone called to him, challenging him to do it. He closed his eyes and resting his forehead against the window pane, tried not to speculate on where she may have gone last night. The name Roger scratched at his inner ear and he turned away, trying to lose the man but the gawky fucker would not let him go.

She wouldn't go with him!

How could he be sure after what he'd done? She knew about it, so could he blame her if she did?

"She wouldn't!"

He pictured himself returning home, eager to join her, running upstairs to be in her embrace and there she was, writhing on the bed with Roger.

"Fuck off!"

He managed to expell the man from his mind, thinking about what Hilary had said yesterday, about the possibility of Veronica being alive. The idea seemed fantastic but was it really anymore unlikely than the alternative he was dwelling on?

No, it was a damn sight more credible. And yet...

If she was alive, where the hell had she been all these years and why hadn't she come forward before now?

He dressed, put on his wrist watch. Its face told him it was a quarter to eight. Sitting on the edge of the bed, he reached for the telephone, swining it round onto the mattress beside him. He lfted the receiver, heard the familiar sound as the automatic switchboard down in the foyer connected him to an open line and tapped in the number he knew so well.

"Hello?"

"It's me," he said. "I wanted to catch you before you went to work."

He gripped the receiver, held it close, tense until the sound of her voice freed him and he smiled. She told him she had just got up and sighed.

"Are you alright?"

"Not really." She sounded strange, subdued and he became alert once more.

"What's the matter?"

There was a pause, then, "I was at the hospital until late. Roger tried to kill himself."

"Yeah?" Everybody's doing it, he thought. Some were even succeeding.

"How is he?" he asked, feeling guilty.

"He swallowed a bottle of sleeping pills, but it seems he's going to be all right."

"So how did you get involved?"

"He started having a woman in to clean after his wife went. She found him yesterday morning and called an ambulance. After they had taken him away, the woman called work."

"And you went to sit with him?"

"Somebody had to," she said coldly.

"What about this wife of his?"

"She arrived late last night. That's when I left."

"I called last night," he said.

"I know."

She knew!?

"What do you mean, you know?"

"I was here. I didn't want to speak to you."

What was she talking about? Why did she sound so distant? For all she knew, he might have been in trouble!

She asked, "How are things going down there?"

An after thought.

"Okay I guess."

"Still haven't found anything conclusive?"

He would have told her if there had been. Why was she talking about this when there was obviously a more important matter to address?

"Are things all right with you? I mean apart from what's happened to Roger?"

"Yes."

He waited, the silence on the line filling his head. Every fibre of his being screamed at him that there was something not right here. Words came to him, hovered on his lips and died. There was something she wasn't telling him. Something bad maybe which had frightened her but she didn't want to worry him. What was she keeping from him?

"I was thinking," he said carefully. "Maybe it would be better if you went to stay with Carol for a while."

"Carol! What on earth for?"

"My peace of mind." He hoped she didn't want him to expand on that.

"No."

"Chrissie, I -"

"I am not going to stay with Carol and that's an end to it."

"Look, something's wrong, isn't it?"

"Of course something's wrong! My friend tried to commit suicide."

"I know. I'm sorry. But I'm more worried about you at the moment."

"Danny," he heard the anguish in her voice, "I don't want to talk about it now."

"Listen, I'm not trying to scare you but what I'm doing, what I'm going to do, there may be consequences. I'll call Carol and -"

"For Christ's sake!" her voice sharp in his ear. "I have a very difficult decision to make."

Cold hands around his heart. "What decision? About us?"

"Please Danny, leave it be!" She was getting emotional. There were tears not far away but he had to know.

"Alright, I'll get the first train I can. I'll come to the house. Just tell me, are you in danger?"

"In danger?" she sounded bewildered. "Of course I'm not in danger."

Of course she wasn't. This was something else, something to do with them, their marriage. Was she going to leave him after all?

"Tell me or else I'm coming back today!"

"Danny, please..."

"Tell me!"

A long pause. He heard a sob of breath and then she said, very softly, so softly he could barly hear her.

"I slept with Roger."

A moment of not comprehending, her words seeping into his stunned mind. Then they exploded, four little words that destroyed his world - BAM-BAM-BAM-BAM!

"When?" he croaked.

"Does it matter?"

"Yes, it does actually."

"A while ago," she muttered, trying to get past this. "He wanted me to move in with him."

"Is that why he...?

"Maybe. That and other stuff."

And she was talking fast now - she was sorry - only right she told him - no secrets if they were to make things work between them. The girl who had stood alone at that house party, shy, pretty, the girl who had reached into his chest and grabbed his heart. Now it felt as though she had ripped it from his chest.

Danny slammned the receiver down and sat looking at the phone. It was there, she had said it but somehow he could not accept it as truth. She was just saying it to punish him, wasn't she?

"Of course it's fucking true!" he snarled.

He jumped to his feet and went to the bathroom, splashing cold water into his face then turning sharply, spewed hot bile into the toilet bowl.

"FUCK!" he screamed then lifted his head and stared at himself in the mirror above the wash basin.

It was true and tears burnt his eyes. Another man had slept with her, had wanted her to move in with him and when she had said no, he had tried to kill himself.

Well he should have tried fucking harder!

Raising a fist, he punched the tiled wall to the side of the mirror and felt pain explode in his knuckles. Barely glancing at the thin line of blood slipping between his middle and third fingers, he washed his mouth out with handfuls of water.

Returning to his room, he pulled on his coat and was reaching for his scarf and beanie when there was a knock on the door. Crossing, he opened it and stared at his hostess, looking quite sleepily sexy in her satin dressing gown, hair tousled and wearing no make-up.

"Hello," she said, smiling uncertainly. "I was wondering whether you would like to share an intimate breakfast too?"

The gown clung to her, every swell and curve, every hollow and he felt nothing. He managed a smile and thanked her but said that he had to go out. She looked a little hurt but that was her look out. She meant as little to him as the pattern on the stair carpet at that moment.

Out on the street, he turned towards the Bridge with nothing in mind but out running the pain that threatened to engulph him. He had to put space between him and the hotel, where he'd heard Chrissie say....

The air was bitterly cold and burned his throat as he sucked in great lungs fulls of it. Frozen patches of snow crunched softly beneath his feet but he was careless of it and the cold, the cold could not touch him,he was dead inside and impervious to all feeling. He was walking as fast as he could to nowhere.

And then he wasn't.

He became aware of other pedestrians around him but he didn't care about them, they didn't exist for him. He was concious only of the gnawing hole which had opened up in his centre, where some part of him had been wrenched away.

How could she have done this to him? And with that four eyed bastard of all people!

Had he removed his glasses before he'd fucked her? His socks?

He stared bleakly into the truth of his situation and asked himself whether what she had done was any worse than his own betrayal? She had been lying in a hospital bed having just lost the child she had been longing for and where was he? Screwing some tart he'd picked up in a bar, during his long and cowardly escape from Chrissie's tragic gaze.

He should have been holding his wife in his arms, comforting her as best he could, not clutching the hot, damp flesh of a woman he hadn't even known. His guilt made him sob.

What am I doing?

What they had done to each other, after all they had shared! He groaned at the aching hollowness inside him.

"Shared?"

He reflected on the word and asked himself had he ever shared anything with her, anything that mattered? Once maybe but not for a long while.

He stopped dead, eyes focusing on the here and now. The reality of his situation becoming all too apparent. He had to get things done, finished. Only then could he start trying to put his marriage back together. Which meant filling his mind with the job in hand.

He walked on at a faster pace, eyes and nose watering as the chill plucked at him, He realised that the direction his feet had been taking him in was towards Kavanagh Mansions. That was where the key to everything was, he felt sure now. She had lived there and to all intents and purposes, part of her lingered there still. He felt sure that down in that basement, finding the trunk Ellen Hayden had left behind would, if not be the end what was going on, would somehow act as a catalyst to that ending.

Reaching the corner of Kavanagh Gardens, he turned right and walked swiftly along to the Mansions before he could start thinking about what he was going to do. First he would go and see Mrs.Kershaw, ask her about the basement storage area, learn what he could before descending into it.

He stepped into the porch of the Mansions and was reaching for for the button marked Flat 2 on the security panel, when he heard the front door click. Surprised, he gazed at it for a moment, reached out and gave it an experimental push and it opened. Had she had spotted him again and released in automatically?

He pushed the door wide and stepped into the foyer, into the usual heavy silence, whic quickly enveloped him. He'd been expecting it, yet he still found it unsettling and found himself breathing as quietly as he could in order not to disturb it.

Behind him the front door closed with a click, which was immediately smothered by the silence. He moved across to Mrs. Kershaw's front door and saw that it too was ajar, so she must have seen him and would no doubt be there inside, waiting to greet him with her usual smile.

Smiling a little himself, he stepped into the hall.
"Hello?"

No response. He shut the door gently behind him and felt a cold draught blowing at him from the kitchen.

"Mrs. Kershaw?"

Nothing. No greeting and even more surprising, no barking from Waldorf.

He walked along as far as the living-room door and looked into the room. The outraged stares of the Kershaw ancestors gazed back at him from the line of photographs but otherwise, the room was empty. He looked down at Waldorf's empty bed. Surely she hadn't taken the dog for a walk and left the garden door open?

He thought of Dad, of the way he had a habit of doing a similar thing. It must be a common fault with old people and sure enough, as he turned into the kitchen, he saw he was right, the door to the garden was wide open.

Something was wrong. He looked at the kitchen table, where a plate contained the half eaten remains of a meat pie, some peas and mashed potatoes, smears of congealed gravy.

"Where are you," he muttered.

She was not the sort to leave her dirty crocks for all to see. Had she gone into the garden for some reason last night, had a fall and been lying out there all night?

"Jesus."

Moving quickly to the back door, he stepped out into a world of snow covered undergrowth, skeletal trees and frozen footprints. How long ago were they made? Snow dusted stepping stones forming a path across a white plain, which he assumed was a lawn. He made his was slowly along them, any earlier foot prints having been partially filled by another fall of snow, deeper here than in the streets.

Which didn't look good.

He worked his way towards the high boundary wall at the end, beyond which was Embankment and the Thames.

Always the river!

And was halfway along the path when he saw her, at least he saw Waldorf, lying on his side away from the path, stiff and dead eyed, his head at a very strange angle.

"Mrs. Kershaw?"

He stepped quickly from the path into deeper snow, moving to the spot where the dog's corpse lay. Moving around a snow laden bush, his thigh caught a branch, bringing a powdery cascade down around him and that was then he saw her. She was lying on her right side, knees brought up, one arm thrown out in front of her, as though to ward off an attacker. The other arm was curled beneath her.

What were you doing out here?

He glanced back at the dog. It was possible that Waldorf, out in the garden to relieve himself, had suffered some sort of fit. That would have brought her outside but would she have stopped to put on her coat? That didn't seem feasible, the way she loved that dog, she'd have run straight out in what she'd had on.

He looked closer, trying to see more of her face, then gasped and pulled back. Her expression was much the same as the one he'd seen on Cockle's face, a look of shock and horror. She had probably glimpsed something from the kitchen window, put on her coat and come out for a better look with Waldorf following her.

Had there been an intruder in the garden?

Had the dog set to barking and earned itself a broken neck?

What sort of intruder had it been?

A sudden gust of wind from the river blew snow from the higher branches of a nearby tree, showering his head and shoulders but he barely noticed. Gazing at her waxy face, her wide eyes, contorted face, at her wide, crooked mouth, he was lost in a moment of dread.

What had she seen?

Danny stiffened, suddenly aware that he was being watched. The hairs on the back of his neck bristled and slowly her turned his head. He saw the open kitchen door, a slice of the empty room beyond, a flash of something that shouldn't be there, a figure moving away fast from the door.

"Hey!"

His voice seemed sharp in the brittle afternoon. A few flecks of snow skipped around him. His boot slipped as he started for the kitchen door and he staggered a couple of steps, managed to stay on his feet and ran back to the steps, into the kitchen.

Quiet. Still. Empty.

He looked back into the garden, to the spot where he knew she lay and felt anger building inside him. He'd known her only for a short while but in that time he had come to like her a lot and now she was dead, for what? Seeing what she had seen all those years ago maybe?

Telling him about it?

Turning, he walked quickly up the hall to the front door and into the foyer, just in time to see the lift car disappearing down into the basement.

Was it her?

It had to be her!

He hurried across to the door to the basement and down the flight of stairs that led to the mezzanine floor, where the caretaker's flat was. In front of him was the door marked

BASEMENT - NO ADMITTANCE

He opened the door and listened. Nothing! Not a sound, just dank air wafting up around his face. Opening the door wider, he stepped through onto the small platform at the head of a concrete flight of stairs. Was she aiming to play games with him like before? Deep inside he knew this was nothing like before. There would be no games, not this time.

This time was different in so many ways.

Down there was in darkness, except for the long oblong of yellowish light coming from the lift car, shining through the lift gates, casting a diamond pattern across the basement floor. Beyond this unbroken darkness looking as dense and solid as rock.

There was someone down there, he felt sure of that, someone responsible for the deaths of four people and he didn't want to be number five.

Someone or something?

He shut that thought down. He could not afford to be dwelling on those ideas right now.

Flapping around on the wall beside him, he found the light switch and turned it on A pall of weak light, from a bank of ceiling fitments with green metal shades, each containing a fat, bayonet style bulb, struggled to push back the darkness.

You don't have to go down there.

But he did, even though he would rather not.

He remembered the day he had tried to deliver Cockle's package, he'd noticed a torch on a small table tucked deep in under the stairs, right beside Cockle's front door. If it was still there, there was no reason why he shouldn't borrow it, so he stepped back onto the mezzanine floor and went along to the staircase where sure enough, the torch was still there in the spandrel.

Ducking beneath the stairs, he picked the torch up, weighing it in his hand. It was large, rubber covered and lighter than he'd imagined it would but it would still be a useful weapon if he needed one.

Not against...

He would not dwell on that. Just holding the thing he found reassuring. He turned the torch on to make sure that it was working and returned to the head of the basement stairs and descended carefully to the bottom.

In the space beyond the light from the ceiling bulbs the darkness held solid. He turned on the torch and directed its beam into the blackness, punching a wide circle of light as far as the wall on that side of the space. As though offended by the torches glow, the ceiling lamps flickered and buzzed, then shone steadily once more.

He turned the beam to his right, saw the lift gate, its slats and runners thick with accumulated dirt, showing that it was a long time since anyone had opened the gate down there. He frowned; he'd seen the lift car going down, so if anyone had come down, there should be signs of the gate having been opened to let them out. He swallowed dryly, unless whatever had been in there did not need to open doors!

Beside the gate on the other side of the lift, there was a drain with a galvanised bucket and mop standing beside it, no doubt left there by Cockle the last time he had used it and further over, some old markings on the floor where something had once stood, probably an old boiler judging from the outline. A sizeable thing, judging from its imprint, a greedy monster, requiring constant feeding.

He guessed then what that wide space on the other side of the aisle had been for. Filled with that dank, earthy smell he now recognised as being that of coal and turning the torch beam up the outside wall, located a round metal plate in the ceiling where the delivery men used to empty their sacks into the basement from the street. From the tide mark on the brickwork, the boiler had taken a lot of coal to keep going.

Danny turned the torch off and walked quickly along the aisle with the washed out light from the overhead bulbs enough to see by. If there was anything lurking in the darkness around him, he didn't think he could bare seeing right then.

The light flickered and Danny looked sharply up at the row of bulbs. They flickered again and then resumed their steady glow, just the way those in the train carriage had. Would these suddenly go out leaving him in darkness? The possibility scared him to the core and he tried not to dwell on the memory of the black form developing in that train carriage.

Enough!

Who knew how these things worked. Once his mind lost control, there was no telling what monsters he might see advancing upon him.

The aisle ran along a natural path formed between rows of storage racks on his right side and huge, brick arches on the other. These solid buttresses were keeping the flats above from crashing down into the basement and in the deepest recesses of them, the weak light from the bulbs failed to penetrate.

He did not turn on the torch, preferring for the moment not to delve further and keeping his eyes focused straight ahead, he moved slowly towards the back wall. He glanced into each row of racks as he went by, seeing mostly empty shelves, just a few gallon tins of disinfectant and bags of salt for icy weather left.

No doubt at one time there would have been all the supplies the caretaker would need to keep the building shipshape. Now that Kavanagh Mansions was all but vacant, so too were the racks and as he drew nearer the back wall, he could see through the lower shelf of the end rack, something edging into view with every step closer that he took.

He stopped, turned on the torch and shone the beam between the shelves of the end rack. It was a chest, just like the ones in all those old pirate films he'd seen as a kid. The sort with an oval lid and big, metal retainers which, with the lid thrown open, would revealed a fortune in precious gems and golden doubloons.

Much more credible than Dad's tatty suitcase.

"Pieces of eight," he muttered, not liking the tremor he heard in his voice.

Stepping into the floor space beyond the last rack, he stopped in front of the chest. It stood level with his knees, the lid covered with dust and he guessed that until lately it had stood forgotten in some dark recess. Playing the torch beam along the floor from the chest back to the corner of the wall, he saw where it had been dragged forward, leaving wide marks in the accumulated grime.

By whom?

For his benefit?

He looked quickly behind him but there was nothing to see, just the same empty aisle and behind that, the wall of darkness which wasn't really empty at all.

He turned off the torch and reaching down, grabbed the front edge of the lid, lifting it open. The action drew squeal of protest from the hinges and he let it drop gently back to its limit. Immediately he was engulfed by the smell of mildew, so strong it made him cough.

The trunk had not been opened for a very long time and looking inside, he saw it was filled with linen, curtains by the look of it, moldy and cold to the touch.

He had no intention of delving deeper but of course, he didn't have to. What he was intended to find was sitting on top of the curtains waiting for him.

It was an old Sharps Toffee tin, rusted around the edges, a colourful picture on the lid showing a schoolgirl against a wintery snow scene, wearing a scarf, bobble hat and mittens. She had a huge grin bunching her apple-cheeked face and behind her, too one side, stood a snowman, complete with pipe, carrot nose and beady coal lump eyes.

Nineteen fifties, he thought, picking up the tin and giving it a gentle shake. There was movement inside, stale toffies or something else? He tucked the torch under his arm and moved his thumb tips to rest beneath the rim of the lid. He drew in a deep breath and was about to open it up, when the lights went out.

Startled, he cried out and dropped the torch. Plunged into total darkness, terror grabbed him. He fumbled with the tin, managed to drop that as well and was floundering around on the floor when common sense finally gained a hold.

Think!

The wave of terror, which had threatened to take him, subsided enough for him to get a hold of himself. There had been no sound, either of the torch or the tin hitting anything, they must have fallen into the chest.

Shoving his hands down into the curtains, he shuddered as the heavy, dank material touched his skin. Moving his hands around stirred up great wafts of mildew but eventually one hand found the torch immediately.

The tin?

He turned the torch on, thankful it had landed inside on the curtains and not on the floor. Directing its light into the trunk, he searched around for the tin but could not find it. It had vanished. He thought about shoving a hand under the curtains again, in case it had somehow slipped down there between the curtains but that it wasn't likely, as they were quite densley packed.

When something shifted behind him, he span round, pointing the torch beam at the darkness, waving it about wildly over walls and floor, all the way down to where the racks stopped.

"Jesus..." the word barely a breath.

He moved quickly back along the aisle, following the torch beam, to where the soft glow from the lift car fell across the floor in an arc.

Had left the basement door open?

He thought he had but it was shut now, no light from the mezzanine to help push back the darkness. All the same, he could make out the stairs in the light from the lift and was moving swiftly towards them when he tripped on some obstacle and just managed to stay on his feet.

The torch shot from his grasp, hit the bottom step and this time there was the sound of breaking glass.

"Damn!"

To his utter dismay, he was left with only the light from the lift car to see by. Standing there as the chill darkness rolled in, trying to smother the light there was, he became chillingly aware that he was not alone.

A strangled mewing noise fought its way up his throat and out through his clenched teeth. He edged towards the domed arc of light from the lift, terrified that his slighted move might bring something springing from the darkness.

And then.

"Daniel!"

He yelped and his blood became ice water.

"You're - dead!" he said.

She giggled.

"You can't be here!"

Backing up he reached the light from lift the car, his bulging eyes scouring the darkness for any sign of movement. When she giggled again, he scampered backwards, not daring to look away from that balck wall. He felt the lift gate behind him when its hard knuckled grid joints dug sharply into his shoulders.

"Daniel."

He stared wide eyed at a point dead in front of him, where the light from the car stopped.

"Get away! I don't believe in you."

Another soft giggle and this time much closer than before.

"Of course you do."

He heard something moving closer. He had to get out and there! Turning, he grabbed the gate handle and pulled but the gate barely moved. With desperate eyes, he looked down at the runner, set into the concrete and blocked by an accumulation of old grease and fluff.

She must have opened it earlier!

But he knew that wasn't so. She didn't need to open anything. She could go wherever she wanted. And he finally faced up to the full enormity of what he had tried for so long to deny.

A wild feeling of release rushed through him and he let out a loud yell. Yanking at the gate again and again, he managed to open it some thirty centimeters or so.

Too narrow for him to squeeze through!

He shot a look back over his shoulder and gasped when he saw a pair of black, highly polished shoes standing right at the edge of the light.

"Welcome to the lion's den."

She stepped closer still, so that he could see white socks pulled right up to a pair of pink knees.

Danny yanked at the gate until his wrists, his arms and shoulders screamed out in protest and finally it opened a fraction more. Space now which he might just squeeze through.

Turning sideways, he shoved a shoulder through the gap, then pushed and wriggled and puffed until he finally stumbled into the lift car.

"Daniel," she said reproachfully.

With a mighty shove, he closed the gate. Through the metal grid, he saw her step clear of the darkness, her smile wide, her eyes devouring and he felt the breath being sucked from his lungs.

"I've waited so long."

"It can't be..."

But it was.

Veronica, just as she had looked in the photo he'd seen at Mrs. Hayden's home. It was impossible. She was dead! Had been dead for a long time, yet here she stood, just the same as in real life.

"But this is real life," she said.

Lifting her arms towards him, she showed him hands holding the Sharps Toffee tin, proffering it to him. Then, ever so slowly, she started to open the lid and suddenly he knew exactly what was inside. He stared in horror at the shrivelled pieces of human flesh.

"No..." His throat tightened. Tears stung his eyes. He threw himself at the control panel, stabbing at the button marked G until the car jerked and started up and he heard her laughing as she disappeared beneathe the lift car floor.

When the car reached the foyer, he threw the gates open and ran from the building as fast as he could.

Outside the cold hit him like an icy fist and he gasped. It was snowing again and quiet, so quiet. He pulled his coat tightly across his body but nothing would warm the dead chill he felt inside.

Was he going mad?

He made his way up Kavanagh Gardens to the main road and stopped. He had to call an ambulance for Mrs. Kershaw, he couldn't just leave her out there until someone else stumbled upon her body. This time he would do it right. There was a phone in her flat but he didn't want to go back into that building ever again.

He'd seen a dead girl smiling at him!

And she *was* dead, he was certain of that.

There was a call box across the road, up the side of the Half Moon pub. He hurried over the road without checking the traffic, pulled the kiosk door open and stepped inside. Tapping out the digits 999, he told the operator he wanted an ambulance and the police, giving the next voice he heard the details.

Chapter Twenty Two

It took just under half an hour for the police to finish with him and for the ambulance to take away the body of Mrs. Kershaw. They all agreed that it looked like she'd had a heart attack, although the doctor who received the body would determine that.

He didn't see what happened to Waldorf.

Finally Danny stepped out of Kavanagh Mansions and sucked in greedily of the ice cold air in an effort to clean the taint of the building from him. What had happened in the basement, the memory of those shriveled organs and the fact that Veronica had seemed as corporate as any of the people walking past him on the street, would not let him go.

But he did not believe in ghosts!

He had always been sure of that. Now though...

Wandering along through the snow, he went over the same argument again and again, trying to convince himself that what he had seen had not been real, couldn't be real. Veronica had grown to womanhood, had born a child that was, to all intents and purposes, an exact replica of herself.

There are no such things as ghosts!

Now that he was out of that basement, away from what had scared him so much, he should be able to feel reason returning. But...

She had been there!

He had seen her!

He knew now why Cockle and Sarah had killed themselves, confronted by someone they knew had died years ago. And even if they had not wanted to do it, she had been able to force them down that road.

And Murkin, he had seen her too? Had she made him start the fire? His wife thought she had seen an old woman in the burning room.

But why is she haunting me?

He hadn't been one of the Tykes. He'd had nothing to do with anything they had got up to. But he had cheated her in other ways, he shouldn't forget that.

He needed a drink!

He'd not so much as thought about boozing since this affair started but right then, he could think of nothing better. Of course, he wouldn't throw himself into it, lose himself in an alcoholic stupor, as he sometimes had when overwhelmed by problems. One drink though. A little something to keep his moral up, that wouldn't hurt.

He made his way along the main road towards the common until he came to The Cricketers. Walking around the side of the pub, through the deserted beer garden with its snow covered benches and tables, abandoned until spring.

Kicking snow from his boots against the high doorstep, he entered the saloon bar and let the thick fug of cooking smells and beer envelope him. He felt a sudden rush of love for the long bar, its polished wood and shiney pumps, which seemed to welcome him back to a world of normality.

At the bar, he ordered a whisky, which he knocked back in one go, and a pint of bitter to chase it down. The whisky was warm in his throat but it could not rid him of the lingering chill he felt inside. Ordering sausage and chips from the menu, he took his pint to an empty table to wait for the meal.

He swallowed a quarter of the beer, thought about

ordering another whisky but decided it wasn't a good idea. He had never been good with spirits and felt needed to keep a clear head the way things were turning out.

"Here we are."

A pretty young woman brought his food, cutlery and napkin, which she placed on the table in front of him. She put down the plate and with a big smile, asked if he wanted any sauce.

At a different time, he may well have told her that he was saucy enough already, the sort of stupid comment men of his age often made to nice looking women young enough to be their daughters. Now though, he did not have an iota of humour in him. Twenty years ago and a hundred miles away from what he was going through at the moment, it might have been nice to get to know her.

He watched her walk away and disappear round the end of the bar, taking with her the glow of warmth she had momentarily brought him. Chrissie had filled him with much the same warmth when he first knew her, only in her case, the feeling had been real and lasting. It had changed over the years, matured into something deeper, stronger, or at least he thought it had.

She'd slept with Roger!

He stabbed at a chip with his fork and contemplated the cold, grey light filling the two big pub windows at the front of the bar room. The pub door opened and to his surprise, he saw Hilary step inside. She spotted him and lifted a hand in a half-hearted wave as she came to join him.

"I saw you come in but had a job finding a parking space."

"Do you want a drink?"

"I'll get it."

He cut the end off a sausage and popped it into his mouth, chewing perfunctorily as he watched her go to the bar. She ordered herself what looked like a glass of bitter lemon, paid and then came to sit opposite him. Taking a swig, she put the glass on the table and looked at him.

"What's happened?"

"How do you mean?"

"It's in your eyes. You look as though you've had the fright of your life."

He swallowed the piece of sausage and said, "That clear, is it?"

"Tell me."

He looked away. "You'll think I've lost my mind."

She took out her cigarettes. "Tell me all the same."

He put down his knife and fork and wondered what part of his delightful morning he should start with. Not Chrissie, it wasn't her problem and if he started down that road, he would have to tell her everything. He already had enough people thinking he was some kind of low life, Carol, Chrissie, not to mention himself. Telling Hilary would make it a quartet.

He started with Mrs. Kershaw because, in spite of what had happened to her, that was the easiest. While she smoked her cigarette, he took her through it all up to seeing Veronica in the basement and she did not interrupt him. When he had finished, she stabbed her cigarette into the glass ashtray on the table and took a chip from his plate.

"It was Veronica."

"It couldn't have been." She added a piece of sausage to keep the chip company, pausing in the middle of chewing it. "You know that "

"I know what I saw."

"You were stressed, the lights going out and the stuff with the tin," she shrugged. "The mind can play tricks."

"I didn't imagine the trunk. Someone had pulled it forward from where it had stood for decades, right at the time I would be down there to see it."

"Yes, a living human form."

"You really think I saw her daughter!? That she is alive and well and laughing at us?"

"I don't know. But it couldn't have been a dead person."

"It was her!"

"You know what you're suggesting?"

Danny shoved the his glass away from him.

"I've been seeing things since I first came back to Putney. I know what are memories and what aren't. This wasn't imaginary. This was real. Happening in real time, there in front of me."

Hilary didn't believe him, he could tell by her face and could he really blame her? Just a short while ago, he would have reacted in the same way had she told him something similar.

And then he realised there was more to it than that. Some part of her did believe him and that frightened the hell out of her. She was terrified of even considering what he was suggesting might be true.

She glanced at his plate and for a moment, he thought she may reach for another morsel. People cope with fear in different ways.

"Help yourself."

She shook her head.

Danny reached for his glass and drank some more beer but it tasted different, like it had gone flat and he left it.

"How come you're here so early?"

"Carol phoned. She tried to get you at the hotel but the woman said she hadn't seen you since you left earlier."

Immediately he thought of Chrissie, "What's happened?"

"Singleton called. He wants you to go to his place today."

"His place?" He felt relieved, at least there was no bad news from home, or at least no worse than he already knew. "What time?"

"Anytime. Carol said he sounded edgey and wondered whether you'd upset him."

"She would."

"He's off work at the moment and wants you to go to the house instead of the office. I have his address in the car."

"Okay."

Danny paid his bill and followed her into the street, already worrying about Singleton. Something must have happened to spook him? When they had last met, he'd been less than helpful, now he wanted them to go to his house. Had something happened, made him realise the danger he was in?

Hilary led the way around past the beer garden to a small street edging the common where she had wedged her car awkwardly between two others. Waiting for her to open up, Danny looked over the car roof at the building facing him across a short stretch of common.

"Putney Hospital."

She saw where he was looking. "It's used for convalescence and rehabilitation these days. They'll probably pull it down eventually, the way things are going."

In his dream the place had been derelict, all except that one room where Chrissie had given birth to -

He shut that thought down and drew upon another memory, a child running down a long hospital corridor in pyjamas, desperate to catch up with his retreating parents who were getting further and further away. He knew a sudden, intense pain in his throat, so bad he could hardly swallow. Then the memory faded. The pain vanished and there was just Hilary's pinched face looking at him.

"I had my tonsils out in there." he said vaguely touching his throat.

"Good for you. Now can we get moving?"

She climbed into the car and Danny got in beside her. The heat she had built up driving there had all but gone and he saw a faint mist starting to line the inside of the windscreen.

She started the engine and the blower came on, driving the mist outward towards the edges of the screen.

"I need to stop on the way."

She looked at him, questioningly.

"Murkin's shop. I need to see his wife."

She worked the gear stick and Danny directed her along the quickest way he knew to Stacy Road. He told her to stop and she parked at the kerb a little way along.

"I won't be long."

Climbing out of the car, he paused for a moment looking across at the plumber's shop. There was a light on in the shop window and above, the burnt out room had been boarded up. He saw movement inside the shop, a shadow on the smoke glass window. Mrs. Murkin, he hoped but would they have let her out of hospital so soon?

He walked across the road, tapped on the shop door and a moment later it was opened. Mrs. Murkin stared at him, looking like an angry stork.

"Do you remember me?"

She continued to stare at him for a moment, then stepped aside and let him in. He watched her close the shop door. She seemed even thinner than before and there were dark patches beneath her eyes. She was wrapped up in a heavy looking coat and wore a grey woollen hat on her head.

"I know you," she told him.

"I called before."

"To see him. Before the fire."

"That's right."

"About this lot?"

She indicated the racks behind the old worn counter, racks overloaded with lengths of pipe, copper and heavier, galvanised stuff that must have become obsolete ages ago. It was all diferent diameters,with boxes of joints, knuckle bends, all sorts of materials, mostly covered in dust.

"No. I just wanted to talk to your husband."

"Trains, I suppose." She was already wandering aimlessly back behind the counter so Danny didn't correct her. She stood there looking at the jumble, shaking her head. "I don't know why he didn't get rid of this before. I kept telling him. He didn't take on heavy jobs any more, so most of it could have gone. He wouldn't have it though." She looked at Danny, direct and unblinking. "He's dead, you know?"

"Yes, I heard. I'm sorry."

"You're not the man I spoke to on the phone then? You don't want to buy this?"

"Somebody else."

"Oh. I thought..." She looked around helplessly, "I'm expecting someone."

"I won't keep you long."

She continued to gaze at the racks, waiting, rocking gently, heel to toe and back again. Now that he was here, Danny was not sure where to begin.

"Do you remember much about the fire?" he said finally.

She turned to look at him. "I could have died too. Smoke inhalation. If I'd stayed there much longer, I'd have gone with him."

"The hospital discharged you already?"

"I took myself out. I have to get rid of this lot."

There was a momentary lull as she once again surveyed the racks.

"How did you escape?" Danny asked eventually.

"Neighbour saw the smoke, called the fire brigade."

"Ah!"

"They broke in and found me...us. Up there,"she pointed at the ceiling. "I don't know who fixed my front door."

"Police, I expect."

"They do that, do they?"

"Yes. At least, I think so."

"Well, it's fixed, whoever did it."

She broke into a loud bout of coughing. When it had passed, she went back to looking at the racks. Her breathing sounded hoarse, as she continued rocking backward and forward. Danny watched her, wondering if she had been like this before the fire or whether this was how the trauma had left her.

"I'm sleeping in the parlour. Can't go up there."

"Do they know what started it?"

"Haven't heard."

"Takes time, I suppose."

"Does it?"

"I guess." He glanced at the shop door. How could he make his escape? Why had he bothered coming here in the first place?

"Suppose there will be some sort of inquiry?"

"Bound to be," he said.

"What with him being dead and all."

He opened his mouth, shut it again and watched her nodding to herself. He wondered what Hilary was doing.

"I'd gone to bed," she said eventually. "I was listening to my late night drama."

"I see."

"We slept seperate. On account of his snoring. He was in there with his trains."

"How did you know about - ?"

"Heard him shout."

"You don't know what he -?"

"Just heard him shout. Thought he was calling me. He had fits, you see. I thought he was feeling bad again. He'd had one earlier."

Danny didn't say that he already knew that. That he may have caused it.

"I got up, went next door. The door knob was brass and burnt my hand. " She looked at her bandaged palm for a moment. "Door was already ajar. I hadn't noticed that. When I pushed it open, woosh! Knocked me back across the landing."

"It would."

"Heat. Smoke. Banged my head on the bannisters."

"The fire was already blazing?"

"The whole room was full of it. And I could hear this sound." She stopped, a confused look on her face.

"The fire?"

"No. Like someone was laughing. Horrible" Her eyes
had widened, as though she was seeing the whole thing
again. "And then - I saw someone in there with him."

Danny felt a tight hand at his throat.

"All bent up and in this big black coat. It was a very
old woman."

Coldness flooded his veins and he was back on the
Norwich train, facing that dark figure at the other end of
the carriage.

"I don't see how I could have though."

He managed to force his attention back to her. "Why?"

"They only found him in there, no one else."

Before he could say anything more, a knock came at
the shop door and Mrs. Murkin hurried round the counter
to open it. It seemed as though she had already forgotten
they had been talking.

Danny nodded to the middle aged man at the door as
he went out into the street. He heard the door shut behind
him and then he was on his own on the pavement with
snowflakes falling gently around him.

An old woman!

"Singleton lives in Southfields," Hilary said as he
rejoined her in the car. The address is in the dash
compartment."

He looked, saw a piece of paper sitting on top of all the
other junk in there and took it out. "You know where this
is?"

"I looked it up earlier."

She turned the car round and drove back the way they
had come, leaving Stacy Road and finally joining the
Lower Richmond Road at the common. She took the left
fork across the common, passing the tree festooned with
Bolan memorabilia, then Roehampton Lane to the A3.

Turning back towards central London, they left the main road at Tibbet's Corner roundabout and were driving through quieter, tree lined streets, making their way towards Singleton's address.

"Danny?"

He looked at her.

"You haven't said anything since you saw that woman. At least, nothing important."

No he hadn't, simply because he had no idea where to start. She had been eying him differently since he'd told her about the basement at Kavanagh Mansions. If he told her what Mrs. Murkin had said, if he told her that he thought the woman had seen another manifestation of what they were up against in the burning room, how would she look at him then?

"About what you told me. The basement. I don't know what to think."

"Join the club."

What could anyone think? A sane person would dismiss it out of hand but he had been through it over and over again, desperate to find another, more logical explanation for what he'd seen and had failed to find one.

"Not far now," she said.

They drove through a smart estate of council properties, modest tower blocks and terraces, then into a warren of quiet avenues lined with 1930s houses, detached place mostly but with a couple of semis thrown in for good measure.

"It should be along here somewhere," Hilary said, driving at a snail's pace.

Danny checked the piece of paper, counting off house numbers until he saw the one they wanted.

"Here!"

Hilary turned off the engine and looked out at the thick hedging shielding the house from the road. The number was on the front gate, which was good because otherwise they may have driven right by it.

Outside the car the snow was starting to ease but they lingered, neither of them eager to get out. Danny glanced over at her and knew that she shared the same feeling of trepidation which was holding him in his seat.

The air outside looked sepia coloured, adding a sense of melancholy to the afternoon which wasn't helped when an ancient street lamp across the road came on.

"This is - unreal," Hilary said.

"Like the rest of it's so normal."

After a moment, she released her seat belt and said, "I still think Veronica's alive. I know it's a wild shot but this... Give me a better alternatine. One that doesn't involve seeing... "

Danny sighed, looked at her, saw the pleading in her eyes for something that he couldn't give her.

"I can't," he said wearily and climbed out of the car.

The snow was falling light but steady and althought the wind had lessened, it was still sharp enough to keep him huddled down inside their coats.

Hilary got out into the road and locked her door. They walked across to the front gate without speaking and went up a slab path to the front door, which was sheltered by a small porch. Fresh snow sat innocently on top of the older stuff, which had iced over and Danny felt his foot slide as he stepped on it.

"Careful here!" he said. "He could have cleared this!"

"The curtains are closed."

Danny looked at the windows, up and down and saw she was right.

"Perhaps he's the shy type."

"Or scared."

He moved up to the front door and rang the door bell. When he heard nothing from inside, he used the door knocker to rap twice.

"Nice street. Lot of money tied up in these buildings. "

The front door opened a crack and Singleton peered out.

"It's me," Danny said.

"Who's she?"

"A friend."

"Just a second," he said, continuing to eye Hilary while he fiddled about behind the door. They heard a security chain being released and then the door finally opened. Singleton waved them quickly in, took a look out at the street and shut the door.

"You expecting someone else?" Danny asked.

The man's eyes flicked between the two of them, then he looked away. "Just you."

"Well here I am. Are we going to stand in the hall all afternoon?"

"Sorry," Singleton said. "Come through to the kitchen, it's warmer in there."

They followed him through to the back of the house, which smelt of stale cooking and fresh coffee. The kitchen was a sizable room, decked out in dark pine against light coloured walls. There was a pile of unwashed crockery on the side and a couple of dirty pans in the sink.

"You want coffee?"

Danny nodded. This Singleton was not the smart, assured man he'd met before, his confidence bordering on arrogance. This one wore a bathrobe over a scruffy shirt and trousers he seemed to have slept in. There was a few day's stubble on his chin, his hair was a mess and from the shadows beneath his eyes, it looked like he'd been having a troubled nights.

They sat at the kitchen table while Singleton searched about for a couple of clean mugs Giving up, he rinsed two from the draining board under the hot tap, wiped them and spooned instant coffee into each. Waiting for the kettle to boil, he turned to look at them.

"I live alone now," he said, as though this explained the pile of many unwashed utensils.

"Divorced?" Danny asked.

"Seperated."

"It's a bitch, isn't it?" he said, feeling some resonance with his own situation.

When the kettle had boiled, Singleton made the coffee, plonked the mugs on the table and added a plastic milk bottle, which Danny was tempted to sniff, just to make sure the milk hadn't gone off. He refrained though, opting to take it black the same as Hilary.

"I think it's time we were straight with each other, don't you?"

Singleton sat down opposite them and met his gaze. After a moment, he nodded and started blowing at his coffee. Danny pushed the milk bottle towards him but he ignored it.

"Who did you say she is?"

"I didn't say."

Hilary introduced herself while Singleton eyed her suspiciously, as though he wasn't quite sure whether he wanted to know her or not.

"So," Danny said. "What are you afraid of?"

"Nothing," Singleton said quickly, "I'm not afraid of anything."

"Not a very good start," Hilary said coolly. "You lie badly."

"Come on, Joe. We are here to help you."

Singleton looked at Danny for a moment, then nodded once and getting up, went over to where a pile of mail sat on the worktop. He pulled free an A4 envelope, which he held out to them.

"When did it arrive?"

"You know what it is?"

"I know," Danny said, taking the envelope from him. He dipped two fingers into it and pulled out another copy of the Tykes photo, which he tossed onto the table in front of Hilary.

"When?"

"Two days ago," Singleton said. He looked down at the floor. "Ever since, someone's been hanging about outside."

"Someone?"

"Just a shape. The light's been bad. Just a shape."

"All the time?"

"I think so. It's hard to tell without going out there. I can see from the upstairs window but... The light's not been good these last couple of days. Even when it's near a street lamp, there's no definition."

"Could it be a woman?" Hilary asked. "Or a child, maybe?"

"Just a shape. Like seeing someone through thick fog, changing, bent then upright."

Danny exchanged glances with Hilary.

Singleton dragged a hand across his stubbly chin, avoiding their eyes. "A couple of times, glimpses of what could be a face. Pale and..."

"Any - features?" Danny asked tightly. "Eyes?"

Singleton groaned and buried his face in his hands. "An eye. Possibly. The blackest, coldest eye. Penetrating."

"Hence the curtains," said Hilary, quietly.

Danny glanced at the closed drapes.

She said, "What would you say if we told you we think Veronica is alive?"

Singleton stared at her for several seconds, then looked away.

"Is it possible?"

"Come on!" Danny muttered.

Ignoring him, she continued. "If she is, maybe she has a daughter, a daughter that very much resembles her."

"For god's sake."

"Maybe she's using the girl against you and the other members of the Tykes. Frightening you."

"Making them kill themselves," Danny said tiredly. "Have you heard yourself?"

From the way Singleton looked at her, it was obvious that he still wasn't sure about her. Danny could see the doubt in his eyes, smell the fear upon him. But it was not the idea of Veronica being alive that had a grip on him. It was something more than that.

"You're wrong," he said eventually.

"I've seen her," Danny said.

Singleton looked up at him.

"I was a boy in Putney back then. I knew the Rudd Street Tykes. Sort of. I think."

"I don't remember a Danny Stephens."

"I don't remember much about him myself. Not back then."

Singleton didn't understand and why should he? Danny told him about the meningitis, his memory loss and the problems it was causing him.

"Recently, things have started to come back to me. Memories. Jumbled, yes. But I believe now that I was in the Tykes orbit."

"It's a long while ago," Singleton said wearily. "There must be lots of kids I can't remember."

"Where is Rudd Street?" Danny asked after a moment. "I've looked at my A-Z but I can't find it."

"Gone."

"Gone?"

"Swept away in the early sixties. It used to be near Ray Murkin's place. A short street, little more than a wide alley really; thirty small cottages. It was a bit of a dump but I was sorry to see it go."

"What's there now?"

"Couple of low rise council blocks."

Danny knew where Singleton meant, he'd noticed the flats when he visited Murkin's shop.

"Let me be honest with you," he said after a moment. "I think you know more about what's going on here than you're letting on."

Singleton shifted, eyes roaming everywhere but he said nothing, just sat there chewing his lower lip.

"We need to trust each other."

Now the man's eyes came back to Danny had stayed there.

"I think I'm as involved in what's going on as you. As the others were." Danny glanced at Hilary, who was sipping coffee, her attention centred on him.

Singleton looked interested. It was clear that the man wanted to unburden himself, he just needed to be sure that he could trust them.

"When I came to deliver that package to Alan Cockle, I went inside his flat and found him."

"You saw him?"

"He looked terrified. Like he'd seen something he knew was impossible."

Singleton made a strangled sound and jumped up fron his seat. He walked across to the sink and stoodd there, a fist pressed to his mouth. He remained like that for several seconds, then turned and looked at them.

"He called me. He said that Sarah had phoned him. That she'd received a copy of that phtotgraph. He sounded hald out of his mind."

"Had he seen something too?" Hilary asked. "Outside I mean, like you have?"

Singleton stared at her as though he had forgotten she was there, then shook his head. "Alan was always getting in a state about things. I told him to leave it to me and called her myself that evening but there was no reply."

"Did you tell him?"

He looked at Danny, miserably. "I was going to. I thought I'd leave it for a while. Give him a chance to calm down. The next thing I heard, he was dead, killed himself. I should have spoken to him sooner."

"You weren't to know."

"He was my friend. I should have been there for him."

"Sarah Eadel was dead when we got to her farm," Danny said. "It was impossible to see any expression on her face."

"Sarah wouldn't have done that!"

"Murkin's wife thinks she saw a figure in the room with her husband while the fire raged."

Singleton groaned. "We should have talked. All of us, together. Now three of my friends are dead."

"And Brian?" Hilary asked.

Singleton shook his head, "I don't know."

"What you saw outside," Danny said. "I saw it too, on a train to Norwich."

"How?" Singleton stared at him. "Why?"

"The light was bad. You said you were in a highly emotional state." Hilary's voice was clipped.

"I wasn't seeing things! Why are you so negative all the time?"

"I prefer to call it realistic."

"Like a mother and daughter hit squad, for god's sake!"

"It's a more feasable idea than what you're suggesting."

"You really think Veronica's alive?"

"I don't know. I'm just saying, it's a possibility."

"It isn't!" Singleton's voice stopped them. "She's dead. I saw her dead."

They looked at him. Seconds ticked by. Finally he sighed and said woodenly, "Brian killed her. We all helped bury her."

Chapter Twenty Three

So there it was, Veronica was dead, just like everyone had assumed over the years. She was dead, not at the hands of some faceless killer but of those regarded as her friends?

Had they thought of her as a friend? He didn't think so. How had she thought of them?

But she *was* dead, which knocked all the elaborate theories into a cocked hat.

"There it is then," Danny said.

They fell into silence, each knowing there was much more to talk about, each knowing that none of them wanted to at that moment.

They sat there for some while, each with their own thoughts and the afternoon light grew dimmer and dimmer, until Hilary finally roused herself.

"It's almost four o'clock. I suppose we ought to think about eating. Even if we're not hungry, we should eat. Something tells me we're going to need our strength."

"She's right," said Danny.

Singleton dry washed his face in his hands. "We could cook something. I haven't done much shopping lately though...."

"Get a take-away." Danny said.

"Fish and chips?" Hilary suggested.

Singleton told them there was a good chippy opposite the Underground station in Southfields, a short drive away. "I could pop down there."

Danny laid a hand on his arm, "I'll go."

"Take the car," Hilary told him, handing him the keys.

Outside the cold air snatched at him as he walked briskly across the street to the car. Glancing round as he opened the driver's door, he was sure he saw an indistinct shape move in the twilight. Climbing in behind the wheel, he shut the door firmly and inserted the ignition key. He had volanteered to fetch the food, partly because he knew Singleton was scared to leave the house but also because he wanted to phone Chrissie and would rather do it away from them.

Starting the car, he pulled away gently and turned left as Singleton had instructed. He found it tricky going along those those narrow back roads, where the gritting lorries had not ventured and there were cars parked both sides.

Driving like a little old lady, out for the first time on the public highway, he finally reached the mini roundabout which took him onto the steep hill down to the station. The car slewed and kicked all the way down as he worked brake and clutch, letting it find its own speed to the bottom.

The kerbside was clear outside the station, so he parked close to the entrance on what he could see were double yellow lines. With the wind pressing against him, he climbed from the car and shut the door. The shop was across the way, bright light through steamed up windows, the air filled with the smell of fish and chips.

Locking up, he risked a small trot across the road and entered the shop, where the air was warm. He was the only customer and giving his order to girl behind the counter, saw a man in a white hat and apron set to preparing the food immediately. Both him and the girl looked like Danny had made their day just by being there.

"I won't be long," he told the girl and paying her, left the shop.

Outside, he crossed over to the station vestibule, where he had spotted a call box. Stepping into the box, he

He held their house another, looking onto into the dirt
when she answered.

"It's me," he said.

"Oh, Danny," her voice sounded husky.

"Are you okay?"

"Yes," a slight pause, then, "I sure were of you might not
call, after our date."

"None of that," he said quietly.

"We have so much to get through. Can we do it?"

"Of course we can. I'll be here soon. We can start
then."

She was quiet for a moment, then said, "Have you
found what you wanted?"

"I think so. I'm close anyway. It doesn't be correct
now."

"Is it dangerous?"

"I'm not sure," he lied. He was certain that it would in.

"I'd better go," he told her. "I want you to go and stay
with Carol. Don't question me, please. It will be better
for me knowing you are with her."

"Alright." He knew she wanted to talk more but had
deferred something to the tone of her voice that stopped
her. "Take care, Danny."

He said her words and rejoined the reaction. Here he
dialed Carol's number and she answered on the third
ring.

"It's me. I don't have time to talk, Carol. I've told
Christine to come and stay with you. Is that alright?"

"Of course." She sounded worried, "Is here something
I should know?"

Nothing. And I believe, he thought. "I'd just feel
happier knowing she's with you."

"I'll go and pick her right away."

"It took a breath, "Simply now, Carol."

How could he explain the sheer weight of anxiety he felt inside him? He was stepping into a reaction that he didn't understand, one he never would have believed possible just a short while ago. Veronica was dead, no doubt about that now and yet he had seen her, heard her voice. He had to accept the interruption, there was no other choice.

Replacing the receiver carefully, he stood for a moment looking at it. There was much more to say but right then was not the time to say it. He couldn't have explained a thing.

He moved quickly out of the station and back over to the shop, clinging to the thought that at least Chrissie would be safe at Carol's house. He had no certainty that things might get dangerous for her but he would feel easier in what he had to face knowing she was with Carol.

In the shop, the man behind the counter wrapped up the order in three packages. "Sorry mate, no bags."

Danny said that was fine and left. He popped the bundles inside his coat to shield them from the weather and walked quickly across the road to the car. Dumping the food onto the front passenger seat, he climbed in behind the wheel and started the engine. Outside the snow had eased but it felt colder inside the car, which was already filling with the smell of fish and chips.

He fitted his seat belt and sat looking out at the gathering gloom and thinking of Chrissie. He wished with every fibre of his being that he could give this up, go home to her, hold her close. He needed her.

What they had done to each other tore him up inside and it would take them a while to work through the mess but he was sure they could do it. They just needed time and if he came through this, it would be as a different man, a man who would give her that time she needed. The man he should have been had his life taken another track.

He turned on dipped headlights and flipped the wipers switch to clear what snow had gathered on the screen while he'd been in the shop. Releasing the handbrake, he edged gently away from the kerb and made a U turn in the deserted road. Keeping the car in second, he gently accelerated up the hill, sticking to the middle of the road, where the snow was negligible.

The truth of the matter was, none of them had any idea what they were dealing with. How were they supposed to fight against something that wasn't there, not in the real sense? They might go blundering in to whatever course of action they decided on and all be killed.

Singleton had said that Brian had been resposible for Veronica's death, then maybe Brian and not Sarah had been her first victim. Could what she had become move anywhere it liked across the country or even abroad?

What boundaries were there for something that did not exist as a corporal being?

The car started to slide and he quickly brought it back on course with a gentle half turn of the steering wheel. When he reached the mini-roundabout at the top of the hill, he breathed a sigh of relief and made a right turn towards where Singleton lived, moving the gear stick into third.

Late afternoon had almost slipped into evening when he turned at last into Singleton's road. Parking across from the house, in almost the same place he had vacated earlier, he turned off the engine and released his seat belt. He engaged the handbrake, gathered the food bundles from the seat next to him and stepped out of the car. As he was locking the door, the snow suddenly started falling heavily. Turning towards the house, he found it coming at him as though it had some personal grudge to settle.

"Jesus!" he muttered.

Raising his spare hand in front of his face, he bowed his head and peered through his fingers. Carefully he made his way across the road and was near to Singleton's front gate when he caught a fleeting movement over by the lamp post across the road.

He stopped and stared over there and the snow attacked him mercilessly. It came to him strongly then that he didn't have to stay here. He could collect Hilary, get in the car and drive away. He hadn't been involved in what happened to Veronica, let Singleton deal with the situation alone.

The thought died as quickly as it had grown and he opened the gate. There was nothing to see over there, at least nothing that was showing itself at the moment. He stepped through the gate onto the front path to the house and without warning, his foot shot out from under him. He fell heavily onto his left side, squasing the food packages against his chest.

"Fuck!"

He scrambled about in the snow, desperate to get up, terrified of what might be bearing down on him. Looking back wildly, he was sure something moved in the darkness.

"Who's there?" Singleton barked in a voice that did not sound like his.

"Me," Danny answered sharply. Why hadn't the idiot cleared the path!? "Who did you think it was?"

Light from the hall poured out over Singleton's shoulders from his position on the doorstep. Danny got up and walked as fast as he dared up the path, his arm and shoulder aching and the food packets deverely squashed.

"Did you see - anything?" Singleton asked.

Danny stepped smartly into the hall and waited for him to close the door. When he had, he thrust the food into his arms.

"Plate those up."

He busied himself removing his coat and beanie, hanging them up without worrying about the snow falling from them. When he walked into the kitchen he saw they had washed the stack of crockery from the draining board and Hilary was taking warm plates from the top oven of the cooker.

"No problems?" she asked.

"Apart from slipping arse over tit, no."

She met his eyes, saw his warning look, then glanced to where Singleton lingered nervously in the kitchen doorway.

"I don't know what state the food will be in. I landed on it."

"That doesn't matter." She took the bundles from Singleton, "Let's eat it while it's hot."

The fish was broken, a lot of the chips flattened but they ate it anyway, quietly around the table, just the occasional clink of gutlery breaking the silence. Later, Danny and Hilary moved into the front room while Singleton remained in the kitchen making fresh coffee. He told them to help themselves to the good whisky he kept in the sideboard but neither of them thought it wise to start drinking.

As soon as they sat down, Hilary turned to him, "Something did happen out there?"

Danny said quietly, "There was a shape - a figure."

"The weather's turned worse. Are you sure...?"

"As I can be."

Which was not sure at all.

She withdrew into herself and sat looking into the fire, which was now orange embers. Danny watched her, seeing in the glow from the embers her fear plainly showing in her eyes, her tight mouth. Was she starting to accept the unacceptable?

Singleton joined them, depositing a jug of coffee and three mugs on the coffee table in front of the couch, he poked at the fire and added more coal.

"If you want milk..."

None of them did. Hilary asked if she may smoke and he said he would join her, accepting one of her Gauloise.

"I've been keeping a packet on my desk at work, just to tempt myself," Singleton said.

"Don't you ever lapse?"

"All the time," he tried a grin but it looked more like a grimace.

"I couldn't see clearly out there," Danny said, pouring coffee for them from the jug. "The light is dim and the snow was blowing right at me."

"But you saw...?"

"Nothing. I saw nothing."

Singleton blinked, then shot nervous glances at each of them. "Sure about the whisky?"

When they both said they were, he decided not to drink alone and sat opposite them in an armchair. "So now what?"

"I think you had better tell us exactly what happened back then," Hilary said.

"Yes," he said. "I suppose I must."

He sat for a while staring unhappily at the steam drifting up from his mug. Beyond the curtained window, they heard every so often, the snow being thrown against the glass by the wind.

At length, Singleton sighed and looked at them. "It's been a long while. I'll do the best I can."

Chapter Twenty Four

"There were five of us at first," he said. "We were called the Rudd Street Tykes because four of us lived on Rudd Street. We'd been friends since primary school, Alan, Ray, Sarah and me and that was where we met Brian. He wasn't a Rudd Street kid but it was like he was the missing part of our bunch.

398

"So there was just the five of us and we went everywhere together, playing on the common or just mooching around the streets. Saturdays we would go Saturday Morning Pictures at our local ABC cinema, the Regal, which was a real treat to look forward to every weekend.

"It's gone now, demolished back in the '70s, along with the Odeon, which was next door. They replaced it with that horrible concrete slab of a place that's there now but we all had good memories of the Regal."

He offered them a shade of a smile, a little shrug, such is life. "I'm digressing."

"That's fine," Danny said.

"It was a really good time for us. We had a lot more freedom than kids seem to have these days, as to where we went to play and how long we could stay out for, which really mattered during the long school summer holidays. We got up to all sorts and didn't want to go home until the very last minute. And then she came."

He changed his mind about the whisky, pouring himself a hefty shot.

"We first became aware of Veronica in the winter of '54 - '55, just before Christmas, at the Carol Concert held in our school hall. The other junior schools in the area were invited to join in and there was a lot of us packed in there.

"She was older than us by a couple of years and already going to her second school, some private place in Kingston I think, but her mother knew our head teacher and Veronica, who had a very good voice, had been invited to sing the solos for that year.

"I remember she sang, 'In The Bleak Midwinter' on stage with such feeling, everyone in the hall was impressed. It occured to me later that she'd probably had a different kind of bleakness in mind while she was singing it."

"Which had nothing to do with Christina Rossetti," Hilary muttered but Singleton either didn't hear or didn't understand the reference.

"It snowed in January and one Saturday morning, larking about on our way home from the cinema, we got into a snowball fight along the High Street and into Stacy Road, right where those tarted up little shops are.

"Back then, they were run down places, second hand books and old clothes, like you get in the charity shops these days. There was a curio shop selling all sorts of junk and outside, the bloke who ran it had one of those laughing dummy machines you used to see in arcades and amusement halls."

"The laughing policeman," Hilary said.

"That type of thing, only this one was a sailor, 'Jolly Jack Tar'."

"Drop a penny in the slot and make Jack happy," said Danny.

Singleton looked at him, "You've seen one like it?"

"Oh yes."

"Well, none of us had a penny to spare and we were about to move on when the next thing we knew, Veronica was there, talking to us like she'd always been one of the gang and showing us a handful of change. She said her mum could afford to give her plenty of pocket money."

Danny thought of the boy with the bleeding face and the look Veronica had thrown his way.

"She got the machine going and Jack went through his routine," Singleton continued. "Which wasn't much, looking back on it, but it had us kids laughing along and when it was done, we meandered our way back to Rudd Street with Veronica tagging along.

"From then on, she was around most of the time. Clinging on to us. Like a parasite, feasting on our happiness. Things weren't the same with her there. It was like she had brought a shadow over us. We still hung out, had fun, but there was always felt as though something at the edge of things was waiting to close in and spoil our happiness.

"One afternoon after we'd been playing some game or other, Brian told me he'd been watching her and didn't like what he'd seen. The others had gone in for lunch and we were on our own. He said she frightened him and he wished we could get rid of her."

Singleton realised wht he'd said could be misconstrude and held up a hand.

"I don't mean he wanted to harm her in any way, just stop her keep hanging around with us. I think it was because she seemed to like best and was always getting herself near him and he didn't like it.

"I think she scared all of us to some degree, especially Alan. He was the youngest and shyest of us and tried to avoid her, which was difficult as she was always there. Somehow he always managed to keep himself in the background, out of sight, out of mind, so to speak.

"Ray, who was odd even then, was mad about trains, collecting engine numbers and things like that. He used to come in for lots of bullying from her, like calling him a spas or a dunce. Brian called her out for it a couple of times and she would say she was only joking, then ruffle Ray's hair to show she hadn't meant it. Ray wasn't stupid at all, just odd, quiet; you could be in his company at times and he would be in some world of his own."

He smiled, remembering.

"He used to have a whole lot of routines he would go through before doing things. Like, we all were mad on

Jubbly orange drinks. You could buy them frozen from the shop's ice cream freezer. They came in these pyramid shaped packs and we'd suck them like ice lollies.

"Ray had his own way of opening his and where the rest of us just tore across the top edge, he would have to go through the process of opening the folds in the same order until he'd exposed the ice.

"This one time, I went and bought them and opened his for him the wrong way. He wouldn't touch it and in the end, Alan, who hadn't opened his, swapped with him, so that he could go through his routine and he was happy.

"Now Sarah was different again. She was a tough little thing, pretty but a tomboy and she could fight like a lad. Of all of us, it was Sarah who Veronica mostly left alone, as though she knew she wouldn't get away with any of her nonsense.

"I couldn't imagine Veronica ever fighting, at least, not face to face, she had more devious ways of working. If she had though, Sarah would have taken her apart. I saw her once wrestle Brian to the ground and he was pretty handy himself."

"You were closest to Brian?" asked Hilary.

Singleton'e face sobered. He looked sad.

"Yes, he was my best mate. We just sort of bonded from the start. Which I guess is why I was so hurt when he went away that summer of '55, without saying a word to me. That stayed with me for a long while, that sense of, I don't know, betrayal, I suppose. Without him there to hang out with made the rest of that time very hard to bear."

"You've no idea where the family went?"

He looked at Danny, made a kind of so be it face and looked away.

"They moved up north. For a while, I thought I might hear from him, a letter, Christmas card, my birthday but no. I never heard from him again."

For a moment, he was back there, re-living the way he had felt then then. Finally, he shrugged, sighed.

"But we're getting ahead of things. We must go back to the start of the school summer holidays; six long weeks of lazy, golden days, at least it felt that way when we were eleven years old. That year, things to last as long as possible because September would bring big changes to our lives, leaving primary school, starting secondary education, no longer all together. It was the end of an era, although we would never have expressed it that way back then.

"Sarah was off to the local girl's school while we boys were bound for Wandsworth Secondary Modern, so that last long summer break was special. Happy and sad at the same time and when the fair came, as it usually did every July for a two week stay, it felt as though it was going to be better then ever.

"I remember watching it arrive, all the pieces that made up the rides and sideshows strapped to lorries, driving in convoy along Lower Richmond Road towards Putney Common. It was a ritual, all gathered there on the corner of Brian's street to see the show, a kind of hors d'oeuvre to the main event, the fair opening.

"We always went on the first Saturday afternoon. The school break didn't start until the second week of July and we could only go to the fair in the evening if our parents agreed to take us, which meant we weren't altogether. So we made the most of that first Saturday and were there ready for the opening at one o'clock, all so excited, even Veronica's presence couldn't put the dampeners on our afternoon.

"As usual, we pooled our coins, mostly coppers saved from weeks of pocket money, paper rounds and things. None of us had parents that didn't have to watch every penny they spent. I mean, my dad was a postman and Mum had a couple of part time jobs, cleaning other people's houses and the others weren't much better off.

For Alan though, it was worse. He only had his Mum. His dad was always away and wasn't much good when he was home. You've met him I take it?"

Danny said he had.

"Well there you go then. He was much the same back then.

"Sarah's dad had been an ARP warden in the war and been killed by a VII rocket, just before it ended. Her mum was a school dinner lady, so like Alan, she had less than the rest of us. Ray's parents both had low paying railway jobs. So we used to pool our money in order that everyone had a fair chance of getting their share of the rides."

"Socialism in action," Danny said and smiled but Singleton didn't seem to have heard him.

"Veronica's mum was a widow. She had a government pension for herself and for Veronica's dad, because he'd died in Germany just after the war. She worked for the London County Council, quite a good position at County Hall, so they were fairly comfortable by comparison to the rest of us. That afternoon, Veronica put a half crown into the kitty, then beamed at the rest of us, like she was Lady Bountiful, doing her bit for charity. We didn't like it much but that didn't stop us making the most of it once we started on the rides and the stalls."

"What was all the business with the coconut shy?"

Singleton looked across at Danny. "How do you know about that?"

"There's a photograph."

Singleton nodded. "Yes, Veronice took it on that bloody camera she was always carting around.

"It was another of our rituals. Every year, on the first visit to the fair, we'd gather around the coconut shy before anything else to watch Brian win a coconut or two. He had an eye for it and I can't remember us ever being without a coconut to share among us on the way home."

He smiled, "Funny really, none of us liked coconut much."

"Veronica was mad on that old camera of hers," Singleton resumed. "She didn't like other people touching it. I must admit, she had the knack for taking photos though. She was a pretty good artist too. Used to sketch us from time to time, mostly focusing on Brian. She had this thing for him, as I said, which was odd, him being three years younger than her."

"And he didn't like it?" Hilary asked.

"He was always trying to put her off but she did what she wanted and it wasn't always a good idea to try to stop her. I think she even lured him back to her home one time. He went but he didn't stay long. I tried winding him up, saying that she had come on to him and he couldn't handle it."

"How did he take it?"

"Brian could usually take a joke but that time, he got really angry and we had a bit of a falling out."

Singleton stopped and looked around, as though expecting to find something hostile lurking in the corners of the room.

"What's the matter?" Hilary asked.

"Nothing," he said shortly and poured himself a stiff whisky. He offered the bottle to them and when they shook their heads, put it down on the table with a bump.

"It's brining it back, talking about it," he said and drank some whisky. "I believe that day at the fair was the last truly happy time we had. I've always thought that something happened that day at the fair. I don't know what it was but I suspect it had something to do with Veronica. Only Brian knew the truth and he wouldn't say but whatever it was, it changed him."

He took another pull from his glass.

"And then all that was overshadowed by what else happened the same afternoon, although we never heard about it until later."

Wind threw snow at the window, which sounded like tiney fingers tapping the glass. Singleton shot a frightened look across the room and reached for the bottle again.

"Take it easy," Danny said, putting a hand on the bottle. "I think we may have work to do tomorrow."

"I'll be alright!"

Danny exchanged looks with Hilary and slowly removed his hand. Singleton refilled his glass and took a messy drink, some of which rolled down his chin and he wiped the back of a hand across it.

"There was this little kid started at the school. A Turkish boy, called Berat. He was deformed, hunchback, skinny arms and legs. His torso was so small, it made his limbs seem longer than they were and kids used to call him spider."

"Kids, eh?" said Danny.

"Berat would tag along with us sometimes, mostly because he didn't seem to have any other friends, which was a shame because he was a nice enough kid once you got to know him. He was always smiling."

For a second, he refelected, thinking about the boy, the time, everything overlaid with sadness.

"His father was something high up at the Turkish embassy, so he had more pocket money than the rest of us and that afternoon, he treated us to several rides. The horses, was his favorite and the Whip, which used to throw you about and have the girls screaming."

He showed that same mirthless smile.

"The gang wasn't together all the time, some of us wanting to do one thing while others favoured something else. We would break up and meet again later. Nothing organised, only where we'd meet up at home time.

"Alan and Ray always went to ride the Ghost Train, because anything to do with things moving on rails attracted Ray and Alan enjoyed harmless scares.

"Me and Brian would make the rounds of the main rides, while Sarah, who was pretty good with an air rifle, usually went for the rifle range. She's spend ages trying to win one of the cheap bits of crockery or an ornament for her Mum.

"I remember that afternoon, Berat paid for Danny to go on the horses with him and afterwards, stuck with us for a while, watching us on the dodgems and the chair-o-planes and the rockets, all of which he didn't want to go on. Sometime there, he drifted away and we didn't see him again.

"I don't know what Veronica did."

But I do, Danny thought, grimly. It must have been that same afternoon she'd tracked him to the copse and tried to get him to expose himself.

"At home time, we would meet at the place we'd agreed, generally scoffing toffee apples or a hot dog maybe, anything but bloody candy floss, which none of us liked. We'd amble our way home, all excited, talking about what we had done and looking forward to our next visit the following Saturday."

Once again he had that wistful look on his face and then it slipped away.

"It was like old times that Saturday, as Veronice wasn't with and it felt like a weight had been lifted from our shoulders. We were all larking about, except Brian. He was very quiet, dragging along behind the rest of us, Making like he was joining in now and then but his heart wasn't in it.

I asked him what was wrong but he wouldn't say, just kind of froze me out. I'd never seen him that way before and I was hurt. When we reached his street, he just left without saying much at all and I watched him walk off, burning with angry that he hadn't confided in me."

The next morning he forgot about Brian's mood because Berat had disappeared.

"The police were all over it, his father being who he was. Had the boy been kidnapped by some group with an axe to grind against the Turks? or was it a case of ransom? Plenty rumours circulated but that all changed when Berat's mutilated body was found in the old parish cemetary."

Danny glanced at Hilary, who looked away.

"The police came to the school two days before the end of term. The whole school wasd gathered in the assembly hall and asked whether anyone had any information about the boy that might help the them in their investigation. The five of us went as a group into the class room that had been set aside for interviews and told them that he came to the fair with us. They asked us questions, together and individually but all we could tell them was that we had lost sight of him.

"Not long after, the school holidays started and our mood lightened a little, although the shadow of what had happened was never far away. Brian seemed something like his old self again, quieter but we all were and none of us thought anything of it. Berat was our friend and now he was dead, murdered in the most awful way, so it was natural that things felt a little different.

"Then one day, Brian said he didn't want to meet up with the others and I knew that whatever had been on his mind that day at the fair was still there. We went back to my place and settled down with our new comics, intent on spending the afternoon reading them.

"He didn't talk much, even when I tried to get him interested in our football team's prospects for the new season, he'd say a couple of words and that was that. It wasn't until later, just as he was leaving and he stood in our front passage and told me he'd seen Veronica walking in the woods behind where the fair with Berat following her.

"He hadn't said anything to the police in case it got her into trouble with her mum. He said couldnb't believe she had anything to do with what happened and I agreed with him. I mean, it was beyond awful to think sin spite of everything I knew about her, I didn't either. I could tell that there was something that was bothering him to do with her but he wasn't saying anything, no matter how hard I tried to get him to open up. All I know, he was as cold as ice with Veronica after that.

"So the holidays ran their course, trips to the cinema, games in the park and down by the river, along the water front, even though we'd been forbidden by our parents to play along there since a girl from our school had drowned a couple of years earlier.

"Gradually the days slipped away, hot and lazy and, terrible as it sounds, Berat's death faded a little from our minds. And then we reached that day. The worst day of our lives. The day that has haunted us ever since."

Singleton needed a break. It was obvious that remembering had taken a lot out of him. Hilary made tea, bringing the three steaming mugs through to us on a tray she had found somewhere.

Danny, who had been trying to fit what Singleton had told them together with his returned memories, came back to the room with a start. Singleton had produced a pack of cigarettes and was puffing at the flame from a small, chrome lighter.

"There's no sugar in any of them," Hilary said, placing the trey on the coffee table.

Neither of them responded and after she had sat down, the trio sank into an uneasy silence to drank their tea until eventually, Singleton leaned over and tossed his cigarette butt into the fire.

"I guess it's time for me to finish the story."

"In your own time," Hilary said.

"I'll do it now, otherwise I might never do it."

As the night closed in around the house and snow flicked gently at the window, he took a deep breath and resumed his tale.

"It was hot that day! I mean really burning hot. One of those days when the air seems so thick with heat, it seems like you can't get enough air into your lungs. All you feel like doing is throwing yourself down in some shady place and closing your eyes. Laze away the remaining hours until a modicum of coolness arrives with evening.

"As usual, Veronica had met up with us early in the morning, waiting for us in the street where Brian lived, like she knew we intended to pick him up there. She wanted to play Tin Can Tommy, where we all lined up against the high wall at the bottom of Brian's road and whoever was Tommy would throw a tennis ball at you,

410

trying to hit you. If you were hit, you were out of the game.

"None of us liked playing with her because she would always play rougher than we did and throw the ball hard enough to hurt when it hit you. And she always aimed for the face, which was not allowed and if she hit you there, she'd be all apologies, but all the time we knew she was really enjoying it.

"She caught me a good one that day, smack in my left ear and after that, Sarah said she'd had enough and walked away from the wall. It took some doing because Veronica could get quite scary if you didn't do what she wanted and I remember her looking daggers at Sarah. But nothing came of it, as she knew Sarah wouldn't take any of her shit. If it had been anyone but Sarah, there would have been troubel, although maybe Brian could have got away with it.

"We played some other games but the weather soon tired us out and after a morning running ourselves silly, we all needed time to rest up. Fractious and sweaty, we went in for luch, having already decided between the five of us to go to the Ranelagh in the afternoon. It was shaded and peaceful there and we go alone, without Veronica hanging on.

"That was when the photograph you've got was taken," he said to Danny. "We were just dropping Brian off at his place when his dad came out on his way to work. We all like his dad and someone suggested we had a photo done with him in his uniform. Veronica was reluctant at lending her camera to another person but finally agreed that this other bloke, a bus driver friend of Brian's dad, could use it to take a photo.

"It turned out to be the last film on the roll and Brian's dad offered to get it developed, as he had a mate who would do it for nothing and - "

"Wait! WAIT!"

Hilary and Singleton looked at Danny, startled by his tone. He was wild eyed with shock.

"What do you mean? Jack Reed was *my* father!"

They stared at him in silence until Singleton found his voice. "P.C. Reed was Brian's dad."

"He was my dad! I was Danny Reed back then, not Stephens."

Danny touched his brow, feeling the familiar tightness around his skull. The echo of his own words reverberated in his head. Of course, Jack was his father, he'd always been his father. What was Singleton trying to pull?!

"I saw him die! I was there. I watched him plunge into the Thames to save a girl."

"Did Brian have a brother?" asked Hilary.

"No brother. He was an only child." Singleton looked at Danny, "Brian's name was Ellis, not Reed."

Danny saw that Hilary watching him, nervously , questioningly. Singleton regarded him in that same strange, searching way as he had before, back in his office the first time they had met.

"When Brian was six he fell over in the kitchen," he said at length. "He cut himself pretty badly on the edge of his Mum's boiling copper. It left a crescent shaped scar on the left side of his jaw."

Danny had forgotten the scar, hidden for so long by his beard. He raised a leaden hand and traced the shape of it below the hairs with his fingers. All at once, pain swelled within his skull and then diminished just as suddenly leaving him light headed.

"Brian?" Singleton said softly. "Is it... Are you...?"

"My name was Reed," he said uncertainly. "Even if my Christian had been Brian, I'd still have been Reed."

"Brian's mother wasn't married to P. C. Reed," Singleton said. "Brian wasn't Reed's son. His mother never called him anything but Ellis."

Memories seeped into his head, sharp as a knife blade, stabbing his consciousness with fragments of memory. Mum telling something quietly, just the two of them there. Whispering secrets that she knew he was too young to remember.

"Brian's father - died in the war," Singleton said. "D-Day. On the beaches at Normandy."

Danny listened to the ghost of his mother's voice, snatches of sentences, names. places, long locked in the confines of his brain. As she spoke, he saw the photo he'd found at the bottom of Dad's case, taken outside Waterloo Station. Two soldiers with two young women, laughing, having fun, like there was no war going on. A precious moment snatched for posterity. It hadn't lasted long, fate had seen to that, just long enough to seed him and then...

"My father was a Canadian," he said quietly and felt invisible shackles fall away from him.

"Your mother must have loved him a lot," Hilary said. "Refusing to change your name, knowing the condemnation she would have to face, the stigma."

Hilary was right. An unmarried mother was considered the lowest of the low in those days, condemned more for the fact that she defied convention than having conceived him. Had she married, changed his name, her disgrace would have been grudgingly accepted.

Had there been no family to help her? Had her sin been too much for them to overlook? Mum had told him once, when he was older, that she had lost touch with her family, some unexplained and apparently unrepaiable fracture in their relstionship. Now he wondered whether if, as far as they were concerned, both mother and baby were dead. Living with Jack must have had tongues wagging all around the neighbourhood. All those bloody hypocrites who had led such stainless lives.

Danny gave a bitter laugh. "I've been called a bastard many times in my life without realising just how accurate the description was."

"Danny - "

He wanted no words of sympathy, he didn't need them. He gave another bark of ironic laughter. "I've been looking all over the place for Brian and he was here all the time! I've been looking for myself!"

But there was nothing new in that, he'd been doing it for as long as he could remember, although he hadn't know it.

"It's getting late," Hilary said. "Should we leave this for now?"

"I think we should hear everything."

"You're right," Singleton said. "The next part is the hardest. You're both welcome to stay the night if you want. It may take a while and I want to tell it properly. Accuracy might be important and it's sbeen a long time."

"If I'm writing about this later, I'd certainly appreciate as much accuracy as you can give."

"I mean for what we may have to do."

Danny felt that familiar shifting inside him.

"I don't understand," Hilary said. "What may we have to do?"

"Stop her," Singleton said quietly.

She looked from one to the other of them, "Stop her? How?"

"Let him finish the story," Danny said. "After all this time, it has to be told. Then maybe we'll know how."

Chapter Twenty Five

The room suddenly seemed glommier as Singleton emptied his glass, stood it on the table, then pushed both it and the bottle away from him.

"So, we'd had a belly full of Veronica in the morning and none of us wanted her coming to the Ranelagh with us. It was dangerous over there and with someone like her around, there was always the chance of something happening. She never hurt any of us badly but there was always the sense that, if we didn't do what she wanted, that might easily change."

Danny drew away from what was being said as his mind reeled at what he'd just learned. Brian Ellis was as unfamiliar to him as the man in the moon and yet, that was him. He moved to the end of the couch and tried to lose himself in the corner. He had to listen to what Singleton was telling them, it was important but he just could not free himslef from the truth of who he was.

"The Ranelagh Club had been a swish place before the war," Singleton continued. "With polo grounds, croquet lawns, tennis courts and a golf course and the well-to-do flocked there from all over London and the home counties at weekends; sports events and parties, dancing into the early hours, you can imagine the type of thing.

"I think Edward VII and George V both visited at some time, as there were often touring polo teams from India, Germany and even the USA, playing against various home sides.

"The club also hosted the annual Ladies Open Golf tournament for several years and there were often noted college sides rowing on the sizeable lake the owners had had constructed.

"The club closed at the outbreak of war and remained that way for the duration, the intention being to re-open when hostilities ended. No one had foreseen how much society would change after the war though and the place fell out of favour. Somehow the building caught fire in the late forties and burned down, after which the blackened shell was boarded up, the grounds forgotten and left for nature to re-claim. By the time it became our secret place. it was an overgrown wilderness, full of pitfalls for the unwary but we loved to play there, in spite of the warnings from parents and authorities alike.

"The site faces out over the Thames, with Beverly Brook running along one side and the main road through Barnes to Hammersmith Bridge on the other. By the mid fifties, the local authority had erected a wire fence all around the site, but we found a way in, through a gap in the the fence along the brook bank.

"There's a dirt path beside the brook that runs alongside the old playing fields from the foot bridge that crosses the brook at its mouth. The bank up to the field was steep and uneven, so the wire fence couldn't follow the contours of the ground. There was a gap just big enough for kids of our size to squeeze through.

"Inside, we'd made a pathway through the under-growth, a jungle of nettles and cow parsley, blackberry bushes and grass as high as out heads. It took ages to get through, with a fair bit of damage to our arms and legs, so every time we went there afterwards, we would make sure to clear away new growth, so it would never be as hard as that again.

"On that day, the air was heavy, oppressive, and filled with a cocktail of scents from the wild growth around us. There wasn't a breath of breeze to cool us and by the time reached to the ruin, we were sweaty and covered in insect bites. It was as though that jungle of vegetation was trying to stop us in a way it never had before, almost like it knew how the day was going to end.

"The air was thick and particularly heady near the lake and passing it, we were forever swatting away mosq-uitoes and there were wasps too, which always seem to go a little crazy as autumn approaches, stinging for no reason at all.

"I tell you, it was a treat when we finally reached the blackened remains of the building, emerging from the jungle at the rear of the ruin, where the fire had done least damage. There was a covered patio area fronted by an arc of ten thick pillars, which vertually untouched by the fire, leant a little normality to the scene.

"The patio overlooked what had been the playing fields and the lake, with a bank of French windows letting onto a loung area cum function hall, where members could sit and watch the activity on the fields while enjoying a drink in the shade. If you were of a mind, you could imagine exactly how it must have been but when you turned round and faced reality, all you saw was glassless window and blackened frames.

"It was there we'd found a way into the building, where the boards fitted across the windows when the place had closed had come away. It led into the lounge, which Sarah insisted on calling the ballroom, a large space that had once had a parquet floor. It was still possible to see sections of it if you looked hard enough, beneath the fallen debris from above.

"The bar area had been at the far end and the blackened stump of the bar itself was still there. The mirrors which had lined the wall behind it had gone, just bits of burned frame hanging patheticall from srew in the wall. The ceiling had mostly fallen in, exposing the floor joists of the room above and all over, the floor was a thick mix of rain soaked plaster, burnt wood and weeds.

"It was relatively safe in there and only dangerous once you went through to the rest of the building, where the roof had caved in, bringing down most of the upper floors. There was a mass of debris, scrappy vegetation and blacked brickwork. Some sections of the upstairs rooms clung on, scraps of flooring, joists, a few charred floor boards.

"Brian, Ray and myself used to go up there during our games sometimes. The grand staircase in the front hall was still standing and was navigable, if you stuck to one side and were careful. A stretch of the upper landing remained in places, with a couple of rooms still having sections of their flooring which was quite solid.

"It sounds pretty precarious, doesn't it and I certainly wouldn't try the things we got up now as I am now. We were children though and those upper stretches were safe enough, if you knew what you were doing - "

"You could stand at the top of the staircase and get an idea of how the place must have looked in its heyday," Danny said quietly.

Singleton looked at him, nodded. "Yes, that's right, if you could look beyond the forlorn, forgotten wreck that it had become."

Danny smiled forlornly, held his hands out, palms up and shook his head, saying he didn't remember anymore right then.

In a moment, Singleton continued. "We'd found the remains of couch on our first visit and dragged it through to the ballroom, parking it beside a smashed up piano. The old thing was still working, after a style and Alan used to tap out the opening bars of the Harry Lime Theme on it from time to time. Butt not that day. That day it was like an oven in there, with the air hanging dead upon the place and the stink of charred wood and mold permeating everything. We mooched around for a bit, throwing something here, kicking something there, maybe tearing off clumps of hanging plaster held together by a flap of wall paper.

"It was no ideal hideaway that afternoon, as we should have known it wouldn't be. No cool areas to stretch out away from the heat and really, we'd have been better staying round the streets where at least one side of the pavement would be in shade. There was a lot of complaining, some arguing, some taking out their irritability by digging at the remaining walls with a stick or some hard implement dug out from amidst the rubble.

"When Sarah, removing the cowboy hat she inevitably wore, suggested we play a game, we thought she was mad but in the end, we agreed, just for something to do, although Ray wanted to go down to the grotto. That was nothing but an old brick construction beside the brook which housed a big, concrete pipe that ran underground, all the way back to the lake.

"We thought the pipe was probably used to drain the lake it if necessary and to us kids, it became a grotto, another place for adventure. Ray, who had taken a real liking to it, used to climb into the pipe and see how far he could get along it before losing his nerve. It was wide enough for a ten year old to climb into quite nicely, if that ten year old was reckless enough to do so except Ray.

"Brian used to stop him doing it too often, as he was our de facto leader." Again he looked at Danny, "Youe weren't comfortable with it, but we mostly listened to what you had to say."

"And now, Hilary said. "At least, to a certain extent."

"Then don't," Danny told them. "Back then, I can't say, but it's definitely a bad idea now."

There was a pause, as though to let the echos of his words fadse, then Singleton carried on.

"Alan was youngest, not much past his tenth birthday, while Sarah and I were ten and Brian was just eleven, so I guess that's why we tended to listen to what he - you had to say. Maybe that was why Veronica took a shine to you. Do you remember that?"

"Some," Danny said shortly and turned his face away. "It's all a bit vague still."

"She was always trying to get close to you. She was only fourteen but she seemed a lot older sometimes. She knew about things we'd never even dreamed of." He pulled a face. "She was always smirking at some private thought or other. I think she was amusing herself with us."

"But that day, she wasn't with you," Hilary said.

"No. I need a glass of water," he said edgily. "Damn scotch has dried my mouth."

Singleton lurched to his feet and hurried from the room. In the quiet that followed, Hilary watched Danny, saw him lower his head, stare at the floor as though staring into damnation. She reached across and touched his forearm.

"Are you all right?"

He gave a deep sigh and looked at her. His face was anguished. "Not really. I'm scared stiff."

"Well, all of this. It's bound to..."

"Not just about this." He sucked in a long, seemingly painful breath. "I'm scared that my memory's returning. Of what I may find out. Of what I did back then. Of who I am."

Singleton returned opening a packet of cigarettes he had found somewhere. He tossed the cellophane into the grate and shoved a cigarette between his lips. Sitting down, he used his lighter to get the stick going, puffing at one nervously.

"Sorry about that. It was just... I couldn't - my mouth was so dry."

"Okay," said Hilary, wearily.

He tried a reassuring smile but it wasn't clear whether it was for them or himself. Hilary reac hed over and helped herself to a cigarette from his pack.

"You's better go on."

"Yes." He tapped ash from his cigarette and took a moment fiddling with the ash tray. "We settled on a game of, 'Tag'. That's where everyone hides and the one chosen as 'It' has to find them. Off we went while Sarah, who was 'It', started to count to a hundred and once she was done, she would come and find us."

"I used to play that too," Hilary said. "I can't remember what we called it. The last one to be found was the winner and became 'It' in the next round."

"Yes, yes," Singleton said irritably and looked at Danny. "I saw you going up the main staircase and was tempted to follow. You were the best at the game and nearly always the last to be caught."

Danny shook his head, no.

"Well, I changed my mind. It was hot and I couldn't be bothered to climb up after you. I think the rest of us were looking for obvious places to hide, so the game wouldn't go on too long.

"I settled on the large kitchen area. Being at the back of the building, it had missed the worst of the blaze, but there wasn't a lot of room to move around, as part of the ceiling had fallen in, so I hid behind the door of a larder, just inside the room.

"Sarah, who had suggested the game in the first place, soon lost interest, so it was a good thing we all wanted to get caught. She found Alan and Ray first. They always hid in the same places, so that was easy. I was soon fed up in the kitchen and gave myself up and we went through to the ballroom to wait for Brian to show himself.

"We were all sticky with sweat, dirty and miserable, so that I finally told them he was upstairs and we nagged Sarah to go and find him. She was sick of the game now and had already torn her new shorts on a nail. She knew her mum would give her hell.

"We started calling out to Brian, telling him he'd won and that we wanted to go to the grotto to hang out, paddling and looking for tiddlers. No matter how much we shouted though, you didn't give up and we got pretty annoyed about it. We decided to go on ahead and wait for you there, when ...."

Singleton stopped, rubbed a hand across him mouth, eyes darting from one to the other of them.

"Christ! This is harder than I thought it would be. I've managed to keep it out of my mind all these years, well, most of the time. Now it's all coming back, stronger than ever."

"Yes," Danny said. "I think...it's all shadows...

Singleton glared at him and for a minute, looked like he might lose his temper. But he controlled himself and after a few more seconds, continued.

"It was just as we had started for the French windows. There was a loud scream. God, what a scream! It filled the building. The next thing, Veronica came falling through the air, arms waving wildly and falling - falling - like she was in slow motion. It was as though a spell held us there, watching her body descending, her arms flailing helplesly... And then, she crashed down on her back a few feet away, on top of a pile of charred joists and the spell was broken."

Danny's head, already aching, felt suddenly numb. A a hot tingling sensation began to build at the base of his skull. All at once, his mouth and nose filled with the stench of burned wood and he could see...

"She just lay there, staring up at me through the joists."

The other two looked at him but when he said nothing more, Singleton jumped in.

"There was a sharp crack when she landed, then she just laid there. It was horrible. Her head was thrown back at an awkward angle, her eyes gazing at nothing."

"At me! She was staring at me. Time ticked away and we all froze, gazing at her, waiting, praying for her to move. Slowly we began to realise that she would never move again."

"Didn't any of you check, see if she was alive?" Hilary asked.

"Yes," Singleton said quietly. "Finally. Somehow, I found the nerve to edge closer and the others followed me. They shuffled around uneasily, suspecting she might jump up. Laugh at us for our concern. I think we all knew though that that wasn't going to happen."

Danny said quietly. "She just lay there, broken and floppy. Like a marionette with its strings snapped."

"You remember?" Hilary said.

"I think we'd have stayed like that forever if it hadn't been for your voice coming down to us," Singlton told him."

Danny continued in that same hollow tone. "I asked if she was dead. You thought she was but none one wanted to get too near to her."

"Sarah got the nerve up in the end."

Danny nodded, remembering her reaching over, touching one of Veronica's wrists, then snatching her hand away.

"She said she felt clammy. I asked if there was a pulse but she wasn't sure and refused to touch the body again."

"In the end, I did it," Singleton said. "I'd been in the St. John's Ambulance Brigade for a while, so I had some idea what I was doing. I felt both her wrists and her throat but there was no pulse. She was dead."

Danny closed his eyes for a moment, saw them beneath him, frightened, fidgeting, wondering they should do. Someone made a whimpering sound, certain they would be in big trouble for what had happened.

"Alan started crying," Singleton said. "He was terrified the police would come to his house, of what his dad would do when he came home from sea and found out. Ray said we might be hanged."

Danny remembered going down to them, as shaken as they were, more so. It was him that... that what? He shook his head, as if to clear it and knew that he'd been angry at them for looking to him to make things right, when he was just as scared as they were.

"We asked you what had happened," Singleton said.

"I couldn't think. Not with her lying there."

They had gone outside to the patio and after a few minutes it had started coming back to him, blazing at him in giant, technicolour pictures on the screen of his mind.

"I had been hiding upstairs."

"Because we were all scared of going up there."

"I'd known that you would all give up and start shouting for me to come down, as always."

"You shouldn't have gone up there!" Singleton snapped. " Maybe she wouldn't have..."

"I know."

Singleton had a hand covering his eyes. Danny reached out and squeezed his arm.

"I know it was my fault, but I'm seeing it again through the eyes of a stranger."

"Don't you remember any of it?" Hilary asked.

"Bits and pieces. Some as clear as day but others... There's a lot of empty spaces."

He knew that he'd been as tired of the game as the rest and was already thinking of coming down. He remember how dangerous it was up there. How careful you had to be, with hardly any floor left.

"The air was so hot, heavy, like a blanket. The overriding stink of burnt wood. I'd been watching you lot down below in the ballroom. I could see you through the joists."

He'd got to his feet on the back section of the existing flooring, back near the wall, where it was safest. He had turned towards the door when - .

"Someone was there with me."

A creak from the landing flooring. He'd stepped close to the door and peeping through the carck where it met the jamb, saw a blur of movement.

"The door opened and she stepped into the room."

"Veronica," said Hilary.

"She was a clever bitch," Singleton said harshly. "She had guessed we would go to the Ranelagh and followed us there."

Danny moaned softly and closing his eyes, saw images coming at him fast. Her in front of him, as clear as if she stood there now, angry but hiding it behind a sharp smile. She had told him she thought he'd chosen the perfect place to hide. Somewhere they could be alone.

"The others are just downstairs."

She had smiled even more. "There's not one of those chickens could find the guts to come up here."

She told him it gave them time to finish their other little game.

I've shown you mine. Now it's your turn to show me yours.

"She wanted me to - show her - to expose myself."

"Jesus!" said Singleton.

"She was furious at being left behind. Her eyes... I was too scared to call out to the rest of you."

Singleton muttered something about it all feeling too close but that was all. Danny stared at him. *Too close! It's playing inside my fucking head!*

Veronica had come at him then, bigger and stronger and he'd struggled to get her off. All the time she was pulling at his shorts. He couldn't hold her back.

"She had me down on the floor."

He swallowed dryly, feeling her hands on him, pawing at him. He felt again the panic he had felt them, the terror that she would get his clothes down and see him. That she might do to him what she'd down to Berat.

Danny reached over the table and snatched up the whisky bottle. The top was still off from Singleton's last top up and he swigged straight from the bottle. When the spirit was burning its way down inside him, he gasped and stood the bottle down.

Across the table they were watching him with frightened eyes. He nodded that he was okay to them and closed his eye for a moment. The pictures played on but he was able to handle them better now.

"She'd had to release me a little, so that she could get to the button holding my shorts, get at my fly. I could smell her sweat, feel her breath on my face."

"God!" Hilary looked pale.

Danny remembered the weight of her on top of him. He could smell again the hot smell of her, not unpleasant, the smell of a young female body close to him, sweat and soap.

"Lifting herself, she gave me the briefest chance to bring a leg up between us and I shoved as hard as I could."

It wasn't enough to get her right off but it was enough to dislodge her. She held on to him, trying to stop him from getting up but he was quicker than her and was on his feet before she could get her weight over him and push him down.

Her eyes flashed, her teeth snapped, her hands, still interlocked with his, pushed them back until his wrists cried out in pain. It was that pain which spurred him on, the fear that she might break his wrists let him duck towards her, bringing his head close to her breasts.

He actually heard now the savage noise she'd made back then, as he lunged forward with all of his terror driven strength, sending Veronica staggering backwards. Her left foot came down on empty air and she released his hands, her arms windmilling in an effort to keep her balance as she tottered backwards. Then, one small squeak of panic as she ran out of floor space,teetering on the edge of the last board for a moment before falling into oblivion.

"She had nowhere to go," he said. One second she was there, the next she'd vanished through the joists. A moment later, I heard her land."

Singleton said, "She didn't even scream, not really, just a kind of shocked snort and then she was spread eagled over that pile of joists with a thin trickle of blood running from her ear into her hair. Afterwards, there was a such silence. All dense, we could hear was the noise of insects from outside. Then you came down and got us moving out onto the patio.

"We were devastated and for once, you didn't come to our rescue. You couldn't, you just stood there, gazing out into the jungle of weeds. In the end, I managed find my voice, asked what we should do with her.

"Alan and Sarah wanted to leave her there. Just go home and not say anything to anyone but I was certain that someone would know we played over and that Veronica was always with us. I knew the police would find out evenntually and search there.

"Looking back through adult eyes, it's obvious we should have owned up. Said it was an accident, that she fell while playing a game. But of course, we weren't adults and we were terrified. It was finally agreed to put her in the grotto."

"Jesus!" Danny said and looked away.

"Do you remember?"

Danny nodded, "It's vague. I remember the heat."

"It was bloody gruelling, I can tell you. Lugging her body through that tangle of vegetation in the full heat of afternoon."

"Yes," Danny said. "Who would have thought she could be so heavy?"

Pictures came jumping into his head, plodding through a jungle of tall grass and nettles, flies buzzing around them, mosquitoes biting them. Every time they stopped to get their breath, they had descended in swarms, drawn in by the smell of their sweat and her blood.

"It was worse near the lake," Singleton said. "The vegetation was spectacular there, right up tp the water's edge. The water was stagnent and the was filled with living things, which rose up in swarms when we disturbed them.

"By the time we got down the brook bank to the grotto, most of us were either crying or close to it and now we were faced with the job of getting her body into the tunnel and along to the drainage pipe."

Danny remembered them agreeing that the pipe was the best place to put her. The grotto was actually a squat, brick built structure, with a flat roof and flint covered walls.

"Once we'd rested, we carried her inside, albeit in fits and starts. It was actually relatively straight forward moving about in there, as it was wide enough for a couple of men to work comfortably and we were kids. It was a lot more tricky getting it inside the pipe because tunnel tapered as it reached the pipe mouth and there was limited space to manoeuvre.

"The place had been neglected since the fire and the elements had littered the inside with fallen leaves and rain, blown in through the entrance. Crumblkings from the roof had mixed with it and turned to mush, which coated the floor in a slippery carpet."

"There were tree roots," Danny said, remembering dangling fingers touching his face.

"Broken through from above," Singleton confirmed. "It was clear that, unless something was done to maintain the place, the roof would eventually give way.

"We took turns getting the body as far along the tunnel as we could, then just stood around staring at it. None of us wanted to touch it again and no one wanted the job of manhandling the corse into the pipe, when we would be close up to it. It was only when some of the fatter flies began finding their way in there that I said we should get on with it."

In his head, Danny was back in that tunnel and knew that they had all wanted to run away, especially when the idea of flies laying maggots on Veronica, of them eating into her, worked on their minds. It had taken a lot of argument, of accusation and finally appeales to their friendship to keep them there.

"Getting the body close enough to the pipe in order to fit it inside proved harder than they had tought, as the tunnel narrowed considerably and with all those tree roots hanging down..."

There had been room for just three of them to gather around the pipe mouth, Danny knew. The walls were rough and to rub against them was enough to remove skin from bare elbows and knees.

The speed with which his memorey threww picture at him was enough to make him reel and he had to keep a firm hold on himself. One second, all he saw was blackness, a wall that the next second would come tumbling down to show him what was behind it.

"The smell of rotten vegetation was sickening, and of course, every step we took through that slimy sludge stirred it up more." Singleton's expression showed he could all but smell it again. "Alan was the smallest, so he climbed into the pipe while Brian - you and me lifted her feet first over the concrete rim."

Danny remembered they had lifted her body, holding it as level with the pipe as possible while Alan inched back, dragging her feet, legs and finally by the hips until he and Singleton finally steered her shoulders and head inside.

"Thankfully she was wearing shorts and not a skirt," Singleton said. "There was no problem with excess clothing snagging as we inched her along the pipe."

"That was when you banged your head."

"Yes," Singleton raised a hand an stroked the back of his head at the memory of it. "I had to get outside after that. I felt dizzy and thought my head was bleeding."

Once Joe was outside, Danny remembered Sarah had hurried out after him and was splashing brook water onto his head. It was a good job there had been no cut, that water wasn't the cleanest in the world.

"After you'd gone, Ray came up to help. There was a ridge inside the pipe that we hadn't spotted, a section of piping had dropped slightly causing the adjoining section to protrude by about four inches, thereby snagging the body."

The pictures playing in his mind began to flutter and distort, like the picture on an old TV set that needed the aerial adjusting. He was still there, in that stinking tunnel, aware of leaning into the pipemouth. He guessed that he was still shoving.

"When I was sure that my scalp wasn't cut, I came back inside," Singleton resumed. "Ray was in a state and went out and I stepped up beside you. We kept pushing at her shoulders but no matter how many times we pushed, we couldn't get the body past that ridge."

"Did her head fall back and crack againt the outside rim?"

Singleton looked at Danny. "Yes, but she was beyond feeling anything."

Talking about it was beginning to take its toll of Singleton. His hands were trembling and he kept licking his lips to moisten them. Danny felt he should stop, take a break but did not say anything. His memory was clearing all the time they were talking, He was afraid that stopping might cause it to shut down again.

"This is the worst bit," Singleton said shakily. "Alan was till inside and close to flipping out, he was so scared. We had to bully him into staying, of lifting her nips over that blockage and we said some horrible things to make him do it."

Whatever they had said worked. Alan was whimpering but he remained where he was and somehow managed to manouever her hips and buttocks enough and one last push by them did the job.

"Once she was inside, Alan couldn't wait to get out," Singleton's voice sounded thick with the memory of it.

"Luckily, he was the smallest of us, so when his panic took over, he managed to scramble out along her body. How he'd managed to hold it together for so long, I don't know."

He hurriedly poured himself a big drink and swallowed half of it in one go. He said to Danny, "In some ways, you're lucky your memories are sketchy. I can see it all, like it happened yesterday."

Danny did not comment, the pictures were coming freely again now and he saw Cockle clambering across the corpse and them, him and Singleton pulling him free of the pipe.

"He was almost out of his mind," he said. "He kept saying that her eyes were open."

Singleton choked on the whisky, spluttered, coughed and quickly wiped his chin clean of dribble.

"We just stared at him, shocked I suppose and he kept on saying it, over and over, that she'd looked at him!"

"Her eyes were closed!" Singletonn snapped. "I saw them closed before we pushed her in there. You saw them too, for god's sake!"

Danny shook his head, "I can't see that."

"Maybe you don't want to!"

"Maybe I don't," Danny snarled. Maybe he didn't want to remember any of it, but it was too late for that now.

"Could they have been open?" asked Hilary in a tight voice. "Could she have been alive?"

"No! She had no pulse. I checked."

"Maybe we were wrong," Danny said.

"Maybe I was wrong, you mean." He attacked the whisky glass again. "Anyway, if you hadn't pushed her, we'd never have been in that position in the first place."

Hillary said quickly, "This is pointless."

"Is it? What was he so frightened of? I mean, if she really wanted sex, she'd hardly have come to any of us."

"It wasn't sex," Danny said.

"So what then?"

"Power," said Hilary. "Dominance."

"And humiliation. Of course she didn't have the hots for me, for any of the Tykes. We were kids, for Christ's sake."

"She wasn't. Not up here," Singleton jabbed a forefinger at his head.

"No. She was - more."

"Well then."

"It was," he searched for a word, "subjugation she wanted. She'd exposed herself to me, knew that buried in the mass of conflicting emotions I'd felt there was some degree of excitment. She wanted to humiliate for it. She wanted me to know rub my nose in the fact that I was just a child still. She wanted me to know her scorn."

Singleton stared at him for several seconds, then let out a great expulsion of air. He rubbed his face, started to reach for his glass but changed his mind.

"I'm sorry," he said.

Danny nodded, OK and the tension, which had been building between them, evaporated. In a moment, Hilary spoke.

"What happened after that?"

"We gathered debris," Singleton resumed. "As much as we could find and threw it into the pipe. We wanted to hide her as best we could, in case anyone did look in there. After that, we went home."

They sat quietly reflecting and the shadows in the room grew longer around them. Singleton reached for the bottle again, offered the bottle to them and this time, they each had a small amount.

"Our friendship changed that day," he said. "We were no longer the same kids."

"There was the knife."

Danny could see it plainly. Veronica had always carried a pen knife, it had a white handle, with pictures of horses on each handle panel. They had started for home when he'd seen the knife lying on the path.

"It had fallen from her pocket."

"Yes, that's right. You just keept staring at it and I asked you why it was so important."

"I think I must have known, even then and the thought of it horrified me."

Singleton moaned softly, "Berat."

"We stopped on the footbridge and I threw it as far out across the Thames as I could."

Hilary said, "If she had used that on the boy, the police might have been able to... "

"Now maybe, not back then. Anyway, I was a kid. I just wanted rid of it."

"After doing that, you said it was the finish of her."

Danny, without irony said, "How wrong you can be."

They say there thinking about that until Singleton roused himself.

"We didn't see much of each other after that. I spent most of that last week of the holidays at home. I think we all did. There were no more gatherings."

Danny said, "The days of the Rudd Street Tykes were over."

He closed his eyes and leaned back gainst the chair. In the darkness behind his lids he saw them all, five happy children laughing together as they went looking for adventure and a great ache started up inside him.

Chapter Twenty Six

Early morning was struggling to lift the darkness in the room. Danny turned over on Singleton's long couch and gazed at the glowing embers of last night's fire. All around him the grainy light from outside fell over the humped shapes of furniture, standing like tomb stones in the gloom.

At length he sighed and sat up. The room was cold so he dragged the blankets Singleton had supplied around his shoulders. He had barely slept, tortured by the things he'd learnt and now felt lost in a confusion of facts he was trying to get straight in his head.

They had talked into the early hours about what they should do, Hilary suggesting they should go to the police, tell them everything. Yes, they may well be prosecuted but at least it would all be out in the open then, over and done with.

"This thing seems to thrive on secrets."

And she was right, whatever dark thing Veronica had become had grown out of their guilt, but both he and Singleton believed it was going to take more rthan a confession to placate it. She had her own punishment to deal out and no amount of public condemnation would alter that fact.

Hilary came into the room carrying two cups of what turned out to be tea, handing one to him and standing the other on the coffee table.

"Did you sleep?"

"Some."

"Same here."

She walked to the window and pulled the curtains back. Cold grey light fell slab-like into the room. Danny shivered and drew closer to what was left of the fire, holding his hands towards the warmth that struggled from it.

"Are you alright?"

When he didn't answer, she sat down and quietly drank her tea.

How was he? The sixty-four thousand dollar question. There was so much to take on board. He felt like a man with no past, or rather that the man he had known had been blown into a thousand parts and he had no idea of how to bring all those parts back together again.

His real name was Brian Ellis. He had been one of the Rudd Street Tykes and not just an outsider looking in, observing things they had done and before he could even start to come to terms with this, there was still the other thing to deal with.

"I've been trying to feel like Brain all night but he's still a stranger."

Hilary, holding her mug in two hands before her face, had been considering the dark places they were heading into, blinked, looked at him.

"Last night was difficult. All those things that were said."

She shut her eyes and pinched the bridge of her nose between a thumb and forefinger. Danny knew that however hard it was for him and Joe Singleton to face what they were up against, it was even harder for her. Hilary knew what they knew but still could not accept the reality of it.

"Perhaps we should delay our plans."

Singleton came into the room at that moment and stood inside the door looking from one to the other of them. Finally he said, "Do I call you Brian or Danny?"

"Danny. I don't know Brian." Managing a smile, he said, "I'm not even sure I know Danny anymore."

Singleton nodded. "She used to call you Daniel. It was your middle name and she knew you didn't like it."

Daniel in the lion's den.

"Do you remember anything more this morning?"

"Remember? It's all bits and pieces. I know it happened but can't actually *feel* it, if you know what I mean."

"I think I do."

Hilary cleared her throat. Her voice had a rough edge to it, as though she had sat up all night smoking and thinking. "I was wondering whether we should put this off."

Singleton looked at her, then at Danny. "We can, if you're not up to it? Personally I'd rather get it over with. If we don't do it the way we agreed, I don't think I'll have the nerve to do it at all."

They had run through the possibilities last night, whether it was likely Veronica had only been stunned by the fall through the floor, woken up later and somehow managed to get herself out of the drainage pipe.

Singleton had insisted she was dead and Danny thought he was right. Hilary tried to persue the argument but even she knew how unlikely it was to have happened that way. Singleton had felt no pulse and her eyes had been closed when they had pushed her inside the pipe.

"She may have been stunned," Hilary had persisted.

"She'd have needed medical help after a fall like that," Danny explained patiently.

"She'd have been more than hurt," Singleton had added. "She'd have been angry. She wouldn't have chosen to wait thirty years to avenge herself. Not the Veronica, I knew. She'd have started as soon as she could."

Seconds had passed, then Danny told her, "The child I saw in the basement was her. No one else."

"So what then?"

"I think you know. I think we all know. Veronica is dead. She was then, she is now. What we're dealing with is something else."

Oh yes, he could guess what a night she'd had trying to accept the impossible. He knew the battle she had gone through and felt sorry for her. It was the same battle he'd been through himself.

"I don't need convincing," Singleton said. "I've been wondering whether Alan decided to cut his throat when he saw her or whether she made him do it. The same with Sarah."

Danny said, "I think she made them do it. She probably forced Ray to start the fire too."

Hilary said, "If she has such power. What do we do? What can we do?"

"Go to the Ranelagh," Danny said.

"Oh, Jesus!" Singleton shrunk in on himself and gazed at the embers in the grate.

"What good will that do?" Hilary asked sharply.

"Maybe if we find her, if we bring her remains into the open and then tell the truth about what we did, maybe that will satisfy her. Give her some sense of justice."

"It's not justice she's after," Singleton muttered. "It's revenge."

Danny did not have any more confidence than him that what he had just suggested might be any good but it was the best he could come up with. From what he knew of Veronica, he doubted she would be satisfied, but what else was there to do?

"Do we start now?"

"I guess so. But first, we go to Kavanagh Mansions."

"Why?" asked Hilary.

"I need to look in the basement again."

"For what?"

"A sweets tin," Danny said.

They both gazed at him miserably.

"She showed me what was in it."

"What?" Singleton asked.

Hilary said, "A trophy."

"Yes." Their faces were grim.

"What trophy?" Singleton demanded. "I don't understand."

"There are killers who take things from their victims. Trophies, to remind them of the moment - of what they have done."

"Christie took samples of pubic hair from each of his victims," Hilary said.

Singleton looked at her, then at Danny and finally the penny dropped. "You mean, Berat?"

"Yes," said Danny.

"Oh, dear God!"

"I think we should get started, " Danny said.

He wasn't relishing the thought of going down in that basement again but it would be even harder if Singleton went to pieces on them.

"Supposing she's down there?" Singleton said, with an edge to his voice.

"You needn't come down."

"I'd prefer not to. But I'll come all the same."

"Afterwards, we go to the Ranelagh. If the grotto is still there, we go in and look in the pipe."

"And if she's not there?" Hilary asked. "If the tunnel has been flattened?"

"You're guess is as good as mine."

"If we find her, we come clean?"

"It was an accident, Joe."

"You don't think they'll charge us with anything, do you?"

"Possibly."

"We were kids."

"We haven't been kids for a long while," Danny said. "We'll have to take our chances."

The room seemed suddenly darker, colder and loaded with unspoken feelings. They looked at each other and saw the same fear reflected in the eyes that gazed back at them.

"I can't believe I'm going along with this," Hilary said but her heart wasn't in it.

Singleton shifted, stood up. "I think we ought to eat before we go."

In the kitchen, Danny cut some stale bread for toast, while Hilary grilled the last of a pack of bacon. Singleton went out to his garage to sort out some tools, loading them into his Land Rover.

"It belonged to my father," he told them when he returned.

"Did he have a farm?" Danny asked.

Singleton forced a grin. "Allotment."

When they had eaten, they drank fresh coffee and then climbed doggedly into their outdoor clothes.

Outside the sky was threatening. There hardly a breeze blowing and the cold, dead heaviness of the air seemed as though it wanted to drive them into the ground.

Hilary sat in the front of the vehicle beside Singleton. Danny climbed in the back with the tools; a shovel, two crowbars, a club hammer and a couple of cold chisels. There was also the coal shovel from the fireplace, which Singleton had had with him when he'd climbed into the driver's seat.

"The standard shovel will be useless in there," he said.passing it back to Danny. "The space is pretty tight."

"We'll have to get inside the pipe?" Hilary asked, alarmed.

"I meant in the tunnel," Singleton explained. "We were children the last time we were in there. But one of us will have to go into the pipe."

"Let's go," Danny said.

The ancient engine sounded extra noisy in the quiet morning, belching clouds of near black exhaust into the air. Danny watched it roll away through the small rear window of the vehicle until his eye was caught by a movement of another dark shape near the gate.

"My dad loved driving this," Singleton said, crunching the gears. "God knows why."

Danny hefted a crowbar, which had a chisel head at one end and a snake's tongue at the other. Then he weighed the coal shover in his hand, as he found Singleton's eyes in the rearview mirror.

Had he noticed the movement too?

If he had, he didn't show it. One of them, he thought, would have to crawl into the pipe, Joe had been right there. He was the slimmer of the two and there was no question of asking to go in. It was his problem when you got right down to it. He had killed her and his friends had only been helping him.

And look where that had got them!

"Look at the sky," Hilary said.

Peering out, he saw low hanging clouds, purple dark and ominous. It was already trying to snow again and the light was so poor, Singleton had to turn on the vehicle's dipped headlights.

The Land Rover climbed labouriously up a short hill to the top of the road. The inside had already started to stink of exhaust fumes and Danny pulled his coat tighter around him. He eyed the tools doubtfully. Would they get to use them? Not if the tunnel had been flattened when the site had been renovated to create council playing fields.

The snow was falling faster and a moment later, Singleton flipped on the wipers. The blades started a laboured zinc-zonk back and forth across the windscreen, which suggested that, should the fall increase, thay might give up altogether.

He looked out at the passing street and wondered, if the tunnel was still there, what state would it be it after all this time? It had been bad enough back then and it can have only got worse in the meantime. He humphed irritably and sat back in his seat. There was no point worrying about it, whatever was there was there and they would have to deal with the reality soon enough.

He thought about the photograph, the wartime one taken outside Waterloo Station, mum gazing up at the Canadian soldier, blind to everything else around her, eyes only for him. His name had been Ellis and he had gone back to war leaving behind a little more than he had brought with him.

Me?

The roads had been gritted that morning traffic and they arrived at Putney Bridge around half an hour later. It was snowing steadily now, medium sized flakes that looked like they meant business. Singleton turned the the reluctant vehicle onto Embankment and Danny stared gloomily out at the brooding Thames.

"I'll park along here," Singleton said.

He pulled in at the rear wall of Kavanagh Mansions and shut off the engine. They sat there in the new quiet for a moment, saying nothing, thinking their own thoughts, addressing their own fears. Singleton pointed towards a tall old wooden gate in the garden wall.

"We could get in that way but the bloody hinges have gone. Can't get them mended until summer."

"It's a walk then," Danny said and a sudden gust of wind threw snow at the wind screen. He sighed, "This shouldn't take long. If you want to give me the door code, Joe, you two can wait heree."

Singleton was already unbuckling his seat belt. He grunted and reached into the dash shelf, fetching out a hefty torch.

"I'm not staying here on my own," Hilary said and they all got out into the cold

"Well!" Singleton locked the vehicle, then stared into the falling snow, his eyes and mouth narrowed slits. "Here we go then."

They walked along until they reached a short stump of a road that swept up a steep slope to the main road. They climbed it quickly, then turned back on themselves at the top, walking along to the corner of Kavanagh Gardens. They went to the bottom without speaking and saw the Mansions at the far end.

Waiting for us, Danny thought. Ready to swallow us up, which of course was ridiculous. It was only bricks and morter. What might be waiting for them inside was another matter and when they arrived at the front of the building, he automatically looked up to the top floor landing window.

"Did you see something?" Hilary asked in an urgent whisper.

"No."

Singleton was already at the front door , punching in the security code. They joined him, following him inside to the foyer once the doors had clicked free.

"God!" Hilary said as the wall of silence descended upon them.

"It's always the same in here," Singleton said, nervously. "I've never taken much notice before."

"Over here."

Danny led them across to the door to the mezzanine. He was breathing in short, rapid breaths and he knew that he would never be truly ready for this. She had shown him that tim the last time he was here and although he didn't understand why, he knew it was important, so he had to check the trunk again.

"Dangerous?"

"What?" Singleton was staring at him in alarm.

"You said something about it being dangerous."

"Did I?" Danny frowned, had he been thinking aloud?

"Can we get on with this? Hilary said in a harsh whisper. "The silence in here is hurting my ears."

Danny opened the door and watched Singleton, who pushed past him, start down the stairs. He fell quickly in behind, joining him on the mezzanine in front of the basement door.

"Do we all go down?" Hilary asked as she stepped down beside them.

"No," Danny said. "You wait here and make sure the door doesn't close."

"You think it might?"

"I know it might."

"Okay." She reached inside her coat and looked put out. "Damn! I forgot my little camera."

"I shouldn't worry. I don't think you could photograph what we're after."

Singleton was gazing along the mezzanine to where the door to Cockle's flat stood half hidden by the stairs they had just used.

"Is that -?" Hilary asked.

Danny nodded shortly and took Singleton by the arm. "Come on, Joe."

He found the switch inside the Basement door and turned it on. The place was bathed in the same watery light from the line of bulbs in the ceiling.

"You may need your torch down there."

It took Singleton a second to process what Danny had said, then he nodded and half raised the torch like a club, as though to reassure them.

"Jesus!" he said. "Was it this cold before?"

"No." Danny said, tightly and found that the smell of coal seemed stronger too.

They went down the stairs quickly and stopped at the bottom. The aisle was facing them, the weak light inviting them to step into its chilly glow.

"Down there," Danny told him and Singleton gazed miserably at the space between the storage racks and the arches. He hefted the big torch in his hand, as though for reassurance and followed Danny past the first rack of shelving.

As though playing with them, the lights flickered and Danny shot a look up at them. To one side of them, beyond the empty shelves of the rack, he could see the lift shaft, although the car was at another floor. Behind the gate, the dark coils of cable hung down from the black shaft, poised for action.

"Down the end," he said and walked quickly along to the back wall.

"Will this take long?" Singleton asked, throwing glances into the black depths of the arch they past.

Danny stopped at the end of the aisle and saw the trunk standing where he'd left it. He was staring at the closed lid when Singleton stepped up beside him.

"The lid was open when I left it."

"Right." Singleton followed the tracks in the dirt with his eyes, all the way back to the dark corner the trunk used to stand in. "Did you pull it out?"

"It was already like this."

"As though it was waiting for you."

Danny didn't comment. Bending over , he took hold of the edge of the lid and lifted it back to its maximum. A great breath of fusty air wafted up around the two of them.

"Ugh!" Singleton said, stepping back.

Danny was already digging down the sides of the curtains, searching for the tin, which was not on the top of the pile as he had anticipated. He was sure she wanted him focused on that tin and had been certain he would find it this time, sitting there waiting for him. If it wasn't here, then she must have it with her *and want him to take it from her!*

He had to make sure it hadn't somehow slipped down into the trunk and the cold, tacky touch of the mouldy fabric revolted him.

"It's not here."

"Did you think it would be?"

Danny straightened up. "I wasn't sure."

"You said she had it. When you were in the lift car, she showed it to you."

"Perhaps it was never really here in the first place? Maybe she had it all along. Maybe it's been with her all these years."

She couldn't have had it back then. We'd have seen it."

"I didn't notice anything. Did you?"

"Alan got the closest to her."

"Alan was in a panic. He would't have seen anything other than the way out. Would you have, under the circumstances?"

"Her eyes being open, you mean?" Beads of sweat broke out on Singleton's forehead. He looked back over his shoulder, searching for something. "I won't believe it!"

The lights flickered and they both looked up.

Danny said, "Let's get out of here."

He took Singleton's arm and they moved quickly back along the aisle to the stairs. Hilary was waiting just inside the door and was staring past them, deep into the basement.

"You okay?" Danny asked.

She continued to search the space behind them. "I thought I saw something, a movement."

"Don't look!" Singleton said harshly in Danny's ear.

"I don't intend to."

Singleton seemed to pull himself together to a degree. He stepped away from Danny and started up the stairs. In spite of what he'd said, Danny cast a quick look back but all he saw was the trunk sitting on the floor at the end of the aisle. The lid was closed. All at once, the lights went out and he hurried up the stairs in the glow coming from the mezzanine floor.

"Come on," Singleton said, already mounting the stairs to the foyer.

Danny shut the basement door and followed, pushing Hilary in front of him. They reached the foyer with the cold, tainted air from the basement seeming to follow them. The top door clicked shut and it seemed that an extra dense silence fell over them, heavy and hostile. They didn't linger, just moved swiftly across the fading carpet and out into the street.

"When does the renovation work start?" Hilary asked.

"Spring," Singleton told her.

"Might be a better idea to pull the place down."

He didn't disagree with her.

"She lived here," Danny said. "She brought me here once but I didn't stay long."

Singleton said. "I think she still lives here."

A wind had picked up since they entered the block and was driving the snow flakes into their faces as they walked away from the Mansions. They bowed their heads and narrow their eyes against the icy pellets. It was slippery underfoot, with fresh snow settling on the frozen remains of older falls falls. Trudging miserably along in a tight little group, they eventually reached the vehicle and climbed quickly inside.

Singleton turned on the engine and wacked the heating up to maximum. "I can't remember seeing snow as dense as this before.

"Not in this country," Hilary said. "And never in the city, not in my lifetime."

"It's almost like it was trying to stop us," he said softly.

The others didn't comment. Something similar had passed through each of their minds.

Singleton crunched the vehicle into gear and they started slowly away, along Embankment. Outside, even the Thames seemed cowled by the force of the weather, its grey waters rippling angrily in the strength of the wind.

Watching the river, Danny was siezed by a sense of hopelessness at what they were about to attempt. So many years had passed since the day they had interred her in that pipe. What he remembered of it, the structure had been bad enough then. How would it be now, even if it was still there?

Chapter Twenty Seven

Singleton let the Land Rover move gently into the kerb outside a small park and turned off the engine. At once snow began building up at the bottom of the screen and cold fingers reached out at them as the warmth of the cab rapidly dissipated. Yanking on the hand brake, Singleton released his seat belt and got out.

"Pass the tools."

Danny handed him the crowbars, the shovel and club hammer, feeling his doubts tugging at him. What if they did find her, none of them knew what they were dealing with, not really? They were acting mostly on his say so when, up to just a few days ago, he would have dismissed all this as nonsense. Maybe he should tell them to leave well alone, go there by himself.

Hilary got out of her side and walked around the front of the vehicle to stand on the pavement besside Singleton. Pulling her gloves tighter, adjusting her coat collar around her throat, she peered in at him through the screen, wondering why he wasn't moving.

"Here," she said, passing her bag inside to Danny. "I don't need to take that with me."

He took it and dropped it onto her seat. When he looked bac, she was shoving her small camera into a pocket of her coat.

"Are you coming?" Singleton asked.

Hilary was wearing a woolen bobble hat, which she quickly pulled down to cover her ears and then grinned at him, a grin saying it was all right. That they knew this would be dangerous.

Danny asked Singleton to tilt the back of the seat forward so that he could get out, then emerged clutching the cold chisels and the coal shovel. He almost slipped as his foot touched the pavement and would have gone down had Singleton not grabbed him by the elbow.

"Thanks."

He looked through the park railings, across a covered lawn area to where a children's play area was located, a few swings, a roundabout, a see-saw and a slide. In spite of the snow, he had no problem matching the scene to one of Veronica's drawings they had seen in Bournemouth.

Singleton moved slightly beside him, following his gaze with one of his own. "We had some fun there. Seems like only yesterday."

Danny smiled until a fierce blast of wind rocked them where they stood. He looked beyond Singlton's shoulder, along what was left of Embankment to where a small footbridge marked what he guessed must be where Beverly Brook met the Thames.

"She knows we're here," he said quietly.

"She wants to stop us, maybe?" Singleton shot a nervouse glance towards the bridge, then looked back at Danny.

"No. I thinks she's saying hello."

"Give me those," Hilary said after a moment.

He let her take the chisels and then in turn took the shovel and the hammer from Singleton, leaving him with the crow bars.

They set off without a word along the pavement. At another time, Danny might have enjoyed the wintery scene but now there was only a solid, cold block of dread where his heart should be. What would they find there? Would she be waiting for them?

In answer, the wind increased, pelting them with small, icy pellets of snow, making them bunch together as a blind, shuffling mass. Finally though, they reached the point where the tarmac ran out and Embankment disappeared at the brook. An unadopted tow path took over on the other side of the stubby footbridge and ran off in the direction of Hammersmith Bridge.

"There!" Singleton said and pointed across the brook to where a brand new plastic chain link fence enclosed a wide, flat, snow covered area.

"Is that the Ranelagh?" Hilary asked, raising her camera for a quick snap.

"It was," Singleton said. "Now it's Municipal playing fields.

Danny was seeing a heavily overgrown jungle and in the distance, sticking up like a few blackened teeth in rotting gums. Thereality was another place, acres of flat, snow bound land stretching away into the far distance.

"We have to go down here."

Singleton was pointing to a steep bank leading down the water of the brook. The bank was densely covered with growth, all heavy with snow, but Danny thought he could discern a narrow path at the bottom, running away along the edge of brook bank.

"Recognise it?" Singleton asked.

"Sort of."

A line of tall, naked trees stretched along the top of the bank, skeletal limbs reaching into the air and marking the edge of the playing fields.

"There's been a lot of heavy work done on that ground. The bank is higher than it was."

"Let's hope they haven't buried the grotto."

Beneath them, the brook was flowing steadily along towards the Thames and for a moment, Danny thought he remembered standing on the bridge, throwing stones at rats foraging in the mud at low tide.

"We never hit any,"

Singleton spoke quietly, as though reading his mind and looking at each other, they smiled. For a moment it was Brian and Joe again, best friends.

"Hey!" Hilary said, as the wind suddenly dropped and a dead, cold hush, filled only by the almost imperceptible sound of falling snow surrounded them. They stood for a moment longer, a forlorn little bunch, seemingly lost in the storm.

Singleton, rousing himself said, "If we're going to do this, we'd better get down there."

They followed him across the bridge to the point where the corner concrete post stood, close to the bridge support on that side. Telling them to wait, he put down the crowbars and swung himself around the side of the parapet, moving surprisingly smoothly for a bulky man.

"Be careful here," he said. "It's pretty slippery."

"Careful!" Hilary said, as his feet shot out from under him and he went tumbling down the snow covered slope. At the bottom, he sat for a moment on the footpath, seemingly disorientated.

"Are you okay?" Danny called.

They watched him get carefully to his feet. Bending over, he started brushing snow from his trousers, then the sleeves of his weatherproof jacket.

"Another few centimeters and you would have been in the water"

He said, shakily. "I think I've bruised my hip."

"Can you walk?"

"Yes, yes. I think so."

Danny turned to Hilary. "Are you coming or are you staying here?"

Giving him a hard stare, she put down the tools she held, she swung around the parapet the way Singleton had and let go. Danny watched her descend, holding a crouched position as she followed the path Singleton had made through the snow. Being lighter than him, she kept her balance better and reached the brook bank without mishap.

"Throw the tools down," she said.

Danny tossed the crowbars down first, lightly, so that they landed safely in the snow within reach of Singleton and Hilary. He did the same with the shovel, the hammer and coal shovel, but held onto the chisels, shoving them into his pockets.

When he was ready, he swung himself round the parapet and started down the slope in a sitting position, legs doubled up beneath him, sliding in fits and starts all the way down to the brook bank.

"Can you manage?" he asked Singleton, who was favouring his right hip.

"I'll be okay."

Danny could smell the Thames strongly down here and glancing over his shoulder, saw beyond the bridge the great spread of sullen water stretching away from them towards the Fulham side of the river.

"Let's go."

Singleton led off, picking his way carefully along the narrow, snow covered path which allowed single file only. Hilary went next with Danny bringing up the rear, trying to remember how far it was from the bridge to the grotto through a haze of ghostly images.

Would the structure be there and if it was, would the tunnel even be navigable? The constant worry, the thing that nagged at him on and on was, would bringing Veronica's remains to light stop her or would there be consequences? He smiled grimly to himself as it occured to him what Carol would say if she could see them now.

The snow kept coming relentlessly, blown by a sharp wind which seemed to find them face on wherever they went. It seemed as though the elements too were their enemy, freezing faces, getting into eyes already narrowed to slits. It made walking difficult, the narrowness of the path they trod forever on their mind, as one careless step could see any one of them fall into the brook.

The pace was slow then and it was clear that Singleton was suffering, picking his way along, favouring his injured side. Hilary, sandwiched between them, kept raising a hand in front of her face, in order to shield her eyes from the snow and when Singleton stopped suddenly, she cannoned into him, almost overbalancing him.

"Jesus! Take care, will you?"

As he said this, she moved instinctively to save him, twisted sideways and one foot shot out from under her. If it hadn't been for Danny grabbing her arm, both of them would have fallen into the water.

"Calm down," he said.

She nodded, quietly thanked him and turned helped Singleton regain his footing.

"It must be somewhere along here," he said, irritably.

Danny seemed to remember a wide curve in the bank, where the path dropped into a steep dip in the ground. He pictured a hollow filled with brambles, hot and buzzing with insects. He saw them in his mind's eye, five children hacking their way through waist high undergrowth of nettles and doc leaves, blackberry waiting to snare the unwary. And flies, dozens of them buzzing annoyingly around his face.

"There's an dip up ahead," said Hilary. "You can see that the trees drop."

"I can't see a bloody thing," Singleton complained. "Not with this shit in my face."

Danny could see she was right. Standing sideways on to the wind, he raised a hand to shelter his eyes and followed the line of snow covered undergrowth along the face of the bank to where it dropped away steeply.

"I think that could be it," he said.

Singleton looked at him for a moment, then said, "Let's take a look."

They moved along the path until it too dropped into a dip. Clambering up the bank beside them, Danny stood on the edge of the decline, looking into the dell. The growth was thicker here, the snow deeper, it almost covered the tops of the bushes.

"It all seems smaller," Singleton said, dragging himself up to stand beside him.

"We were kids then. Everything seemed larger than it really was."

"No, no," Singleton cried angrily. "They've filled the fucking thing in!"

Danny leaned forward, craning his neck and peering through the falling snow and saw a slice of brick wall showing through a snow clad covering. The slope of the bank loomed over it, sweeping up to the trees and the playing fields beyond.

He was slightly higher on the slope than Singleton from his vantage point, could see the lower part of the structure, hiding behind brambles, a large gate fixed across an open mouth, cosing the tunnel to anyone curious enough to want to venture inside.

"Bastards!" Singleton whipped at a bush with the crowbar, sending a shower of snow through the air. "All this fucking effort and..."

"It's okay. We can get in." Danny said.

Singleton looked at him angrily, then walked a few paces on towards the structure. He seemed pretty strung out and Danny exchanged glances with Hilary before following him down the slope.

"This is all different," Singleton said, miserably. "It's been filled in."

"It's almost thirty years since we were here. Of course it's different and the snow doesn't help." Danny grabbed his shoulder, pointing towards the structure. "The tunnel's still there, beyond that gate."

They drove forward, through snow and undergrowth until they came within striking distance of the brambles which grew in front of the entrance. Immediately Singleton began hacking at them with one of the crowbars, sending cascades of snow in all directions.

"Steady," Danny said.

Singleton glared at him but took several deep breaths, which calmed him somewhat. He resumed hitting at the nearest bush, slowly breaking it down enough to expose the tunnel mouth and the gate properly.

"It's locked," he said. "Of course, it would be."

Danny saw the gate was fastened by a large padlock to a thick eye, which was cemented into the wall on the opposite side of the entrance. He picked his way slowly through the remainder of the bramble until he stood in front of the gate and tested the padlock with a hand.

"Even if we had the key, I doubt it would be any use," he said. The lock had been there so long without maintenance, the hasp had rusted into the body.

"Good job we have the perfect master key, then," Singleton said, hefting one of the crowbars.

Danny took it from him and glanced through the bars of the gate. He couldn't see far inside, so he took Singleton's torch from the others coat pocket and shone it between the bars. At once the forward edge of darkness retreated and he could see what looked like a mound of earth about a meter inside.

"There's been a cave in."

He caught the damp, earthy smell coming from in there and heard the slow but steady dripping of water. No one had been in there for a long, long while and no doubt there were all sorts of obstacles there to hinder them.

"Do you think it's safe?" Singleton askedd softly.

"We'll soon find out."

Singleton called to Hilary over his shoulder. "There's been some sort of cave in."

"Has it has blocked the pipe entrance?"

" Can't make out how bad it is until we get inside."

"Let's not worry ourselves until we get in there," Danny said.

He slipped the torch into a pocket, took the crowbar from Singleton and hooked the chisel end beneath the hasp of the padlock and the body of it. It was a tight fit but he did manage to get good enough leverage to snap it open. At least, that was the theory of it.

"Give me room," he said.

He braced himself, pressing firmly down on the metal body, testing the torque. Tightening his grip on the crowbar's shaft, he took a deep breath, lifte the implement up until it met the hasp, then jammed the crowbar downwards with both hands. The chisel end slipped from its purchase and he fell forward, cracking his forehead on the edge of the gate.

"You okay?" Hilary called.

He raised a hand to let her know he was, then repeated the same action, trying to ignore the pain in his bitterly cold hands. Walking there, snow had caught in the fibres of his woollen gloves, melted in the warmth from his fingers and had then proceeded to soak through to chill off again against his skin. His fingers had numbed and now, the ache was bone deep, each jolt making it worse.

"Give it to me."

Singleton took the crowbar from him and pushed Danny away. He watched, shoving his hands into his coat pockets as Singleton lined up the crowbar. Glancing behind him, he saw Hilary looking back towards the bridge.

"What is it?"

She shook her head uncertainly and he looked off in the same direction. There was nothing of note to see.

"You look perished," he called. He almost told her to go back to the Land Rover but he guessed what her answer would be.

"Christ!" Singleton cried as the crowbar jumped its purchase and fell to the ground. Danny picked it up, saw him gripping his right hand in his left, then noticed his gloves had torn through and the skin of his knuckles was bleeding.

"Trust me," Singleton said. "All this undergrowth and I have to punch brickwork!"

"Move back."

Singleton nodded, moving away, as Danny turned the crowbar in his hands, fitting the two prongs of the snake tongue around the hasp of the padlock, with the shaft angled upwards this time. He tested it to be sure it wouldn't jump off again and then threw all his weight into the motion - but the lock held!

He glanced at Singleton, "This time."

He took a deep breath, bunched his shoulder muscles and did the same thing again and this time, the hasp snapped open. For a second the lock dangled from the metal eye then fell to the ground.

"Try the gate," Singleton said.

Danny stepped back from the gate and yanked at it, seeing it move a reluctant couple of centimeters before jamming against the base of the bramble.

"Here!"

Singleton stepped in quickly with the shovel, hacking at the snow covered stems with awkward swings until most of them came away, clearing a space for the gate to open. He finally stepped back, his damaged knuckles bleeding again.

"That should do it."

Danny patted his shoulder, moved past him and grabbed the edge of the gate with both hands. He pulled as hard as he could and felt the hinges giving grudgingly on their rusted spigots but the gate opened just a crack. He pushed it to again, then pulled once more with all his body weight behind it. This time the hinges gave a nerve jangling screech and the gate opened enough for them to to get inside.

Singleton squeezed his bulk through the opening and Danny followed. The moment they were inside, they were engulfed by a cloud of foul air, bearing all the evils of that long dead tunnel. Danny glanced at Singleton, saw what he was thinking.

"Nothing," he said. "Stale mud. Seepage from above."

In order to lay the playing field, the workmen had needed to level the ground. They had drained the lake and filled the hollow, which was why the brook bank had seemed higher than back then. It wasn't his defective memory playing tricks but something real. The ground had been built up, hence partially buried structure they now stood in.

Singleton took out the torch and shone it into the tunnel, trying to locate where the walls and roof narrowed towards the mouth of the drainage pipe. Numerous cave-ins over the years had partially blocked the tunnel, the mounds of debris obscured to a degree by a curtain of dangling tree roots.

"It looks dangerous down there. If we're not careful, the whole sodding roof could fall in."

"That smell is awful," Hilary called to them. "I can even smell it out here."

"What is it?" Singleton asked, gazing at a slimy, rust coloured ooze colouring the mud at their feet.

Groundsmen responsible for the playing fields over the years had been treating the surface with some kind of manure based product. Over time it had been seeping through into the tunnel, as was evident from the viscus lines of muck lining the old brickwork.

"Basically, it's shit," Danny said. "And we're going to be walking through it."

"Great!"

But he was more concerned with the fragile look of the structure. Earth still dribbled in from the spaces where the bricks had fallen in and others, especially in the roof, looked ready to follow. Singleton was right, one bad move could have more then just bricks falling on them.

Danny called through the gate to Hilary. "You had better stay out there. We'll need you to keep watch in case anything happenes."

"Such as?"

"Who knows? Anyway, the space in here is limited and the more of us milling about, the more dangerous it becomes."

She didn't like it but saw his point. "Okay. But shout if you need me."

Singleton gave a loud grunt and said, "Let's get this done."

"Hold up," Danny said following him along the tunnel.

Singleton shone the torch ahead of them, its beam playing over the curtain of roots, which seemed to be reaching out for them like tentacles of some emaciated sea creature.

"There!" Singleton said, pointing to the beam shone at a spot some way along from them. "That's where the pipe mouth has to be. The tunnel looks narrower down there than I remember it."

Danny lifted an arm and gently moved some roots aside, in order to get a better view. Their passage along the tunnel would be difficult, but he beieved they would be able to get through. That would be it though. There was no way that either of them was going to fit inside the pipe.

Singleton said, "We'll never make it."

"Let's get there first, then we'll see."

"We'll have to crouch right down to get up to the pipe."

They were already walking in a semi-crouch, soon they would have to get so low, their knuckles would be dragging in the muck.

"You or me first?"

Singleton half smiled. "Toss you for it."

"My hands are so cold, I couldn't find a coin, let alone spin it."

At that moment, a brick fell from the roof and splashed in the mud at their feet. Singleton gasped and looked up at a fresh dribble of ooze hanging down like a long candle of snot.

"Whatever we're going to do, we'd better do it quickly."

Danny grunted and watched him start off down the tunnel in an exaggerated stoop. He noticed that somewhere along the way, he had abandoned the crowbar and was now advancing carrying just the short handled coal shovel.

464

"Watch this," Singleton said, picking him way around a mound of debris from an old fall.

Danny watched him edge his way around a far larger pile of debris almost blocking the path. It had been quite a hefty fall by the look of it, brining down a lot of bricks and earth. Jutting up at an awkward angle was a flat, stone seat, protruding from the fall like an admonishing finger.

"Where the hell did that come from?"

Singleton told him there had been stone benches around the lake edge. "I expect it got pushed through when the machines filled the lake in."

Edging round the chunk of granite, Danny hoped nothing else of that size was poised to crash down upon them. He carefully parted another curtain of roots and saw the torch beam dancing erratically over the way ahead, which was getting narrower all the time. He could feel feel his boots squelching slightly with each step he took and kept reminding himself that, should he slip, not to grab at the roots for support.

"This is it," Singleton said and aimed the torch beam at the place where the rim of the pipe mouth protruded into the tunnel. He looked back nervously at Danny, then kneeling down, tried to look see the pipe.

"This shit is freezing," he complained, his knees sunk deep into the slimey muck. "The smell is stronger here."

Danny had noticed and was breathing through his mouth. He nestled himself as close to Singleton as he could in the confines space. His back was already starting to complain. It was a snug fit, their shoulders touching the brickworkl on either side of them.

"You don't think this stink could be...?"

"Not after this long," Danny said.

"I don't know.

"Anything like that, to do with the remains, would have stopped years ago."

"Normally, yes. But this situation's hardly normal, is it?"

Squatting down, Danny looked where the torch beam was pointing into the pipe and saw just mess of debris plugging the pipe.

"We didn't put all that in there, did we?"

"Some," Singleton looked nervously back along the tunnel.

"What?"

"I thought something moved back there."

He shone the torch behind them but all they saw through the hanging curtain of growth was faint light from the tunnel entrance.

"I wondered... Hilary maybe..."

"Possibly." Danny knew she wouldn't have entered the tunnel but he wanted to reassure him.

"I heard something," Singleton insisted.

"I'm hearing things all the time."

Reluctantly, Singleton turned his hand towards the pipe again and the torch beam showed them once again the plug of debris.

"Looks like a build up of silt. Drainage possibly, running along the pipe from where the lake was."

"Seems a lot," Singleton said doubtfully.

"It has been over twenty years."

"Right," Singleton muttered. Right or wrong, they would have to clear it.

Getting his feet beneath him, he passed the torch back to Danny, then leaned cautiously into the pipe mouth with the coal shovel thrust out before him.

"I'll need the torch beam to see what I'm doing."

Danny directed the beam over Singleton's shoulder, saw him stab the shovel carefully into the wall of muck, which seemed to have the consistency of wet clay and the blade sunk into it about four centimeters.

"It's thicker than I thought," Singleton said, as he wiggled the shaft about, working the blade free. A loud splash from behind them made him start violently and he threw a wary look over his shoulder.

"That doesn't sound too good."

"It's nothing," Danny said. "Do you want me to take over?"

"Keep the torch still!"

Singleton bent into the pipe again and struck at the muck, this time causing a fat wadge of it to break free. Water spouted from the hole but soon decreased to a trickle. He stepped back.

"There seems to be a lot of water."

"Like I said, seepage. There's probably all sorts of shit back there."

"And her."

They looked at each other, the realisation of how close they were to Veronica's resting place dawning on them. After a moment, Danny took the shovel.

"I'll take a turn."

They managed to squeeze passed each other, noses just a centimeter apart.

"It's tighter than back then."

"We were smaller back then," Danny said and bent into the pipe.

The smell of stale mud was stronger inside and he breathed as shallowly as he could. He picked up the coal shovel from where Simgleton had left it and struck at the blockage with hard jabs. On the third blow, more mud fell out and he shuffled forward as far as he could, taking himself into the pipe as far as his waist.

"How is it?" Singleton's voice souded shaky, like he was shivering and who could blame him, the temperature in there seemed to have dropped quiet a lot.

"There's more of that brown water back here."

"Much?"

"Not sure."

He pulled out and shuffled round to face Singleton.

"I think there could be a fair amount just below the level of the hole we've made. It might be better to clear just the upper portion of the blockage."

Something shifted at the corner of his eye and staring over Singleton's shoulder, he saw a trickle of dirt falling from an exposed section of earth, where the roof bricks had fallen in. He held his breath for a moment, fearing a larger fall but when nothing more happened, he breathed again.

"What was that?" Singleton asked, to scared to look back.

"Nothing to worry about."

He turned back to the pipe with a groan and carefully dragged the mud they had cleared so far out. It fell about his feet and he stood for a moment brushing muck from his coat. His trousers were beyond help so he cleared as much as he could from his hands, which were covered with the stuff.

"We've opened the plug enough to look up the pipe. Give me the torch and I'll see if I can spot anything."

Singleton groaned, straightened as much as he could in that confined space and moved his head from side to side. "How did we manage to get her in there?"

Looking at the mouth of the pipe, Danny thought it seemed an impossibly small space in which to do what they had done. He could imagine how close Alan Cockle would have had to get to Veronica to move over her and shuddered. Intimate was not the word for it.

"We put her in feet first?" Singleton said unnecessarily.

"On her back," Danny remembered. "According to Alan, with her eyes open."

"You weren't in here for all of it. Once we'd got her inside, you began to shake and cry, so we sent you out. Some sort of delayed reaction."

Leaving them to clean up his handywork.

Singleton said, "I'll go in. Take a look."

"Are you sure?"

"As I'll ever be." He saw Danny hesitate and said, "I'm alright! I can do it!"

Reaching into the pipe. he lifted the shovel, just as a thick line of the black, glutinous liquid began leaking out onto the floor. He barely looked at it, just took the torch in his other hand and crouching down, inched himself into the pipe, until the tops of his thighs pressed against the rim.

"I'll just clear a little more fron the top of the hole."

Danny heard the dull thunk and scrape of the shovel as Singleton worked and bending over, he tried to see past the other's heavy body to the hole.

"Ugh! It's in my mouth!" Singleton screamed suddenly.

"Come out then," Danny said, watching the other's legs working, slowly backing himself out of the pipe.

"Okay! I think I'm almost there."

He stopped and Danny bent down over his calves, still marvelling at how he had managed to fit himself in there in the first place.

"Should I pull you out?"

Singleton muttered something and a wave of the thick liquid oozed fell from the pipe.

"Joe?"

"Not yet," came the muffled reply.

Danny leaned forward until his head was close to Singleton's knees and watched the man's shoulder shifting awkwardly as he brought the shovel blade into play once more.

"That's it," Singleton shouted. "I can almost see..."

All at once Danny was forced to back up as Singleton began to struggle violently to free himself from the pipe. Danny grabbed the thrashing legs and pulled as hard as he could and Singleton popped from the pipe like a cork from a bottle.

He went down, face first in the sludge and then came up again just as quickly, spluttering and wiping at his mouth, turning awkwardly to face Danny.

"I think - I saw her."

He grimaced and shuddered violently. He shuffled forward as speedily as he could, in the same hunched position they were both forced to adopt.

"Are you positive?"

"I think so - yes."

"Give me the torch, I'll go in and make sure."

Danny reached for the torch but Singleton took his arm in a vice like grip.

"It's my fault she's in there."

"You don't understand," Singleton said in a strangled voice. "She moved! She's just bones but she moved! Dear God, she was grinning at me!"

Danny stared at him for a long moment, as a tight hand closed around his heart. After a few seconds, he managed to control himself.

"We have to know," he said, trying to get around Singleton to the pipe mouth.

"NO!" This time, Singleton pulled him back forcibly. "Both Alan and Sarah tried to tell me they thought she was alive. I dismissed their fears out of hand. If I'd listened, they would still be here."

"She's not alive. You know that."

"She is," he said, desperately. "Something is!"

Danny stared at the pipe mouth. Even now, after all that had happened, he still needed to see.

"None of this would be happening if it weren't for me. I need to know."

But Singleton was unrelenting. He met Danny's gaze with one of fierce resolve. Danny looked at him, his dirty face, his hair plastered across his forehead and nodded.

"All right."

He inched his way round to face the entrance and started moving towards it. He could sense Singleton close behind him, heard him say in a hoarse, frightened whisper.

"It seems darker in here."

The next moment, he heard a faint rumbling sound coming form behind, getting louder all the time as possible causes for it rushed through his mind. He turned his head as a rush of foul air belched from the pipe, then Singleton screamed.

All at once, there was a loud sucking sound from inside the pipe and the next second, with unbelievable force, a jet of black liquid spewed from the mouth. Danny jumped away from it, caught his heel on something beneath the slime and grabbed at a hanging tree root to stop himself falling.

"Get out!" Singleton screamed, a noise that was taken up by a high pitched keening that filled the tunnel, only not a scream of terror but one of raging triumph.

Another spout of muck burst from the pipe, hitting Singleton square in the back and knocking him from his feet. He grabbed for support, caught a tree root and this time, it triggered a fall from the brick roof of the tunnel.

"Watch it!"

Danny turned his head in time to save his eyes and felt something sharp graze his cheek. He scrambled through the muck, already feeling the pressure of the released flow on the back of his legs. Clearing the last curtain of roots, he saw the entrance just a few feet in front of him.

"Come on, Joe," he called without looking back.

Launching himself towards the half open gate, he tripped, splashed down to his knees and pain shot up through his hips. But he couldn't stop, he knew that; to stop was to die. He scrambled forward on hands and knees until he was able to get up again.

"Joe!"

The torch had gone out, submerged beneath Singleton, who had been floored by the tide. Danny saw him flailing about, in panic and moved back, deeper into the tunnel once more. He grabbed a waving arm.

"Come on!"

With Danny's support, Singleton regained his feet. He was completely covered in black slime and was looking about him stupidly.

"Okay. Okay," he muttered, finally focusing on him.

Danny nodded, started back up the tunnel when a third wave erupted from the pipe, which knocked Singleton off his feet again. Danny turned, saw him roll onto his back and then saw something that would haunt him all his days.

Within the tide gushing forth was a shape, a thing in human form, a flash of white, a grinning skull, a crouching form that seemed to pounce from the pipe onto the struggling figure before him. Singleton screamed as he struggled with the thing, then his head went beneath the surface.

Danny took one faltering step towards the writing mound, then another, forcing himself to go back. Then the skull emerge from the muck, with thin straggles of something flesh like stuck to it and turnedits empty, obsidian eye sockets upon him. A moment later, as though in recognition, the large teeth seemed to stretch into an impossible wide grim before it sank down onto its prey like some demonic carnivore.

"Joe!"

Danny hesitated on the edge of going to help when there was a wrenching sound and the next second, a large portion of roof caved in, crashing down on the place where Singleton had fallen, burying the scene in a mound of earth and bricks.

"JOE!"

Hands grabbed his arm and Hilary's anxious face appeared by his shoulder. She stared at the mound, at the theick, black wavelets running around their feet.

"Come on, Danny. Move!"

She dragged him towards the gate and out into the white snowscape beyond the structure, away from the shallow tide of ooze snaking its way towards the brook. She pulled him up to the crest of the dell, although by now, he was barely resissting. At the top, they paused, stared at each other with bleak, bewildered eyes, then turned their faces back the tunnel house.

"Joe?" she asked.

"Back there... she..."

She stared at him, horrified, finally believing. Then she tuned away, started back to the brook path and a moment later, he followed. There was nothing else to do.

He almost fell a couple of times on their way back to the bridge. The brook bank path seemed narrower than before. At one point, overcome by what had happened, he dropped to his knees in the snow and it took Hilary several minutes to get him up to his feet again

"Get up!" she barked. "We have to get back to the Land Rover."

The muscles in Danny's arms and leg had never felt so useless, heavy lumps of flesh without a spark of life left in them. When they reached the bridge, he stopped before the climb up the bank.

"I should have gone back."

Hilary looked anxiously back towards the grotto. "Was she...?"

"There was... something, It jumped...out of the pipe...onto him."

Her mouth moved soundlessly, he gaze fixed at where they had come from. After what seemed an age, she found the will to move. Stepping behind him, she started him up the bank, pushing at his behind every time he stopped moving.

"There's a call box back near that park. We need to get help."

It took them a while to reach the top of the bank and to get onto the bridge. The snow fall had moderated, large, wet flakes drifted past their faces, touching briefly from time to time like dead kisses. Plodding off towards the park, they finally reached where Singleton's Land Rover stood lonely sentinel.

"Did he lock the door?" Hilary asked.

Not expecting any answer, she walked round to the off side of the vehicle and tried it.

"Locked?"

474

Danny was standing at the front of the vehicle, looking across the bonnet with paained eyes. She went and joined him, pulled the front of his coat closer around across his chest. Reaching into her pocket, she found a crumpled tissue and dabbed at his cheek, showing him a slight smear of blood on the paper.

"They're all dead," Danny said. "She killed them all but she let me go. Why?"

There was no answering that and Hilary just shook her head. Danny stared at the river. His whole body ached with weariness and his feeling of desolation was deeper than at any time in his life.

"She was there," he muttered. "She was grinning, like she was meeting old friends after a long absence."

He supposed that in a way, she was.

"Look, why don't you go, Danny?" Hilary said.

It took a second for her voice to reach him. When it did, he gazed at her blankly. She was pale and drawn, with deep track marks under her eyes which he hadn't seen before. She was waiting for some reaction from him and didn't know why.

"I'm going to call the police...ambulance...Christ, I don't know!"

"They'll want to speak to me."

"They don't need to know you were here."

He gazed at her, not quite understaanding what she meant and her eyes in turn searched his face. He couldn't quite pin down what he saw in them, pity? kindness? concern? maybe all three.

"You've paid your dues," she said softly. "Let me handle it from here on. As far as the police need to know, there was just the two of us, Joe and me."

He was so tired, he couldn't think straight.

"Go, back to the hotel now and tomorrow, Norwich."

Forget this, is that what she meant? He wanted to laugh. He didn't think he'd forget any of it, ever again, and why should he be allowed to? It had all been his fault.

He tottered slightly and she put a hand on his arm, steadying him. God! He felt exhausted and still there was something trying to grab his attention, something he couldn't pin down but that seemed vitally important. Maybe a bath and some sleep would do him good.

She walked him as far as the call box, where they stopped. Looking at each other, they each tried to find words to express what they felt but could not. It had all been too big. Eventually she managed a weary smile and they hugged each other tightly.

"Goodbye, Danny," she said when they parted.

He turned and walked away. He didn't look back.

Chapter Twenty Eight

Danny shifted his chair out of the May sunshine, which was strong through the pool house windows and glanced over at Dad. The old man had fallen asleep in one of the cane chairs on the other side of the anteroom and was snoring quietly.

Danny sighed, looked at the supplement from the Sunday paper lying on the cane and glass coffee table between their chairs. Dad had brought it through with him after lunch with the intention of reading Hilary's piece on the disappearance of Veronice Hayden but had fallen asleep before getting started.

Danny had not read it himself, he didn't need to. He already knew the gist of it, as Hilary had come to town the previous week and he'd taken her to lunch in the city. He had been dreading reading the article and was surprised at how glad he was to see her.

"How are you?"

"Better," he'd told her.

"Good."

He'd said how was looking forward to starting work. Carol had been as good as her word and taken him on as a trainee.

"I have six months to prove myself, starting when we get back from holiday."

"We?"

"Me and Chrissie, we're back together."

"I'm pleased."

He had told her all about the cottage Chrissie had booked in North Yorkshire, not far from Scarborough sounding like a teenager on his first holiday with his girlfriend.

Thinking about it now, he felt embarrassed, shifting uncomfortable inside his shirt. He'd been nervous about the article, about it stirring everything up again, of opening half healed wounds and told himself he might have said anything under the circumstances.

"I went to Joe's cremation," she had said eventually. "His wife asked me to go and it seemed only right."

He was glad. He'd wanted to go himself but couldn't face it so soon after being ill.

"And the others?"

"No."

He'd nodded. At some time in the future, when he was sure he was strong enough, he would visit each of them to say his goodbyes. Mrs. Kershaw too.

He glanced again at Dad, who had slipped into sleep the minute his backside touched the chair. It was to be expected he supposed, someone of his age, just out of hospital following a mild stroke. The doctors weren't sure but said it may well have been brought on by the beating he had taken.

The heat in there was becoming uncomfortable, even with the top windows open. If he sat there too long, he might start to doze off himself, which he didn't want to do, so he took himself to the patio. There was a garden bench on the edge of the lawn and he walked over and sat down.

It was better out here, a gentle breeze from the river to temper the warm sun. The garden was rapidly coming into its own and he reflected on how quickly the weather could change in Britain. After January's snow, February's wind and rain had roared into March, knocking down trees and removing several roof tiles from properties right across the country, from the Atlantic to the North Sea. Now they were enjoying this early warmth, offering the promise of a fine few days to follow.

All a long way away from those bitterly cold weeks in London.

A shadow touched his mood and he and he thought about Hilary's article. Her version of the events leading to the discovery of Veronica Hayden's remains, a story of five children and a tragic accident that had haunted four of them until the end of their days.

"Five children?" he'd asked.

"Alan, Sarah, Ray, Joe." She had looked at him, "And Veronica."

She had turned he gaze away from him, across the restaurant.

"And Brian?"

"I said I'd keep you out of it. Brian didn't exist."

He thought about that now and let it go. Brian hadn't existed for a long while, not really. Why not keep it that way? She said he had paid his dues and she was right, so why should dhe feel guilty about it? There was no reason Brian should be brought into the frame, there was no one left to worry about it. It was over, done, he could put it away with all his other nightmares and hopefully it would fade away the same as they had.

Hilary had waited until the case had been officially closed before writing the piece and had wanted him to know what was in it before it went to press. In case there was anything he rather not have out there. Truth know, he'd rather not have any of it out there but he owed her too.

He gazed at the sunny lawn and tried to ward off the feelings of doubt as they threatened once more to assail him. Why shouldn't he take this opportunity to start again? It wasn't as though anyone would be hurt if her truth wasn't the full truth.

"Just say the word," she'd said and he'd made a smile, shaken his head.

He had recovered from the illness which had afflicted him for weeks after returning from London. At least he thought he had. He'd soon discovered, during that luch date with Hilary, that he wasn't as healed as he thought he was. Reliving even a sanitised version of what had happened had awakened memories, threatening his flimsy defences.

In some ways, he didn't care what she had written. He would have been glad to agree to anything so long as he didn't relapse into that twilight world he'd been lost in during those long, dark and miserable weeks when he first came home.

He'd managed to reach the hotel after leaving Hilary by the river, arriving in a daze, hot and giddy and had collapsed on the stairs, which was where the blonde hotelier had found him thirty minutes later. Somehow she had got him to his room.

Waking briefly at some time that eveing, he'd managed somehow to convince her to call Carol, before falling back into the twilight world he'd been inhabiting since passing out earlier. The next thing he remembered was Carol and Chrissie manhandling him down stairs and into Nick's Mercedes, where he had zoned out again in the back seat.

They had brought him back to Norwich, Carol driving and Chrissie keeping a nervous watch over him, asleep in the back. Later they told him he had been muttering deliriously about all kind of strange things, prompting Carol to call her doctor the minute they reached home.

It turned out he had suffered a complete mental and physical collapse, medication was prescribed and bed rest was ordered. The doctor had called in regulary after that and finally, weeks rather than days later, he had started to get better.

"Welcome back," Chrissie had said tearfully and hugged him. He had smiled stupidly and fallen asleep again.

The following weeks went by in a blur of nightmare images, of shadowy figures and strange noises. of a violent struggle in a sea of black muck. Even in his lucid hours, when to all intents and purposes he led a normal life, he was convinced that something terrible was with him, lurking just out of sight at the edge of his eyeline.

And then that phase had pst too, he was out of it, better, thanks to Chrissie who had nursed him and Carol, who had kept visitors away, Roy being the only one. He had been wrapped in a protective blanket from which he gladly broke free at the end of April. He was still a little weak but according to the doctor, past the worst of it and Chrissie had taken him home to their house.

He saw the doctor one more time, visiting him on this occasion at his surgery. It was for a final check up and the man had told that he would continue to improve over time. That the further he drew away from whatever had caused his suffering in the first place, (which he had not divulged to anyone), the stronger he'd become. It was all but over, finally, irrefutably over. All he needed to do now was sit back and enjoy life.

And then he'd met Hilary that day in Norwich.

He gazed across Carol's lawn to the high hedge at the bottom of the garden. Beyond it people walked, out of sight in the warn Sunday sunshine, but for him there was now the suggestion of a frost to follow. It was that day, sitting eating lunch, that it was brought home to him that he was not as cured as he'd believed. From the moment he had touched those loosely bound sheets of A4 paper, he had been troubled by doubt; maybe things were not as over as he had thought them to be. That the world of sudden noises and swift, disconcerting shadows was still there, just waiting to draw him back in.

Muted laughter from the kitchen window. Chrissie helping Carol clean up after a lunch which she herself had prepared. He turned away, telling himself to stop being so pessimistic. That he had always know he would have to face up to the memory of it again one day. He'd wanted to know about his past, about who he really was and now he did. He couldn't select the bits he wanted to remember and consign all the other parts to oblivion.

Hearing their laughter gave him a comfortable feeling inside, another small thing to cling on to. Later, at home, he might suggest a stroll before the warmth of the day gave way to a chilly night. Chrissie might enjoy that. He would smile and do his upmost to deal with the shadows lurking at the edges of his consciousness. Things had been good between them since his illness and he would do nothing to jeapodise that. She seemed to have reached a place at last. a place from which she could see a real future for them.

His memory block had all but gone. There were still some shaded areas, his past would not lay itself out for him in linear procession, but it was more than just a series of sharply defined moments, punctuated by empty spaces, any longer. If the shadow dispersed completely some day, he rest of them should slot themselves into the whole, like completing a jigsaw.

Hilary's story was the feature in this weeks supplement, a scoop from the woman who had actually been there at the end. A mystery answered, a grieving mother given closure at last and all the other newspapers falling over themselves to cash in on what she had revealed. She had been anxious for him to read it first, hence the lunch in Norwich last week ago, in case he had concerns about any of it. With what he owed her, he would hardly have raised objections, even if he'd had any.

True to her word, she had kept him out of it. He believed she felt that she had involved him in the first place, putting suspicions in his head at Carol's luncheon. This of course was nonsense, he had been involved since the beginning. Now she was standing between him and the police, the Coroner's Court and of course, the newspapers.

To all intents and purposes, Brian had never existed. Danny's only official involvement was as a peripheral character, being one of two people who had discovered Sarah Eadel's body at her farm house.

Peripheral? Christ!

He thought back to that cold Putney morning, standing outside the telephone box, wet and tired to the bone, no doubt already feeling the onset of what would hit him later. All he could think of at that moment was what he had seen in the tunnel, running it over and over, like film on a loop. Something had sprung from the mouth of that pipe and fastened itself to Joe Singleton's back!

Turning his head, he looked through the pool house window and saw Dad stirring in his chair. The Old Man had been in a more conciliatory frame of mind since leaving hospital and hopefully, he would continue to feel that way. It was time for him to tell his story, after all it was Danny's story too, one he was long overdue in hearing.

On the other side of the hedge, a child screamed and another shouted before the voice of the mother rose up, quietening them both.

Lunch with Hilary.

He sighed, there was no avoiding it. They had sat looking at each other over a polished wood table top, him with some sort of salad in front of him, her with a steak sandwich.

"I told them, Joe approached me," she said. "Knowing I wrote about unsolved murders."

Her voice had been low, not wanting other customers to hear, but clear enough for him. She had taken a thin, plastic folder from her brief case and slid it across the table to him.

"I said he asked me if I would be interested in hearing the truth about the disappearance of Veronica Hayden. He said things had gone on for too long and it was time the truth was told. He claimed to know where the girl's remains could be found and the truth about how they got there."

She said that he agreed to reveal everything, provided she promised not to go public until after they had uncovered the bones.

Hilary took a large bite from her sandwich and spoke around it, "Of course, I agreed."

Opening the folder had set Danny's nerves on edge and as he'd lifted out a thin A4 manuscript held together by a paper clip, he had felt all the old tensions coming back. He opened the first page and started to read.

Her article took the reader back to the hot school summer of 1955, to the penultimate week of the school holidays, when Veronica had gone missing. She explained to the reader how the disappearance had triggered a massive hunt for the girl with police forces all over the country looking out for her and of how, after almost three months, the inevitable scaling down of the investigation had started when no results were forthcoming.

She then returned to the week in question and day five friends, Alan Cockle, Sarah Eadel, Ray Murkin, Joe Singleton and Veronica had gone to their favorite hideaway to play, against the express orders of their parents and the dire warnings from Police Community officers who had visited all of the schools in the area.

The warnings had been against playing in dangerous places, such as anywhere along the river, on any of the various bomb sites that still existed in the borough at that time and especially, over the vast, overgrown site of the Ranelagh Sports Club, the burnt out ruins of which were a deadly lure to the children of the area.

She explained the overgrown acreage of the Ranelagh, its all but inpenatrable foliage and the blackened stumps of the building rising up from that jungle. At once, Danny could feel the intensity of the heat, the thick air filled with a dozen scents. He could taste the musty dampness inside the ruin, smell the stink of charred wood.

"We'd loved it there."

He could hear the cries of joy from his friends.

"Not Veronica."

"No," she said. "Only in my account."

She had written that that holiday had been special, Their primary school days were over and September meant starting secondary school and not all at the same school.

"We knew things may never be the same again."

How right they had been, only not just in the sense they meant at the time.

Danny laid the article aside and stood up. "Excuse me."

He'd left her there, struggling to contain the thoughts rushing through his mind. When he made it to Gents, which was mercifully empty, he splashed cold water into his face, then stared at his reflection in the large mirror behind the hand basins, water dripping from his jaw.

"Calm down!" he hissed.

The memory of what had happened in that ruin had returned fully. He knew what came next, her falling, screaming and then the dull thump of her landing on the mound of rubble below.

"You're alright," he told himself and eased his grip on the basin edge.

He'd thought he was past reacting like that, thought he could look at the whole incident clearly, for what it was, an accident. Reading what she'd written, even her adjusted version, had sosmehow made the whole thing seem more real.

When he had finally returned to the table, he found she had finished with her food and was smoking one of her inevitable cigarettes.

"Better?" she asked, gently.

"Yes." He sat down and after a second, reached for the article. "I think I'll skip to the end, if that's okay?"

"That's fine."

It was clear that the remainder of the story would be laid out in the same way, substituting Veronica for Brian as the fifth memeber of The Tykes. Her fall and accident, no more, no less. The terrifyed kids, the internment in the pipe, everything just as it had been but without him.

He took the article up again with Joe Singleton telling her that the matter had faded into the background of their minds as they had grown to adulthood. Not going completely, lingering there in the subconscious, all but forgotten - until now. For some reason, with them all pushing middle age, it had reemerged and started to swallow them up.

"Guilt took them over."

"Of course, I wasn't around by then," Danny said. "At least, Brian wasn't. He was locked up inside my skull."

Problems had started to affect them and the more discomforted they became, the more the memories started to haunt them. They tried to ignore it, get on with their lives, work, relationships, marriage - but it didn't leave them, it worked on them in different ways; depression, alcoholism and pills.

"Sarah's marriage folded, her farm failed. Alan's relationship fell apart and Ray...who knows what was going on inside his head? The accident could have been just that or - not."

She had come for them all, but not in the article. In the article, it was all grounded stuff, the grind of everyday routine, the sort of thing that was happeneing to people all around the world. The pressure of modern living.

"Jesus!" Danny said quietly and stood up.

It was so wrong to him. He knew why she had written it that way and he was grateful. He had no intention of saying otherwise. All the same, the truth would eat away at him for the rest of his life and was just going to have to get on with that.

He walked down across the garden towards the rear gate, then changed his mind as he thought of the river outside, flowing beneath hanging willows, of people strolling, completely oblivious of what dark things there were in the world on a day like today.

His friends had paid the ultimate price for something he had done, while he had escaped virtually untouched.

Was this her punishment for him, to live with the guilt for the rest of his days? And if not, what then, had she really spared him for some other twisted reason of her own?

The inquests on Alan and Sarah had taken place, with the coroner in each case returning a verdict of suicide while their minds were of a unsound disposition. Carol had given evidence in the case of Sarah, while he had been excused due to his illness. No mention had been made of the photograph in either case, it no doubt being considered to have no baring on what had happened.

In the case of Ray Murkin, it was agreed that the old fire he was using in his room was way past its safety limits and was no doubt responsible for the tragic accident in which he had died.

In Hilary's account, she aquiesced with these finding and then turned to what happened to Joe Singleton. He had been in a bad way when he contacted her, she had seen this. His life had been in free fall, with the deaths of two of his friends and his marriage in a bad place. He believed that the only way he could put things right was to reveal the secret they had been keeping all those years.

With this intention they had set out, on what had to have been one of the worst days of the winter, for what had been the Ranelagh sports ground, and the long abandoned tunnel house. Built in the 19th century as an artistic feature, the small brick building had been erected to hide the drainage pipe for the artificial lake and it was here, in the concrete drainage pipe, that the body of the girl had been hidden.

Danny had skimmed through the rest, the breaking in through the padlocked gate, the deteriorating tunnel, and the black filth they had walked through inside the tunnel. All this, she had written, had been completed by Joe Singleton and herself but what they hadn't allowed for was that the structure had been weakened dangerously by the heavy plant used to create the playing fields, which covered the site today. During the uncovering of Veronica's remains, the roof had partially collapsed, killing Mr. Singleton.

The medical report on Veronica's remains confirmed she died of a broken neck and fractured skull, both synonymous with falling from a high place. What was left of that unfortunate child, who had died so tragically while enjoying a game with her friends, had now been laid to rest at a cemetary in Bournemouth. The site was close to where her mother now resided with her step daughter, the famous writer of children's books, Paula Heffingham.

After their meeting, Danny had accompanied her to the station. Her London bound traim was due to leave in ten minutes, so they had stood on the platform to say their goodbyes.

"There's something else," Hilary said, then looked away uneasily. "They found an old sweets tin in the tunnel where Veronica's body had lain."

He closed his eyes now, remembering how those words had fallen upon him, chilling him to the bone.

"Did they look inside?"

Her eyes fixed on his, she nodded. "The contents are being analysed."

"I see." They had both known what the investigation would reveal. "More questions then?"

"Possibly. But not for you."

"No," he said, finding no comfort in the truth of that.

They had stood together quietly for a while, Hilary lighting up the inevitable cigarette. For a moment, Danny almost begged her for one but managed to resist the temptation.

With half the cigarette unsmoked, Hilary dropped it on the platform, trod it out and kicked it down onto the track bed. It was time to board the train. She opened the carriage door and stepped up into the lobby between carriages.

"Thank you," Danny said. "For everything."

She made an attempt at a smile which didn't quite come off. "There's Something..."

He watched her, waiting.

"Do you think...I mean, what happened..."

"Was it real?" He felt a shudder run up his spine. He pushed away thoughts of what he had seen. "I think so."

"Me too," she said quietly and turning, had walked into the carriage.

Chapter Twenty Nine

Danny listened to children laughing excitedly beyond the garden and felt no joy in the sound. The sun on his head and shoulders suddenly held no warmth.

Was it real?

It was the same question he'd asked himself a dozen times since he'd recovered and every time, he'd come up with the same answer. He'd seen her in the basement, he'd seen what had jumped on Joe Singleton in the tunnel and he knew he would never forget it. And yet still he questioned the veracity of it and probably always would.

He re-joined Dad in the pool house, needing the accumulated warmth in there to drive the chill from his bones. The old man was gazing wistfully at his pipe when he walked in and with a deep sigh, laid it down unlit in the ashtray on the table beside his chair.

"You've been told not to smoke."

"Am I smoking?" he answered sharply. "Do you see smoke?"

The doctors would have told him to quit even if he'd had an ingrowing toenail and anyway, Carol didn't like him stinking up her house with pipe fumes. Any puffs he managed to get away with had to be taken outside.

"I thought you'd gone," Dad said.

"I was enjoying the sun," Danny told him and sat down. Soon the warmth would start to drain out of the afternoon and then evening would close in beyond the window.

Danny sat down in the same chair he'd had before, feeling Dad's eyes on him all the time. When he looked at the old man, the rhumey eyes slid away across the room and fastened on the window.

It took him time to collect his thoughts. The stroke having left him virtually unscathed, could be detected in his cognitive speed.

"She met him in the January of 1944," he said finally. "He was stationed in Britain, part of the build up to D-Day, an NCO in the 3rd Canadian Infantry Division. His name was, Vincent Ellis and your Mum said he was all that a girl could want. She fell for him straight off."

Their relationship was strong and immediate. It was the way back then, when there was a good chance of being killed, either in battle or by a V1 rocket attack at home.

"There's a photo," Dad said.

"I've seen it."

Dad blinked, then nodded understandingly. He said, "He died on Juno beach. Shot in the first wave hitting the shore. She made enquiries after the war, after she'd had you. The Canadian authorities eventually told her what had happened."

They weren't married, so there was no pension. The consulate had arranged for her to write to his family in Winnipeg, explain to them who she was and about the baby. They would probably draw some comfort from knowing that their son had fathered a grandchild for them.

"Or not. They might think she expected them to help her out financially, which she didn't. They might want her to move to Canada. They might want to take the child anyway."

"She should have written," Danny said quietly.

"She couldn't see the point. Their dead son had fathered a child by a girl he had barely known. How was that their problem?"

"A grandchild. Their flesh and blood. She should have written."

"Well she didn't!" Dad snapped.

Danny thought about the soldier in the photograph, posing for it, then hurrying off into Waterloo Station, turning for another look at the girl he was leaving behind.

Doubtless they had both believed they would be seeing each other again.

"She should have given them the chance of knowing us."

Dad snatched up his pipe and clamped it between his teeth but made no move to light it.

Danny knew what attitudes were like back then towards unmarried mothers. There was no reason to think these had been any different in Canada than they were at home. In fact, some of those younger countries were even more narrow minded than here at home. All the same...

Out on the river, a pleasure boat went by. Danny could see the top of it above the tall hedge. He reached down to pick up the glass of wine he had brought there earlier, which was white and warm by now. Dad wasn't allowed this either and Danny saw him eyeing the drink from floor to mouth and back again. He humphed around the pipe in his mouth.

"I'm nearly eighty," he said. "I'm a too long in the tooth to worry about prolonging my life."

But still he left the pipe unlighted.

Dad had been out of hospital since the middle of February and would have been discharged earlier had it not been for the stroke. Carol had insisted he came to stay with her, which was probably one of the reasons Nick gave for making himself scarce.

"I met her first," he said and thought about that for a while, turning glassy eyed as he stepped back in time.

Danny saw a crow land on the lawn. It looked imperiously around before stabbing at the turf a few times with it large beak. When its head came up, it caught sight of him watching, regarded him beadily for a few seconds, then threw itself into the air and flew off.

"Carol's mum was killed when a doodle bug hit my mother's house. Carol was just a few months old and had been out for a walk in her pram with my mum."

This was new to Danny. He knew Dad had been married before, obviously but this was the first time the he'd heard the details of how his first wife had died.

"When the war in Europe ended, I was demobbed and came home with all the other ex-squaddies returning to civvie street. Mum was living in a new prefab by then, up near Wandsworth Common. It was a nice place, three bedrooms, kitchen, bathroom. Better than most had been used to before the war.

"Jack didn't get home until September and we were surprised that he looked so well. I mean, he was skinny and worn, silent a lot at first but much better than we'd imagined he would be.

"I was on the buses then and I suggested he should apply for a job too but he said he wanted to join the police force. It surprised me a bit, as I'd never thought of either of us being a copper but his mind was made up. He went for it too, after he'd been home for a while and he got in.

"I met your mum about a year later. She'd started working in the canteen at Jew's Row garage in Wandsworth, part-time. She used to leave you with a friend who had three kids of her own, two of them at school. She had to collect them when school finished, so needed your mum to pick you up before then.

He was smiling dreamily and for a moment, Danny almost glimpsed the younger man beneath the age worn face. It was strange to think of Dad being young, with all the hopes and aspirations of those other young men just back from war. They were going to build a new and fairer country. Pity the people gave up so quickly and threw away all their hard earned possibilities.

"An old army mate of mine was on the railways, ticket collecting at Waterloo Station. He told me about a social coming up at the NUR's social club at Vauxhall. Would I like a ticket?"

"Dancing?" Danny grinned, trying to imagine it.

"I've had my moments!" Dad took the pipe from his mouth, studied the bowl and then returned the mouthpiece between his teeth. "I bought four tickets, one for Jack and the girl he was knocking about with and one for me and your Mum, hoping she'd agreed to go with me when I asked her."

She did and they'd had a great evening, dancing to the five piece band, enjoying a few club priced drinks in the bar. By the time the band returned for its second set, Dad knew that Jack had taken a shine to his girl and that she seemed to feel the same way about him.

"After that, they became a regular thing. By the summer of '47, they were living together and he became your step-father."

"But I wasn't adopted?"

"No. You stayed Brian Ellis. Your mother thought it was only right by your father's memory; Brian Daniel Ellis to be precise but you didn't like being called Daniel."

"No," Danny said. "So I've heard."

Dad shook his head, his face shining with admiration as he said, "She took some stick, I can tell you. Not being married, one kid. The gossips worked overtime, people looking down their noses at her, barely concealling their contempt. She looked right back and thought sod 'em! Of course, it helped a bit, Jack being a copper. No one said anything to her face."

And so they had gone on, a nice little family, P. C. Reed, his 'wife' and her son, living in Galvin Street, in Putney. He'd attended the local school, St. Mark's, made friends there and around the neighbourhood, everything was fine.

"I'd hooked up with a few women over the years and we would go out as a foursome but none of the girls meant much to me."

He had still been carrying a torch for Mum. They had remained close, Dad showing his feelings for her in platonic ways because Jack was his best mate and he would never have done anything to hurt him.

"Then there was that day in September '55. It had been an unbearably hot few weeks and the weather finally broke after August Bank Holiday, thunder storms, hailstones, you name it. By the start of September, things turned much cooler. mists over the river, autumn knocking at the door. By then though, Jack was dead, you were ill; everything had gone to hell."

Danny saw the shadows of grief in the old eyes. It was still a raw subject for him, even after so long. He had masked it well over the years, for Danny had never seen it so clearly displayed before.

"The photograph," he said, quietly. "Who took it?"

"Me," Dad focused on him. "I had a day off and went to Galvin Street to keep an eye on you while your Mum and Jack were working."

"She had a job at some factory, I think?"

"The Veritas factory in Wandsworth, making gas mantels."

Jack was on lates that week, starting work in the afternoon and even though her son just turned eleven, mum didn't like him being left on his own.

"You could look after yourself but she was a worrier, so I agreed to come over. I brought Carol with me, although she thought she was too grown up to play with the rest of you. When you and your mates came along, you wanted a photo taken of you all with Jack. Some girl had a camera..."

"Veronica," Danny said.

"You mean the one who...?"

"Went missing. Yes."

"I hadn't realised." He thought about that for a moment, then said, "She wasn't too happy about letting the camera go."

He remembered vaguely, Dad holding the camera while the gang sorted themselves out, who was standing where and Jack, waiting patiently, smiling at them. They had wanted Carol to stand with them but she had turned her nose up and gone inside. Veronica was arguing with him when the photo was taken. He could guess about what.

"I moved," he said.

Dad looked at him.

She had whispered threats in his ear, calling him Daniel, reminding him of what he owed her. She was just being spiteful because of her camera and he'd reacted angrily, right when the camera had clicked.

He looked at Dad. The Old Man knew what had happened at the Ranelagh but no more. None of them knew did.

"You turned inward after she disappeared."

"Yes," he said. He did not want to go into that part of things right then.

"Jack and your mum were worried. It was obvious that something had happened and they did their best to get it out of you."

Danny was now able to remember the days after they had hidden Veronica. The turmoil he'd suffered, torn between keeping their vow of silence and talking to Jack, the nightmares. It had been following one of these, a particularly intense one, that Jack had come into his room. He had sat on the edge of his bed and asked quietly if he was all right, almost like he knew something terrible was haunting him. It was almost two o'clock in the morning and Jack had just returned from work.

"I heard you cry as I was passing your door."

And after a while, with Jack still sitting on the bed, patiently waiting, Danny had told him what he'd done. He told him why and how it had happened,and what the gang had done for him afterwards. When he had finished, Jack had put a comforting hand on his shoulder.

"You know, you are going to have to face up to this sooner or later?"

Danny realised that he'd even then that one day, they would have to account for their actions, he just didn't want to admit it to himself. It was as though, by keeping it quiet, he could make the whole thing simply go away.

"I'll tell you what," Jack had said. "I'll give you a couple of days to think it over. You're old enough now to do the right thing. When you're ready, I'll come to the station with you and you can tell the detective in charge of the case what you've told me. Okay?"

And suddenly it had been.

But they had never got to the station. Three days later, a Saturday in early September, Jack had taken them as a family to the cinema as a treat. The film had been a Walt Disney live action adventure, '20,000 Leagues Under The Sea' and he had been looking forward to seeing it for weeks.

Mum was fully aware of what had happened at the Ranelagh but had pretended she wanted to know what the occasion was. Jack told her that he had earned a treat and her curious act had been easy to see through.

"Danny?" Dad looked worried, no doubt guessing he was re-living that evening, seeing it as clearly as if it had happened only yeaterday.

"We were walking home," Danny said, seeing that fateful evening clearly at last in his mind's eye. "We were walking home from the pictures and I was exceited the giant squid grabbing the Nautalus in the film."

And there it was, playing before him, Jack stopping, mum asking what was the matter and then hearing the girl crying out for help. Then Jack was running across the road with him following, towards Embankment, towards the river.

"Mum called me, trying to stop me but she was already running herself."

"There!" Jack shouting, pointing, then he was tearing at his coat, his jacket, kicking off his shoes. Before anyone could say anything, he was climbing up the safety rail, theree bars and balancing on the top.

"I saw her face! She was there, in the river!"

"Who?" Dad asked. He could not understand the emotions playing across Danny's face.

"Her," Danny said, his voice strangled. "She was already dead."

And there it was, the thing that had eluded him on the Embankment. The full horror of the scene but not the last one. It had not been over for him, could never be over until - what?

She smiled at me and her smile had been that of a shark.

Dad was staring at him searchingly.

"Your mum told me that after that, you shut down. That you were in a terrible state, much like the one you've just been through. When you came out of it, you didn't remember a thing."

Of course he didn't, What he'd seen with his eleven year old eyes had been the consequences of his own actions being visited upon the man who he'd called dad.

"No menigitis?"

"NO."

Just an overwhelming weight of guilt and horror his young mind could not handle. So it had just shut down tight for the next twenty five years.

"The doctors eventually diagnosed dissociative amnesia," Dad said.

The cause of which could never be revealed.

"We invented the illness. Your mum knew what you'd go through if the truth were known and she would have done anything to protect you."

"She didn't see...the girl?"

"No. At least, she never said had."

As far as everyone was concerned, it was the shock of seeing Jack drown that had caused his mind to shut down.

"They said your memory might come back in time, or not."

"And you kept up the lie for all these years."

"It was what your mother would have wanted. Your memory might not have come back at all. What would have been the point of me telling you the truth?"

He was right of course there would have been no point, but that didn't stop him feeling anger. He swallowed it as best he could.

"That's why you didn't want me to go to Putney. Just in case what happened, happened."

Dad said it was and fiddled with his pipe again, the fingers of his other hand twitching above the pocket in which he usually kept his tobacco pouch. Finally, he gave a sharp sigh and pushed the pipe away from him.

"We were settled. You were settled, new school, new friends. You were happy."

Was he? Yes, he supposed he had been - for a while, until things had started happening inside his head. They had cooked up his life story on the grounds of his memory not coming back. They hadn't planned what to do if it did. Then mum had died and Dad had had to take the resposibilty on himself.

"I was scared that going down there, to Putney. In case it freed up your memory. And I was right, wasn't I!?"

"Yes, in a way," Danny said. "But I think it had already started. Going to Putney just accelerated things."

With a little help from an outside source.

"After Jack died, I still used to visit."

Helping with the arrangements for Jack's funeral, which had been a police affair with all the trimmings. Then supporting her through the nightmare weeks that followed and sure enough, always close, they had grown closer. By December, Dad had asked her to marry him and two weeks after Christmas, they were wed.

"We moved up here soon after. I'd set everything up, new house, new job, a new school for you. We adopted you in the following summer and since then you've been Danny Stephens."

"There are no papers," Danny said.

"Not in my case. I have them elsewhere," Dad gave one of his rare smiles. "You think I didn't how much you you and your sister wanted to look inside there? I kept the important papers somewhere else. Safe."

Danny waited for more but soon realised that the Old Man had said all he was going to say for now. Standing up, he looked down at the shrunken figure, who seemed to have aged tremendously in the last few weeks. He wondered whether Dad would see another summer and if he didn't, would the papers be found?

Whatever the answer to that was, he was not going to press for them now. He said goodbye and walked back through the house, thinking about what he had learned, the sense of loss he felt now that he could remember everything about Jack's drowning. Had Jack seen her face the way he had, or had she reserved that pleasure for his eyes only.

He paused before going into the kitchen, wondering whether Carol knew the full story. She'd read Hilary's account over her high fibre breakfast and had acted as though she believed it. But Carol was Carol and she could surprise him with what she did know at some later date.

Of one thing he was sure, whatever she thought she knew, he was happy to let her believe that. If she once found out the full breadth of what had happened, that knowledge would destroy her understanding of everything she held rational.

"Would you like a beer?" she asked, as he opened the kitchen door.

He watched her walk across and take a can from the fridge. She popped the tab, holding the can over the sink and asked him if he wanted a glass. He could have drunk it as it was but said he would like a glass to ease her sensibilities. She brought the can to him with a glass, both of which he accepted graciously.

"Nick called last evening to tell me that work has started on Kavanagh Mansions."

"What about the people still living there?" Chrissie asked.

"They went a while back."

He didn't comment. Kavanagh mansions was the last place he wanted to talk about. He poured his beer down the inside of his glass, feeling Carol's eyes on him all the time.

"I was down there last Monday," she said when he had finished. "For a look round with the architect."

"And Mrs. Kershaw's flat?"

"All taken care of by some legal firm. She has relatives abroad who hired them to look after her affaires."

He nodded, thinking fondly of the elderly woman. Would she still be alive if he hadn't come into her life? Maybe not, as Veronica had scores to settle there too.

"There was a lot of junk in the basement," Carol continued and he felt a cold shadow roll over him.

"What sort of junk?"

"Boxes of all sorts. It seems they have been there for years, forgotten by the people who owned them. There was a rather nice trunk, which might restore well. Full of mouldy old curtains, which I told them to dump."

Danny shifted, tense, but he didn't say anything. There couldn't be any danger there, not any more. The tin had been found in the tunnel after all.

"Everything else was rubbish and the bulders skipped it. I've told Nick to claim the trunk and get it refurbished. It might make a nice Christmas present for you two?"

"Yes," said Chrissie obliviously. "That would be lovely. We could use it as a blanket box."

But he was wondering now how the sweets tin could have turned up in the tunnel, when he had seen her with it it in the basement. Under no circumstances did he want the damned trunk in their house. By rights it belonged to Ellen Hayden and he would use that argument to change Carol's mind.

Chrissie was watching him questioningly and he forced a smile.

"Tired?" she asked.

"A little."

"Nick's selling the flat in Fulham," Carol continued obliviously. We took the time to have a long talk, I mean a real discussion, not just using words as weapons in the usueal way."

"And?"

Chrissie seemed genuinely interested but Danny knew it was just another in the long line of new starts which peppered their marriage. Sooner or later, Nick would find a new pierd de terre to carry on his philandering.

"It seems we both want things to work better. We aagreed on ways we might try to put our relationship on a stronger footing. I don't know whether we can succeed, but we're both going to try to make a go of it."

"Both?"

She stared at him. "Nick is going to cut back on the drinking, spend more time at home."

"And the women?"

A shadow darkened her face, not an easy thing to put behind her. "I told him I would cut them off if I caught him at it again."

"Keep your knife sharp."

"Well, I hope it works, I honestly do," Chrissie said, quickly.

Carol smiled, "Thank you. That means a lot. Anyway, it's partly down to you two that we're trying."

"How so?"

"The way you have patched things up."

Chrissie said, "So far, so good."

"Hey!" Danny said and she smiled at him.

"You know, if we succeed it will mean more work for you," Carol told him.

Danny raised an eyebrow questioningly.

"I won't be at the office so much, you'll have to take on more work to cover for me."

He grinned. "I haven't said I'll stay yet."

"You will," Chrissie said. "Believe me."

"You're not joking, are you?"

"No."

Carol walked them out to the Cortina, which he'd parked close to the house. Chrissie kissed Carol and climbed into the front passenger seat. Carol closed the door for her, then turned to Danny.

"I'm proud of you the way you handled things in London."

He muttered something, not wanting to get into it.

"No, credit where it's due. I think it all ended very well."

She took the glass he was still holding, stood on her toes and kissed him.

Danny said, "What did you tell them, about the woman who hired you to deliver Cockle's photo?"

"Nothing," Carol said. "The subject never came up. No need to open up another mystery. I don't suppose there's a lot to it anyway."

"No," he said. "I shouldn't think so."

Chapter Thirty

"Can you pull in over here?" Chrissie said.

She was wearing the ring. In fact, had been wearing it for some weeks and every time he looked at it, glistening on her finger, he filled with contentment.

Now though...

He had felt out of sorts since they left home hours ago and experienced a further dip in his mood when he heard her tone. He looked across at her and she showed him a tight and distant smile, which only increased his unease.

What had he done?

What had he not done?

He'd said or done something, obviously.

His general sense of wellbeing receded, dwindled towards non-existence. This holiday was supposed to be something special, a high spot, a time to celebrate their new start. Now for some reason a cloud had fallen over it and no matter how hard he tried, he could find no reason for its presence.

"I'm hungry," she said.

"You can't be." He grinned. Never a big eater, she had scoffed a huge cooked breakfast before they had left home, one that would normally have kept her going until the evening.

"I just said that I was!"

"Okay," he said, with a breeziness he did not feel.

He saw a large pub coming up on their left and indicated to make the turn. No, he decided, hadn't done anything to upset her. Which meant this mood must be down to something else and he could rest a little easier.

He slipped the gear stick on their newish car down to third and drove into the car park of the establishment.

"Your wish is my command."

He parked in one of the many empty spaces. Chrissie released her seat belt before he had turned off the engine and, reaching for the door catch, threw him a stiff smile over her shoulder.

He sat watching her through the windscreen for a moment as she walked off towards the building, then removing his own seat belt, he got out of the car.

Should he stop worrying?

Maybe it was a woman thing?

Whatever, sonething was getting her down and no doubt it would pass in its own time. He would do better to stay out of it.

He locked the car and set off after her at a slow pace. Thinking about it, she had been acting oddly for a week or so now, a couple of weeks at least and he had been waiting for her to either speak about it or for it to disappear. He's been hoping that the holiday would perk her up a bit, but so far there was no sign of that happening.

Drawing nearer the entrance to the pub, he saw a board outside, announcing in chalk that they were now serving lunch and naming today's 'Special'. Had she spotted it from out on the road, driven by this seemingly insatiable appetite, decided she needed to eat?

They had been driving since before eight this morning, stopping just once for a pee and a tea a mile or so short of Newark. He had decided to avoid the A1, expecting lots of traffic, as it was the Sunday before the schools went back after the Whitsun holiday.

He'd taken the slower route past Kings Lynn, through Newark and on to Lincoln by the A19, then over the Humber Bridge. Now, toll paid, they had crossed the border into Yorkshire and were closing in on Beverly.

Another hour and we'll be there.

At least they would have been, if they hadn't had to stop. Now, who knew what time they would arrive? Did she have a tape worm or something?

The car park was a big space, room enough for a good number of vehicles and was a little under half-full at the moment. He looked back at the Ford, another Cortina, where he had left in a slot facing a stream. It was just four years old, a blue 1600 with very low milage, bought from a local dealer with a loan he'd taken from the bank on the strength of the job Carol had given him. It drove well, looked almost new, both inside and out and had that new car smell from whatever the dealer had used on it before putting it out for sale.

He felt Chrissie watching him, saw she had stopped and half turned to see where he was. He walked quickly to catch her up and realised as he drew closer that her eyes were searching his face.

What *had* he done?

But he had exhausted that avenue and just had to settle for the fact that somehow re-awakened her doubts about him? He couldn't think how, the relationship had been going so well since he'd moved back in. So well in fact, it was almost possible to forget they had ever parted. It made him anxious to think she might be questioning the wisdom of taking him back.

His pace faltered momentarily, then he saw her continue on past the entrance to the pub and around the side of the pub. Hurrying after her, he saw her moving towards a shaded area beneath a large tree, which overlook the stream on this side of the building. When she stopped on the bank, he steeled himself for whatever might be coming and walked quickly to join her.

"Is something wrong?"

She stood there, staring into the stream and he drew closer. The water bubbling over its rocky bed stopped him and just for a second, he was back beside Beverly Brook, as it flowed steadily towards the Thames.

Pushing the image from his mind, he gazed at Crissie until she turned to face him and he was startled to see she was on the verge of tears. He moved quickly towards her, reaching for her and she let him take her in his arms. Whatever it was, he was sure they could fix it.

"I'm pregnant," she said softly and pushed her face into his chest.

For a second, he thought that he'd misheard her. He took a step back, holding her away from his as he studied her face. She stared up at him, eyes wide, nervously waiting to see how he would react. So this was what had been on her mind for the last few weeks, he thought and relief flowed through him.

"It is yours," she said.

"I never thought otherwise," he objected loudly.

"Don't lie."

She was right. Three things had passed through his mind in rapid succession.

Could she carry it full term?

Was it a boy or a girl?

Was it his?

"It's natural," she said. "After what happened, and us still working together."

To hell with Roger! he thought and looked at her.

"I promise, I never think about - "

"You do. That is also natural. After all, I sometimes wonder about you."

"God," he said. "We must spend our time doubting each other."

"I suppose it's something we have to grow through."

She took his arm and they began strolling slowly back towards the pub along the side of the stream.

She said, "I'm happy the way we are."

"So am I."

"All the same, it's bound to take a while - for both of us."

"To hell with it! We're having a baby."

"Are you pleased, really? I mean...after the last time, I wasn't sure..."

"More than pleased. I've turned a page since then. A lot of pages."

They walked a few yards in silence, listening to the water bubbling and feeling the warmth of the sun on their faces, until they were forced to move away from the stream by a fence around the rear of the pub building.

Danny stopped them and looked at her. "What about you? Have you spoken to the doctor?"

"Of course. He said things have come a long way in the last few years. He can see no reason I shouldn't carry full term."

He her close too his chest, quietly digesting what she'd said and wondering at the excitement he felt spreading through him. All at once, he realised just how much he wanted this, needed it. It was vitally important to him to be a father and this intensity of feeling made him gasp.

Near the front of the pub, she stopped and looked at him with suddenly frightened eyes. "I hope..."

"Ssh!" He gathered her in his arms,

"Sorry. For a moment I felt something..."

"Don't think about anything like that, not for a moment. The doctors will know your history. They'll look after you, take the necessary steps."

"And you - do you really want a child? We said no more lies."

Danny felt sick with shame that what he had felt back then should still be haunting her.

"I'm more than sure. Much, much more."

She kissed him, then said, "God, I'm hungry."

They moved towards the door of the pub, grinning like a pair of idiots. "We'll have to think about names," he said.

Chrissie stopped, looked at him gravely. "I don't want to talk about that yet. Not until we're sure it's going to be alright. I want to keep it to ourselves too. No telling Carol or anyone."

"If that's what you want."

"Promise?"

He dragged a finger across his chest to form an X and she smiled. "Let's get lunch. You're eating for two now, don't forget."

"Danny, wait!"

"What's the matter?"

"I want you to tell me all of it."

"All of what?"

"What happened in London."

"I've already told -"

"Not everything. Please. I know you're hiding something. What you told me was bad, so I'm guessing the rest is even worse?"

He'd known this moment would come and hads been dreading it. But they were so happy in this moment, so here was neither the time nor place.

"Yes, it is."

He would not go into it now, not when things felt so good. Yet his joy was already tinged with regret and he eyed her sadly, knowing that by telling her, he would introduce a darkness into her life which could never be removed.

He said quietly, "Wait until we're in the cottage. Once we've settled in, if you still want to know, I'll tell you."

She went ahead of him into the pub. He followed a moment later, knowing that some of the warmth had gone out of his day.

Later, back on the road, he drove steadily, trying to shake the dark mood which had settled upon him. He should be looking forward to reaching the cottage, to starting the holiday proper, but the weight of what he'd promised to do there could not be dispelled. How much should he tell her? Would she know if he held some of it back?

The Truth!

Christ, the truth was enough to crush any spirit!

Chrissie had consumed a large steak, a pile of chips and several grilled tomatoes, two crusty rolls, buttered and a half pint of local bitter. When she had seen him watching her over his glass of lime and soda, she had grinned and he'd grinned back, determined to hide the shadow in his eyes.

Now, with the traffic light and moving freely, he tried to lose his doubts by speeding up. They had already left the York road, joining this one, which would eventually lead to Scarborough. He intended to turn off at Malton, cutting in across the North York Moors National Park, heading for Goathland and the cottage that was theirs for a couple of weeks.

The sun was bright, filling the car with warmth. He lowered his window rather than turn the fan to blast in cold air, as the noise of it would disturb Chrissie, who had dozed off. Just two weeks ago, following that hot spell in May, the rain had seemed never ending. Looking out the kitchen window, Chrissie had sighed heavily.

"Sometimes I hate this country. One day I'll fly south and stay there. Buy myself a villa in Tuscany and spend my days drinking wine and lying in the sun."

"The council doesn't pay you enough for that," he'd told her. "Anyway, I can't speak Italian."

"Who said you'd be there?"

He smiled to himself, thinking about it now. She had been happy then, more than happy actually and he guessed now that she already thought she might be pregnant. Once it was confirmed, the worry had set it about how he would take the news, for which he felt guilty. Now that was done and she was light hearted once more, looking forward to the holiday and much more to come.

They were heading through some beautiful countryside, the sort of terrain that always came to mind when thinking about the Yorkshire moors and he remembered another holiday, when they had stayed inland from Whitby. They had been lucky with the weather then too, taking long walks down narrow lanes and through beautiful villages.

Well that's what he intended this time too. Just maybe he could put off telling her the darkness in his soul and hold on to summer warmth, for a little while at least.

Chrissie stirred, yawned, sat up. "I must have dropped off."

"I kept thinking there was a motor bike coming up behind us."

"Liar!" she punched his leg

"I thought you'd want to see this." He nodded out of the window, "Do you remember?"

"I remember," she smiled.

Danny turned the radio on, a local station playing old hits and she sat there, watching Yorkshire and swaying her body in time to the music.

"My mouth is a bit..." She made a smacking noise with her tongue against her palate.

"Have a drink then."

She reached for her bottle of water, which had slid down between their seats. "I think this is going to be a good holiday."

He glanced over, nodded, saw her open the bottle and take a swig. "Ugh! It's warm."

"It's wet, isn't it?"

"Do we have any sweets?"

"In the dash."

He stared up the empty road in front of them, a two lane backroad, and increased their speed. Beside him, she had found the sweets and was rustling paper. He was getting a little weary and was looking forward to reaching the cottage, stretching his legs.

"I would have thought you'd eaten enough. You'll be getting fat."

"That happens when you're pregnant."

The road dipped and turned, then it shot up in a steep incline. When they reached the top, it plunged down again and into another awkward turn. He took it slowly and found himself looking at a familiar sight, a metallic blue Granada towing a caravan.

"Oh, great!"

He had grumbled some miles back, where the road had been wider and the driver of the Granada had pushed the speed limit for towing in order to get past them. Now the Granada slowed a little now and Danny eased off the accelerator. It was no problem. Let the idiot go. He was happy to poodle along at just on the forty mark and he watched the other car inch ahead.

"Danny?"

"It's that bloke with the caravan."

Chrissie sat up in her seat. "There were two children in the back seat."

"Probably driving him mad," he said.

"Children do that sometimes," she said meaningfully.

"Other people's children might. Our son won't."

"Son?"

"What else?"

Suddenly the Grenada breaked sharply. The caravan buckede, swayed its rear from side to side, as the driver swung the whole caboodle into a sharp right turn, onto an even narrower road, running off through a wood.

"Twat!" Danny touched the brake, increasing the space between them so as not to clip the off side corner of the caravan. He checked his driving mirror and saw a black Mercedes way back, not hurrying in spite of being such a powerful car. He increased speed a little.

"Did you see that?"

"What?"

She was frowning. "I'm sure there was a child in the back of that caravan. I glimpsed her face at the rear window as they turned off."

"A child?"

"I think so."

"He'll cop it if he's stopped."

He was not really listening. A dull ache had started beneath his ribs, quickly growing to a pretty fair sized discomfort that made him draw in air through his teeth.

"What?"

He thought of the pie he had half eaten earlier and wished that he had ordered a salad instead. "Indigestion.

I'll pull over when we reach the next lay-by. I've got some Rennies in my bag in the boot."

"I'll see if there are any peppermints in here." She dived back into the glove compartment.

He took the next bend smoothly, squinting as the sun dipped below the sunshield, blinding him for a second. Then the glare was gone and he saw a long, straight stretch of road ahead. There was bound to be somewhere where he could pull over.

He glanced in the rear view mirror again and saw the road was clear behind them.

"What's this?"

He looked at her, saw her raised eyebrow and then looked at what she had brought out of the glove compartment.

"Keeping these for yourself were you?"

He felt as though the breath was being sucked out of his lungs. The tin she held had a snow scene on the lid, a rosy cheeked girl, a snowman with beady black eyes and a twisted mouth.

What?" she asked, suddenly anxious.

He stared at the tin, horror mounting within him, unable to believe his eyes.

It couldn't be here!

It was impossible!

But so many things he'd witnessed recently were too.

"Daniel."

One whispered word and ice grabbed his heart. He looked in the rearview mirror and Veronica smiled at him from the back seat.

"DANNY!"

The crack in Chrissie's voice reached him. He tore his eyes away from the mirror, saw her terrified face and looked at the road in front, just in time to see the huge farming vehicle pulling out of a parking area onto the road in front of them.

"Jesus!"

An opening appeared at the corner of his eye, an expanse of broken ground but an opening all the same. He wrenched the steering wheel left, sending the car barreling into the gap, the off side wing catching the bank and then they were bucking and fishtailing over uneven ground as Chrissie screamed.

The Ford hurtled forward, seeming to find every mound and pothole possible in its mad rush towards a copse of fir trees at the far side of the space. Danny hit the brake hard, felt the car lurch sideways in a juddering skid and a moment later, the violent shock as it slammed near side on into the trees.

Chrissie cried out in pain, as he was thrown towards her, only to be yanked back the other way. His head slammned against the driver's side doorpost and the world rushed into blackness.

He groaned, opened his eyes slowly and for a second, didn't know what had happened. Then it rushed in on him. The impact had thrown his door open and he was hanging out of the car, held fast by his seat belt. He tried to move, feeling the pressure of the belt tight against his chest. Pain screamed in his shoulder and he stopped moving, holding his breath until it subsided.

What about...?

He couldn't think. Peering through grey fuzziness, he managed to find the seat belt lock, pressed it and the belt sprang open. Rolling from the car onto the ground, his right side hit hard on packed dirt and the shoulder pain erupted again. He gave a loud shout, dragged his legs out and struggled round onto all fours, favouring his right side as he moved slowly away from the wreck.

What about...?
There was something...

He disgorged the contents of his stomach onto a floor of pine needles in a hot, steaming jet, then he slumped to the ground. He closed his eyes until he registered the sound of music, soft but steady and felt confused. Then he remembered the radio was on in the car and that it was this he could hear playing.

Chrissie!

His whole body tightened. He'd forgotten her! How could he do that? He struggled to move, to get up but he couldn't make it and turning his head to one side, dry retched. Eventually he found a mouthful of bitter juice to spit onto the ground, then rolled away from the stink of what he had brought up, slumping sideways against the gnarled and twisted trunk of a fir tree.

He would go back to the car in a minute, when he could stand, when his bloody shoulder stopped hurting so much. Chrissie was still inside, safe in her seat, held there by her belt.

'Clunk, click, with every trip!'

He almost wished that he still smoked, because the taste of tobacco would be a thousand times better than the taste of vomit.

Er, what's up, doc?

The cartoon voice was clear in his head and looking sideways, he saw the carcase of a dead rabbit off to his right. It was lying on its side in yellow scrub, shrunken to nothing, a spent vessel. Its fur was patchy and lustreless, its long ears had fallen flat across its collapsed shoulders and were starting to curl in upon themselves. It looked back at him from empty eye sockets, grinning at him with its skeletal grin.

Welcome to my world!

It all came in at a rush then, the sweets tin, the farm vehicle.

Veronica looking at him in the mirror!

She was dead and buried and still looking at him from the back seat of his fucking car!!

"Chrissie!"

His voice sounded old, croaky but that didn't matter because that was how he felt.

With effort, he peeled himself away from the tree trunk, gasping at the white hot shafts of pain that lanced his shoulder. He tried to stand, staggered, almost fell, catching at the tree trunk to hold himself up with his left hand. He tried again, managed to keep his feet, this time, stooped and wobbly but on his feet. Now all he had to do was move.

When he did, he found he could walk after a style, bent low and taking short, deliberate steps that didn't jar his shoulder. Somehow he had to get back to the car, cover the distance, lower himself into his seat.

"Chrissie?"

The sun was hot in that space, already starting to burn his neck and his stumbling feet kicked up little puffs of dust into the thick air. Some got into his mouth to mix with the vomit tasting saliva but bit by painful bit he went on, each step an achievement until at last, he was there.

"Hey, darling..."

Bending painfully to get himself inside, he fell into the driver's seat. She was slumped sideways, held by her seatbelt, head at an awkward angle over the gearstick. He could almost imagine she was looking for a new station on the radio if it wasn't for her eyes, which were fixed and glassy. He whined softly. Her face had taken on a deathly palor.

"Chris?"

Reaching out to her.

"Chrissie...."

"Are you all right?"

It was a man's voice, the sound of others behind it, talking in whispers and all the time a bloody siren was getting louder and louder. The man said over his shoulder to those gathered behind him that he couldn't see any blood.

"Wait for the ambulance!" said another voice, female this time.

Danny eased himself over on the seat, until his face was level with Chrissie's head. He managed to lift her back with his left arm until she was more upright in her seat. Then he held her close, feeling her dead weight pressing against him. The man said something behind him, which he didn't hear.

"She's my wife. She's carrying our child."

And he held her proudly, turning away because he just wanted it to be the two of them, the way it ought to be. He lifted her hand and the sun light pouring into the car sparkled off the ring on her finger.

24918214R00288